SOME SHALL BREAK

BY ELLIE MARNEY

None Shall Sleep
The Killing Code

SOME SHALL BREAK

THE NONE SHALL SLEEP SEQUENCE

ELLIE MARNEY

LITTLE, BROWN AND COMPANY
NEW YORK   BOSTON

Little, Brown and Company
Hachette Book Group
1290 Avenue of the Americas, New York, NY 10104
Visit us at LBYR.com

First Edition: June 2023

Little, Brown and Company is a division of Hachette Book Group, Inc.
The Little, Brown name and logo are trademarks of Hachette Book Group, Inc.

The publisher is not responsible for websites (or their content) that are not owned by the publisher.

Blood drip (title type) © halimqd/Shutterstock.com

Quote on page vii from the poem "Making a Fist" by Naomi Shihab Nye, from *Everything Comes Next: Collected and New Poems* (2020), published by Greenwillow Books. Used with the permission of Naomi Shihab Nye.
Quote on page 148 from the poem "Power" by Adrienne Rich, from *The Dream of a Common Language* (1978), published by W. W. Norton. Used with the permission of W. W. Norton.

Little, Brown and Company books may be purchased in bulk for business, educational, or promotional use. For information, please contact your local bookseller or the Hachette Book Group Special Markets Department at special.markets@hbgusa.com.

Library of Congress Cataloging-in-Publication Data
Names: Marney, Ellie, author.
Title: Some shall break / Ellie Marney.
Description: First edition. | New York ; Boston : Little, Brown and Company, 2023. | Series: The none shall sleep sequence | Audience: Ages 14 & up. | Summary: Travis Bell and Emma Lewis reunite to help the FBI capture a serial killer in Pittsburgh, and they must again turn to a notorious teenage sociopath and his twin sister for help finding the murderer.
Identifiers: LCCN 2022030339 | ISBN 9780316487719 (hardcover) | ISBN 9780316487818 (ebook)
Subjects: CYAC: Serial murderers—Fiction. | Twins—Fiction. | Brothers and sisters—Fiction. | United States. Federal Bureau of Investigation—Fiction. | Criminal investigation—Fiction. | Pittsburgh (Pa.)—Fiction. | LCGFT: Thrillers (Fiction) | Novels.
Classification: LCC PZ7.M34593 So 2023 | DDC [Fic]—dc23
LC record available at https://lccn.loc.gov/2022030339

ISBNs: 978-0-316-48771-9 (hardcover), 978-0-316-48781-8 (ebook)

Printed in the United States of America

LSC-C

Printing 1, 2023

For all the survivors

"How do you know if you are going to die?"
I begged my mother. We had been traveling for days.
With strange confidence she answered,
"When you can no longer make a fist."

Naomi Shihab Nye, "Making a Fist"

CHAPTER ONE

In a dark, unfamiliar bedroom in Beechview, Pittsburgh, Patricia Doricott, a twenty-year-old Duquesne poli-sci major, wakes up groggy.

She lies there for a second until her brain regurgitates the cab ride to Stanley Theatre with Fletch and Lori. The concert. Patricia's older brother, Tom, bought the tickets for her as a gift, so she was glad Elvis Costello delivered. The music was great.

Her memory is hazy post-concert. She remembers afterward, another cab to Zack's on Fourth Avenue. Then another club: getting drinks, chatting to a guy at the bar. It was crowded. There were any number of drinks. She's gone home with someone, which is not a first, but it's the first time she can't remember the guy's name.

The bedroom she's in now smells of some kind of nauseating air freshener. She makes out a nightstand but no lamp. The room is damn dark: Maybe she just can't see the lamp? Her mouth tastes terrible and her head hurts. Fumbling off the blanket, she realizes she's still in her clothes. Not the typical Walk of Shame scenario, then. Patti stubs her toe on the way to the door, then twists the handle and opens onto—

Light, god.

A white hallway with dark dado and beige carpet, wincingly bright. She has the world's most awful headache. Framed pictures in the hall show her reflection in the glass. Her dark hair has gone from tousled to bird's nest, yeesh.

But framed pictures mean she's in a house, not a dorm room. Okay, this is better. Easier, in some ways. Just say hi to the guy, thanks for being a gentleman, ask to call a cab, get home.

Patti walks onward until the hallway reaches stairs. She descends slowly, holding the banister, turns right past a front door, walks until the trail spills her out into the kitchen. A plain wooden table with one place setting: a bowl, spoon, glass of water, white coffee cup in a saucer. A box of Cheerios and a carton of milk on the table. Maybe the guy has gone to work. She's honestly trying to remember his name, but that information lives somewhere just out of reach.

She sits at the table and drinks the water, wishing her head wasn't fracturing everything into bright, painful prisms. Low music, somewhere farther away—KC and the Sunshine Band. Jesus, how much did she have to drink?

The sound of a door opening, closing, and a young man walks into the kitchen. Tallish, medium build, brown hair, white dress shirt and dark trousers, cute professor glasses. He looks like the guy from the bar, but she can't be sure.

"Hi, honey," he says cheerfully.

"Hi," Patti replies, but she is thinking, *What?*

He takes the chair opposite, across the table. "How are you feeling?"

"Uh, yeah." Her tongue, thick in her mouth. "Like my head got steamrollered."

"Oh, would you like something for that?" He grubs in his trouser pocket, pulls out a blister pack of tablets. Pops two and pushes them across the tabletop. "Here you go. Tylenol."

"Thanks, it's fine. I'll wait until I get home." Better not to accept strange tablets. *Nice place, do you mind if I call a cab?* She rehearses mentally as she sips the water.

The guy cocks his head and smiles. "You do look so much like her."

"Pardon?"

"It's nothing. Would you like me to show you to the bathroom?"

"Uh, if you wouldn't mind. Then I should probably call a cab."

"Sure." He smiles again as he rises from his seat and hurries over to help ease Patti's chair out from the table. "Follow me."

He leads her back the way she came. The music murmur fades the farther they get upstairs. Patti's trying not to trip over her feet. How embarrassing. No wonder she woke up in her clothes.

Confession time. "I'm sorry, but what was your name again?"

"Peter." He looks over his shoulder as they reach the hallway, walk past the pictures. "And you're Patricia?"

"Patti. Yeah."

"Peter and Patricia. Sounds nice together, don't you think?"

"Uh—"

"Here we are." He angles to open a door on the left side of the hallway.

White bathroom, not huge, compact. A showerhead on the wall over a bathtub. A toilet, a freestanding sink. Security bars on the window, which is pretty standard for Pittsburgh, although not usually on the second story.

"I'll just leave you to freshen up," Peter says, smiling away.

He closes the door. There's no lock but Patti needs to pee, so she uses the toilet, washing her hands after and splashing her face for good measure. This headache is not going anywhere, god. Another twenty minutes of polite conversation while she calls a cab and waits, then skedaddle. She's looking forward to getting in the cab.

Half her makeup comes off on the hand towel. She can't see her panda eyes because there's no mirror in here. Weird.

A knock on the bathroom door, and it swings open a foot. Peter, smiling again—he has a real commitment to smiling. It's a bit more than she can deal with right now.

"Brought you something you've always wanted…" His voice is singsong.

"Sorry?"

Peter bites his bottom lip. Swings the door wider. He's holding a clothes hanger up high, and suspended from the hanger is a long white dress. "I know, I know—I'm not supposed to see. But it's a special occasion."

"What—"

"I don't want to hurry you, but you should get changed quick so we can get started."

Peter is smiling now in a different way. His eyes are glinting. The dress has pearlescent sequined roses around the bodice. In Patti's fuzzy state, it takes a moment to register.

Then it all comes into focus.

The white dress. News reports.

When she looks back at Peter, he's got a long-barreled gun of some bright metal in his other hand. He holds it across his chest. The cock of the trigger echoes loudly in the security-barred bathroom.

"Come on, Patricia." He smiles and smiles. "I can't wait to get started."

Patti Doricott begins to cry.

CHAPTER TWO

Kristin Gutmunsson, twin sister of the most infamous juvenile serial murderer in American history, watches the oak trees through a window one floor above the Quantico library. The outside leaves ripple in a breeze. Insulated behind the window, Kristin cannot feel the breeze, but she can imagine the coolness of it.

Kristin has a richly developed imaginary life, and right now she is using it to tune out the people talking at her.

She feels nostalgic, looking at the oaks. In her mind, she and her brother, Simon, are lying down together under the big oak in the back garden of the Massachusetts house. It is the end of the summer of '78, and they've played croquet all afternoon with Janet and Marlowe. Once their friends left, Simon and Kristin finished the game without them. Now, with the sun lowering, the grass is pleasantly shaded.

Simon reclines with the bottle of lemon water from the tray. Kristin flops beside him, her hair spun out like a silver fan. Simon plays with it idly as they pass the bottle back and forth.

"You've got grass stains on your skirt," he notes.

"And a sweaty face." She swipes the long cotton sleeve of her blouse against her forehead.

Simon gives her the handkerchief from his trouser pocket. His snowy hair matches her own, and they are both wearing croquet whites. Against the bed of verdant lawn and fall's first russet oak leaves, Kristin imagines that she and her twin look like a sculpture of marble angels.

"You were very mean to Marlowe," she says. "I think that's why he and Janet went home."

Simon shifts to lean on his elbows, looking at the sky. "I'm not mean to Marlowe. He brings it on himself. I wanted to play, not watch Marlowe make cow eyes at you all afternoon."

"I like the cow eyes."

"Good god."

"I like Marlowe." Kristin traces a gnat's flight in the air above them with her finger. "I think he wants to ask me out."

"It's a shame, then, that he's already dating Janet."

"I know." Kristin makes a vexed frown. "It's most annoying."

Simon laughs. Kristin loves to see him laugh more than anything. She loves her brother most when he is at his most free. Every pointed edge of him seems to smooth away. At fifteen, she senses him becoming sharper.

And he grew up to become the keenest blade. The knowledge of what her brother is tinges Kristin's thoughts with melancholy. A few short months after this pastoral scene, Simon will lead Marlowe to a small clearing at the edge of the woods outside town and open up his innards to the air. . . .

"Kristin? What do you think?"

She looks away from the window, half-tumbled in the memory. Travis Bell is the person calling her name. She understands why Bell sometimes seems uncomfortable working with her. Yes, they both survived the fiasco of the Butcher case, three months ago. But she is the sister of his father's murderer. Socially, it makes things rather awkward.

They also look like perfect opposites, her white skin and hair next to his dark Mexican American coloring. He's standing now in his G-man suit, jacket open and hands on hips. Bell's father was a US Marshal, and Bell has inherited a measure of law enforcement attitude. But his social intelligence is above standard, and Kristin is intrigued by his personal development. She wonders if he's aware that his empathy—and his attractiveness—may be a liability in the bureau. Bell is young, but he has one of those faces that will become even more rugged and interesting with age. He is still in training and doesn't yet have the closed-off expressions of a proper FBI agent.

Kristin looks back to the window. "I don't think you need more explanation from me. I mean, I appreciate that you've kindly allowed me to visit you here at Quantico, but I've already given you my opinion about what you have to do."

Special Agent Howard Carter's baritone. "Miss Gutmunsson—"

"I knew it after the first girl's case appeared in the newspaper, of course, but I wasn't completely sure. By the second girl, I was sure. That's why I contacted Mr. Bell last month, to give him my instinct. I asked to come here today because I wanted you to confirm it, and act on it."

"It can't be just about instinct, Miss Gutmunsson."

Kristin turns again to face the room. A long table of some beige wood runs down its length, a Rolm business-phone unit set in the middle. The briefing room is this afternoon's temporary location while the basement area of FBI Behavioral Science is being fumigated. Light from the windows makes the blond brick walls and tan carpet glow.

"Instinct is only useful with evidence," Carter reiterates. "We have to compare the evidence."

Special Agent Howard Carter stands at the opposite side of the table to Bell. Carter is a Black man in his early fifties, with a close-cropped beard and mustache. He is wearing a brown three-piece suit, and his glasses are on a chain. Carter is reasonably smart, Kristin suspects. He presents as reserved and calm, even when he is frowning like this. His facial expressions are much more standard FBI.

Kristin tries again. "Then examine the evidence—I'm sure you've started doing that already. Because I know what this is, and I think *you* know what this is."

Carter nods, slow and reluctant. "We have been tracking some superficial similarities between these new murders and the Huxton case—"

"You see? So you already know. And you know you need to call Emma."

"Kristin," Bell says. Low, warning.

"The flowers at the crime scenes are a different touch, certainly. So is the posing and the locations of the bodies. But even without all the same elements, the flavor is the same."

The mention of flavor seems to make Bell uneasy. "Daniel Huxton died in 1979. We've got photos. We've got autopsy reports—"

"Obviously I'm not saying it's the same *man*. But I know it feels similar enough. You should call her."

Bell chews his bottom lip, exchanges a look with Carter. "Is Agent Martino still on the ground in Pittsburgh?"

Carter nods. "Day after Labor Day though, he'll be trying to get caught up on any backlog. He might be hard to contact. You want to talk with him about it?"

"Maybe, yeah," Bell concedes.

"You reviewed the Huxton case file?"

"I had to." Bell doesn't seem very comfortable about it.

"Did it feel disloyal to Emma, to read the file?" Kristin asks. She is not interested in procedure, only in feelings.

Bell ignores her question, directs his words to Carter. "I'll talk to Martino."

She prods again. "Did it make you angry, to read it?"

A fast glare from Bell. Yes, angry.

Carter seems to settle something in his own mind. "All right, thank you for your…instinct, Miss Gutmunsson. I'll order a thorough literature review. Everything we have on Huxton, cross-referenced with what we have on this case."

Kristin isn't sure why they're being so dense. "And who's going to call Emma?"

Bell sighs. "Emma deserves a break. I'm not gonna call her just on a hunch. She doesn't need to deal with all this stuff again—"

"Are you being deliberately stupid?" Kristin blinks at him. "Travis, you've *seen* the pictures of the victims. Small, slim, dark-haired, college-aged…"

Something crackles behind Bell's eyes. "She's in Columbus."

"That's only three hours from Pittsburgh."

Now, at last, a little panic in his face.

"Okay," Carter says. "I hear what you're saying, Miss Gutmunsson, but let's not rush into anything. Let's complete the review, the cross-referencing—"

"You really think she's in danger?" Bell blurts.

Kristin is saved from replying when the phone rings.

CHAPTER THREE

Once Emma is settled in her favorite chair in the living room, Audrey Klein brings out a bowl of fresh raspberries. "Here, enjoy. Last crop of the season."

Emma Lewis knows Audrey has kept the fruit because she cares, that it is a gift freely given. "Ah, geez. You know I love these."

"Go on, eat as many as you want." Audrey settles carefully into her own comfortable wingback, with the crocheted lap blanket. The blanket helps with the arthritis in her knees. "Thanks for making time for our session today."

Emma shrugs. She and Audrey are friendly because the therapeutic relationship is an exercise in trust, but this is a scheduled appointment, not a social call.

"How was Labor Day with your folks? Roberta's all right?"

"Yeah, everyone's good. Robbie said she's seeing someone. Won't tell me who, though."

"Big sisters like to torture you with that stuff." Audrey smiles. "Now, have you been trying to walk, like I suggested?"

"Yes." Emma eats another raspberry, corrects herself. "I mean, I start off walking. I always start that way."

"And then what happens?"

"I get a...It's like an itch. A burn in my calves." She looks out the window, thinking of the long, late-fall grass brushing her legs. "One minute I'm walking. And then I'm striding. And then I just... It's like all this energy comes to the surface and I have to move. Like something inside me is saying, *Hurry, hurry.*"

Audrey pours them both tea from the big jug. "When you came back from Virginia you were running every day."

"Yeah."

"Sometimes twice a day."

"I know." Emma accepts her glass.

"Until you threw up." Audrey sips from her own glass. "So sometimes running brings no relief."

Emma tries to think of how to phrase it. "Some days I run, and that's all there is. Just the road, and my feet, and it's quiet. Other days it's like...something is pulling me forward. Like I could run forever and never find it."

"What are you thinking you'll find?"

"I don't know."

"Do you think the running helps somehow?"

"I don't know if it helps." Emma's eye turns inward. "I don't know what it's supposed to help *with*. It just is. It's just what I need to do."

"Okay, let's talk about something else now. I want to ask you whether you feel you're regaining balance."

Emma's grateful they're not talking about running anymore. Talking about running makes her want to run. "I'm doing okay. I'm keeping up with my classes."

"Well, I already know you're a good student. Do you feel your career goals have changed?"

"No. Maybe. I still want to help kids."

"Your goals are your own, Emma." Audrey sits back, her glass of tea held over the lap blanket on her crossed knees. "And your goals aren't dependent on anyone else's approval. What's important is that, whatever direction you choose to go in, it's one that makes you happy and brings you satisfaction."

"You believe that?"

"Yes. Part of my job, as your therapist, is to help you make the choices that *you* want to make, that feel right for you. To give you room to grow—and change. It's about evolving, Emma."

"Okay." Emma's hands are cold where she clasps her glass.

"Are you still comfortable talking?"

"Yes. I just never really questioned what I want to do before."

"But your experience at Quantico changed that?"

Emma has a sudden flash of memory: Agent Ed Cooper in his meticulous suit, dead teenagers in a warehouse, the horrifying grin of the man who killed them. A white-haired boy with blood on his teeth. The sounds and smells of the Jefferson building at the FBI base come back to her. It hasn't really been that long.

"Quantico was...I felt useful. But I also felt used."

Audrey inclines her head. "Can you say more about that?"

"I've just been wondering whether I made the right decision, to reject the FBI's job offer. Stuff like that." Emma rubs at the condensation slipping down the side of her glass. "My first reaction was *No way*. But that was just after St. Elizabeths, and I was raw. Now I feel like I'm healing."

"That's good." Audrey takes another sip. "But there's a balance in that, too. You have to examine if you're knitting back together or if you're simply growing defensive armor over the wound."

"The result is the same, though, right? You can get by."

"There are some differences. And one is healthier than the other, long term. What still attracts you to the FBI program, d'you think?"

"The idea of saving other victims." Emma's voice is firm.

"Delivering justice?"

"Maybe." Emma fidgets, hesitates, sips her tea. "Being the hunter instead of the hunted."

"I can see the appeal of that for you. It's good to acknowledge that the offer is tempting. And it's an intellectual challenge, which I know you like." Audrey cocks her head again. She's pushing sixty years old, but her eyes are sharp. "You seem restless, honey."

"I feel a little like that," Emma admits.

"Can you say a bit more about what you're feeling?"

Emma tries not to frown. The feeling is there: amorphous, opaque. "I don't know."

"Is it a physical feeling in your body? You mentioned your sister is dating—is the feeling related to dating?"

"What? No. You know I don't..." Emma shifts in her chair. "I'm not ready for that."

"Aren't you?" Audrey smiles. "You're nineteen years old. Healthy. It wouldn't be unlikely if you were feeling that urge."

"It's not that. I've just been wondering if maybe I should have accepted the offer from Quantico."

"Well, I know you still have some connections there. Have you heard from Travis?"

Emma startles. She only ever lets herself think of him as Bell. "No. I don't think he would do that."

"Contact you?"

"We never . . . I just don't think he would do that."

"Would you like him to?"

Emma shrugs. "I mean, I miss him. I miss . . . the partnership. Teamwork. But I don't think he would contact me unless it was some kind of emergency." She presses her lips. "Not like some other people."

"You've had another postcard from Simon Gutmunsson?"

The last card had been addressed to her care of the psychology department at Ohio State University. It read, *Dearest Emma, Are you still shining? Thinking of you, Simon.* Emma put her winter gloves on, took it downstairs to the basement incinerator, and burned it. Then she burned the gloves.

Remembering the handwriting now, she sets her glass aside and wipes her palms on her jeans. "I don't want to talk about Simon."

"No, and we don't have to. Let's talk about something else, then."

"Okay." Emma knows what's coming.

"I know your birthday was last week. If you're feeling vulnerable on the tenth, you know you can come see me, or call."

"I want to try something different this year," Emma says. "I've got a good schedule on Fridays, lots of classes. I'm going to try to keep real busy."

"Sounds good. If you need me, though, I'm right here." Audrey makes the offer seem casual.

Emma knows that Audrey clears her day on the tenth of

September—the anniversary of Emma's abduction—every year, just for her. The knowledge makes her feel grateful but also pathetic. She eats one last raspberry to get rid of the feeling.

After the session, she lets Audrey gift her a small container of raspberries. Then she walks out of the turreted house, down the steps, heading for her car. The Rabbit is parked by the curb, getting some sun. Audrey's street in Mount Vernon is lovely: double-lot blocks, plenty of grass around the houses, graceful, widely spaced trees. The dogwoods are starting to change color.

Emma turns her face toward the sky. Her parents will be out in the yellow leaves, thinking about harvesting apples and cutting pumpkins. It makes her consider growth, and whether she's really evolving. She'd like to think so. She's been seeing Audrey for almost three years now. But there are no real markers with therapy, nothing to say, "Here, I've reached this point, I've made progress." It's just a gradual shift so that one day you wake up and realize you don't think like that anymore, or you've slept through the night for a while now, and maybe this is the new normal. Emma wonders if she's plateaued, and if such a thing happens, or if she would even know if it had.

She gets in the Rabbit and takes it out past Sears to the Texaco on West High Street, gases up the car. It runs better since her father replaced the carburetor in August. She eases onto Old Delaware Road toward Route 71 for the trip back to OSU. It's about an hour of potato and corn fields, peaceful rolling country. She could drive like this all day. Then the concrete and asphalt of the highway, and she's finding her way home.

She manages to get a parking spot under one of the old ornate streetlamps on West Tenth Avenue. When she gets up to her dorm room, she discovers her roommate, Leanne Frome, is painting her nails with some kind of disgusting glitter polish that makes the whole room smell like sour lemons.

"There's mail on your bed, I think it's from your sister. Oh my god, isn't this the worst? Open the window for the stink, I've still gotta do the other hand."

"That stuff reeks." Emma puts the raspberries on the dresser— she'll share them with Leanne later—throws her knapsack on the bed, and grabs up the mail, checking the sender addresses. Since Simon's postcards, she always checks the addresses.

"What I get for buying cheap." Leanne shakes her hand and blows on her fingers. "I don't know why I'm going all out, we're only going for coffee."

"You got a date?"

"Yeah. But I haven't had a date in, god, a while."

"Then . . . congratulations?"

"Thanks." Leanne's a redhead, and pleased embarrassment looks good on her. "Hey, how were your folks?"

"Oh, fine." Emma shucks her jacket and pulls sweats out of her drawer. "Gonna run. Maybe do a wash when I get back. You got anything?"

"In the hamper." Leanne waves at it. "Thanks—you got change?"

"I'll check the jar." Then Emma has her running shoes on and she's gone.

She runs for three miles, just to take the edge off. Talking about her running habit with Audrey always gets her like this. She reminds herself to slow down and walk the final quarter mile back to Hanley

House, but it makes her feel twitchy. She's hoping to channel that into a study session later this evening.

When she gets back from putting in a wash load downstairs, she takes a shower, scrubbing her scalp and thinking over what Audrey said about physical feelings. She's nineteen. Hot-blooded as any teenager. It's not her body that's stopping her, it's something in her mind. She's had a few offers in the last three months from guys in her classes who aren't put off by her buzz-cut hair. The girl who works behind the counter at the grocery store sent out tentative vibes, too. Emma doesn't even know if her reluctance is confusion about her sexual preference, because she's never let herself date, and how fucked up is that? Maybe she should start saying yes. The idea is slightly terrifying.

She towels off to dress, dumps her shower caddy in her room, pulls a robe on over her pajamas to go shift the laundry into the dryer. When she returns with the basket, Leanne looks up from where she's piling all her things into a shoulder bag. She's wearing jeans, but her makeup's done and she looks nice.

"Phone for you. Sylvia was holding it."

"Ah crap, thanks." Emma leaves the basket, reverses course.

Downstairs, Sylvia is waiting by the communal phone in the dingy hall, holding a palm over the receiver but still talking sotto voce. "He said he couldn't leave a message."

"Thank you, much oblige." Emma takes the phone. "Hello?"

"Emma."

A voice she hasn't heard in three months. It stops her cold and warms her at the same time. Five whole seconds pass until she gathers herself. "Travis?"

"Listen. I didn't want to call you. I've been . . . I've been trying to get them to leave you alone." His voice is low and urgent.

She's immediately alert. "What is it?"

"Special Agent Carter's on his way to you. Don't freak out, okay? He's an okay guy. Emma, they want to take you into protective custody."

All the hairs on her body prickle up. She hears herself take on a tone she never uses in the dorm. "Travis, what's going on?"

"Have you been reading the news, Lewis?" He pauses. "Read the news."

He said *protective custody*. Emma makes herself follow the logical thread of that, gets a bitter taste in the back of her throat. Braces her hand against the wall. "What about my family?"

"They're sending people out. Lewis, are you with me?"

"Yes."

"Stay in the dorm. Carter needs to find you. He'll tell you some of it. The rest of it . . . I'll be there, okay? At the Pittsburgh field office. You'll have backup."

Pittsburgh. They want her in Pittsburgh. She needs more information, which she's unlikely to get over the phone. She'd prefer to know how bad it is, though. "Do I need backup, Travis?"

"Yeah." He sounds deeply regretful. "I'm sorry, but yeah, you do."

CHAPTER FOUR

Howard Carter lifts the black carry-on bag that Emma Lewis has brought aboard and stows it for her in the overhead bin. She's already got the window seat. He sits by the aisle so there's a seat between them. He thinks she might appreciate the space.

He needs to talk with her, and there's not a lot of privacy in coach. But there are agents in the rows ahead and behind, and the rest of the flight is only half-full. He waits until everyone's seated and the Delta staff are busy with pre-flight checks.

He keeps his voice quiet. "Miss Lewis, thank you again for agreeing to do this. I'd like to brief you a little more, if that's all right."

She is not looking at him at all, is focused instead on the wing of the plane out the window. "What's happening with my family?"

"I've got people at your parents' house, and there's an agent with your sister."

"Okay."

"We'll take care of them. That's what we do."

"Okay."

He's very aware of her lack of inflection. "Miss Lewis, we will do our utmost to ensure your safety and the safety of your family. I'm sorry we've had to do this, in this way. But I'll make certain they're looked after."

She nods. Her arms are tightly crossed, and she looks tense and closed off, a little underfed. She's a small white girl, with a runner's wiry build. Tiny silver hoops at her ears, no other jewelry, and her dark hair is buzzed.

He wasn't surprised by her hair—he's met her once before. But she was dressed formally then, for Ed Cooper's funeral. Now she's in jeans and a gray Henley and a green down vest, and she looks much younger.

She's just a teenager, Carter thinks. But Carter has raised two children to adulthood. Emma Lewis is more self-contained than any teenager he's ever encountered.

"Miss Lewis, we don't know each other very well," he starts carefully. "I only know of you from Mr. Bell, so I have secondhand information at best. But he says you're smart, and pretty tough. I'd like to think we can cooperate to get this situation resolved quickly."

Finally, her head turns. Her eyes are spooked and wary. "Bell said that about me?"

Carter nods. "He said you're strong. He also said you don't trust the FBI. I'm sorry you've had bad experiences with the bureau in the past. I know we let you down during the Huxton case, when you had to save yourself. I know our agents were very…tenacious when they pursued you for more information afterward. And I know former section chief Donald Raymond made a lot of bad decisions during your involvement with the Butcher case. So your impression of the FBI is tarnished. But I want to try to improve that impression.

And we need to work together on this. The only way we can do that is if we talk with each other."

A long beat as she presses her lips together. Then she says, "You remind me a little of Agent Cooper."

"Well, I'll take that as a compliment." He makes a soft smile, settles back in his seat. The plane is taxiing and the cabin lights are dim. "Ed Cooper was a good man. I miss him a lot."

"How long have you been with the bureau?"

"About sixteen, seventeen years? Closer to seventeen. I started out as beat on the street, took the long road up to federal. Law enforcement's the only job I've ever known. I'm a career cop, Miss Lewis."

For whatever reason—his manner or his words—she seems to be thawing. Her arms are still crossed, but she looks less stiff. She's pale, and he can't blame her for that. This situation would frighten anybody. For someone who's survived what Emma has, it must feel like a horrifying regression.

"Again, I'm very sorry we had to do this. If we could have transmitted photos of this new victim for you to view, that would have been preferable, but a fax picture—"

"A fax picture is useless for detail," Emma says. "It's better if I see things for myself."

He nods because she's right. "And we're on a tight timeline with this case. I'm relieved you agreed to come to Pittsburgh. But look, I'm hoping we'll get there and find something that defuses it all. I can't make guarantees, but that's what I'm hoping."

She visibly steels herself. "I think you'd better give me all the information, if you want me to make a call on it."

"Okay." The lift in his stomach as the plane takes off. He waits until they're coasting. "All right. As of today, we've got three victims. We called in Mr. Bell a few months ago, when we realized the perp was targeting college-aged women."

"I thought Bell was already in training with you."

"No, it's a flexible arrangement. He's been completing some units for his pre-USMS training. We brought him in at the end of July. He's due to go back to Wisconsin in October for second-session classes."

Emma looks at the back of the seat ahead of her. "He's doing okay?"

"He's doing very well. He's bright, disciplined, and he's committed to the work. And of course, he has a good track record." As if it's an afterthought, Carter adds, "He healed up fine after St. Elizabeths."

She pauses, nods. "Good to know."

"I'm afraid I vetoed him meeting us in Pittsburgh. I wanted only essential staff on this trip."

"Oh. Okay."

"I'm sorry. You're stuck with me."

"That's fine."

He thinks she is more disappointed than she's prepared to say. Better to press on with the details. "So it was the appearance of all three victims, plus some particular elements at the scenes, that made us pull the lever and come get you."

"They're all young."

"Yes. And they all fit a type."

"White, slim, dark-haired," she recites.

"You know the pattern."

She looks out at the flying night. "It's Huxton's pattern."

"Yes." Carter senses that Emma's reactions are on a cycle: withdraw, approach, withdraw. Her comfort zone is narrow. He needs to share this information, though, so she's prepared for what's to come. "But it wasn't just the physical similarities that made us jump."

"What are the other elements?" Her voice is toneless again.

"He puts them in bridal dresses, with flowers."

In the window's reflection, he sees her cope with that. She holds firm. "What else?"

"Sexual assault."

"And he holds on to them a while."

"Yes," he acknowledges. "About five days, on average. We also believe he drugs them on capture, like Huxton."

"Is there anything new?"

"They're posed crime scenes."

Emma gives him back her gaze. "Huxton never did that."

"No. He buried his victims in the area around the mountain house. There was no posing." He thinks how to phrase this. "Miss Lewis, I put you into protective custody because there's enough resemblance to the Huxton case to warrant concern for your safety. But I'm taking you to Pittsburgh to see the body of the latest victim, the victim discovered today, because I'm hoping we can rule out a copycat. If we're able to eliminate the copycat theory, I can send you back to OSU and dial down the security around your family."

"So if I see important differences, you'll let me go home?" Her eyes are hopeful.

"Yes. I'm not prepared to do that, though, until I know for sure what's going on." He checks her face. "Did you think I would try to hang on to you? To give advice on the case?"

Emma says nothing.

Carter is abashed. "If that strategy has been used on you before, my apologies. But that's not how I operate. If I want your help, I'll ask for it straight out, like I'm doing now. I prefer to deal with people who have some honest interest in the work."

"Not just a talent for it?"

He knows he has to tread carefully here. "Miss Lewis, I would appreciate your perspective. I would. But like I said, I'm not going to strong-arm you into cooperating. That usually turns out to be counterproductive for everybody."

She looks as if she's weighing this up. Deciding whether to trust it, checking underneath for the hidden trap. Damn, but he wishes this girl had been properly treated in the past. It would make his job a lot easier now.

He sinks back farther into his seat, removes his glasses to clean them. "Now I don't know about you, but I'm planning to catch a nap sometime in the next three hours. I encourage you to rest. It may be a long night ahead."

She scans him slowly then turns away, leans her head back. Her arms are still crossed. But it's a start.

They get into Pittsburgh about 20:30 and are met by a car from the local field office. Emma carries her own bag and refuses to let the Pittsburgh agent, Novak, put it in the trunk. Carter waves him away.

Traffic on the I-376 is sparse at this time of night. Carter looks out the window, or checks the information in the folder on his lap by penlight, so Emma won't feel like he's studying her. The Fort Pitt Tunnel is lined with white tile, which makes him think of the place they're about to visit. They come out over the river, and the lights of downtown are sparkling. Another ten minutes and they're passing the tattoo parlors and pizza shops he's familiar with on Smithfield Street.

Shored up with white mortar, the red stone walls of the Allegheny County Health Department glow under the streetlamps on Third Avenue. All the big windows and turrets of the old building look slightly out of plumb, most likely from the time it was moved in its entirety in 1929. Carter directs Novak to park on the street—they can go in via the back entrance. A light drizzle is dusting down from the dark sky.

Emma looks around a little wildly. "I thought we'd be going to the Pittsburgh field office."

"No, ma'am," Carter says. "The morgue is at county health."

"Oh, right." She says it like she should've remembered.

He wants to check she's okay, but that might translate as being an offer to back out. He's sure this is going to be difficult for her, but he's hoping she won't lose her nerve now they've come this far.

They're met at the little red rear door by Dr. Karl Friedrich, the venerable county medical examiner, who's wearing a suit and a burgundy bow tie. "Hello, excuse me, you must be Special Agent Carter."

"I am." He shows his credentials. "We've spoken a number of times on the phone, Dr. Friedrich. It's good to meet you in person. Thanks for letting us visit at this hour."

"Of course, it's no trouble. Come on in, get out of the rain."

Friedrich ushers them into a tight hallway and past towers of cardboard file boxes, through a corridor with a freight elevator, and onward. He has not yet acknowledged Emma, although he casts curious glances.

"Any early news on the victim identification?"

"Not yet," Carter admits. "We're door-knocking at the colleges. After this, you're free to do a full examination, take prints and so on. Then I imagine we'll know soon after."

"And this young lady is…" Friedrich's tie twists a little as his head turns.

"This is Miss Lewis. She's going to be viewing the body and providing some insight."

"And Miss Lewis's area of expertise is…"

"Serial killers." Emma, tired of Friedrich's trailing sentences, perhaps. She has her hands deep in the pockets of her vest. "My area of expertise is serial killers."

"Ah." Wisely, Friedrich doesn't push further. They've reached a set of tall white wooden doors. "Well, here we are."

"Here we are," Carter says. "Could you excuse us for a moment, Doctor? If you'd like to get set up, we'll be right in."

"Certainly, certainly," Friedrich says. He opens one of the white doors and slips inside the autopsy room.

Carter shuts the door carefully behind Friedrich before turning to Emma. "Are you cool to do this, Miss Lewis? I'm serious. I didn't want to ask before, but if you're really struggling—"

"I'm not." Emma looks at the door handle, away. "I mean, I'm struggling. But I'm cool to do this."

"Okay." Carter puts a palm on the white wood. "Would you prefer Dr. Friedrich not be in the room?"

She swallows. "I don't know. Maybe? I don't know."

"Let's play it by ear, then. All right. We're going to go in now."

"Okay."

He looks at her carefully: Her breathing is short and high, her shoulders tight. But she said she's okay. Take it slow.

He opens the door. In the old autopsy room, the tiles on the walls are a dingy white. Large ventilation units are set over the autopsy tables, like range hoods over a home stovetop. The tables are of the obsolete porcelain type made in Chicago in the 1930s—solid, thick-edged, and chunky. Less industrial-looking than the modern metal tables.

Dr. Friedrich stands on the far side of the second table. He has opened up the long black body bag and laid a drape over the form inside. Carter walks closer, Emma Lewis matching his echoing steps. By the time they reach the table, she has slipped her hands out of her pockets, clenched them into fists at her sides. Her face, since they came in the door, has the expressionless cast of the condemned.

Friedrich holds the edge of the drape. "She's intact as she was found. Not the positioning, of course, they had to lay her straight to put her on the stretcher."

Carter knows this is a very long way from standard procedure. Typically, the body would have been autopsied by now, and fingerprints and dental shots taken for a fast identification. He was the one who gave the order putting a hold on all that, sacrificing the crucial first hours of early victim ID to give Emma Lewis a chance to look, and hopefully rule out a worst-case scenario.

"How was she found?" Carter asks for Emma's benefit; he already knows.

"Propped up on the curb by a bus stop. The exact location is in the report, with the photographs. She's holding a small bouquet—I asked them to bring her in with it still in place."

"Okay, thank you, Doctor," Carter says.

"Are you ready for me to..."

Carter nods. Friedrich checks Emma's face, then draws the drape aside.

Oh, Lord—behold, I tell you a mystery. Here she is now, this poor young woman, in blue-gray tones. Her mouth and eyes are open, one iris milky in death. The other iris is a watery green. Carter can see the blood shot through the sclera. Bruising shows at the neck, on her face, and down her arms.

The autopsy room has a faint scent of decay, stronger since Friedrich lifted the drape, but Carter's trying to block it out. He wants to focus just on the victim. The body smells of damp, from the situation she was found in, and of mothballs, probably from the dress. Friedrich has exposed her all the way to her hips. She looks cold. Even though he knows that this girl is beyond feeling it, Carter's own flesh goose bumps in sympathy.

Emma Lewis stands absolutely still beside him. Carter has read Ed Cooper's old reports; he knows Emma is a soldier in this war. They have a chance now, to catch the man who did this, to hold him to account. The girl laid out before them is gone, but she can still speak and tell her story, if someone cares enough to listen close.

He angles his head. "Miss Lewis, what do you see?"

There's a long pause, and then—

"Bridal dress." Her voice is faint. "He's put a veil on her."

"Yes, he has." The veil is drawn back. It's really just a white headband with some tulle attached.

"There's the flowers."

They droop loosely in the girl's hands. Her wrists are tied together to keep them in the correct holding position. Carter makes a mental note to ask Scientific Analysis about the ligatures.

He watches Lewis. The control in her is intense. He speaks quietly, calmly. "Just tell me exactly what's on your mind, Emma."

"She's got...He's taken out her earrings. Or maybe he got her to remove them."

"I see it." The girl has two holes in each lobe.

"Pink nail polish. Makeup, too. It's worn off, mostly, but there's a little eyeshadow still at her brow. Mascara streak, there on her cheekbone."

"She was going out, maybe, when he caught her?"

Emma opens her mouth, closes it. A little head shake. Impossible to perform the detached mental scan necessary for deductive reasoning while she's looking at this.

"I'm sorry. Go on."

"That dress don't fit her right." Lewis's accent coming through. It happens sometimes, when folks are in distress. "He's not buying made to measure. He's getting them from a charity shop, maybe."

"Mm-hmm." That's consistent with what they surmised from the other two victims. Something else to file.

"She was strangled, wasn't she?"

31

Carter checks with Friedrich. The man nods, solemn. "I won't say categorically, but it looks like manual strangulation, yes. There's no blunt-force trauma I can make out."

Carter indicates with his chin. "The bruising. And the cyanosis on the lips."

"And you can see the petechiae in her eyes. We'll have a cause of death determination once we do a proper exam. There's another obvious injury here, consistent with the other two victims."

Friedrich lifts the girl's hands gently to show them. Carter sees the pink polish on her nails, then beneath the covering bouquet, a neat chop below the biggest knuckle of the left ring finger, where the digit has been removed. Carter thinks of his wife, how she prunes the rose bushes out front with shears.

Beside him, the sound of Emma Lewis's breath stoppering. She turns sharply sideways and walks out of the room.

Dr. Friedrich says nothing until the door closes. "Hard on a young woman, to see this kind of—"

"Excuse me, Doctor," Carter says, and he goes after Emma.

The corridor outside is warmer than the autopsy room. A framed print of the Precious Blood of Jesus faces the doors. Emma is leaned back against the wall, not looking at the Savior's heart ringed with thorns, staring up instead at the ventilation pipes near the ceiling.

"Are you all right, Miss Lewis?"

"He cut off her finger." If Carter thought she looked pale before, now she looks like a ghost.

"Is that significant?"

"To take off the ring."

"The ring?"

"The wedding ring." She takes low, deep breaths to stabilize. Now she's focused on the stack of boxes near the floor. "We...we each got a wedding ring."

"Huxton used to do that?"

"Did you even read the file?" She looks at him now like he's stupid. He knows this deflected anger is keeping her together.

"Not in enough detail, apparently." He addresses the obvious issue. "You don't have a missing finger."

"I didn't *die*." Emma closes her eyes and scrubs her hands over her face. "He only took the rings back from the girls who died."

This brings him alert very quickly. "Was this something that came out in the papers? Is it something the police withheld?"

"I don't know. I don't remember."

"Okay." They both know what this means. "So is this it? Are you sure?"

Emma kicks herself off the wall, her voice rough as dirt. "Take me to Quantico."

CHAPTER FIVE

They're met at Pittsburgh International by Special Agent Mike Martino. When he sees Emma and Carter approaching across the concourse, he wipes his mustache with a napkin and then dumps it and his coffee in a trash can.

"Okay, we're cleared to board. Hello, Miss Lewis."

"Hey." Emma has met Martino before, and she finds him bluff, of average competence. If the rest of the team is made up of people like Martino, she doesn't trust the FBI to resolve this quickly.

Not without her help.

"Straight to base, Mike." Carter passes Martino a thin folder of paperwork. "There'll be a car set up for you at Washington National. Check in with Jack Kirby at the office. Miss Lewis, I'll be in touch by phone tomorrow."

"Sure."

"We're going to figure this out." Carter holds her gaze. She thinks he probably knows she doesn't trust him yet. "We're going to work this out, and we're going to get you back home."

"You'll make better progress with me on the team." The words tumble stiffly from her mouth. "You said you'd appreciate my perspective—well, you've got me now, like it or not. Don't make me sit in a room under protection, that would drive me crazy. Let me do something, or send me back to Ohio."

Carter considers, finally nods. Emma wants to slap him for putting on the pretense of thinking it over. He's got what he wanted without any expenditure of effort. She knows that's not his fault, but she fusses with her overnight bag anyway so she doesn't have to shake Carter's hand.

She's not feeling very charitable toward the FBI as she and Martino make for the boarding area. The lights are always too bright in airports. Emma feels sticky from so many hours of stewing in her own perspiration. Walking past the Military and Family Courtesy Center, she has the strongest urge to just go on into the little rest area and lay her head down on the couch.

Martino makes a noncommittal gesture. "Want me to take your bag?"

"No."

Emma gets the window seat again, and the view outside is like the landscape of her mind: black and vast and furiously cold. How is she back here? Only this morning she was considering working with the FBI again, but not like this. Not when she doesn't get to set her own terms. Last time, she was motivated by survivor's guilt; this time, she's compelled because of the danger to herself. She's chosen participation over helpless inaction. The result is the same. It's like one of those kaleidoscope toys, where you twist it and the colored chips fall into different patterns, the same components in endless variation.

She thinks about the dead girl's ring finger all the way to Washington National.

The flight is just over an hour, then it's another hour in the car to Quantico. Fleetwood Mac's "The Chain" plays softly on the radio. They roll past the military police guard station about 00:30—at this time of night they have to leave the requisitioned vehicle parked in the outside lot. Emma assumes all the oaks around the base have changed their seasonal colors, but it's hard to tell by moonlight.

In the Jefferson building, they go through the process of signing in, and she has to show her driver's license. The agent at the desk already knows her name. The interiors here are chillingly timeless: the same hollow sound of footsteps in the atrium, the same long windows. This is a nightmare she's having. She just wishes she knew how to wake up.

Martino seems to be always reaching for her elbow to guide her, hastily pulling his hand back. Emma wonders who gave that order, the "give her space" order.

He leads her to the elevator. "Okay, we're going to see Special Agent Kirby in Behavioral Science."

"So I'm allowed into Behavioral Science now?" She hitches her bag higher on her shoulder.

"Yes, ma'am."

"Because it's my case they're studying."

"Uh, yes, ma'am. I'm afraid so."

The rest of the trip is in silence. Emma feels her stomach hover a little with the elevator's downward fall. Her mind is whispering as the car descends, and the whisper says, *Huxton, Huxton, back from the dead.*

When they get out of the elevator and past the vending machine, Emma turns ahead of Martino and goes left.

"Miss Lewis—"

"I want to see the Cool Room."

"We're expected at Behavioral Science—"

She ignores him, walks on without pausing. Suddenly she is in the correct hall, and away farther down on the right is the door to what used to be her office. *Their* office. She is running on the dry edge of her nerve now.

When the door opens and Travis Bell steps out into the hall, she feels a jolt.

He does not see her for a second—she has a moment to take in the sight of him. He looks tall and serious in his dark suit. His hair is cut regulation-sleek at the back and sides, longer in front. His eyes are shadowed, and he looks tired.

She wasn't expecting this intensity of emotion on seeing him, but there's a lot of emotional stuff inside that she usually avoids thinking about. Mainly it's like she's been staggering under an oppressive weight and now, finally, she can put it down. The relief is sharp as a knife cut. It stops her in her tracks.

Bell looks up at her arrested movement. She sees him mouth her name.

Her bag slips to the floor, then she is covering the last few steps. Her hands are lifted weirdly, but Bell doesn't seem to notice, and they clasp forearms in the way of people who do not hug.

The first thing he says to her is, "It's okay. It's gonna be okay."

"It's him," she blurts.

"It's not him. Emma. Look at me. You know it's not him."

"I know," she says. Her face feels frozen with the effort to appear neutral. "I know."

"Emma. It's okay. It's gonna be all right...."

He hangs on tight, glances over her shoulder to nod Martino away. Bell is the only person who violates the "give her space" order, and Emma is shocked to realize how much she needs human contact.

I've got my partner back. The thought grounds her enough that she can draw breath. "I know. I know it's not him. But it feels the same."

"That's what *I* said. Hello again!"

Emma's attention is dragged sideways. Kristin Gutmunsson steps from the Cool Room into the hall. She is wearing midnight blue trousers and a matching jacket, a white shirt with a sharply pointed collar. She looks elegant and lovely with her long white hair loose.

"Kristin." Emma stares. Dredges her voice up from somewhere. "Hey."

"It must've been an awful shock," Kristin says. "And you had to look at the bodies."

"Emma—" Bell starts.

"One body." Dazed, Emma lets go of his wrists. "There was only one body."

"Of course!" Kristin flaps the lanyard around her neck. "I've been helping with the case. Look, I have a special permission card from Chesterfield, and my own ID."

Emma glances between them, composing herself. "Carter said there's been three victims."

"Yeah. Lewis, I'm sorry." Bell shoves his hands in his trouser pockets. For a moment, she's not sure what he's apologizing for. "I didn't want to call you, I know you didn't want to get pulled back in—"

"It's okay. You didn't have any choice."

"There's more you need to know."

"Travis, stop it," Kristin says. "Look at her, she's definitely too tired to deal with all this now. Emma, how are you? Have you eaten? Goodness, it's nearly one in the morning. Can we still get her some food?"

Kristin puts her hand on Bell's arm when she speaks to him, and Emma feels it like a hard punch in the solar plexus.

"I'm fine." She steps back. "I'm not hungry. Let's get moving, I want to start putting everything together."

"Are you sure? Okay, then." Bell nods to the open door of the Cool Room. "Go on in while I fetch the other files from Behavioral Science. Grab a chair. Yeah, they're the same chairs. We've got a permanent phone now, at least."

Emma peers into the room. "You got an upgrade."

"If you can call it that," Bell says grimly. "Hang tight, I'll be back with the files in five."

"I'll get your bag!" Kristin bustles in that direction.

Emma swallows everything down, even the feelings she doesn't fully understand, and steps inside.

The Cool Room has changed subtly from the last time she was here—it's been three months, and change was inevitable. The file boxes from the time she and Bell spent interviewing juvenile killers are all gone. There are desk lamps now, and a cup full of pencils and a typewriter. There's the telephone, in industrial brown. The room smells like it's been recently fumigated. Someone has laid beige carpet tiles on the floor to make it look less bleak, and there's an old, hard-looking couch against one wall.

The room is still gray, though: a basic, windowless concrete bunker. It's not the same space she remembers, but it's familiar enough, which lessens the sting.

Emma collects one of the metal folding chairs by the door, opens it out near two desks, their front ends pushed into cooperation to make a table. Two other chairs sit adjacent. She looks at how closely they're positioned before shoving that thought aside.

"Yes, it's still like a *dungeon* in here, if you were wondering." Kristin talks as she moves around the space, sweeping back her hair and setting Emma's overnight bag near the leg of the desk. "Oh, Emma, it's so good to see you! Horrible circumstances, of course, but still. How have you been? You've been at college, is that right? How are your studies?"

"It's, uh, it's good. Fine. Everything's been going fine. Up until now."

"Oh, yes—sit down, you must be quite exhausted. Would you like coffee? We have a filter pot. I don't like brewed coffee, but you might."

Emma cuts to the chase. "How long have you been working with Behavioral Science?"

"Well, I'm not actually *working* with them." Kristin has found a chair, but she doesn't settle in it, more just flutters around the edges.

"I'm not *employed* by the FBI, I should say. But I contacted Travis—Mr. Bell—in July, after I saw the news reports about the first girl. Then I contacted him again after the second girl, because the similarities to the Huxton case were just so striking, and at last he agreed I should come in and explain it all to his superiors, as he had been thinking the same thing, of course. And I kept telling them to call you, but they wouldn't listen. It was like nobody would *listen* until they found this new girl today, and then finally people seemed to sit up and take notice." She has been touching small things on the desk: a pencil, a chain of paper clips. Now she stops fidgeting and shrugs. "Anyway, I've given them—Mr. Bell and Mr. Carter, that is—all my thoughts on the matter, and I'm very glad you're here. Now they might start listening to sense."

"They might." Emma's getting used to Kristin again, the way the girl talks, that peculiar cadence and syntax. It reminds her of Simon, and Emma knows that's a block in her, a natural revulsion. She has to fight it. Simon Gutmunsson is a serial murderer, and Kristin is not. Kristin is eccentric, but she is not her twin. "You knew it was a Huxton copycat just from reading the newspaper reports?"

"Well, yes, but I wasn't *sure*, that's the thing." Kristin sinks at last into the neighboring chair, takes Emma's hand. Kristin violates the "give her space" order, too. Emma reminds herself that Kristin is like this: She likes to touch, and she doesn't mean anything by it. "I didn't know for certain until I read your file. Oh, Emma, I'm so very sorry. I had to read it. Mr. Bell has read it as well. I'm sure that will feel awkward and uncomfortable—"

"It's necessary. Don't apologize." It's hard, though, the awareness that everyone knows. That they're viewing her through that lens. Emma experiences it like a wave of numbness, of absence.

"It made Travis angry. But I felt a kind of sorority." Kristin's grasp on her hand is gentle. "Isn't that strange? I don't want to presume, but goodness—between the two of us, we've gone through a lot, haven't we?"

Emma returns Kristin's clasp to show that she's reciprocating. She doesn't want Kristin to feel like she's alone. Since Simon's imprisonment two years ago, Kristin has been living in an expensive "mental health spa" facility near Richmond. Emma's been there: The individual bungalows are exquisite and discreet, but solitary. Once part of an inseparable unit with her brother, Kristin is now a girl who's been alone for too long. And in Emma's experience, the Gutmunsson twins react poorly to isolation.

When the door clicks open, it's Bell, laden with paperwork.

He dumps the files on the corner of the desk. "Here's everything. I checked in with Jack Kirby, too, so that's one less thing you have to do. Lewis, what do you already know?"

Emma finds this quality in Bell the most reassuring—that after everything, after months of separation, he can reintegrate her almost seamlessly back into the team, back into the work. Work is good; it's focusing.

"Assume I know nothing, because that would be accurate. I haven't been checking the news, and I have no information beyond what I know about Huxton and what I just saw in the Allegheny County Morgue."

"Okay." He pulls up his chair, kitty-corner from her and Kristin. "Here's the timeline. The first victim, Geraldine MacIntyre, was found on July twenty-first. She was dumped under an overpass in Seldom Seen Greenway, so she wasn't discovered for three days, and he had her for probably five days prior. You ready for this?"

He means the crime scene photos, and Emma nods. He passes them to her. The pictures are stark, but there's a certain remove. They're nowhere near as disorienting as the body she saw on that table in Pittsburgh.

She's sure her face looks dismayed all the same. "The wedding dresses."

"Yeah, he's following the same pattern."

"The veils and bouquets are different from Huxton, though." Kristin touches the photos. "And the posing. Looking at these pictures, I'd say the most recent victim was the most posed."

"He's refining a little each time," Bell acknowledges.

"Does he cut the ring fingers on every victim?" Emma's soul, suspended just outside her body as she asks.

"Uh-huh. Was that the thing that ran up your flags? Okay, let's come back to the significance of that in a minute. He took the second girl, Marilyn Preston, on the fourth of August. Her friends reported her missing early. That let us figure out he held her for seven days."

"Carter said about five days."

"It's variable." He sifts through the file papers. "This new girl, we don't have an ID yet, but if we count back, then she was probably taken no earlier than last Wednesday."

For Emma, the scent of the hunt is the smell of human putrefaction. "What do we have on him so far?"

Bell peels a page out of the file and hands it to her. His gaze is intent. "He's a white male. Twenty-five to thirty-five years old. He has a house and a vehicle. Organized. He's got brown hair. Type O secretor. Extrapolating from his hand size, he's between five-seven and six-two."

They know so much already. It's still not enough. "How is he replicating the details of the Huxton case?"

"Apart from keeping you safe," Bell says, "finding out the answer to that question is the reason I brought you in."

CHAPTER SIX

There was no way she was going to be able to sleep, Emma thought—right up to the moment she rested her head on the desk, before being woken with a startle, Bell's hand on her shoulder.

"Lewis. Hey. Have they given you a room? I can walk you up."

Of course, once she's installed in a single room on one of the upper levels of Jefferson—the FBI have put her, Travis, and Kristin all in the same building this time, to keep things streamlined—she finds sleep elusive. She lies under the comforter, wondering if a hot shower would settle her or make her feel more awake. She's running on adrenaline.

The room smells faintly of carpet shampoo. It's a world away from her homey dorm at Hanley...where she forgot to share the raspberries with Leanne. Dammit. She hopes Leanne's date was successful. Someone should get a victory out of today. Although it's not Tuesday anymore: Dawn will be peeking over the Quantico oaks in a few hours.

Emma talks herself out of taking a Valium, thinks about the case and Leanne's glitter polish. In her ragged state, Leanne's face is replaced by the face of the girl in the morgue, her ring finger chopped clean off and the rest of her fingers tipped in pink.... *Pink nails—did they all have pink nails?*

Her eyes feel dry, and she dozes a while, until the sun hits the curtains and bounces off the mirror near the study desk. By the time Bell knocks at 07:00, she's washed and dressed and mostly alert.

"Did you sleep?"

"A little." She tosses the towel she's using to rub at her hair through the nearby bathroom door. "Bell, the latest victim, her nails were done. I think he painted her nails."

"Okay."

Emma looks at the way he's holding himself. "What's happening?"

"Carter called. He wants us in Pittsburgh for a police briefing at nine."

"He couldn't have thought of this last night?" She sees Bell's face. "Ah geez, fine. Let me get my bag."

It's anyone's guess if she'll be back in this room again. Habitually meticulous in her packing, now she's jamming underwear and toiletries together in Bell's presence. Great.

She makes small talk to reduce the discomfort, although small talk was never really their thing. "So, um, you're doing okay here? The job is okay with study and stuff?"

"It's good, yeah." He stands by the door, eyes politely averted. "I get the theory in school, and now with the case, it's all practical. I was in Pittsburgh last week, pounding pavement like everyone else—door-knocking, taking witness statements, helping with street searches. The fast track is kinda brutal, but it's okay. And Carter's one of the good guys."

Emma examines him this time via a series of glances. Apart from signs of fatigue, Bell looks good. His eyes are clear and he's put on some muscle—they're surely sending him to physical training classes, but that was always something he enjoyed. He looks strong. The work obviously suits him, and if Carter's been honest, Bell's good at it. He's turning into a proper law enforcement officer, which is what he's always wanted.

It shouldn't create a pang, that he looks like this. She should feel happy for him.

She refocuses on her packing. "How are your mom and your sisters?"

"They're well. Your family's okay?"

"Yeah. You know, I just saw them on Labor Day. They're fine." Maybe not so fine, these last twelve hours. Better not to think about it. Emma rolls a pair of socks, shoves them down. "So we're heading for Washington National?"

"We're heading for the roof. Carter's ordered a Marine helicopter."

She twists around. "Pardon?"

"You need to collect your ID from Behavioral Science first, though."

"Okay. That's fast."

Bell shifts from foot to foot. "The perp abducted this third girl three weeks after the second. We're racing the clock here, Lewis."

That moves her along.

Bell takes her bag, and Emma shoves her arms through her down vest on the way to the elevator. "All right, so we go to the basement, I grab my ID, you grab Kristin—"

"Kristin's not coming." He moves her bag from his right hand to his left, slaps the elevator button.

"Excuse me?"

"Carter didn't mention her."

"And you didn't think to ask?" Emma pulls the collar of her shirt straight, keeping her eyes on him. "What's the problem, Travis?"

"No problem." His expression is mighty neutral.

"Look, I know it must be weird, working with the sister of the guy who—"

"It's not weird." He polishes his back teeth with his tongue. "All right, fine, it's weird. But she reached out to me months ago. And we get along okay. We've been discussing the case together, I don't know, she's . . . She's been here."

Ouch. Emma doesn't want to do this now, but it's better to deal with it. "And you needed to gap-fill. Right."

"Yes." Bell turns to face her straight on. "Because you left a gap. Why didn't you accept the FBI's offer to work with the bureau?"

"I don't know." She should give him more than that. "I talked about it with Dr. Klein, my therapist. I didn't feel easy about it."

"We made a good team."

"We did." They brought down the Berryville Butcher together. They used to be partners. A unit. The memory brings an ache. "But after what happened during the Butcher case, and at St. Elizabeths . . ."

She can't speak of it without remembering it: Anthony Hoyt smiling, injecting blood into his arm. Anthony Hoyt screaming, as Simon tore him apart. *She* was the one who let the genie out of the bottle by releasing Simon Gutmunsson that night. She's still coming to terms with that decision.

Bell's mouth is tight. "I know you had a good reason to walk away, after St. Elizabeths. But I thought..." He looks elsewhere. "I thought you liked working with me."

"I did." She corrects. "I do. And my decision wasn't a reflection on you—it wasn't personal."

Now he's looking back at her. "It felt personal."

"No—Travis, it wasn't about you. I just...wasn't sure." She glances down, scuffs the corridor carpet. "Anyway, I'm back here now."

Bell's expression is conflicted, but his voice softens. "Look, I get it. Working with the FBI again, especially in these circumstances, isn't what you wanted. I'm sorry about that. And I'm sorry I wasn't in Pittsburgh. I was set to go, then Carter vetoed."

I needed you there. I needed you with me. Emma puts that thought right in the garbage, where it belongs. Soft feelings have no place in Quantico. Theirs is a professional relationship, nothing more.

"Don't worry about it." She composes herself. "But listen, I'm not the only resource you've got. I don't think we should leave Kristin behind. She was onto this copycat business from the start. She's got insight into the killer mindset, from a different perspective than you and me. She's very articulate about it. I think she'd be an asset."

"I agree." The elevator doors open.

"You agree. Great." Emma gestures for her bag as they step into the car. "So call Carter back. Tell him we need her."

Bell sucks his teeth again. Waits for the doors to close before passing her bag over. "All right. Fine."

The car begins its descent. Emma waits, knowing there's more.

"There's another thing," Bell says.

She's prepared for it, busying herself with the zipper on her vest. "You read the Huxton case file. I know. Kristin told me you both read it."

"Emma—"

"It's fine. It's what you had to do." If he apologizes, if he sounds—even for one instant—like he feels sorry for her, she doesn't know if she'll be able to handle it.

There's nothing like that. But his voice holds a warning. "We're gonna have to talk about it."

"I know."

"We might have to talk about it *today*."

"Yeah." She stares hard at the fascinating buttons on the elevator control panel. "Who else has read it?"

He hesitates before the admission. "Carter has a copy. Martino. Jack Kirby. The Pittsburgh chief of detectives, Clyde Horner, has excerpts."

Everybody, then. She swallows that down, nods. "Right. Well, plenty of law enforcement people have read the file. It's been across a lot of desks."

The sound of the elevator's hum in the pause. "I had to listen to the tape of your deposition, Emma."

Her gaze jerks over. Bell's eyes are very dark and deep. No pity there, but something else—something vigilant. Appalled. A burning fury, almost as hot as her own profound anger. And something else, an emotion she can't plumb the reaches of. The intensity of it resonates in her bones. She has to look away.

"We'd better . . ." They've reached the atrium floor. She clears her clogged throat. "We'd better move or we're going to miss our ride."

They congregate on the roof. Wind is snapping Emma's jeans against her calves, and the noise of the chopper is ridiculous. Whatever Bell had to do or say to get Kristin on the flight, he got it done, because she's standing there looking like a kid in a candy shop.

Her hair gets in her mouth as she yells, *"I've never been in a helicopter before!"*

"You'll be fine," Bell yells back. *"Hold on to your skirts. Lewis, have you flown before?"*

Emma nods. She was evacuated by chopper to Cleveland after she collapsed during the raid on Huxton's cabin. She was in the hospital for a month. It was three years ago, and she doesn't remember much about that flight at all.

This flight is different. A SWAT officer is accompanying them—Emma suspects he is part of her protection detail while she is off base without a qualified field agent. She's strapped in, given a headset with earmuffs, squeezed between Bell and the SWAT officer, whose name is McCreedy. She can't really see much. She experiences a lot, though: the heaving rotor thrum that seems to embed itself in her marrow, the whining roar of liftoff, the gut roll as the huge machine banks and turns.

Kristin looks gleeful the whole time, and Emma focuses on that. Someone else is finding the experience pleasurable; it puts her own nausea into perspective. She watches Kristin exclaim and smile around, as her hair whips in the cabin like white seaweed. Bell finally slides an elastic band off one of the file folders in the satchel at his feet and passes it over.

The helicopter cuts flight time from an hour to thirty-seven minutes, and there's no talking en route. When Emma is finally unstrapped, once she has crouch-walked on wobbly legs to the car that's taking them to the location, she has plenty of questions that need answering.

"Are we going to the Pittsburgh field office?"

"No, ma'am." McCreedy tosses their luggage into the trunk, moving fast. It's beginning to rain. "I'm supposed to escort y'all to the Pittsburgh City-County Building on Grant Street."

"We're not stopping at county health?"

"No, ma'am." He opens the door of the Plymouth for her. "My orders are to deliver you to Special Agent Carter, and I'll be following those orders directly."

She and Kristin pile into the back seat as McCreedy jogs around to the driver's side. Bell slides into the front passenger seat and immediately turns around to speak to Emma. His hair has been blown a little wild from the helicopter. "You're thinking about the autopsy results?"

"Yes."

"Has the new girl been identified yet?" Kristin is disentangling the elastic band to return it.

Bell shrugs. "Carter said yes, but I've got no more details."

The streets are slick, and McCreedy drives fast and careful. Bell explains that police operations units in Pittsburgh are divided into zones, but for a citywide operation like this, they're using the big City-County Building on Grant Street as home base, and that's where the briefing is being held.

Carter meets them inside. Pittsburgh COD Clyde Horner, in his gray and black uniform, with the puffy eyes of the overworked, is ushering stragglers through the door. Carter flags his attention and they organize, through a series of gestures and facial expressions, that Emma and Bell and Kristin are supposed to sit somewhere at the back.

The interiors are grand and, in Emma's view, jarringly opulent—the briefing room has buffed dado walls and a high ornate ceiling. None of the two dozen or so congregating officers seem to pay the surroundings any mind. It'll look impressive for the press conference to follow the briefing, so that's useful.

Emma scans the crowd, trying to screen out the overwhelming odor of male perspiration from all the polyester-blend duty shirts. Dr. Karl Friedrich is standing near the front in his bow tie and a sports jacket. Carter stands between Friedrich and a red-faced man in a gray suit. She sees McCreedy take up position across from her and Bell and Kristin, near the back wall. She doesn't recognize anyone else.

Bell squints at the red-faced man, leans in close to keep his voice quiet. "Alan Kraus, Pittsburgh public safety commissioner. The woman on his right is his PR staffer. She's all right, he's a pain in the ass. Hold up, looks like they're getting started."

"Okay, everyone shut your traps." Horner has a booming voice, and his tie seems tight at the neck. "Yes, Fitzgibbon, I mean you, too. You men at the wall there, find your seats. We've only got limited time and I want to get moving, so have a look up here."

He steps aside to give unfettered line of sight to a large portable corkboard with a series of photos tacked up, including pictures of all three victims as they were in life. Emma sees a photo of the newest victim, obviously taken in the morgue, juxtaposed beside a picture of her that looks as if it was cribbed from a college yearbook.

Horner raps his knuckles on the desk in front. "Gentlemen, listen up. We have an identification—Patricia Doricott, twenty years old, originally from Akron. She was enrolled at Duquesne. Her body was found yesterday afternoon, at the bus stop on Pine Hollow Road in McKees Rocks. The parents have been notified, they arrived in town late last night. We're interviewing them for any relevant details. This brings us to a total of three victims in the past three months."

Horner gives everyone a significant frown, consults his notebook.

"State of play at the moment—we're conducting interviews at Duquesne, and door-knocking a three-block radius around Pine Hollow Road and McCoy Road, including the small businesses there. We're also talking to regular patrons along the twenty and twenty-two bus routes. If you're on this detail and you find a useful witness, you know the drill, refer them on up the line. Some of you are also taking interviews at charity shops in the general Pittsburgh area about the, uh, wedding dresses. We have some cooperation from out-of-town homicide units on this front—he may be getting the dresses from another county, or even from out of state."

Horner glares around at the gathered men. "Before I turn over to the commissioner, a brief word. I know some of you have been bitching about the shoe-leather work. While I appreciate there's been more cold calls and street checks on this case in the past few weeks than in the last year, I don't want to hear any whining about it. That's the job, gentlemen, and we do the job until this jagoff gets caught. You want to claim overtime, be my guest, but don't get too excited about it. All right—Mr. Commissioner?"

Alan Kraus steps forward, looking uncomfortable about Horner's cussing, being overly polite in response. "Uh, thank you, Chief, hello, folks. First, I want to say that the city appreciates your best efforts on this. This is a terrible thing Pittsburgh is dealing with, and people are worried. A public safety broadcast will go out on local television and radio tonight, and we're setting up an information hotline—I know some of you will be manning the phones, that's much appreciated. We're also cooperating with the colleges to warn young women to attend to their safety."

Kristin looks around Bell to catch Emma's eye. They both know what this means for women. "Attending to your safety" is code for not wearing short skirts, or drinking in bars, or having any kind of life.

A detective in the front row raises his hand. "These safety broadcasts, are they mentioning this guy has a specific type? Or are we casting the net wide?"

Kraus exchanges glances with Horner. "We're warning all women, of every type and every age. Just because this perpetrator is focused on one type of lady at the moment doesn't mean he won't switch things up at some later point. We're also doing a newspaper appeal for more information from the public. Dr. Friedrich, is there anything you'd like to add?"

Friedrich straightens his bow tie. "Not really, at this stage. We're still waiting on results from toxicology and trace examination from the body. We'll send out a bulletin if there's any variation on what we already know."

As Friedrich finishes, Horner fills the gap. "Gentlemen, you've got the profile. Don't rule out suspects from surrounding counties—the computer banks say he could live within a two-hour radius of Pittsburgh. He's got a vehicle, he's mobile. He may work in town or commute. Keep your options open, is what I'm saying. Anyway, Special Agent Howard Carter, from the FBI task force, would like to say a few words."

Carter looks more like an academic than a field agent, with his rumpled suit and his glasses, a folder of paperwork under his arm. His baritone gives him a dignity and solemnity appropriate to the subject matter.

"Good morning. First of all, I'd like to express my appreciation for the level of coordination we've got going here between Pittsburgh PD, the local bureau field office, and consulting Quantico staff. That's really positive. Last time I spoke to you, I said it doesn't bother me who gets the collar—Pittsburgh cops, FBI—so long as the perp we're hunting gets caught. I still hold to that. Good cooperation between agencies leads to good information, and that's something we want to encourage. What's important is that we grab this guy fast."

Carter catches eyes around the room to drill the message home. Pittsburgh has its own FBI field office, which has made liaising on this case easier, but interagency cooperation is always delicate. If the Pittsburgh detectives aren't enthusiastic about visiting Quantico agents on their home turf, they're keeping a lid on it.

"I also want to say something real quick about timing. There were three weeks between the abduction of victims two and three, but only two weeks between victims one and two. It seems like he's waiting slightly longer between kills, but he's hanging on to them a few days more. We're still on a tight timeline. Safe to say he's going to do it again as soon as he's given the opportunity.

"Now we've got some new insights that suggest the perp might be taking the victims in a social situation, at a club or a bar maybe, so this guy presents okay. Don't assume he looks like a maniac—he might look like Leif Garrett for all we know. We all learned that lesson after Bundy, I think."

A general murmur of agreement. Another detective from the front has a question. "Excuse me, where'd we get this 'new insights' stuff?"

Emma shifts, uneasy.

Carter takes off his glasses. "We've been tracking the similarities between this case and the Daniel Huxton case in Ohio '79. The presentation of the victims, the dresses and the sexual assault aspects... It's all looking a little familiar, and we've been consulting in that direction." He looks toward the back of the room, and Emma's heart stops. "Miss Lewis, would you like to add anything here? Whatever you can add would be helpful."

There's a lurch in her stomach, like she's on a boat. She wishes to god that Carter had allowed her to write up a report so she could've relayed relevant information to Horner without the glare of the spotlight. But now heads are turning, seeking her out.

It seems to take ages to get to the front. There's no podium, and she sees forty-year-old detectives craning their necks from the back rows to get a look at her. Her throat is very dry.

"Um. Good morning." She avoids looking at specific faces. "Okay. My name is Emma Lewis. I don't have the experience that you detectives have in investigation. What I have is personal experience of dealing with a perpetrator like the one you're tracking."

She clears her throat, and her voice comes out stronger. "He's most likely local and blue-collar. He probably won't have a record, or if he does it will be for something unrelated. He won't sweat under questioning—he'll have good answers. Like Special Agent Carter said, he'll seem normal, or close enough to normal that you probably won't look twice. But something about him will seem off. If your radar pings, then I suggest you take a second look."

She has to say it. She meets the eyes of the men in the room, to make it count. "Daniel Huxton was questioned twice by detectives while he had women—including me—stashed away in his basement. Both times, he was released. Don't be the guy who lets this perpetrator walk out of the station to find another girl to abduct and rape and torture to death. This is going to sound like lame advice, but trust your instincts. Listen for the ping. And good hunting."

When she returns to her place, she's shaking. Kristin squeezes her hand.

"You did good," Bell says quietly.

"Great." Her armpits are drenched. "Get me the fuck out of here."

CHAPTER SEVEN

Travis Bell has shucked his jacket. He glances at the view through the window, his attention spliced between hunched pedestrians scuttling in the rain on the streets below Pittsburgh police headquarters and the current conversation inside the squad room bullpen.

"Respectfully, Miss Lewis, the public service broadcast won't be a waste of time if it helps keep people informed."

Lewis is a small, severe figure beside Clyde Horner's gray bulk. "*Respectfully*, Chief Horner, I said the broadcast is a waste of time if it isn't clear about the victim profile."

The bullpen bristles with the sound of typewriters, telephone noise, and detectives—some of whom Travis has come to know personally—moving around the space, talking over the top of one another. Kristin is sitting at Detective Kowalski's vacant desk nearby, combing through the old media reports on Huxton to find out if the cut-finger detail made it into the papers in 1979. The humid fug of cigarette smoke in the room gives Bell the sensation that he's underwater.

They've been going hard for hours: meeting with Dr. Friedrich to discuss the autopsy results, talking to point men like Kowalski and Simmons about the street searches and leads, standing under umbrellas in McKees Rocks as the first responders stepped them through the most recent crime scene. Now they're back at headquarters to talk strategy.

Horner tries again. "Kraus said—"

"Kraus is wrong." Emma's tone is sharp. "The killer targets slim, white, long-haired brunettes aged eighteen to twenty-five. It's *that* specific. He's not going to deviate, he's not going to 'switch up.' He's following a victim pattern, probably for reasons even *he* doesn't understand. A general announcement is just going to terrify every woman in Pittsburgh."

"She's got a point, sir." Travis steps closer. He knows his height gives him an edge with Horner; it makes him look older. Having a family background in law enforcement and an understanding of procedure gives him an edge, too. "That broadcast goes out after the news at seven. I'm betting by midnight you'll be following up a half dozen reports of men getting shot at by their own wives when they come home off the late shift."

Horner scratches his stubble. "Okay, look. I'll talk to the commissioner about it. But we've gotta say *something* to the general public."

"Then say something right." Emma turns to Travis. "What's next?"

"Coffee. Excuse us, sir." Travis nods at Horner in apology and steers Emma toward the Brewmaster station over near the wall.

Rain is sheeting down outside the windows, washing the streets gray. Pittsburgh looks miserable, and Lewis looks exhausted as she takes the mug he pours for her. "Thank you."

"Emma, you can't win all these battles." He keeps his voice low as he pours his own. "Let me talk to the chief about it some more."

"Why? Because you're a guy, and you can convince him in a manly way?" Her tone has tipped over from sharp to caustic.

He knows where her anger's coming from, so he stays mild. "Because I'm law enforcement. I know how these people work, I understand the system. Some things Horner can't back down on, especially not here in the middle of his own squad room. And this isn't Quantico turf—Carter's working adjacent to the Pittsburgh FBI field office on this one, he's here on Horner's sufferance. We don't want to give the local chief of detectives a reason to block us."

She presses her lips. "Okay, I didn't think of that."

"We've each got stuff we're better at, Lewis. A diplomat you are not."

"I can be…less than diplomatic." Her expression relaxes by one degree. "I just want to stop this guy."

"That's what we all want. That's the goal."

Travis sips his terrible coffee. He's seen her like this before, and he admires it: her focus, that bulldoggish way she has. That first sight of her yesterday was a shock because she's so unchanged. Only the little silver hoops in her ears are new. His eyes keep snagging on them, falling away.

Emma's strong; she's always been strong. He can't remember ever seeing her this tense, though. This is personal to her, all her emotions hovering just under the surface of her skin. Her energy is like a hot thin wire pulled taut, waiting to snap. The anticipation of it makes him tentative around her. It's a new feeling, and he's uncomfortable with it.

Kristin walks up, still flicking through the loose photocopies in the folder she's carrying. "My word, the media are awful, aren't they? I knew that, of course. But some of these headlines are putrid."

"Find anything?"

"The finger-cutting detail was withheld from the media by authorities in 1979, but then I had to check if it was discovered by accident." She consults notes she's made on small squares of colored paper. "No references in any news reports that I could make out. Lots of speculation. Wedding dresses were mentioned...and details about zip ties. Some other information about the types of girls Huxton was kidnapping, that was after the fourth girl, I think. A short description of the inside of Huxton's house—by one very tenacious and horrible tabloid reporter—when it was all over. That's all I could find."

Emma scoops up the forensic paperwork they received from Friedrich. "The pink nail polish is consistent with the other two victims. No clue about whether it's the same polish, though."

Travis squints. "You think it's significant?"

"I think, apart from Kristin, I'm the only female in this room, and I'm the only one who noticed the nail polish." Emma's voice is dry.

"Fair point." He gives her one of Kristin's spare colored notes. "Write it down, we can talk to Scientific Analysis about it tomorrow."

"We're flying out tonight, right?"

"At seven-thirty. Now it's time to go meet Carter. You done with that coffee?"

Travis shrugs back into his jacket as he hustles the girls out of the station and into the car McCreedy has waiting—they're only going three blocks, but it's better than walking in the rain. Kristin commandeers the front passenger seat as he and Emma pile in the back. The interior of the Plymouth smells of damp clothes and vinyl and Marlboros.

"Emma, a question." Kristin twists around to talk as the car pulls out. "You said earlier today, when the detectives were showing us around the crime scenes, that this killer is smart. Is it something to do with the way he's evading law enforcement?"

Travis feels Lewis shift beside him, close enough that he can feel her warmth.

"Maybe." Her fingers are tight on the folder of notes in her lap. "Or maybe it's the posing, the nature of displaying the bodies... It's like the fantasy is more detailed, more complex. All the literature we have on serial predators says that a more complex fantasy indicates a more intelligent perpetrator. But it's just my hypothesis. I don't know exactly. It's just a feeling."

Travis has his own question. "At the briefing, you said he's local and blue-collar. Where did you get that?"

"The previous girl, the second victim, was arranged in an alley in Southside. The first victim was beneath the overpass in the... place with the weird name...." She checks the notes.

"Seldom Seen Greenway," he provides.

"Right." She passes him the folder. "I mean, those seem like street-smart, local-knowledge locations. But this new girl is the kicker. Patti Doricott was arranged at the bus stop."

"You can look up the timetable to get the route."

"But would a white-collar person choose a scenario like a bus stop? Risking being seen by waiting commuters, timing the body dump between bus pickups…No, he knew the route. And public transport means blue-collar."

"He caught the bus before, maybe?" Travis tucks the folder into his satchel.

"It's possible."

"But we know he's got a vehicle."

"I don't know. Something happened. He got access to a vehicle."

Travis is thinking about it. "And he's got a house where he can take the victims."

"Maybe the house *with* the vehicle."

Kristin weighs in. "Inheritance? The death of a spouse or a parent, and he inherited means?"

"That sounds plausible." Emma swipes her face on her sleeve against the humidity. "These guys don't just wake up one morning and decide to go on the rampage. There's always a trigger—a breakup, a job loss, a death. Something sets them off."

Travis gives her a hard stare. "How do you know all this?"

"I studied it."

"You studied it. What, as part of your psych course?"

"No." She is determinedly looking away. "I…researched it. Out of personal interest."

"Oh—you *researched* it out of personal interest." He can't help himself. "But you still say you don't want to be involved with the FBI."

The blushing glare she directs at him is oddly satisfying.

"Okay, fine." Travis rolls the window down an inch, for fresh air and a diversion. "So here's another question—how is he choosing the victims?"

Emma composes herself. "That I don't know. The killer's following a really specific set of criteria. It's linked to something in his mind, something..." She shakes her head. "I'm stuck on that, but the posing is important."

"And the pink nails? That's part of it, right?"

"It's got to be."

Kristin's eyes drift north when she's thinking. "The way he dresses and prepares the girls, it's definitely something to do with obsessions around marriage and love.... Is that consistent with Huxton?"

"Huxton put us in white dresses. He gave us all rings. He never called us brides, that was all the media after the fact, but that's what he was doing." Emma stares out the car window at someplace horrific, and her hand makes a nervous detour over her dark scalp stubble. She blinks herself out of it. "For Huxton, it was like a cruel joke. But for this guy, the bridal image is meaningful. It's important—ritualistic. It's part of the staging he needs to play out his fantasy."

Travis gets the static-electricity jolt of a connection. "That's another clue to his age. He's looking for someone closer to his *own* age. A life partner."

Emma nods. "And he's giving us the key to his motivation in the posing. I don't understand much about posing, though."

Rain drums on the car roof. Kristin wets her lips. "I know someone who does."

Travis feels another kind of jolt. He sees Emma's eyes snap wide.

Emma says, "Your brother's not in St. Elizabeths anymore," at the exact same time Travis says, "Let's hold on now."

He does a double take right in her face. "You're considering that?"

"I'm considering everything." Emma's gaze is still trained on Kristin. "I know Simon's in Philadelphia. He wrote to me."

"He *what*?" Travis's stomach drops, like he's just fallen out of the moving vehicle.

"He sends me postcards sometimes," Kristin says softly.

Emma nods. "I got two."

Travis turns Emma's way on the back seat. "You got *two postcards* from Simon Gutmunsson."

"Yes." She focuses back on Kristin. "Where is he?"

"He's in Byberry," Kristin says.

One of the most notorious mental institutions in the country. *It's not enough*, Travis thinks. For the perpetrator who murdered his father, it will never be enough.

Simon Gutmunsson is like the bogeyman: a name invoked to frighten children. During the course of his "career" he murdered eleven people—twelve, if Anthony Hoyt, the Berryville Butcher, is added into the mix.

One of Gutmunsson's victims was US Marshal Barton Bell. The time after his father's death, the impact it had on his family, is something Travis still struggles to talk about. He isn't the kind to hold grudges, but he wishes more than anything that Simon Gutmunsson was in the ground.

"He's been declared criminally responsible for the death of Anthony Hoyt at St. Elizabeths." Kristin's face angles down. "He's on death row, basically."

Emma reaches across to take the girl's hand. "Kristin, I'm sorry."

"Yes." Kristin's white hair spills forward. "I get very sad about it sometimes. But our lawyer is appealing, and he's very clever. Simon might just get another life sentence...."

Kristin trails off and looks out the window. Travis can't decide what's more awful: how distressed she is, or how confused this clearly makes her.

"Would he talk to me, do you think?" Emma asks.

Travis experiences sharp, unfamiliar anger, like a lick of flame.

"He would talk to you." Kristin looks over at Emma. "If he wrote to you, he'd talk."

"Folks, we're here," McCreedy announces.

CHAPTER EIGHT

McCreedy parks the Plymouth across from the bar, nods them in the right direction as he gets a pack of Marlboros out of his jacket pocket. Emma feels the spatter of drizzle on her cheek as she crosses the street, watching for traffic.

Inside, the Grant Street Tavern has brick walls and big burnished wooden arches separating the bar and the lounge. Varieties of whiskey populate the spirits shelf; the TV set in the top right corner is playing a Steelers game. Hooks at knee height in front of the counter stools show where you can hang your gun belt. Bell immediately loosens his tie. Other detectives are drinking in their shirtsleeves.

"You made it." Carter comes over, also in shirtsleeves but still in his suit vest, his cuffs rolled. "It's like a flood out there. Come in, I'll find you a table."

He walks them to a high round table with stools, excuses himself for a moment to check on something. Emma takes a stool for herself, still wondering what the hell they're doing here.

She leans over to Bell. "Does Carter know we're all under twenty-one?"

"It's a cop bar." He undoes the button at his collar. "I don't think anyone expects us to be drinking."

"*I'd* like to be drinking," Kristin pronounces. She tucks back her hair and puts her elbows on the table. "I'd very much like a Long Island Iced Tea."

"I don't think they serve tea at the bar," Bell says, distracted by what Carter is doing.

Emma and Kristin exchange glances.

Bell looks back. "Okay, heads up, Carter's bringing the public safety commissioner over here."

Emma's spine stiffens automatically.

"Miss Lewis, Miss Gutmunsson, Mr. Bell," Carter says. "I'd like to introduce Alan Kraus, the local commissioner. Mr. Kraus, these young people are part of our consulting team."

Kraus is an unfortunately strong-chinned man with styled red hair and a florid complexion. "Mr. Bell, we've met, good to see you again. Miss Gutmunsson, thank you for coming. Miss Lewis, that was a very brave speech you gave this morning."

Emma decides she is never shaking this man's hand. "It wasn't a speech. I didn't know I was going to be speaking."

"I'm very sorry I put you on the spot this morning." Carter sounds sincere until he turns to Kraus. "We were a little pressed for time, so I didn't get a chance to brief Miss Lewis on how things would play out."

"Which is convenient, because if you'd asked my permission, I would have said no."

Carter's face falls. "Miss Lewis—"

"Excuse me." Emma slips off her stool. "I'm going to get something nonalcoholic to drink. Kristin, I'll ask about the tea."

She walks over to the bar. A group of plainclothes detectives stands in a semicircle, talking and knocking back shots with beer chasers. The barkeep is busy farther down the line. While Emma's waiting, one of the men beside her turns and notices her hair.

"Whoa, Miss Lewis, how you doing? Joe Kowalski—me and Simmons stepped you through the leads today." Kowalski is a jovial, heavy-set guy in his thirties, already half in his cups.

"Oh right," she says. "Yeah, hi. I think we borrowed your desk this afternoon at headquarters."

"You can have it." Kowalski guffaws. "You trying to wash down the road dust?" He gestures to the barkeep. "Hey, Stu! Lady here's trying to get a drink."

"Oh no, it's fine—"

"Nah, don't worry about it. You want a beer?"

"Just orange juice, really it's—"

"Man, you need something stronger, after that shit today." Kowalski pushes a shot glass across the bar, fills it from the bottle of whiskey they've bought. "There you go—on the Pittsburgh PD."

Emma regards the shot glass and has just decided that honestly, she wouldn't mind, when Bell arrives near her elbow.

"Carter's waiting for you back at the table," he says.

"Really." She picks up the glass. "That's nice."

"C'mon, man," Kowalski says to Bell. "Let the lady finish her drink."

"Yeah, Bell. Let me finish my drink." Emma knocks back the

shot. It makes her eyes water a little. Kowalski and his crew let out a ragged cheer.

Bell glares at Kowalski. "Lay off. She's only nineteen."

"Ah shit. Sorry! I totally forgot." Kowalski looks repentant.

Bell's face is stormy as he turns back to Emma. "Can we talk? Like, right now?"

"Sure," Emma says, even though she doesn't want to.

They walk out the front door, where the concrete smells of dumpsters and drain water. The overhang protects the sidewalk from the main brunt of the rain. Night is swarming through the gloomy clouds.

Emma can see the red flare of McCreedy's cigarette inside the Plymouth across the street. She has a sense that something is coming—something unacknowledged between her and Bell is starting to take on a solid shape, but it's too big and too near, and she can't make out the details.

Bell's hands are on his hips as he rounds on her. "What are you doing?"

"Did it not look like I was having a drink?" The alcohol has made her a little loose. "You're not my guardian. Why do you care?"

"You're my partner. And you're not gonna be any use on this case if you can't keep it together."

"Oh. Well." Emma crosses her arms. "So long as I'm *useful to the bureau.*"

"What? Emma, what is going on with you? I know you're here under duress, and that's shitty. But why antagonize people like Horner and Carter, who're trying to help catch this guy? If it's something to do with why you turned the FBI down—"

"It's not about that."

"Then *what*?" His eyebrows knit. He seems genuinely confused. "They're trying to help, and I'm trying to look out for you, and we're making progress. But you're walking around lighting fires, and talking about consulting with *Simon Gutmunsson*—"

"He might be able to help us with this case," she insists.

"I still have a bullet-hole scar from the last time Simon Gutmunsson helped us with a case." Bell's expression is very dark. "It's a bad idea, and you know it."

"All our ideas are bad right now!" She's having trouble keeping her voice regulated. "And if we don't make some progress, we'll get another dead girl!"

Bell steps closer, too close. "Did you report Gutmunsson's postcards to the bureau?"

"Don't try that 'big man in a suit' routine on me." Emma's eyes harden and her spine gets poker-straight. "Why would I report the postcards? What would be the point? It's not against the law to send postcards."

"You *really* want to consult with him again, after St. Elizabeths?"

"Of course I don't want that! But the police here don't seem to have the first damn idea about how to find this killer, and Simon has an understanding of posing that might—"

"You watched him take a man to pieces." Bell's lips are thin.

"Anthony Hoyt was a serial murderer."

"So he deserved vivisection?"

Her enunciation is clipped. "I *know* Simon is dangerous. I haven't *forgotten*."

"If you go see him now, he'll drill into your skull with this copy-cat stuff."

Emma feels the cold weight of that in her stomach. "If I have to deal with that I will."

"That's what I'm *saying*." Bell makes a sharp, frustrated gesture with one hand. "You don't *have* to deal with it. Why is dealing with Gutmunsson even *necessary*?"

"Why is it *necessary*?" Emma gapes. "Jesus, Travis—have you been looking at the same crime scene photos as me? Dead girls at bus stops. Dead girls in alleyways. Dead girls beneath overpasses..." She can hear her voice climbing, is powerless to stop it. "You think I'm worried about talking to Simon Gutmunsson, if it will help solve this case? Women are *dying*. Women all over Pittsburgh are terrified. You don't know what that feels like!"

"I know Gutmunsson is a sociopath and a liar, and you'd be putting yourself deliberately at risk." Bell has snapped at her, which is something that never happens.

"Er, hello?" Kristin pokes the edge of herself out the door of the bar. "Mr. Carter is wondering if you're coming back to the table? I'm quite a good conversationalist, but it's a little awkward—"

"Oh shit," Emma says. "I'm sorry, Kristin."

Bell sighs. "We'll be right there."

"What were you talking about?" Kristin steps out fully, lets the door close behind her. If she heard the tail end of their discussion, she's not giving it away. "You can ask me, too, you know, if there's something you're trying to figure out—"

"I want to go see Simon," Emma blurts. "I think we need more insight on the posing at the crime scenes. I think it could be really important."

Kristin brightens. "I could go with you! Would they let us visit him, do you think?"

"We're supposed to be flying back to Washington tonight," Bell grates.

"Then we should ask Carter to switch the tickets." The idea is solidifying in Emma's mind. "We could do a hop from here to Philadelphia, then return to National."

Kristin claps her hands once then stops. "Would Mr. Carter allow it? He'll have to telephone through to Byberry to obtain the permissions...."

"I'm sure he can make it happen if we say we need it. Bell?"

"You want me to go convince Carter." His voice is flat.

"Look at me, Travis." She lets him look, lets him see what this is costing her. "I'm not trying to light fires. I'm *tired*. I'm tired of feeling scared of a ghost, and I'm tired of looking over my shoulder, and I'm tired of staring at pictures of dead girls."

Bell says nothing, and the silence has weight. Then he breaks away to walk past her, reaching for the door, to go back into the Grant Street Tavern and tell Carter they need to see Simon Gutmunsson.

CHAPTER NINE

They have to run for the plane. Travis offers Emma the aisle seat so she won't be squashed in the middle, and it's one of a series of small courtesies they've accorded each other since the argument. Each gesture adds a layer, hardens into a kind of impermeable chitin under which their true feelings roil.

Travis is still seething and he doesn't know why. He doesn't want to fight. He could blame it all on Gutmunsson—who he is and what he did—but that's not it either. At least, that's not all of it.

Emma's "big man in a suit" comment still smarts.

He reminds himself why she wants to do this: to stop another man, one who is assaulting and murdering women. He hears the reminder in his father's voice.

It's 1800 hours by the time they're in the air. McCreedy has settled into a spot two rows ahead and opened a well-thumbed Louis L'Amour paperback. A few minutes after takeoff, Emma excuses herself to use the bathroom.

Kristin's voice comes quietly from Travis's right. "She sweated through all her clothes, you know."

He turns his head. "Pardon?"

Kristin leans her shoulder against the porthole window of the plane. Her face is serene and ethereal, her long hair trailing down to her midriff, as white as the shirt she's wearing. Travis always thinks she looks out of place in contemporary settings; Kristin seems like she'd be more at home in some forest scene, dancing with woodland sprites.

"After the police briefing," Kristin notes. "Emma had to change her clothes because she sweated through the other ones. That was very brave of her, to go up there and speak. I could never do that in a million years, goodness. I would lift right off my feet and float away."

"They sprung it on her," he concedes. He remembers Emma's exchange with Carter in the bar. "They shouldn't have done that."

"*They*—you mean Mr. Carter. He wanted to give the Pittsburgh police a sense of urgency, to make them listen." Kristin inclines her head. "People only listen when women expose their pain, I suppose. Why do you think it's like that?"

Travis gets a sudden harsh flash on the Pittsburgh briefing: an image of Emma, pinched and pale and sharply defined, standing in front of all the officers in that huge room in the City-County Building. Then, outside the bar, wind blowing rain against her face, her buzzed hair sparking with it. He thinks of last night when she arrived, her rigid responses, the tremor in her voice when she said, "*It's him.*"

For Emma, this case isn't just about the victims. It's a very personal threat, a constant reminder of what she endured with Huxton. She's scared, and far from home, and trying mightily to hold it all together. There are a hundred different ways she is emotionally heightened right now.

He, on the other hand, is merely angry.

"I don't know," he says finally. "I don't know why it's like that." But observing Emma's experience, he thinks he's starting to.

Kristin is looking out the window again, like there's something to see besides darkness. "Does it make you regard Emma differently, knowing the details about what happened to her?"

Travis gets the urge to straighten, resists. "I'm used to thinking of Lewis as my partner. Not as part of a case file."

"You're not used to thinking of her as a victim."

He cuts his eyes sideways. "I think she'd be really angry if I called her that."

"She certainly does get angry. And there are other feelings. She holds them very tightly inside herself, doesn't she?"

"I'm familiar with her MO." His voice is dry.

"But you hold on to your feelings, too, I think. So you don't come across as unprofessional." Kristin smiles, her expression open. "I suppose we all do it. Even me."

Travis examines Kristin's smile for a moment. "Just because you're smiling doesn't mean you're not feeling stuff, right?"

"Of course." She looks at him, clear-eyed. "I'm not sociopathic, like my brother."

———————————

It's forty minutes from Philadelphia International in a hired car. They head west of the city, following the course of the Delaware River until they hit the Woodhaven Road turnpike. McCreedy drives assuredly in the dark along roads he's never navigated before, a skill Travis envies.

Black walnut trees make a shadowy honor guard along Roosevelt

Boulevard, and then there's the turn onto Byberry Road. The white sign marked PHILADELPHIA STATE HOSPITAL glows a warning.

One checkpoint at the gate. Farther in, the hospital streets are very ordered. Modern-looking building cubes are all aligned with the curbs, and spotlights illuminate the pathways. It's hard to get a proper sense of the place at night. They park near N-8 and N-9, the wards housing the criminally insane, and Travis experiences a heaviness in his chest.

Up the concrete stairs, they're buzzed into the foyer area, a nondescript cream-painted room wider than it is long. Beside an enclosed nurse's station on the left, a white woman in her forties wearing blue scrubs is examining a clipboard.

"Uh, hi." Travis steps forward. "There should have been a call from Special Agent Howard Carter—"

He jumps when the window at the nurse's station slides open. A matronly white woman in a starched uniform and a nurse cap pokes her head out the gap.

"Loretta, give me the clipboard and go back to your inmate chores."

The woman in the blue scrubs pouts and makes a dramatic sigh before handing the clipboard over. She walks to the coffee table on the far right of the foyer area, where she collects a feather duster and begins a desultory flicking at the framed paintings on the walls.

The matron examines the clipboard. "Your names, please?"

Emma recovers first. "Emma Lewis, Travis Bell, and Kristin Gutmunsson, to see Simon Gutmunsson. Special Agent Howard Carter called about the permissions. He said the warden would—"

"Warden Parrish is at his dinner right now. Can I see your credentials, please?" After she's seen all their identification, the woman makes a note and takes out three sets of papers. "Sign these. This is the women's facility. I need to call an orderly to escort you to the men's area."

There's only one ballpoint pen, so they have to take turns. The papers say that in the event of a lockdown or hostage situation, the Pennsylvania Department of Human Services will not take responsibility for a visitor's release, which is certainly reassuring.

A white-uniformed orderly arrives from a hallway somewhere on the other side of the nurse's station.

"Take these folks down to Secure Men's, please," the matron says. She is checking off the papers.

"Yes'm." The orderly is huge, stacked with muscle. Travis wonders how hard he'd go down in a fight. "You want me to take 'em through the courtyard or the tunnel?"

The matron's expression is displeased. "Oh goodness, Chester, use your head. They'd have to go back outside for the courtyard, and they just signed all the paperwork."

"Tunnel, then." Chester seems inured to the matron's displeasure. He ushers with his hands. "Come this way."

A series of corridors. Carpet is replaced by linoleum, and then concrete. They pass through two sets of doors, where Chester uses his keys, then downward via a set of stairs; at the bottom, the air is colder. Travis feels the hairs on the back of his neck rise. Now they have to traverse a corridor underground.

"Stay to the right, please." Like a mother duck, Chester checks to make sure they're walking single file behind. A yellow line on the floor indicates the path of safety.

Pipes and cable lines stretch like jungle vines above their heads;

fluorescent tubes provide dim illumination at intervals. The wall closest to Travis's right shoulder is white tile. On the left, across the yellow line, a series of dingy white doors, each with a slot to check on the condition of the inmate within.

Travis walks behind Emma and in front of Kristin. He doesn't usually have a problem with enclosed spaces, but his breathing is tight now. The fluorescent tubes buzz in their fixtures. Far down on the left, someone is talking in a low constant mutter. Another noise, a woman's pleading. Along the echoing corridor, the sounds of the residents magnify and recede, ghost voices bounced from wall to wall. Travis senses the swirl of many alien minds around him, throwing his balance off.

A hissing from the left. "Hey! Hey, buddy!"

Travis glances over on automatic. Through a slot in one of the doors, a pair of bloodshot eyes. The eyes are quickly replaced by another body part—the flash of a brown nipple.

Travis looks away fast. Chester raps on the door with a baton as they pass, and the slot goes empty. Just the residual sound of hoarse cackling.

Travis fixes his gaze forward as they walk on. His cheeks are hot, while the rest of his skin is cold. He's relieved when they make it to a checkpoint, even though this will deliver them closer to Simon Gutmunsson.

CHAPTER TEN

The checkpoint is a small, white-painted room with two desks, two orderlies, three doors, now crowded with the addition of four extra people as Chester waves Emma and the others inside.

"Late visitors," one of the orderlies drawls. "All my Christmases come at once."

"Folks to see N362," Chester says.

Emma steps up to the desk. "Our paperwork was signed upstairs. Special Agent Howard Carter sent the request through."

"Damn. Special Agent Howard Carter sounds like an important guy." The orderly behind the desk has a lean, hard look, with slicked-back hair and a faint jail tattoo on his left hand.

"Important enough." Emma keeps her face neutral. She doesn't want to antagonize this man, because she might have to visit again, but she's not going to put up with assholes.

The orderly's name tag reads GRENIER. Everything in his manner and his words suggests that Byberry is an institution run not by the warden, but by the staff. Grenier looks at Bell and Kristin, looks back at Emma, does a visual assessment. Emma knows she made the right choice, not to back down.

"Okay, here's the drill," Grenier says. "You stay on the right side of the corridor, behind the yellow line."

"Okay."

"You go inside the yellow line, he can reach you. He's got a long reach." Grenier nods toward the CCTV on the shelf beside the desk. It shows a view of the corridor they're about to enter. "I see you cross the yellow line, I pull you out. Understood?"

Emma glances at Kristin, then back. "Understood."

"If you want to pass him something—"

"There's nothing to pass him."

"Great. He's in the last cell on the left. When you're done, come back and I'll buzz you out."

"Thank you," Emma says.

Grenier pauses. "Watch yourself with this guy. Because sure as shit, he'll be watching you. He's sharp."

"I've interviewed him before," Emma says.

"Then you know to stay frosty." Grenier lifts his chin at the other orderly, who is completing paperwork. "Let this one through."

"Wait," Emma says. She can sense Kristin's vibrations of alarm. "We were sent as a group."

Grenier folds his arms. "Well now, I can't send no groups. I can send one at a time, or two with an orderly."

"That's—" Emma thinks fast. Simon won't talk with an orderly there. "I'll go."

Bell starts forward. "Lewis—"

"I'll go." Emma raises a hand for damage control. "Kristin, you come after me."

The other orderly unbolts the heavy door.

Emma is accustomed to fear. She has felt afraid in a wide variety of settings, but she doesn't know what to expect here. Simon's previous accommodation in St. Elizabeths was an old chapel, like the set of a Calvinist morality play. Byberry is different—modern, but more anonymous, and somehow more disturbing.

The corridor ahead is made of white-painted cinder block, more dimly lit than the tunnel—small night-light lamps glow above each cell. Emma takes the first step, and now that she's broken through that wall it feels easier to keep moving forward.

As she walks on, Emma realizes these cells are not fully enclosed but are fronted by bars, with a steel jail door just off-center. The cells themselves are dark inside, but she hears snuffling noises within. Emma avoids looking toward the noises.

On Emma's side of the yellow line, spaced white radiators are enclosed in wire mesh. The radiators don't seem to be giving off heat. All this dim white, and the cold air, give her a feeling like she's walking into the dark, hollow stomach of an industrial freezer.

There are two empty cells before Simon's. Emma can hear her own footsteps resounding, and she can hear someone reciting up ahead in a clear, cultured oratory style.

"And this is the night..." The voice is a resonant tenor. *"Most glorious night! Thou wert not sent for slumber! Let me be a sharer in thy fierce and far delight—a portion of thy tempest and of thee...."*

Emma finds her breath catching. She has not seen Simon for three months, but his voice often slips into her mind uninvited. It's very strange—and unsettlingly familiar—to hear him speak now, again, in person.

She composes herself for three more steps, four. Then she is in front of his cell.

At first glance, the space seems entirely dark and empty. Emma wants to close her eyes to catch the hum of Simon's presence, but there's no time for that.

She waits a moment before speaking to the darkness in the cell. "Hello, Simon."

There is a long pause. Then—

"You've been eating raspberries, Emma. And drinking whiskey. What a strange combination." A disembodied reply from the black.

"Yes." She wonders how he picked up on the raspberries, then realizes she's wearing the same shirt she wore to Audrey's. "Thank you for the postcards. I'd say it's nice to see you, but—"

"But that would be a lie," Simon Gutmunsson says, and he steps out of the gloom, into the light.

It's exactly like seeing a ghost ship emerge from a night fog. Simon's hair and skin are ice white, and his eyes are a fathomless blue. He is wearing the blue scrubs that are the Byberry inmate uniform, over a long-sleeved white T-shirt. He is angular, and very tall, with his twin's full lips and high cheekbones.

In normal life, Simon would be considered strikingly attractive. But his beauty is a razor; Emma knows it is a type of lure, like the filament of an anglerfish, that draws the hapless prey closer. The last time she saw him, he was ripping chunks off a man's face with his teeth.

"How the lit lake shines...." Simon smiles at her. He is just twenty years old, a murderer of twelve, and he is utterly without mercy. "Hello, Emma."

"I hope you don't mind me visiting so late." Emma thinks he looks thinner than the last time they met, but it's hard to be sure.

"Is it late? There are no clocks in jail." Simon steps nearer, into the small bright area immediately before the bars. "In any case, you know I always enjoy visitors."

Yes—you like to chomp them up and swallow them down. Emma pushes the thought away. "Thank you for seeing me."

"It's always a pleasure to see you, Emma. Are you well?"

"I am." Trading banal conversational graces with Simon is disconcerting, like chatting about the weather on Mars, but she knows he considers politeness important. "And you?"

"I'm quite in the pink of health—but somewhat disappointed by your lack of courtesy gifts. No picnic croissants? No contraband alcohol?"

This is a reference to their previous interactions. Emma shrugs in what she hopes is a careless way. "Sorry."

"What a shame." He makes an exaggerated pout. "Aside from the lack of gifts, I thought you'd come visit me sooner. Truly, Emma, you've hurt my feelings."

She's not convinced he *has* feelings. "I didn't know where in Philadelphia you'd been transferred."

"There aren't *that* many high-security insane asylums in the state, surely."

"I didn't want to assume."

"You never kept in touch." In the gloom of the cell, Simon's arctic blue eyes seem darker, threatening to swallow her whole. "No letters, no phone calls, no return postcards…"

"Well, I'm here now." She doesn't want to get drawn into argument or banter. She's not here for that. "And Kristin is with me. She'll come in and talk with you after we're done."

"Kristin is here?" Simon's expression softens into something more human.

"Yes." Emma's glad now that Kristin stayed at the checkpoint; it's good to have that ace up her sleeve. It's important to give Simon some incentive to cooperate.

"There's something happening, isn't there." Simon rolls his eyes. "The FBI only ever send visitors when there's a problem."

"You don't know about it already? I thought you'd be keeping up-to-date via the *Washington Post*." Emma tries to keep the dry tone out of her voice.

"Alas, I'm no longer permitted access to newspapers." He makes an airy wave. All his movements are casual, as if he is perfectly at ease, and not speaking to her through a wall of bars. "You will have to be my herald. Describe the problem for me."

"Someone is killing college girls in Pittsburgh. It's an issue of posing."

Simon's gaze trails away. "Well, I don't really know that much about posing…."

"I think you do." Emma bites her lip, then decides to go for it. "Marlowe Drury—your first victim. He was a friend of your sister. You gave him a soporific and then cut him open under a tree. The investigators described the homicide scene as a 'display.'"

"Oh, *that.*"

Emma pushes on, persistent. "Flora Dearborn and Gregory Northam, in a wilderness area near Exeter. You arranged them on a picnic blanket, in a kind of embrace. That's when the press started calling you the Artist."

She leaves out the part about how the intestines of the two victims were twined in the embrace, too. It's not necessary to give Simon information he already knows.

Simon makes a snort, but his expression is of someone who's been found out. "All right. Point taken. Tell me about Pittsburgh."

Emma feels a soft fluttering in her stomach, like you get after you bet big and win. "Three girls, so far. There are some resemblances to the Huxton case."

"Interesting." Simon tilts his head, presses one forefinger against his bottom lip. "I can see why the FBI called for you. But don't you get tired of it, Emma? Being dragged in to Quantico every time they need a bloodhound with a good whiff of the scent? It must be hard to concentrate on the smell of the quarry with all that police machismo radiating around you, brimming with repressed aggression...."

Dealing with Simon Gutmunsson can be tedious sometimes. Emma forces her expression to stay the same. "Can we simply talk about this case?"

"Did the FBI tell you they *needed* you?"

Emma's tone is flat. "They told me that my life was at risk."

Simon makes a rude noise. "*Pfft.* That old chestnut."

"I don't think I'm in danger," she says evenly, "but I'd rather be with the FBI, and helping solve the case faster, than be worrying about it under guard somewhere."

His smile turns vulpine. "You turned them down, didn't you? They tried to recruit you, and you turned them down."

"Yes." She makes an effort to relax her posture.

Simon leans forward, against the bars. "I'd very much like to know why."

Emma controls her instinct to recoil when he comes closer. She's glad for the gap between the yellow line and Simon's cell. "And I'd very much like you to tell me what you think the posing of the victims signifies."

"The posing is the primary difference between our new friend and your old friend Daniel Huxton, isn't it."

"Daniel Huxton was never my friend," Emma says, unhesitating.

"Would you shoot him, if he was in front of you now? You've learned to shoot since September of '79."

She pushes against the invisible weight on her chest. "What does the posing mean, Simon?"

Simon straightens and looks toward the other side of the cell, seeming to consider his reply. Emma knows he'll only tell her a deconstructed version of the truth. But somewhere along the way, he'll drop pearls of information she can use. It'll be up to her to sniff them out and grab for them.

"Posing has a number of meanings," he says finally, "and those meanings depend, to a large extent, on the personality of the individual artist. Posing originates in fantasy, of course—fantasies of control, fantasies of power. The artist seeks to exercise control over the subject, or the investigation, or both. A certain percentage of posed crime scenes are designed to divert attention to an alternative suspect."

Emma squints. "To confuse investigators?"

Simon smirks. "Hmm. It's a bit gauche, isn't it? It happens, though. Along with a percentage of posed scenes that are about controlling the subject even in death—to make them into exactly the thing you think they should be."

"I can see how you would get off on that." She has a policy of speaking honestly with him as much as possible.

He examines his nails. "I am a sadist, true, but I don't really 'get off on it' in the sense you mean. I find it heightening, but not arousing. My creations were never really part of a sexualized power fantasy, although there are people who are considerably less particular."

"This case involves sexual violence."

"Yes, well. Is he mutilating them in some way? There's a seventy-one percent chance that he is."

"Yes," she says. She wants to know how he knows this, but she doesn't want to interrupt him mid-flow.

"Some artists pose the subject as a form of retaliation," Simon explains. "To degrade them. I admit that many of my models were people I didn't particularly like."

"These victims were all wearing wedding dresses."

He smiles again. "Our new friend is a romantic. But he doesn't bury them, like Huxton."

"No. He sits them up in different locations."

"He leaves them outside? So people can see?"

"Yes. The last girl was found propped up at a bus stop."

Simon's lip curls up slowly in satisfaction. "You didn't find her sitting on the seat, though, did you. Was she sitting in the gutter?"

"Yes." Emma's control slips. "Simon, how did you know that?"

"They were all found in the gutter, weren't they?" He looks at her for a response, and when she's too slow, he turns side-on. "Maybe go away and read the case file properly. You could come back next week sometime. . . ."

"They were all in the gutter, yes."

"Kicked to the curb, as it were." Simon looks back at her with a fond expression. "Our new friend—for convenience let's call him John, shall we?—seems to have had some unfortunate experiences with women, most likely with the first woman he ever knew. John's been rejected before, and now he's doing the rejecting. But he still has hope—every time, he still hopes he'll find the One. He's asking the same question we all ask, Emma."

"What question is that?" Emma's throat is dry.

"It's what you ask yourself sometimes, in the heart of the night— who will love me?" He prowls forward, his eyes glimmering in the dark. "Why *did* you turn down the FBI's advances, Emma?"

She swallows. She tries to tell herself that Simon is a captive here. But this feels very much like his territory, regardless of who is on the right side of the cell bars.

"They want me to be their soldier," she says at last.

"And you don't want to spend your life fighting an unwinnable war. Men and women are different species, you know. Ask the philosophers and biologists, they'll tell you."

Emma holds herself very still. "I don't believe that's true. But if I have to keep looking at this stuff, I know I'll get hardened."

He lowers his chin to study her. "You don't think you are already? Emma, you've been steeped in blood for years. But I can see how living in a constant state of battle-readiness would be unappealing long term, yes."

"Every woman lives in a constant state of battle-readiness." It's very cold in here. The air coming into her lungs is getting thin. "And I don't think talking about my career choices has any relevance to this case."

"Well then, how is the Buckeye State at this time of year, Emma?" Simon is now leaning his shoulder against the corner where the bars and the cell wall meet.

She is reminded of Grenier's comment about Simon's reach. "Fine. Autumnal."

"Have you ever thought about me, since St. Elizabeths?"

"I think about you a lot, Simon." She knows this will appeal to his vanity. "Mostly I think about how I let you out, and what you did to the Berryville Butcher."

Simon shrugs one shoulder. "Anthony Hoyt was a rank poseur. An annoyance."

"And I wonder why you didn't kill me, too, when you had the chance."

"I would never do you injury, Emma." Simon straightens, his face uncharacteristically soft—then his expression changes. "Without you, whatever would I do for entertainment?"

"Kristin said you have a court case—"

He waves again. "Yes, yes, another court appeal—it's very boring. Charges, and intent, and the 'by reason of mental insanity or impairment' defense…" He breaks off mid-flight. "What do you think, Emma? Do you think my lawyers will save me from lethal injection this time?"

"It's the electric chair in Massachusetts," she points out.

"Well, that's appropriately gothic, I suppose."

"Will you help me on this case, Simon?" Emma knows that a direct plea is her last chance. Simon will respond to her, or he won't. She has no way to compel him. All she can do is ask. "I can't get you out of Byberry, I can't stop your court process. I've got nothing to offer, except that you might get to see Kristin a few times before this is all over—"

"And will you come by again, Emma?" Simon's head is gently angled, the sharp plane of his cheek exposed to the light and his eyes taking in her face.

"Yes, if you'll talk to me."

"The best approach is to register your name with Monsieur Grenier at the front desk. Delightful fellow. His hands simply *reek* of Brylcreem."

"If you assist me in this," she continues, "I might be able to persuade the FBI to vouch for your cooperation, to bolster your case in court—"

"Oh, Emma." Simon smiles at her kindly. "Don't promise me the stars. You don't have that kind of authority."

"We want to catch this guy real bad," Emma admits.

"Then you should be looking at who he targets." His gaze narrows. "Didn't you learn *anything* from Hoyt? If you want to find the hunter, follow the prey."

Emma marshals herself. She's got what she needed, now it's time to go. She's not sure why the idea of leaving Simon here, alone, produces a sense of melancholy. "Thank you, Simon."

"And now again 'tis black...." He looks wistful. "Goodbye, Emma. See you next time."

CHAPTER ELEVEN

Travis doesn't take his eyes off Emma. Through the big porthole window in the door, she looks small and far away, lost in the gloom of the asylum's basement corridor.

The glimmer of her profile: Her lips move as she speaks. At this distance and angle, he can't see Gutmunsson, so it looks like she's speaking to nobody. But Gutmunsson is there. Travis can feel it in his own revulsion, the strange yearning awareness of his father's murderer so close by. Travis feels how his mouth has tightened and twisted. He presses his lips together, tries to relax his expression, regain some control.

In the tiny guard room, the scratching of pens as Grenier and his colleague complete paperwork. Chester has returned to the women's facility.

"She's taking a long time," Kristin whispers.

Kristin is standing to Travis's left, gripping her own fingers. Both of them are watching down the corridor.

Travis wants to reply, but he doesn't trust himself.

Now, movement—Emma pivots and walks back. Her face gets more defined as she gets closer.

"Ayuh, let her in," Grenier says, and the other orderly works the clanking metal door.

Travis thinks Emma's expression resembles someone just awakened from a disturbing dream. She has hollows around her eyes; it occurs to him that she probably didn't get a lick of sleep last night.

"You get what you came for?" Grenier asks her.

Emma ignores that. "Kristin, you should go down now," she says. Her voice is a little hoarse.

There are some gestures between the two orderlies, then Kristin is allowed through the door. Travis hears the eager clip of her shoes on the concrete, sees the swirl of her skirts.

Emma looks over at Grenier. "Have you got paper and a pen?"

"Here." Travis takes a small spiral-bound notebook and a pencil from his inside jacket pocket, hands them to her. Their fingers touch as she receives the writing materials.

"Thanks," Emma says. She flips the cardboard cover, finds a fresh page.

She is still in the nightmare country, he can tell. She stands in the middle of the tiny office, motionless but for the short, fierce movements of her writing hand as she pours her notes from the conversation with Gutmunsson down onto the page.

When she's done, she shakes her hand out. Her expression seems clearer. "How long do we want to give Kristin?"

Travis checks his watch. "Five more minutes. Or we won't make the flight to DC."

"Okay." She nods, a little too repetitively. Catches him looking. "I'm okay."

"Good." He knows she's not going to talk about it now.

They have to send the other orderly down to fetch Kristin back, in the end. When the girl returns, she's smiling, but she doesn't look happy.

Her eyes appeal to Emma. "Are you sure I couldn't have just a few more minutes—"

"I'm sure." Emma's tone gentles. "We don't want to miss the plane."

Getting out of the building is easier than getting in. Then there is McCreedy, waiting for them in the parking lot. They have to hightail it to Philadelphia International. The flight attendant holds the door for them, and they're the last passengers to board.

When Kristin goes to the bathroom soon after takeoff, Travis feels it's the right time to speak. "Look, I need to apologize. What I said to you in Pittsburgh was outta line—"

"Stop." In the aisle seat on his left, Emma has turned to face him. "Stop apologizing for things you have no control over. You're reactive about Simon Gutmunsson, for completely legitimate reasons. I knew that, and I pushed. Then I got angry when you pushed back, which...wasn't fair."

Her directness is always so disarming. He blinks at her. "I'm sorry I got mad."

"Me too." She gives him one of those tiny, soft-lipped smiles that always feel like a gift. "Let's forget about it."

"Okay." He says that, but there's something about this exchange that he doesn't want to forget. He's not sure where this sensation is coming from, so he redirects onto safer paths. "Did you get anything out of Gutmunsson about the posing?"

"Yes," she confirms.

"Then I guess it was worth it." He pulls his shirt collar away from his neck. "I still don't know how you can stand to talk with him."

Emma squints at the seat back in front of her. "I have to prepare myself mentally—get in the right frame of mind."

Travis is still struggling with the idea. "Don't you ever get overwhelmed?"

Her head turns and she holds his gaze. "Every single second. When I'm in there, I'm always aware of what he's doing. Of where I am. Of how he looks at me, and what he says. I'm trying to take in everything at once, and there's always this pressure in the back of my mind—the knowledge of his history, and the weirdness of knowing he let me live, back in June...." She looks away and shivers. "It's exhausting, but you have to be that alert. You always have to remember what he is. And what you are."

"What's that?"

"Prey." Emma looks Travis right in the eye. "We're just prey to him."

"But he could have killed you at St. Elizabeths, and he didn't."

"It doesn't matter." She shakes her head. "Inconsistency is his only consistent feature. He let me live in June, he seems to like talking with me, but he could change his mind. He's just playing with me, like a cat with a mouse. He's playing with all of us. That's all we are to Simon. Potential victims. That's all he thinks about."

Travis feels the skin on the back of his neck crawl. "Even still?"

"Always."

Kristin returns from the bathroom, so that's where the conversation ends.

The cabin is dark—Travis registers for the first time that it's late, nearly 10:30 PM. The flight's only an hour; soon they'll be back in DC, but then they still have to drive another hour to Quantico. Travis's exhaustion hits him hard all of a sudden. He's glad McCreedy's going to be behind the wheel once they disembark: Travis doesn't think he'd trust himself not to run their bureau car off the road.

On his right, Kristin leafs through a magazine. At left, Emma is quiet. A few minutes later, he notices her eyes blinking. Her chin drops, jerking up immediately. She rests her seat back. He does a slow count to thirty, and when the cabin gently tilts as the plane banks, Emma's head settles onto his shoulder.

Her breathing is deep and even, but she makes little twitches that he can feel through his suit jacket. Travis finds his own breathing coming in low and quiet. He doesn't want to wake her. He trains his gaze resolutely forward for as long as he can, before an undefined urge gets the better of him, and he looks down.

This is the third time Travis has seen Emma in repose. Her skin is very pale, and her cheek looks soft. The main thing he notices is that Emma doesn't sleep slack-jawed and vulnerable. She looks like herself, except with her eyes closed.

CHAPTER TWELVE

It must be nearly one in the morning by the time they all arrive back at Quantico, but Kristin feels surprisingly awake.

What a day it has been! First, the shock of the helicopter, then the busywork in Pittsburgh, an antidote to the sadness she feels whenever she thinks about the murders. She's noticed how the police avoid personalizing the victims, sticking to anonymous phrases like "Victim One" or "the second victim" or "the third case." But Kristin remembers all their names. To her, they are Geraldine and Marilyn and Patricia, and each of them was a girl, a unique girl, whole and complete and alive.

Kristin wants to be the someone who remembers the details about them when all the other details are smeared together by the "victim" moniker. Emma's presence is a reminder that if the bureau moves quickly, more unique girls may be saved.

But Kristin won't think about that now. Instead, she contemplates the day's final, best surprise: the opportunity to see Simon.

Nobody has asked Kristin what she and her brother said to each other, which she finds curious. She's not sure if she could explain it, anyway—so much of the communication between herself and her twin is about feelings, old memories, lines of poetry, moments in time. Talking to Simon is like listening to music playing just beyond other peoples' aural reach, or standing before a warming fire in the grand stone fireplace at Pippi's house....Although Pippi is dead now, of course.

None of that is pertinent to the investigation, so Kristin doesn't bother to go into it.

But just being near Simon makes her heart resonate with indescribable joy. Even in Byberry, that horrible dungeon where they could not touch, there was something about her brother's presence that Kristin found energizing. These are the thoughts that sustain her as the bureau car pulls to a halt outside Jefferson, as she separates from Travis and Emma in the atrium.

Kristin takes the elevator, goes to her assigned room, and completes her toilette. Then she settles herself in a chair by the window, pulls the curtain to one side, and spends an hour looking at her old friend, the moon.

The next day, she arrives at the basement office at 7:00 AM, but Travis promptly ushers her back from whence she came.

"We're going back upstairs." He has coffee in a lidded polystyrene cup in one hand. His other hand is levering the strap of his heavy satchel onto his shoulder, shutting the door of the Cool Room behind them. "Report from Scientific Analysis just came through. We should go."

"What does that mean?" she asks. She finds much of what the FBI does baffling.

"It means we're meeting Emma in the atrium," he explains

gently. "Then we're heading out. I've been instructed to do follow-up, and I know the lab folks in DC, so I'd like to talk with them in person."

The enjoyable feeling of momentary weightlessness in the elevator. Kristin pushed the buttons helpfully and now stands beside Travis, swinging her hands. "Do you think there will be something new in the forensic results from Patricia Doricott?"

Travis watches the numbers climb. "No idea. But we've got fresh eyes to look at them now."

"Emma might see something?"

"She might."

On the atrium concourse, Emma is wearing the same jeans as yesterday, or maybe an identical clean pair, with a different shirt. Her shorn head gives her a skeletal profile against the pale blank brick of the atrium wall. She looks more rested than she did last night, but there are still shadows around her eyes.

She notices their purposeful, striding approach. "Do I have time to get coffee?"

"Better hurry," Travis says. "Kristin, you want anything?"

It's nice that he thinks to ask. "I would very much like a cream cheese sandwich. No coffee." Kristin considers the Quantico coffee an abomination.

"Gimme five minutes," Emma says.

Travis is already walking backward for the main door. "Meet you out front. McCreedy's got the car."

They nod at each other. Emma walks off to the cafeteria. Kristin finds the way the two of them circle around each other quite fascinating. Something is happening there—she can feel the energy of it, like a heat shimmer in the air—and it's interesting to see the way they're handling it.

They remain highly professional, of course. In the car, Emma holds a file and cups a to-go coffee on her knee while staring out the window, deep in thought. Travis rearranges the paperwork in his satchel. His eyes flit over each of them: McCreedy driving, she and Emma in the rear. Kristin is aware that Travis Bell is singularly observant. She turns her own attention to the outside of the car. The weather is of the not-quite-nice variety: It should be warm, but a layer of cloud creates a flat dispersal of sunlight that eschews warmth.

Kristin would like to eat the sandwich, encased in plastic wrap on her knee, but the scent of Emma's shower gel is interfering with her appetite. "Did you go running this morning?"

"No." Emma blinks back to reality. "They won't let me go without an escort, so I've gotta arrange it in advance."

"But you like to run," Kristin notes.

Emma shrugs. The shrug looks more helpless than nonchalant.

"You get some sleep last night?" Travis's voice is casual.

"Some." Emma sips her coffee, evades his gaze. "Any new leads in Pittsburgh?"

Travis consults his notes. "They got a potential hit at a thrift store in Delmont. Could be the dress was bought from there."

"Any chance they'll get an ID of who bought it?"

"Looks unlikely. It's a cash-only place—no sales records, no cameras."

"But it means he bought local." Emma bites her lip. "It's something."

Travis nods. "It's something."

Kristin watches the interplay of body language. It's like watching a really good tennis match. She sees Emma tear her eyes away from the window again. She swallows more coffee, wets her lips. Kristin wonders why she hesitates, then realizes Emma must be preparing to talk about Simon—that's always a touchy subject with Mr. Bell.

"I've been thinking about the posing," Emma says finally. "According to Simon, posing originates in fantasy."

"Oh yes—I know this." Kristin's pleased that she can contribute, although she only remembers the basics. "It's about control, isn't it?"

"Yes," Emma confirms. "Sometimes it's about controlling the direction of the investigation, to throw the police off the scent. But I don't think this guy is doing that. For him, it's about controlling the victims."

"He takes such care with them," Kristin reflects. "The dresses, the veils, the way they hold the flowers..."

"Simon called him a romantic." Emma's expression flashes briefly, in a way Kristin can't interpret. Then she resumes her neutral tone. "But the places and poses the girls were dumped in suggest the killer is rejecting them. Like they were unworthy in some way."

"So, he has a...a romantic *ideal*," Travis suggests. "When the girls don't meet his standards, he rejects them."

"Simon claims the killer is asking a question—'Who will love me?'" Emma meets Travis's eyes, looks away uncomfortably.

Kristin plays with a strand of her own hair. Out the window of the car, faint mist below, and sun glittering on the brown water of the Occoquan. "Perhaps he gets angry when the girls don't love him back."

"But none of them will ever reciprocate," Emma points out. "He's just going to keep grabbing girls, and they'll all be rejects."

"Which is why he's escalating," Travis suggests.

Emma nods. "He's getting more frantic and angry with each rejection." Her eyes lose focus as she seems to recall something. "It's like...the thing he's doing brings no relief."

"What is he looking for relief from?" Travis asks.

Kristin thinks she knows. "Loneliness."

"Shame." Emma locks eyes with her. "You feel embarrassed when you're rejected."

Travis squints. "So he wants an emotional connection with the girls. When he's denied that, he takes what he wants from them physically—"

"But that's ultimately unsatisfying," Kristin points out. "Finally, he kills them."

Emma's eyes are thoughtful again. "Then he puts his shame back on *them*—he humiliates them publicly, by dressing them up and dumping them in the gutter."

"Like he's jilted them at the altar." Travis chews his lip. "That's a lot of intense emotion. Do you think he might be a suicide risk before we catch up to him?"

"No," Emma says, hesitates. "Maybe."

Kristin thinks it's rather confident of Mr. Bell to assume they'll catch this man when the police didn't catch Simon for ages. But now she is considering it. "I don't think so. I think he's driven by self-righteousness. He displaces his own responsibility onto others—he blames the girls for all of it. He would never blame himself."

"These guys never do," Emma says, her lips thin. She is watching the trees out the window as the road climbs. "But we can catch him. Somewhere in this information is the key. This guy is not infallible. Serial killers have hugely inflated egos—they don't think they'll make a mistake. But they do. That's how I got away from Huxton. He made a mistake, and I saw it. I took my chance and got free. The College Killer will make a mistake, too. We just have to be ready for it, and recognize it when we see it."

"I want all of this down on paper," Travis says firmly. "We should give a report to Jack Kirby at Quantico, and he can pass it on to Carter."

He spends the rest of the trip writing things down in a notebook, asking Emma and herself to supply any details he's missed. In this fashion, it doesn't seem to take them long at all to arrive at FBI Headquarters on Pennsylvania Avenue. McCreedy drives them down into the quiet of the underground parking garage—he gets to sit in the car and enjoy some peace as they sign in.

For Kristin, everything is new: the white corridors, the way they have to swipe their IDs. Interestingly, both Travis and Emma seem more comfortable here than at Quantico. Kristin observes how their shoulders have relaxed. They've moved subtly closer to one another. Travis rakes a hand casually through his dark hair.

In the elevator, Emma says, "We're not getting these lab results before Carter, are we?"

Travis shakes his head. When they're in transit or on the street, he usually seems a little overdressed in his dark suits, but here, inside a federal building, they make him look more agent-like.

"They faxed the lab results to Pittsburgh already. I just want to hear it from the horse's mouth." He turns to Emma. "Look, you oughta know—Glenn Neilsen had a car accident."

Her mouth opens. "Oh shit."

"He's okay, but there's been a few changes—" The doors part, and Travis gestures. "Come on, you'll figure it out."

About halfway down another white corridor, a new door. Travis swipes his ID, and they're met just inside by a short, swarthy man with a dark goatee and imposing brows. He's wearing a white lab coat over a red polo shirt and trousers. He has very nice shoes—a pair of dark brown wingtips that look custom-tooled. The leather has a rich, cognac gleam.

He slaps his hand into Travis's with a wide smile. "Oye, que bueno es verte en persona en vez de hablar por teléfono."

Travis grins as they shake. "No podía quedarme lejos." He angles to include everyone. "You remember Emma Lewis?"

"Miss Lewis, welcome back," the man says, shaking hands with Emma in turn. Kristin has observed her avoid handshakes, but with this man she doesn't seem to mind.

"And this is Kristin Gutmunsson," Travis says. "She's assisting on the case. Kristin, this is Carlos Dixon, he's the foremost trace analyst here at the lab."

"Hello," Kristin says. She makes a little wave, feeling awkward at how Dixon's expression changes at the mention of her surname.

But he seems more surprised than horrified. He gives her a courteous nod. "Miss Gutmunsson, nice to meet you."

"Thank you for accommodating us so early in the morning," she says.

Dixon snorts. "The lab never sleeps. Come into the office."

He walks them through an open area that would be large, except it's crammed full of cardboard boxes and plastic storage containers. Kristin can only see vague outlines through the cloudy plastic lids, but some of the things inside the containers seem very odd—underwear and children's clothes claim space with doorknobs and pillowcases.

Dixon continues talking as they weave their way. "Gerry's not here—he's still en route from Pittsburgh. He was up there yesterday, taking samples, we got everything via FedEx yesterday afternoon. How's the training going?"

"It's going," Travis says ruefully.

"Glenn's got the latest results." Dixon turns his head toward Emma. "Did Travis tell you about—"

"He told me," Emma says.

"Okay, cool. Miss Gutmunsson?" Dixon has noticed her peering around, waves her forward. "This way."

He leads them through a right-hand door, which opens out into a large laboratory. The lab is spacious, with a lot of strange-looking machines and equipment along one side, and at the rear. But it looks efficient, tidy—meticulous, in fact. Half of the lab tables are standard height, and the other half are lowered to accommodate a man in a wheelchair.

The man rolls over to them, navigating smoothly around the

furniture. He's white, and Kristin estimates his age is about thirty years old. He has very fine brown hair that drifts up a little at the back, and he's wearing a white shirt and gray trousers. His hands on the chair's wheels are latex-gloved; once he's arrived in front of them, he strips off the gloves and tosses them into a nearby wastebasket.

He has a puckered scar down one side of his jaw. His eyes don't look toughened or traumatized—just wide and curious, and a little tired. He pushes up his glasses, apparently happy to see Emma and Travis. "Miss Lewis and Mr. Bell, welcome back."

"Good to see you, Mr. Neilsen," Emma says.

"Oh—just Glenn, please." His eyes travel over to Kristin. "You brought a friend."

Carlos Dixon makes the introductions. "Glenn Neilsen, this is Kristin Gutmunsson."

Now Kristin sees a real reaction. Neilsen's eyebrows lift almost to his hairline. "Okay, wow. You're—"

"Yes." But Kristin was brought up to deflect delicate social moments. "You have a wonderful laboratory," she enthuses.

Neilsen is immediately distracted. "Yeah, it's a good setup—centrifuge, gas chromatograph, transilluminators..." He grins at the three of them. "Wanna see something cool? Check it out."

He lifts his chin at a small transparent box, set to one side on a nearby countertop. It's attached to another black box, which is inlaid with a number of switches and dials.

"Gel electrophoresis equipment for RFLP analysis. We're hoping to do more with DNA eventually." Neilsen gets a dreamy look while talking about it, then snaps back as he glances over. "But you probably want to look through the results, right?"

Travis nods, all business. "Is toxicology back yet?"

"We're still waiting on that. But we've got a load of other material—here, take a look."

Neilsen wheels over to a bench on the far side of the room. He seems comfortable moving around in the chair, especially within the familiar environs of the lab, but he does not yet have the developed torso and arm musculature common to long-term wheelchair users.

Dixon, Travis, and Emma follow close to Neilsen; Kristin trails a little farther behind, casting her eyes around. This is where samples come for testing, from the dead bodies in homicide cases. A lab like this one probably examined the forensic evidence that convicted her brother.

The awareness registers in a small way; then, as they navigate through the lab to a low-set table, it increases into a building pressure beneath Kristin's ribs that makes her breath catch. She exhales slowly to will it away, focuses back on the paperwork that Glenn Neilsen is looking through and talking about with the others.

"Your tip about the pink nail polish hit the jackpot, Miss Lewis," Neilsen says approvingly. "Gerry got a partial print from the left forefinger of the Doricott girl—it was embedded in the polish."

"You got a print?" Travis's cheeks flush in his excitement.

Neilsen works to tamp that down. "Only a partial. It's a whorl—probably off a thumb. Gerry says it's unlikely to be enough for an identification, but he's gonna play with it more when he gets back."

Emma's eyes are darting. "Was there any result on the polish itself?"

Dixon clears his throat. "Yeah. It's Revlon brand, but it's old—about seven years old. I didn't know polish lasted that long in the bottle, but there you go."

Neilsen picks up the thread. "We're doing our best to track it, but it's a discontinued line. The color is called Frosted Pink Cloud."

Dixon nods. "We think he might've already had it at home. It's not something he'd be able to buy currently, unless he picked it up at a charity shop or maybe a vintage market."

"If the police found it during a search of his residence, it would be a strong lead," Travis interprets.

"But only circumstantial," Emma notes. She chews dents into her bottom lip. "What else?"

"The bouquet flowers are asters, goldenrod, chrysanthemums, dahlias, and bud roses, as well as some Christmas fern." Neilsen moves his papers around on the table, along with a number of glossy photographs. "They're all seasonal wildflowers or garden flowers local to the Pittsburgh region, which means they're common."

"Oh." Emma deflates a little.

"But they only grow *together* in certain areas, so we're canvassing those sites. It's a guess, but we don't think he's driving all over Pittsburgh to collect the flowers, if he wants them fresh."

"Okay," Travis says. "Any other trace from the wedding dress?"

"Yeah, and the fingernail grit." Dixon's expressive brows waggle. "This is where I get to go into exciting detail about carpet fluff...."

The two men, and Emma and Travis, launch into a conversation about additional trace evidence. As they get technical, Kristin runs her fingers lightly over a nearby lab table surface, tunes out the boring forensic details. The conversation stretches, and she looks around. No one seems to be paying her much attention, and there are no barriers to prevent her from wandering quietly away, so that is what she does.

She meanders back out the door of the lab. Across the corridor, another door, which is closed. On the door is a nameplate panel that reads L. BROWN—DOCUMENTS.

Just below the nameplate, in a frame, is a short length of parchment paper that bears an illuminated quote:

> *For nothing is hidden, that will not be revealed; nor anything secret, that will not be known and come to light.*
> *—Luke 8:17*

Kristin stands before the parchment and loses herself for a while in the curves and strokes of each letter. In her imagination, she traces the artist's movement with the quill nib. She only looks up when she feels a sense of movement to her right. Someone else is nearby.

An elegant Black woman in a burnt-orange skirt and a brown knit blouse has arrived holding a file folder. She looks to be in her forties. Her hair is styled in a flipped bob, and she has simple gold drops in her ears. Everything about her is very uncluttered and orderly, which Kristin likes.

"Can I help you?" the woman asks. Her voice is firm but not unfriendly.

"Oh, hello," Kristin replies. She is still mentally engaged in the bold flourish of an *a*. It takes her a moment to detach and remember that she is on government property. "Excuse me, I hope I'm not intruding—I'm with Miss Lewis and Mr. Bell. They're still talking with the two gentlemen in the laboratory...."

She waves a hand vaguely toward the lab. The woman in the burnt-orange skirt looks between the lab door and Kristin.

"You're not intruding," she says, before pausing. "Were they talking about carpet fluff?"

Kristin's shoulders relax. "Yes! Yes, they were. And it seemed like a rather scientific conversation, to which I could contribute very little, so I came out here. This illumination is lovely."

She gestures toward the framed quote, and the other woman follows with her eyes. Her face softens. "Yes, I've always thought so."

"The calligraphy is so striking."

"It's by Jenny Hunter Groat. It was a gift from a friend."

"What an excellent friend," Kristin muses, caught up again in the certainty and bravery of the lines, the combination of black and walnut inks. She remembers herself. "Oh, I'm very sorry—I'm Kristin Gutmunsson."

As she extends her hand, she notices the woman taking in her white hair, her ID on its lanyard. Only a moment's hesitation before the woman transfers her file folder to her other hand, and shakes.

"Linda Brown. It's nice to meet you."

"Ah." Kristin steps back from the quote, the door. "Then this is your office and I'm blocking your way."

"Not at all. I was just about to join the lab group and talk about nightclub stamps."

"That seems like another conversation to which I could contribute very little."

"Oh, I don't know." Linda Brown smiles. "You might surprise yourself."

Kristin sees Linda Brown's expression alter. There is a shift of awareness between them, an acknowledgment that must be spoken aloud.

"You're Simon's sister," Brown says gently.

"I am," Kristin admits.

This is the part Kristin so often struggles with—when she reveals the connection, and people step back and move away. She braces for it.

"Will you return to the lab with me?" Brown says, and she gestures with her file in that direction.

"Oh," Kristin says, and as she takes a breath, she realizes that she really can't return to the lab. "I..."

She just *can't*. Every muscle and tendon and nerve ending—every particle of her being—rebels at the thought. It's something about the idea of pieces of dead bodies under microscopes, and another gnawing fancy: the idea of Simon being cut up and examined in the same way.

The pressure under her ribs is very strong now, and her entire consciousness just...doesn't want to be here, or to go back in there. It affects her so deeply, she finds it hard to form sensible words to express herself.

"Oh no, I don't think so." She lifts her chin and floats her gaze around, looking at nothing. "I believe I'll just stay here, and..." She swallows. "I think I'll just stay here and look at your lovely illumination."

Linda Brown pauses. Then she steps forward and reaches past

Kristin for the door handle. "Why don't you come on through to my office. You can sit in there, if you'd like."

"Oh," Kristin says. "I certainly don't mean to—"

"It's no trouble," Brown says, and she opens the door fully so they can both go inside.

The office itself is rather like the woman: neat and warm and practical. There is a desk lamp providing low light; the desk itself is mahogany, with a pale leather blotter. More equipment that Kristin doesn't recognize occupies niches on wall shelves. A wooden filing cabinet has a number of framed certificates above it. Brown places her file folder on the blotter and motions to a chair beside the desk.

"Please, sit. Glass of water?" Brown offers, and pours from a carafe on a side shelf, into a paper cup.

"Thank you." Kristin settles herself into the chair. Of all the awkward encounters she has had with strangers who know her name, this is somehow one of the least awkward. She accepts the water gratefully. It does make her feel slightly better, enough to maintain conversation. "So what are you going to say about night-club stamps?"

Brown pours herself a cup of water, too. "That I've identified stamp traces on the wrists of two of the girls. I think they both attended the same nightclub."

Kristin blinks at her wonderingly. "Well, that's very important."

"I believe so, yes." Brown sips as she stands. "It also confirms what Miss Lewis suggested, that the girls are being taken in a social setting."

Brown comes closer, and sets her cup carefully to one side of the desk so she can open the file and slide out a piece of paper.

The paper bears two line drawings absent their original human skin backgrounds. One is only a fragment, with a barely decipherable image, but the other clearly shows a pair of angel wings.

"You said only two of the girls had this stamp?" Kristin leans forward to examine the drawings. At the edges of the file folder, a few glossy victim photos are peeking out, as if they want to see, too.

Brown nods. "For a while, I wasn't sure if Patricia Doricott had the same stamp, but I tried different filters and found enough remnants to get an impression. I couldn't get an impression from the wrist of the second girl, Marilyn Preston. It's possible that a club stamp was worn away."

"He's deliberately wiping it off," Kristin realizes.

"I think so," Brown confirms, "but I don't like to make assumptions. It's possible that Marilyn was abducted at an alternative location."

"But if Geraldine and Patricia have stamps, it stands to reason that Marilyn may also have had a stamp." Kristin peers at the drawings. The stamp image is a delineation of wings, not a cartoon but not much more than an outline. Only a suggestion of feathers remains. "Is the stamp of a particular type or make?" She's not sure how to describe it. "Er, is it—"

"It's a self-inking stamp, not a pad stamp," Brown clarifies, nodding. "Now we just need to narrow down which club in Pittsburgh uses this stamp."

"That's very clever."

"Thank you." Brown smiles.

But Kristin finds herself distracted by the identification photographs of the victims that are spilling out of the file folder. Faces are so much more interesting and revealing than inert facts, and each of the girls in this case has a pleasing similarity. To her eye, they are like a three-part harmony: the same melody sung in a different but consonant key, with the same rhythm....

"Wait," Kristin says.

She slides the photos onto the desk surface, aware that Brown is watching her. Kristin has examined these photos before. But a very subtle understanding is occurring to her now, in this place, in this office. Maybe it's something about the quality of the light.

She tilts the photos, to examine them from different angles. "They're all..."

Brown is a stillness in her peripheral vision. "What do you see?"

Kristin's mind is whirring. "They have the same bone structure. The same build. The same hair."

"We know he's selecting girls of a certain type—" Brown starts.

"Yes, but this is more than just an issue of type." Kristin looks up at Brown sharply. "Do you have identification photos from the Huxton case?"

Brown hesitates a moment, before walking over to a shelf with an expanding file. Inside the file, she collects a folder. The folder is marked HUX-V79, and Brown peels a sheet out of it, places it on the desk. The sheet is a compilation of victim photos from Ohio's most horrifying case of serial homicide.

Kristin scans through the sheet, arranges the current photos nearby.

"Look," she says, pointing. "The Huxton girls are all Caucasian brunettes. But these four have short hair. And this girl has braces."

"She was one of the youngest victims," Brown supplies.

But Kristin is tracking another thread. "This girl has curly hair, which doesn't match. Let's rule out these six. These others most resemble the girls in Pittsburgh."

Brown is beginning to see the pattern. "This girl—the large eyes."

"Yes. And the sharp jawline..." Kristin rearranges some of the photos. "They're all petite, and their bone structure is petite."

"But the Pittsburgh girls all have a distinct look," Brown says, frowning. "The high foreheads, the facial shape..."

"We're missing a photo," Kristin says. She can hear the certainty in her own voice.

Brown looks at her. Then she goes again to the expanding file for a separate folder called HUX-SV79. She takes out a photo and places it next to the photos of the other girls.

Now Kristin sees it in front of her, she can't imagine why it never registered before. The killer has been targeting girls similar to Huxton's victims, and these current girls all have a resemblance, yes. But it's more than resemblance. They don't just look like *each other*. They look like—

"Emma," she breathes. She looks up and holds Brown's gaze. "He's searching for Emma."

CHAPTER THIRTEEN

There were only two photos of me released to the media, that I'm aware of," Emma explains from the front passenger seat of the car, craning her neck a little to talk to Travis and Kristin in the back.

Travis hasn't kept track of the number of photos. He frowns out at a FedEx truck passing them on I-95. "So, one picture released around the time you went missing?"

Emma nods. "And another one of me coming out of the hospital with my parents, when it was all over, but I had a jacket over my head that time."

"No," Kristin says immediately. "There was another one."

"Which one?" Emma asks, her expression confused.

"I saw it when I was going through the media reports," Kristin says. "It's a grainy shot of you in a hospital bed. I believe it was taken with a long-distance lens, probably through a window."

Travis swears under his breath, can't help it. "That's disgusting."

"That's journalists," Kristin says cheerfully. "Horrible little carrion feeders. You're lucky we're not dealing with them directly in Pittsburgh."

They're driving under an overpass, and the sign for LORTON—1 MILE whips by as they make their way back to Quantico. Travis is thinking about the impact of this latest news. Mainly, he's concerned about the impact of all this on Emma.

Right now, she's sitting in the passenger seat, looking out the windshield. She seems entirely normal, which he thinks is unnerving. He glances at her profile from his position in the rear seat, behind McCreedy.

"We need to know why he's got this focus on me, and on Huxton," Emma says. "And if he's so focused on me, why isn't he seeking me out more directly?"

"He must know you're still alive. That's why Carter put you in protective custody in the first place." The idea of Emma being in immediate danger, of the killer seeking her out, gives Travis a sensation like heartburn. He tries to remind himself it's just anger.

"Maybe...Emma's too special." Kristin's head tilts as she considers. "The killer has transferred his attentions to other girls because to him, Emma's not really real. She's a girl in a newspaper report, well out of reach."

"A girl from a fantasy." Emma's still looking at the windshield as if she's talking to herself. "We need to know what triggered the fantasy. And we need to know how he's replicating these murder details. The thing with the rings is too exact. He never got that from the media, so *how did he know*?"

"Uh, excuse me." McCreedy clears his throat. "You folks still want me to pull over if I see a diner?"

Although Emma is closest to McCreedy, she has not responded, still lost in thought. "Yeah, please, that would be good," Travis says.

They stop for lunch at a place called Tastee Diner. Kristin peers around at the black plastic chairs and the '50s-style nostalgic decor, seems delighted to be eating at a place frequented by the general public. Travis is reminded that she's spent two years in Chesterfield, and before that, she grew up rich, and that privilege gives you everything but an understanding of the real world. Emma gets pop and a sandwich, sits beside them and chews automatically while her eyes look miles away.

They're back in the car in under thirty minutes, and arrive at Quantico by 1300 hours. When they get to the Cool Room, Travis finds the phone calls he made from Washington have borne fruit; Mike Martino is in the room, laying an armful of files on the desktop.

"Hey." Martino settles the last folder, straightens and dusts off his hands. "Kirby said you'd need these."

"Yeah, that's great," Travis acknowledges, the girls behind him. "Thanks for the help."

"No problem," Martino says. "You're lucky to get copies—Jack won't let the originals out of Behavioral Science."

Travis thumps his satchel of paperwork onto the desk in the Cool Room. Kristin immediately goes to turn on the lamps. Emma slides in through the doorway like she's trying to avoid notice.

"So what are we doing now?" Kristin pivots on the spot, and her white skirts whip at the hems.

"Full literature review," Travis says, taking off his jacket and hanging it across the top of a chair. "Behavioral Science is running the nightclub angle, so that's covered."

Martino nods. "Yep—and I've gotta get back to it. Let us know what you find."

He exits, and with his burly presence gone, the Cool Room seems very much their own space. There's a united sense of wanting to translate awareness of these new leads into action. Emma is at the desk, separating file folders and laying them in piles.

Kristin selects a pen from a cup and examines the nib. "What does a literature review mean?"

Travis finds a short stack of legal pads in a drawer. "It means it's our job to figure out if what you suggested at the lab and what we discussed in the car has any likely basis. If he's really focused on Emma, then . . . why? How does he know her, what's the connection."

"And what might his next move be," Kristin muses.

"We've got a little time, nobody needs us for anything," Travis notes. "Carter said he wants everything we've got. I think we should just dig in to the information and take notes along the way, see if anything lines up."

The understandings about the killer's use of posing, the new information from Scientific Analysis, and the spin Kristin put on it have changed the ball game. Travis feels like a big pitch is coming up. Until now, he's been unsure of the pitcher's action—all he could do was study the movements and hope they'd positioned themselves right—but this new insight gives them a chance to play offense.

Travis checks Emma as she collects a pen and a yellow legal pad. He thinks she looks pale but together.

"You okay?"

"Sure." Her face is expressionless, and he can't get a read on her.

"Drinks." Kristin claps her hands. "We need more than the coffee from the filter pot. Can we order something at the cafeteria and one of us can collect it?"

"They'll deliver it down here." Travis goes for the phone. "Orange juice and water all right with everyone?"

"Fine." Emma pulls out a chair at the desk.

He holds the receiver in his hand as he dials. "I'm kinda missing the pierogis Horner's team used to order in Pittsburgh."

"I don't know what those are, but they sound lovely," Kristin says. She bypasses the desk and goes straight for the couch. "Shall we flop, instead of sit at the table? I think I might, at least. Oh, this is very nice. Much better than those horrible desk chairs."

Travis turns on the heating, and the room seems more comfortable still. He returns to the desk and digs through files in his satchel. "We'll cover more territory separately. Kristin, I want you to keep looking at the press coverage of the Huxton case in '79. Find out what information about Emma's identity was covered by the media. I've got a stack of press reports here, and there's copies of all the newspaper cuttings, plus some radio report transcripts."

"What are you going to do?" Kristin asks, bouncing a little on the hard couch cushions.

Travis shoves a stray folder down. "I'm gonna check all the details of the crime scene after Huxton's death, and anything new or related that I can find on Huxton himself." He passes her a couple of manila folders, plus a legal pad, before turning back to the desk, and to Emma. "You want to wait for drinks before we get started?"

She returns her gaze from elsewhere. "Nope."

"You gonna be okay with this?"

Her voice is deadpan. "You really need to stop asking me that."

"Okay, fair." He backs off, tries another angle. Right now, she's eyeing the Huxton files like she'd rather take a gutshot than read any of them. He thinks it might be best to give her options. "I figure we need to curate all the connections between this case and the Huxton case, from your own memory. What specific aspects of the profiles match up and which ones diverge. Similarities, differences. Can you do that?"

"I think so."

"Great. And can you tell us what information specifically about you was released by the police and the FBI in '79?"

"Some, while it was treated as a missing persons case," Emma says as she arranges her folders and notepad on the desk. "More during the investigation. But after it was over, there was additional information released during the inquiry."

"Okay, that should help Kristin chase all that stuff." He nods at Kristin, then passes Emma a relevant file. "I want you to give me a list of anything you think might connect, anything you've noticed, any details you judge important."

It's not a total reprieve, but she looks relieved. He thinks it will be strange and difficult to go through the Huxton files with Emma participating. But he also thinks she'd probably prefer to do this research herself, here among friends, than have strangers do it.

He makes another call, to confirm with Kirby that they're dug in here. Kristin fluffs her skirts and finds a comfortable position on the couch. Emma reaches over and pulls the Pittsburgh autopsy file out of his satchel, sits forward on her hard chair, and gets to work.

Travis grabs his own pile of Huxton folders—the report detailing the police assault on the mountain house, the evidence logs, the scene photos—and pulls a chair closer to the table. He and Emma are sitting opposite each other. The room is developing a library quiet: just the hum of the heating, the sound of pages turning and paper flicking. He can hear Emma's soft breathing.

He opens his folder, tries to ignore Emma and focus on the work.

The first two hours are okay. The drinks arrive, and Kristin makes the occasional comment to interrupt the quiet—"I've only found one photograph so far. Oh, tabloids... Why do they *exist*?" But after the drinks are depleted, and the coffee has cooled, all that's left are the typed lines of print, the photographs, Travis's hand moving with the pen as he takes down anything relevant.

He's gone through this material before. But the Cool Room is like a timeless cocoon that seems to create echoes. By the third hour, the low reverb of what he reads, what he sees, blows through his skull like wind through a dark tunnel. The photographs from Huxton's basement are the worst. They make him feel greasy, and there's a limit to what he can look at.

This task is important, and they're on a deadline, so he can't walk away. He tries to compartmentalize, but it's either a skill he hasn't mastered or one he's simply not engineered with. The latter idea he finds unnerving. A good LEO can wall himself off—*this I witness, which I can now put aside.*

But Travis is too inexperienced to have effective boundaries, and he cannot be clinical in Emma's presence. Here is a photograph of a soiled sheet; here, a clump of hair. Here are the cages the girls were kept in. Except one of those girls is sitting at the desk opposite him, and hour after hour, the awareness rasps against his mind.

How in god's name did she survive?

Emma was imprisoned in the ribcage of evil. How she escaped is a miracle to him. But he can't ask her about it. He knows she's haunted by the fact that two other girls had their throats cut when she got free.

He also knows she doesn't really believe in her own bravery. Travis's models of courage include his father stepping forward to bargain himself in a hostage situation, his mother gathering them all to hold together and pray. But Emma's courage was born from a different place: a place of terrified desperation, like a primal scream.

"Lewis?" He clears his throat. "Uh, some of the stuff in the backgrounds of these pictures I can't identify. This looks like a surveyor's tripod. What job did Huxton do again?"

"He was a TV and projector repairman." Emma puts a folder aside and straightens, kneading her lower back. She rubs her hand across her shorn head in a way he's familiar with. Her silver earrings glint in the low light.

Travis sighs. "Okay, I'm gonna have to go back through the evidence logs."

By afternoon, he can feel himself losing his composure. He pushes back from the desk, needing a break. When he looks at Emma, she's stopped writing and is staring into space. He thinks she may have been like this for some time.

"Lewis." When she doesn't look over, he tries again, gently. "Emma."

"What?" She snaps her gaze back, glances around. She still seems unfocused as she pushes away from the files in front of her. "I'm gonna..." She stands on shaky legs. "I think...I think I need to get some air."

He wants to help—and suddenly it occurs to him that he can best do that by giving her license to help herself.

"Emma, how long has it been since you ran?" he asks.

"A few days." She stares at the mess of paper on the desk, wets her lips. "A while."

He checks his watch. "It's getting late—nearly five. If you wanna go for a run, you should go now, while McCreedy's still around to do escort."

Her gaze lifts to his. Her eyes are glassy, her face pale and drawn, and for a moment he gets a raw taste of how she's feeling. Then she breaks eye contact to nod, and leaves the room.

Kristin looks up from the folders over her knees, the paperwork spread across the flat couch seats. "Is Emma going for dinner? I think I would like to go for dinner soon. I've nearly exhausted all my options with these news clippings."

"If you're done, you're done." Travis pours himself another coffee. "Good job, Kristin. Just leave your notes for me—I'm gonna stay on a while."

Kristin leaves her notes and wafts out, shutting the door behind herself.

Travis returns to his spot, but he can't sit. He casts his gaze around the space—Emma's abandoned research opposite his own neat stack of folders, the yellow pages with Kristin's looping handwriting, the paperwork she's left piled on a corner of the couch. He sets his coffee on the desk and does some tidying, telling himself he's giving his legs a chance to stretch. While he's tidying, he tries to think about nothing at all. He just needs his brain to empty itself of horror for a minute. He just needs a place where he can be still.

When the phone rings, he startles, then answers. "Uh, yeah, it's Bell."

"Mr. Travis Bell?" A woman's tentative voice. She sounds older, more like Betty, the receptionist from Behavioral Science. Maybe it's Emma's mom.

"Yes, ma'am," he confirms. "This is Travis Bell."

"Travis, my name is Dr. Audrey Klein, I was transferred to you through the main reception of Behavioral Science."

"Yes, ma'am. How can I help you?"

"Travis, I'm an emeritus professor of psychology with Ohio University in Columbus, and I've collaborated with the Cleveland Rape Crisis Center for a number of years. My work is primarily with survivors of extreme trauma. Specifically, I'm Emma Lewis's therapist."

Travis straightens and puts the pile of folders he's holding down on the desk.

"I have a long-standing agreement with Emma that I should reach out to her if she loses contact or begins missing sessions, and her parents indicated that she may be with you," Audrey Klein continues. "It's nice to finally meet you. Emma has given prior permission for me to talk with you if necessary. She said you were very supportive when you and she worked together last June."

He's not sure how to reply. "Uh...yeah. I mean, I tried. I'm glad she felt supported."

"Is Emma there with you now, by any chance?"

"No, ma'am. She's, uh, not in the office at the moment." He's not sure how much he should share. Then he wonders if Audrey Klein will try to contact Emma through Jefferson residential. "She's gone for a run. But I can get her to call you back later, if you like."

Audrey is quiet for a moment, before replying. "Just let Emma know that I've called, and we've spoken, and that I'm aware she's at Quantico. If she wants to call back, she's got my number. Tell her she can contact me at any time."

"Yes, ma'am." Travis rubs a hand across his mouth. "Uh, ma'am?"

"Travis, you can call me Dr. Klein. Or Audrey. I don't mind." He can hear the smile in her voice.

"Okay," he says. "Uh, thank you."

"No problem. What did you want to ask, Travis?"

There are many things he can't say during the course of an active FBI case. But there are some things he needs to know. He's just not sure how to phrase the request.

"It's tough on her," he blurts. "This case we're working on . . . It's personal. And that's tough on Emma."

"I understand," Audrey says, and her tone is so calming that Travis feels his posture soften. "As I already explained, I've been in touch with Emma's family—again, this is with Emma's prior knowledge and agreement. Her parents said the authorities are concerned about a Huxton copycat."

That Audrey Klein has even this much information makes Travis feel easier in his mind. And it's easier to admit his own concerns.

"I don't know how to help her." He tips his head back, still holding the phone. "It's like she zones out. She gets stuck on a loop with these memories...."

"Okay," Audrey says. "First of all, we all zone out sometimes, to some extent. For a survivor, it's a protection from intrusive memories. But what you're describing doesn't sound like memories. Travis, I know you're in law enforcement, so I'm sure you've dealt with trauma. But you've never dealt with severely traumatized survivors before, have you."

"No," Travis concedes.

"Their experience is different. Some memories are much more real for them. They're not 'remembering'—they're reliving."

"Like a flashback?"

"Yes, that's what it's called," Audrey confirms. "Survivors feel the same emotions, even re-experience the same sights and smells and sounds. It *is* like a loop, one they're trapped in. They relive the original trauma over and over again."

Travis stares into a shadowed corner of the Cool Room. "So every time Emma has a memory of Huxton..."

"Yes," Audrey says. "In her mind, she is back in that basement. Experiencing the event again."

"Jesus."

"It's hard to manage day-to-day, and difficult to treat psychologically because almost anything could push that button. Emma is amazingly level, for someone who's been through what she has."

Travis's first thought is *How can she stand it?* The whole concept makes him want to punch something. Combined with what he read and saw in the Huxton file this afternoon, it makes him feel completely adrift.

He presses the phone to his ear. "How can I help her?"

"Travis, that is a very kind thing to ask," Audrey says gently. "Very kind. And you're probably already doing some of the things required, like being patient, and being a good listener. But a more specific answer to that question isn't something I can just give you. For one, there are doctor-patient confidentiality issues hanging over this conversation, do you understand?"

"I understand," he says dully.

"But there's a way you can find out the answer yourself," Audrey goes on. "And that is to ask Emma."

"Oh. Right. Of course." He closes his eyes.

"Just talk to her, Travis. Ask her what she needs. If you ask in the right way, she'll tell you."

After the phone call from Audrey Klein ends, Travis puts the handset back with a plastic clunk. *Just talk to her.* A red flare of frustration pulses in his chest. The one thing he needs to do, which is somehow the most difficult thing of all.

He sighs, sits back at the desk, and calls Betty at reception, to pass on the message to Emma that Dr. Klein called for her. Then he steels himself and knuckles down again, leafing through page after page. When he resurfaces, it's after seven in the evening and he still wants to punch something, so he goes to the Quantico gym, does a few circuits, and hits the bag for a long while. He thinks that'll be enough to help him sleep.

He's wrong.

After midnight, he gives up on sleep, throws off his bed covers.

He washes his face in the bathroom of his accommodation in Jefferson and changes out of his sleepwear into jeans and boots and a T-shirt, plus an old Harrington jacket that used to belong to his dad.

When he takes the elevator to the basement, it's nearly 1:00 AM, and the entire facility is quiet and empty as a graveyard. He lets himself into the Cool Room, but he doesn't flick on the overhead lights, just a lamp on the desk.

He's been going through reports for about a half hour when a noise makes him look up. Emma is letting herself in, head down, creeping through the door. She's wearing black athletic pants and a gray OSU sweatshirt that's about two sizes too big, the sweatshirt slipping away at the collar, revealing the strap of a white tank. The skin of her curved shoulder has a pale sheen in the low light. Her head is smoked with the dark fuzz of her hair. She's carrying a folded blanket and a cushion, and her shoelaces are untied.

Travis puts down his pen. "Can't sleep?"

Emma jumps with a yelp—yelps again when she bangs her elbow on the doorknob.

He realizes his error immediately. "Oh shit. I'm sorry—"

"*Fuck.*" Her expression is furious. "*Fuck*, Travis!"

"Are you okay? I'm really sorry."

She rubs her elbow, glaring daggers. "Are you testing out my nerve?"

"No!" he objects. But he's stupid—he should've realized she'd react that way. He tries to say something less stupid, more obvious. "You're not sleeping."

She sighs. "Says the guy who's down here in the office at one in the morning."

131

He spreads his hands, unable to think of how else to reply. *Just talk to her.* He used to be able to do that—even three months ago, he could do that. Why it's so damn hard now, he has no idea.

"I guess this is just a tough case." Emma squeezes the edge of her blanket. Her posture is staunch, but her fingers are white and thin as bone, her eyes staring out of dark circles.

Travis nods. "And you're carrying it more than any of us."

"Hey, it's not just me. You're dealing with the fact we're talking to Simon Gutmunsson again."

Travis is too tired to do more than grimace. "If it produces results, I'll wear it."

"I'm gonna have to see him again." Emma hesitates, comes out with it. "Today, probably."

"Today." Travis scratches a hand through his hair. "Okay. I mean, I guess it was inevitable, given that Kristin got in touch with me."

"She's been helpful," Emma points out.

"She likes to be useful." Travis frowns a little. "I still…don't completely trust her."

"You don't know where her loyalties lie," Emma suggests.

Travis shrugs. "He's her brother."

Travis finds he's sharing a protracted look with Emma, and a lot is happening in that look. Finally, he realizes the pause has dragged out too long, and he catches his breath, glances away to the couch.

"You should sleep." He lifts his chin at her blanket and cushion. "You came to sleep, right?"

"I thought…if I tried someplace different…" She clutches

the cushion, presses her lips. "I've tried it before, and sometimes it works."

He picks up his pen, waves at the couch. "Go to sleep. I'll make sure no one bugs you. I'm gonna be up a while, I already poured myself coffee."

She shuffles into the room, closing the door behind her. He should keep his gaze directed elsewhere, but he can't help noticing the way she lays the cushion on the couch and spreads out the blanket, fussing with the corners. She's like a little animal making a nest.

"Will it bother you if I'm here?" he asks.

She glances over her shoulder, her face drawn with tiredness. "Nope."

"I can leave if you want."

"I know this is crazy," she blurts, "but I just want some rest."

"Take it," he says. He keeps his voice and eyes soft. "Go to sleep, Emma. I'll keep the lamp down low."

CHAPTER FOURTEEN

Through the window of flight UA3504, the sun is a pale disk in a cloudy Maryland sky. Emma stops looking at the view when she sees Kristin take an emery board and an orange stick out of her handbag.

The drawstring satin pouch Kristin uses as a handbag always seems to be full of things like drying leaves, handkerchiefs, yellowing photos, rose petals, so the emery board seems comparatively normal. If Travis were here, Emma would exchange glances with him about it, but he's not. He watched them leave for Washington National this morning, standing at the doorway of the FBI motor pool garage, one hand leaning on the bricks. The masculine angles of his posture and the lines of his suit were all sharpened in the morning light. Emma reminds herself to stay focused—she should be thinking about the victims, not about how Bell looks good in a suit.

"Do you think Mr. Bell was disappointed not to come with us on this trip?" Kristin is examining the nails of her right hand carefully.

"No, I don't think Bell was disappointed." Emma drags her

mind back and scans the seat row ahead on the left, where an older agent called Francks is sitting. Francks is the new McCreedy, who's having a service day. "I think he doesn't like the idea of being reliant on your brother for information, which might have been the vibe you got from him."

"Because Simon can be so unreliable, yes, I understand," Kristin says, checking her left thumb. She doesn't seem bothered by the idea. "Give me your hand, Emma, I want to do a manicure and my nails are all quite acceptable."

Emma can't figure out a reason to say no, so she lets Kristin draw her right hand over the seat armrest. Kristin's palms are cool and soft, and she twists at the waist gently to access Emma's hand. Her white hair drifts down over today's ensemble: a dark blue cable-knit cardigan over an oversized white shirt and black palazzo pants. Emma feels drab in her jeans, long-sleeved black thermal, and travel-worn green vest. Instead of a satin handbag, Emma has an old black backpack that Bell scrounged for her from lost property in the Quantico gym.

Kristin examines each of Emma's nails in turn, lifting the soft pads of Emma's fingers from underneath. She seems utterly absorbed in her task. Emma reflects that Kristin is a person who truly lives in the moment. She doesn't seem to worry about the future or hang on too tightly to the past. Like a Buddhist monk. It must be a strange way to exist—unconcerned, unentangled, but also weirdly unmoored.

"When you say Simon is unreliable, what does that look like to you?" Emma asks. Maybe she's reading Kristin wrong.

"Hmm? Oh, I don't think it's really about *looking*." Kristin collects the orange stick and sets about gently pushing back Emma's cuticles. "I think it's more of a *feeling* than anything else, because Simon rarely lies. He obfuscates, or diverts the conversation, or he simply refuses to answer. He'll reply to a question with a question of his own. Emma, I'm shocked—you have nice nails. I thought you'd bite them all very short, but you don't."

"I like to leave a little edge on them," Emma says. "It's useful for scratching. So Simon doesn't lie?"

"Not really." Kristin finishes with the orange stick before picking up the emery board. "Not for important things. But what he *will* do is exaggerate, or dodge, and he's also terribly prone to… I'm not sure how to explain it, but he wields honesty like a sword. And he will cut through your heart with any information you share, which is something he does almost without thinking. Open your fingers for me, just a little."

Emma does as requested, feeling the light rasp on her fingertips, watching Kristin's tranquil expression as she makes smooth strokes with the emery board. "Simon hurt you when he killed Marlowe Drury, didn't he."

"Oh goodness." Kristin's tranquility falters, the sadness shining through as she sighs. "I liked Marlowe very much, and Simon knew that. You have a sibling, don't you, Emma? I'm sure you know what it's like when they play that one-upmanship game with you."

"Yeah, I do," Emma says, although she and Robbie pretty much squared their differences three years ago, and comparing "fighting over who gets the upper-floor bedroom" with "murdering your sibling's romantic interest" is a significant jump. Interesting, that

Kristin finds a correlation. "I'm sorry for bringing it up. Thanks for doing my nails, Kristin."

"That's perfectly all right." Kristin looks up, smiling happily again. "Give me your other hand? I know we're in the middle of an investigation, but we're still girls, aren't we."

Emma gives Kristin her other hand, because she's right, they're still girls. But she isn't sure what that signifies anymore, except that girls are the ones who always end up victimized, abused, tortured, dead. What the advantage of manicured nails might be in those circumstances, she really can't imagine.

On the ground in Philadelphia, Francks drives them to Byberry without a hitch. Because they're visiting during the day this time, and can see the signage, they don't make the mistake of checking in at the women's facility. Emma's skin goose bumps as they step out of the sun off the steps and into the grim austerity of the men's wing. Their paperwork is checked by a male administrative officer at the reception desk. He escorts them down a series of stairs and hallways, and through a number of locked doors, until they reach Grenier's fiefdom underground.

As Emma enters the checkpoint room, she is struck again by the low ceilings and the cramped quarters. At a wooden table near the door to the cells, Grenier's colleague scratches his pen across clipboard forms. Grenier himself is in a white uniform shirt and pants, leaned back in his chair with one foot up on the corner of his desk, reading a copy of *Guns & Ammo*. He's wearing brown Packer Chore work boots, plenty of scuff on the toe. Emma can see him in a corduroy western shirt on weekends, with worn jeans.

Grenier looks over as she and Kristin approach his desk. "Well. If it isn't Miss Junior FBI."

"We're here to see N362," Emma says, and hands him the paperwork.

"Nice to see you've got the lingo down." Grenier is expressionless as he examines the papers, but the toothpick in his mouth wiggles as he speaks. "Do I have to run through the visiting information with you all over again?"

"No."

"Good. But I don't want to have to walk down to haul your friend out, like before." Grenier eyes Kristin balefully. "If she wants to visit, she's gotta play by the rules."

Emma catches Kristin's nervous glance, looks back. "We won't take up your time."

Grenier stays stoic. "Time don't matter to me. I'm just like the inmates here, Miss FBI—I got nothing but time. It's the inconvenience that bugs me." He waves toward the entrance to the cell hallway as his colleague rises to open the door. "Awright, away you go."

"I have something I'd like to give the inmate," Emma says, pulling the package out of her backpack.

Grenier sighs when she shows him what she's carrying. "No can do. We don't allow that here."

Emma speaks quickly. "Could he have one while I'm talking with him? It would make him more agreeable. You can keep the carton, and I'll take one down each time I visit."

She taps the carton of Marlboros, and Grenier's eyes track her fingers. She knows she is supplying the equivalent of a direct offer for him to skim packs for himself.

Grenier sighs again, but it looks more like theater this time. "Well, that's difficult. Not impossible, mind—just difficult."

Emma has thought this out well in advance, and she reaches into her vest pocket to make a demonstration. "Look—I have six cardboard matchbooks. If I take one matchbook in with me, and tear out every match but one, and then tell him to kick the matchbook back…"

Grenier tilts his head, scratches his neck. "That could work. Whaddya think, Randy? Will that work?"

Randy stops fiddling with the door lock to look. "I guess."

"I mean, if he sets hisself on fire, we can hose him down. The folks in the neighboring cells will bitch about how they're missing out on cigarette privileges, but that's not my problem." Grenier considers, finally gives Emma a nod, like she knew he would. "Okay, you've got a deal."

Emma takes a pack of cigarettes from the carton, extracts one cigarette, tears out matches from the first matchbook, turns to the door as Randy opens it. One last glance back at Kristin, who is hovering nearby, hands clasped in front of herself.

"Watch through the window," Emma instructs, passing Kristin her backpack. "I won't be long."

Kristin nods, bottom lip sucked between her teeth.

Emma walks into the cold air of the corridor, and Randy closes and locks the door behind her.

Deep in this basement area, where no natural light intrudes, it's hard to remember it's the middle of the day. It's not as dark as the last time she was here, during sleeping hours. But her footsteps still sound unnervingly echoey, and the dingy white-painted cinder block collects gruesome shadows. The nightlights above the cells are still burning, and suspended above the yellow danger line, a long wire-covered bank of dull fluorescent tubes hums in the corridor ceiling.

Emma tries to avoid glancing into the cells on the left, but her attention is snagged at the second cell in the row, where an orderly is mopping the floor. He looks up, vacant-eyed, as Emma passes by. She wonders briefly where the cell's inmate is: She's aware that the residents of this wing of Byberry are only released by transfer to federal penitentiaries, or by death. The sloshing sound of the mop, the clang of the metal bucket, follows her up the corridor.

When she steps within view of Simon's cell, she feels it like a magnification of the fluorescents' hum.

The white cell is dimly lit. Simon seems to be asleep. He is lying on his side facing the wall, on a thin mattress that decorates a shelf of sheet metal jutting from the rear wall of the cell. While Simon has his back to her, Emma gets a good look at the furnishings of his current accommodation: to the left, another metal shelf for a desk, with a wooden stool; on the desk, a sheaf of paper and a small cardboard box with a collection of soft pastel chalks; above the desk, a metal ledge with three books of poetry. In the cell's far-right corner, a stainless-steel toilet, no cistern.

Simon still has not turned to face her. She wonders if he is annoyed with her, or maybe he is really asleep. The long length of his back is like a skinny mountain range; his hips and ribs and spinal corrugations are clearly defined beneath the blue asylum scrubs. He is wearing white socks, his slippers lying abandoned by the stool.

She thinks it's unlikely he's asleep. He is simply waiting for her to make the first move in this strange game they play.

"Good morning, Simon," she says.

"Hello, Emma." He rolls over to face the ceiling, rests his laced fingers on his stomach. "Are you here to discover more information you could doubtless figure out on your own? Why don't you go back to Quantico and have a discussion with... What was his name? Mr. Bell? I notice you didn't mention him the last time we met—has he been ground up in the FBI machine already?"

Emma is almost used to these conversational parries now. "You seem to be in a bad mood, Simon. Should I come some other time?"

He throws an arm across his closed eyes. "You must excuse me, I was rudely awakened only a few minutes ago."

"You always sleep late?" she asks politely.

"I rarely wake before noon. Evenings are the best time for living."

"So you've become nocturnal."

"*What hath night to do with sleep?* Oh, I beg your pardon, I'm assuming you've read Milton, and that's probably not true." Simon removes his arm and rolls farther until he is looking at her, propped on one elbow. His face does seem drawn from sleep, his white hair sticking up like straw, his eyes narrowed. "But it appears you've brought something to rouse me."

"I have," Emma acknowledges, knowing he can smell it. She holds up the cigarette. "I'm going to toss it to you now."

She tosses the white tube like a dart. The Marlboro sails over the yellow line, through the cell bars, to land on the floor and skid toward the bed. Simon leans over casually and picks it up.

"Am I to eat the tobacco? How charming." He brings the cigarette to his nose for a brief moment.

Emma holds up the matchbook. "You get one match. If you use it to light anything but the cigarette, and if you don't toss the match and the matchbook out straightaway, Grenier will be down here with the hose."

"Very fair," Simon notes.

She tosses the matchbook just inside the bars, fervently hoping this bribe makes him more amenable.

Simon slides his legs off the bed and sits up, slips his socked feet to the floor of the cell. He places the cigarette carefully beside him on the mattress and rubs his face, slides a hand through his white hair. He seems entirely composed of pale limbs, broad shoulders, sharp corners. Emma glances away.

By the time Simon collects the cigarette, comes closer to retrieve the matchbook, he appears entirely alert. Squatting on his haunches, he strikes the match and lights the cigarette, sucking hard. When it's clear the cigarette is not going to go out, he tosses the matchbook out of the cell, shakes the cardboard match, and flicks it through the bars with his fingers.

He makes a happy sigh as he retreats back to the mattress, breathing smoke. "Excellent. Now we may have a proper conversation. What do you wish to ask me?"

The cardboard match, spent but still trailing hydrocarbons, lies in the no-man's-land between the cell and the yellow line. Emma drags her eyes back to Simon. "I've been working through the similarities and differences between Huxton and the College Killer."

"That must have been cheery."

Simon is now comfortable on the bed, his back against the wall, one knee up on which to rest his hand with the cigarette. Every dim point of light arrows to him, as though Simon is the vortex around which the visual composition of the cell revolves.

Emma tries to lead into her questions slowly. "Last time I visited, you gave me some clues about posing. Now I want to know more about motive—because so far as I can see, these men operate in similar ways, but their motivations seem very different."

Simon's eyes glint cobalt. "Congratulations. That was a deduction a two-year-old could have made, but well done."

"So, let's talk about motive," Emma prompts.

Simon does a French draw. The smoke furls between his mouth and nose like dragon's breath, and he holds it for a moment before exhaling to speak. "Do you remember when we discussed the Butcher case? What purpose is served by behavior?"

Emma treads carefully. "Some of the circumstances and behaviors of both Huxton and the College Killer are the same."

Simon makes a magnanimous gesture. "Huxton was blue-collar. Our new man, John, is also blue-collar. Huxton used his own vehicle, and his own home. So, too, does John."

Emma knows this is not a revelation. A private home and a

vehicle are necessary for what John does, to ensure independence and privacy.

She feeds in more details. "They both drug their victims on capture. They both hold on to their victims for prolonged periods. They both put wedding rings on their victims. They both dress their victims in wedding gowns."

Simon raises his eyebrows. "*Who will love me?* indeed."

This is one of the areas in which Emma is seeking clarity. "But Huxton never posed his victims. He never displayed them in public places. He never gave them wedding bouquets."

"Does John do that?" Simon smiles, sharklike. "What a sweet fellow."

"And John is younger," Emma points out.

"His idealism hasn't yet transformed into deep-seated anger."

Emma keeps a firm hold on her outrage. "You don't think killing women shows he's angry?"

Simon waves the cigarette. "Oh, Emma, you know how these things happen—you lose your temper. It's not the same thing at all." Smoke wreathes his head as he stares into her eyes. "Daniel Huxton didn't want a *mate*. He wasn't under any illusions. He exerted power over those he despised."

"You're saying John doesn't hate women like Huxton did."

"Certainly not," Simon declares. "Only the ones that prove unworthy. Unfortunately, that's a large percentage of them." He smirks at her. "I imagine *you* would be very interesting to him, in that regard."

Unsure what to say, Emma opens her mouth and closes it, before realizing that this is an answer in itself.

Simon's eyes flash. "Oh, I see. He likes you, doesn't he? You survived Huxton—John would consider *you* a worthy mate indeed. Are you flattered, Emma?"

Emma hears her voice lose tone. "I don't find the interest of murderers flattering."

"But it's a compliment, isn't it? Pretty girls love to have the boys swooning over them."

"Pretty doesn't matter to me," Emma says flatly.

Simon's smile is broad. "Oh, Emma, how ignorant of you! Don't you remember that beauty is truth, and truth beauty?"

"I'm not interested in listening to you quote Keats. What I'm interested in is the truth of how John is copycatting Huxton." She's trying very hard to control her anger. Simon finds displays of pique amusing, and she's determined not to give him that kind of entertainment.

"Mm." Simon gets up off the bed and prowls forward. He takes up a lot of space inside the cell. His cigarette is almost half-finished now. "How does he know the special details, Emma? It wasn't from you."

"No, I would never." She's frustrated to find her voice has gone husky.

"You would never. . . ." Simon gazes out into the air beyond his cell bars. "Yes, you were very closemouthed to the media. And the 'journalists' "—he makes the air quotes with his fingers—"didn't take many good photos of the house interiors. So how could this killer have an awareness of all the details of that basement in Huxton's mountain house?"

Her concentration wavers. "I don't know. The details he has are…significant."

Simon returns his gaze to her. "One of the details is the way the girls all look like you, isn't it."

"It's not me," Emma insists. She wants to hang on to this information, for reasons she doesn't yet understand. "I mean, it's not just me. We all looked like that. We fit a profile. It wasn't a secret. There were pictures in the papers."

"Pictures of you." Simon tilts his head.

"No, there were pictures of all the other girls, too."

"There was more focus on you." Simon shows his teeth. "But some of the details John could not possibly have known unless he saw inside that basement room."

"Yes," Emma admits. "The wedding rings, and Huxton cutting off the fingers of the dead girls to retrieve the rings—both of those things were details no one saw."

The tip of Simon's tongue flicks out to touch the corner of his lip. "Do you remember anyone coming to visit Huxton during your time with him?"

Emma closes her eyes, reaching for memory, steeling against it. "No."

"While you were insensible, perhaps?"

She opens her eyes, certain. "No."

Simon takes a drag, blows out smoke. "How else might information about Huxton's basement have been shared, do you think?"

Trying to push away those old, awful memories, Emma concentrates her mind. "Verbal or written description."

Simon's gaze bores into her. "Or?"

Emma thinks. It's close now. "Photos. Film."

"Hmm. Huxton was a television repairman, wasn't he?"

"Yes."

Simon examines the end of his rapidly vanishing cigarette. "Do you think his interest in moving pictures might have extended to other forms of visual media?"

Emma stands there, breathing fast. She hears, quite distinctly, Bell's comment from yesterday as he was examining the Huxton crime scene photos: *This looks like a surveyor's tripod.* It wasn't a surveyor's tripod, she realizes.

Her mind's eye clears, and she straightens. "I think it's time for me to go now."

But Simon has stepped close to the bars, his body held with praying-mantis stillness. "Why does the FBI send you to do its bidding?"

"Because you talk to me." Emma fights the urge to walk away fast now that she has her answers. Simon can be petty, and she's always careful to avoid deliberate insult.

"But are they sure they can trust you?"

"I'm sure they consider me to be highly motivated." Her voice is arid.

"Yet you do untrustworthy things." Simon's lips curve gently. "In St. Elizabeths, you set me free."

Emma lifts her chin. "You didn't take advantage of your freedom. You wasted your time dissecting Anthony Hoyt when you could've run."

Simon raises a hand to make a short draw on his cigarette. "I didn't want to leave you to the Butcher's tender mercies."

There's always a risk in being too open with Simon. Emma decides the risk is worth the cost, at this moment. "Maybe that was part of it, I don't know. But I know you lost control. *It's so hard to stay focused when the red is all around you*—it was a comment you made about the Butcher, but I'm sure you were speaking from personal experience."

Simon lowers his head level with her eyes. "Control is only potent when it's wielded, Emma. In that moment when you choose whether to hold on to it, or to release." Without looking, he drops the unfinished cigarette to the concrete floor, grinds it under his slippered heel. "That's something you will have to learn, if you want to exercise any power with the FBI."

"You said it before," Emma reminds him. "I don't have any power with the FBI. I have no authority."

Simon smiles. "But wouldn't you like to have some? Think about it. And about where your power comes from."

Emma swallows. "Thank you for the conversation, Simon. I'll send Kristin down now."

He inclines his head, courtly. "Thank you for the cigarette, Emma. I'll look forward to seeing you next time."

Emma walks away, feeling the hairs standing up on her arms, the shake in her torso and legs, the fine tremor that comes from standing too close to ball lightning. She thinks about power, especially a quote she likes by Adrienne Rich: *Her wounds came from the same source as her power.*

When she arrives back in the checkpoint office with Grenier, she can breathe again. She takes a notepad and pencil from her backpack, writing down everything she can recall from her conversation with Simon.

She is too busy writing to observe the way he and Kristin interact.

CHAPTER FIFTEEN

In the parking lot of the asylum, Francks is standing beside the open driver's door. He's a tall, lean white man of about fifty with a graying mustache and prominent ears. His demeanor is all quiet firmness and pragmatism as he holds up the pager usually clipped to his belt.

"Miss Lewis, I got a page. Special Agent Carter wants you and Miss Gutmunsson back in Pittsburgh."

Emma hikes up her backpack strap, still walking toward the car. "Now?"

"Soon as we can. Arrangements have already been made for flights." Francks gestures to the car. "Hop on in."

En route to the airport, Emma adds details to her written notes and glances frequently at Kristin, who is looking out the passenger window as they make the straight run down Roosevelt Boulevard. It's about one in the afternoon, and the air outside the car is pale, insipid, with the sun in a caul of cloud.

They're not returning to Philadelphia International, Emma discovers, but to Northeast Philadelphia Airport, where they're catching a twin prop, a new experience for her. Francks drives past the little rinky-dink aviation academy at the airport's southeast corner, turns onto the concrete tarmac. Ahead through the car's windshield, a small white plane with a pointed nose and racing stripes, like an airplane version of a Matchbox car.

Emma leans forward from the back seat. "Is that thing safe?"

"Yes, ma'am," Francks replies. "It's a Piper Navajo."

"Are you riding in it with us?"

"Yes, ma'am." Francks is stoic, but he doesn't look entirely happy about it.

The pilot has already started the propellors spinning at the sight of their approach. There's a little set of stairs behind the wing, for climbing up into the plane. The inside windows have curtains against the glare, and there are only four seats, two pairs facing each other. The cockpit is situated directly behind the front pair of seats. Emma can see the piloting array, which she finds disconcerting.

She and Kristin find their places and strap in as the Piper rumbles and blats. Francks settles in with a folder of paperwork. They taxi around a set of orange traffic cones to reach the runway. Emma watches out the window, sees the propellors blur, feels every surface inside the little plane vibrate as they make the impossible leap into the sky.

Once they reach altitude, she looks at Kristin in the seat facing her own. Kristin has been very quiet. "Are you okay?"

Kristin makes a wan smile. "I'm perfectly well. I'm quite adaptable, you know. And any day I'm not at Chesterfield is a good day."

"They were okay at Chesterfield? About..." Emma thinks the words *letting you out* might be inappropriate. "...about you working with this unit?"

Kristin pleats the fabric of her palazzo pants over her knee as the plane buzzes around them. "Well, they weren't excited about it. If it were up to my therapist at Chesterfield Clinic, I would simply sit in my room and *molder*. But fortunately, our lawyer is an old family friend, and we pay him very well, so he's always happy to sign off on me going out for a jaunt."

"I'm sorry I never went to see you in the hospital, after St. Elizabeths," Emma says. In the open cabin of the Piper, she and Kristin have to speak louder, and their conversation is not private. But this is something that has been bugging her. "I didn't really see anyone afterward. Just ran straight home. But they said you had a concussion, and I should've at least said goodbye."

"I didn't mind." Kristin draws her cable-knit cardigan more closely around herself. "You didn't upset me. Honestly, the experience we had at St. Elizabeths...Well, I know it was horrible, and we all nearly *died*. But it was good for me, I think. I'd been just flopping about at Chesterfield for so long, being the perfect patient. St. Elizabeths made me realize I could get out and do things."

Emma takes that in, then considers how to phrase the next question. "Did Simon seem okay to you today?"

"Oh yes." Kristin makes the weak smile again as she looks out the window. "I think the cigarette you gave him lifted his mood. Although he is still dreadfully jealous that you and I get to spend so much time together—because my presence is such a gift, apparently."

Kristin emits a small, self-conscious laugh, and Emma blinks. Allowing Kristin to visit her brother has been a show of good faith. Emma has not considered the flip side before: The idea that Simon sees Kristin as uniquely precious, that giving Emma access to her is a sign of his largesse. That he is favoring Emma in this way, and in the way he shares information, and in the way he killed Anthony Hoyt to save her...

Emma feels a twitchy discomfort. These concepts are rattling on so many levels, not the least of which is the idea of being *favored* by Simon Gutmunsson.

"I really can't tolerate that awful place he's in," Kristin goes on. "But it was lovely to see him, even in such dreadful circumstances."

Emma broaches the next topic carefully. "He should be getting more concessions. They tend to be a bit kinder to death row prisoners."

"Mm," Kristin agrees, still facing away. "His execution is scheduled for November. Our lawyer, Mr. Jasper, says he will be able to make a strong argument for clemency now that Simon is assisting the FBI with this case."

Emma's not sure that such an argument is as powerful as Kristin believes.

"We can try to delay things in court," Kristin goes on, "but it will depend on the judge. For some reason, killing eleven people gets you a criminal insanity plea, but killing twelve people somehow pushes you over the edge of the legal cliff, even if the twelfth person you kill happens to be a mass murderer of teenagers...."

"It seems unfair," Emma says diplomatically.

"It does." The girl looks back, runs a reassuring hand through her long fringe of white hair. Her expression is determinedly buoyant. "But Simon will never let them separate us. It's not in his nature."

Emma thinks on this as they fly the rest of the way to Pittsburgh.

After a somewhat bumpy landing, the Piper taxis away from the main hub of Pittsburgh Airport, closer to a US Air Force facility. They're met on the tarmac by Bell, in dark sunglasses, his suit tails lashing in the breeze. He stands beside a navy field office Lincoln until the Piper's propellors slow. Then he comes closer, takes Emma's backpack as she descends the stairs on shaky knees. The air outside the plane feels warm and damp, and there's sun. It's the first time Emma's experienced Pittsburgh when it hasn't been raining.

Bell speaks at volume over the noise of the Piper's idling engines. *"Glad you made it. The angel-wing stamp had a hit—we think it belongs to a nightclub on Sixth Street, called Paradise."*

"That's good news!" Kristin shouts back.

Bell nods. *"We need to get to Pittsburgh police HQ. Westfall is gonna be on the horn real soon to confirm."*

Francks takes the wheel of the Lincoln, and Kristin takes the front passenger seat, leaving Emma with Bell in the rear. He undoes the button on his suit jacket, hands her a piece of paper from his satchel in the footwell. "Here's the comparison pictures. We're pretty much one hundred percent, but we need Westfall to sign off on it."

They speed past the airport Marriott on the 376 Airport Expressway. It's much quieter in the car than in the plane. Emma examines the comparison pictures, rubs the sleeve of her thermal shirt across her cheek and jaw. She feels grimy from travel. "What will Carter do once we have a confirmation? Organize a stakeout?"

Bell shrugs, noncommittal. But his energy speaks for itself.

"I've got some information that might help with the Huxton analysis," Emma says.

Bell gives her a sharp look. "What did Gutmunsson tell you?"

"Something important." She recalls Simon's contemplative expression as he blew on the tip of his cigarette. "The surveyor's tripod you found in the Huxton crime scene shots—I don't think it was a surveyor's tripod. I think it was a camera tripod, for taking pictures."

Bell leans back in his seat. "You think that's how the College Killer knows the details of the Huxton case."

"Yeah. I think he saw photos." Emma squeezes the back of her neck.

Bell frowns. "Not film?"

"In '79? It would have been pretty unlikely. No, it has to be photos. But how he got access to photos, I have no idea."

"Gutmunsson suggested all this?" Bell's tone is skeptical.

Emma shakes her head. "He gave me some ideas about the College Killer's inspiration and motives. I put the ideas together."

When she looks again, Bell's bottom lip is caught between his teeth. He smooths the front lapel of his jacket. "If you wanted to talk to someone with psychology experience about motive, you could've spoken with Dr. Klein."

"Not for this." Emma waits until he meets her eyes. "I needed someone who thinks like a killer."

They return to police headquarters in the Pittsburgh Public Safety building on Grant Street. The building is twenty years old, but it looks more dated. The foyer is all glass and metal, and 1960s beige easy-wash tile.

Howard Carter—in a different brown suit, no jacket, glasses on a chain—meets them on the third floor after they get out of the elevator. His suit vest is buttoned over his tie, and he smells faintly of perspiration and English Leather. Emma hasn't seen him since they last spoke in the Grant Street Tavern.

Carter's carrying a manila folder, one finger holding his place as he ushers them toward the detectives' bullpen. "Welcome back. Sorry about the twin-prop transport, that was the only plane I could requisition on short notice. Miss Gutmunsson, Miss Lewis, I suppose Mr. Bell has filled you in on what's going on about the nightclub stamp."

Emma has already thought ahead. "You'll be able to narrow down a location. A hunting ground."

"Yes." Carter has a five o'clock shadow, but the new information seems to have given him a core of brittle energy. "That insight—and your input about the killer's targeting, Miss Gutmunsson—could give us a real chance. Come on in, we're waiting on a call from Scientific Analysis. And we have coffee."

"Goodness, yes," Kristin says.

Carter pauses by the glass entryway, beside dusty venetian blinds. "Miss Lewis, before we go in . . . I'd like to apologize for putting you up front of that police briefing on Monday."

Emma doesn't know where to look. "Okay."

"I didn't ask you." Carter's face has deeply weathered frown lines. "It was insensitive. I'm very sorry, and I hope you understand that I'll try to do better."

She'd really like to believe him. He seems genuine. Her habit of not trusting law enforcement is powerfully ingrained, though. Rather than embarrass him, Emma just nods.

Carter extends a hand to encourage them into the bullpen. As Emma walks in, she inhales the odor of Camels and burnt coffee, sees the same bustling movement of plainclothes detectives and duty cops, hears the familiar gruff male voices and ringing phones. The fax machine is chattering, spitting out paper. Under the fluorescent strip lighting, everybody looks slightly jaundiced. At least there are no politicians here this time. Kowalski—the guy who gave her whiskey in the bar—lifts his chin at her and Bell as he pecks at a typewriter. Across the room, the door to COD Clyde Horner's office is open as he talks on the phone.

"So what's the plan?" Emma asks, looking around, looking back at Carter. Bell has broken away to fetch coffee.

"Gerry Westfall has been testing samples of thirteen likely nightclub stamps," Carter says, setting his folder down on the nearest metal desk. "His people are doing a comparison of inks and stamp properties, to give us confirmation that Paradise is the club we want."

"But you feel pretty confident."

"We do. As soon as we have solid information, we can begin arranging—"

"Carter?" Clyde Horner is at the doorway of his office, holding the phone receiver against his chest. The pale curly cord stretches behind him. "I think this is the phone call you're after, Faye sent it up from the switchboard downstairs. You wanna step into the office here?"

Carter's eyebrows have elevated. "Absolutely. One moment."

He gestures to Bell across the room, who abandons the beverages he's pouring and weaves his way between desks and officers as Emma and Kristin follow Carter toward the chief's office. Carter takes the phone from Horner, stands in front of a chair by the cluttered desk. The room is gray and brown and utilitarian, with one half wall of glass facing the bullpen, and a lot of loose paper.

"Gerry, this is Howard. Can you hold on?" Carter grips the mouthpiece and yanks the cord into less of a tripping hazard. He glances at Horner. "I want to put this on speaker. The young people should stay—they were the ones who helped turn up this info."

"Suit yourself." Horner has already moved to the opposite side of the desk and sat down in the swivel chair there. "Speakerphone is that blue button."

Carter hits the button and replaces the receiver in its cradle. "Gerry, you're on conference. Everyone's here, what's the story?"

"The story is..." Gerry Westfall is a longtime chain smoker, and he breaks off to cough. When he returns, his voice sounds wheezy and distant. "The story is that Carlos did the ink sample tests, and it's a positive. The club you're targeting is definitely in the circle. There's not a heap of available inks used in stamp manufacture, though, so it didn't all come down to that—hold on, I want to let Linda talk."

A magnified clunking sound as the phone changes hands. Then Brown's thoughtful contralto voice. "Hello, this is Linda Brown from Documents. Things are looking positive on this end. The ink corresponds, but more importantly, the make and design of the stamp is identical, and the club uses it consistently for patrons, only varying the ink color week to week. I believe we have a match with Paradise."

Carter nods to himself, glances again at Horner. "The Paradise action is going to involve considerable operational weight here in Pittsburgh. Can I say we have one hundred percent certainty from Scientific Analysis?"

"It's a match," Linda Brown says, then the phone is transferred again.

"Howard?" Gerry Westfall's voice is clearer; he's brought the phone closer to his mouth. "Listen, any difference is vanishingly close, and you know what a stickler I am. Call it."

"Thank you both," Carter says. "I'll talk with you again soon." He ends the call, turns to Horner. "Okay, we're on."

Horner suppresses a victory smile, but his weathered face suddenly looks less aged. "Best news I've heard all day. I want a couple units on this. We can get support from the local field office, right?"

"And SWAT backup," Carter confirms. He lifts the phone again as Horner stands. "I'll make some calls."

"Let me get the briefing room set up." Horner heads for the door. "I've already got a list of people I want." He smacks his hands together. "All *right*—I've been looking forward to catching this son of a bitch. Excuse me, ladies."

Kristin and Emma move out of the doorway and into the office to make space as Horner stalks out, a man with a purpose. Carter is speaking on the phone to someone from the Pittsburgh field office.

"What happens now?" Kristin has her fingers clenched in her cardigan.

"Now we organize to get into Paradise and stake it out." Bell seems energized, his cheeks gently flushed.

"Tonight?"

"Don't know. There's gonna be a lot of coordination involved between Pittsburgh PD, the local bureau office, and combined SWAT personnel, and they want to get their ducks in a row. But definitely by tomorrow night."

Carter is still talking. Emma can hear words like *support*, *surveil-lance*, and *tactical*. She feels strangely detached. It suddenly occurs to her that today is Wednesday. Tomorrow is Thursday. Friday is the tenth of September, the anniversary of the day her entire world was pulled inside out.

"What do you mean 'coordination'?" Kristin asks

"A nightclub is tough to surveil," Bell says, glancing at Car-ter, who disconnects and adjusts his glasses, checks his notepad for another phone number. "Lots of people, movement, bad lighting, noise, smoke...We'll have to talk to the management about access-ing spaces, and how to monitor the place. And figure out a way to draw the killer's focus so he reveals himself."

"I know a way," Emma says softly.

"I think we're gonna need field agents in the club, maybe some—" Bell turns to look at Emma. "Sorry?"

Carter halts mid-dial. "What did you say, Miss Lewis?"

Emma swallows. Focuses her gaze on Carter. "I said, I know a way."

Carter holds the phone receiver, his expression forbearing. "Miss Lewis, you're a very intelligent young woman, so you understand why leaving coordinated police operations to qualified law enforce-ment is—"

"Use me as bait," Emma says.

The entire office goes tomb-silent for the space of a heartbeat. Emma can't even hear the bullpen noises over the thrumming of blood in her ears.

"What?" Bell looks confused.

"Oh, *Emma*," Kristin whispers at almost the same time.

"The College Killer wants *me*," Emma says. "He's searching for *me*."

"Miss Lewis—" Carter starts.

"No," Bell says firmly.

"I want to be there." Emma looks only at Carter, who has developed an alert stillness. "I want to be inside the club."

"*No way*," Bell says.

"It makes sense." Emma makes the appeal to Carter with her eyes as well as her words. "He's searching for me. If I'm there, he'll come close. And I know what this guy is like, better than anybody. I'm gonna recognize him faster than any agents in the field."

"Are you *serious*?" Bell says.

"Emma—" Kristin starts.

"What you're suggesting is extremely dangerous," Carter says quietly.

Emma shakes her head, nice and slow. "I think that bullet has already left the chamber, and I'm pretty sure you know that, too." She transfers her attention to Bell, who is practically vibrating. "This case is dangerous for a whole lot of reasons. Only now we know what the perpetrator's after. We have a chance to catch this guy—"

"But you don't have to put yourself *in the line of fire*." Bell's color is very high.

"I'll *know* him, Travis." Emma makes her expression insistent. "If he's there, I'll know."

"She's right." Kristin slaps a hand over her mouth before more words come out. She looks between Bell and Carter, drops her hand away. "I'm sorry, but she's absolutely right."

Carter grimaces, trapped between the thing he wants and the

ethics of it. "I don't know if I can authorize that. I'm not saying I don't want your help, Miss Lewis—"

"If she goes in, *I* go in," Bell declares. His jaw is rigid as he turns to look at Carter. "That's the only way you should do it."

Emma was not expecting this. "Travis—"

"Are you *insane*?" Bell rounds on her, furious. "Do you think there's any *possible* way that I would let you do this alone?"

Kristin glances at them both, then back to Carter. "They... work well together."

That's all there is to say. Emma stands there, clasping her hands into fists. Nausea roils in the pit of her stomach as Carter's gaze takes in each of them in turn.

Finally, he makes a large sigh. "This is... I see your point, Miss Lewis, and it would be safer with Mr. Bell nearby. But you're both under twenty-one. That's too young to be at the center of a high-risk law enforcement operation."

"There'll be other support though, right?" Emma already has her rebuttal. "You said SWAT will be involved."

Carter nods, all his movements considered and deliberate. "This needs some thought." He smooths the chain of his glasses, his frown deep. "I'm gonna think on it. Let me talk to Jack Kirby."

Bell's mouth twists in frustration. "Kirby will back this up. He'd be crazy not to."

Carter's response is measured. "Let me talk to Kirby and Martino. Give me some time."

"Tomorrow will be two weeks since Patti Doricott's abduction," Emma points out. "Time's in short supply."

"Give me some hours," Carter repeats. He pinches his bottom lip between his thumb and forefinger, then he leaves Horner's office.

In his absence, there's a moment of quiet.

Then Bell whirls toward her, his eyebrows dark and drawn. His eyes are livid. "There is no way in *any possible goddamn universe* that this is a smart thing to do!"

Emma digs in with her heels. "Do you *really* think I want to be doing this? Do you honestly believe I feel like I have a *choice*?"

"Please stop." Kristin's voice is a breath of a plea.

Emma takes a step toward Bell, feeling the blood rise in her face, hearing her own voice ring like steel. "He's going to take another girl unless someone catches him!"

Bell matches her, stepping in. He's angrier than she's ever seen him. "There is an entire *team* of people working to catch him! It doesn't have to be *you*!"

"But we have to try *everything*." Emma wants to make this very clear. "We have to use every advantage we have to save possible victims!"

Bell thrusts a hand into his hair. "*Goddammit*, Emma!"

"*PLEASE STOP!*" Once she's got their attention, Kristin takes a breath and quiets. Her pale, long-fingered hands flutter in front of her body. "Please. You're both scared. That's quite understandable. But you need to just...stop shouting."

Emma feels her own energy crest, settle to a simmer. She turns to face Bell again, and this time her words are calmer. "Travis, listen to me. I don't *want* to be there. I don't want *you* to be there. I wish none of us was involved in any of this—"

She halts then, because she can see she's not getting through. Bell's jaw is clenched, and he's breathing hard through his nose, his hands on his hips. He looks at her, into her, in a way she finds unnerving. Eventually he closes his eyes, turns his head to the side.

"I gotta...I gotta be at the briefing. I'll see you both later." His jacket hem snaps against his body as he walks out the door of the office.

Kristin sighs in the wake of his departure. She draws her cardigan more firmly around herself. "For what it's worth, *I* think it's a good idea."

Emma lets her shoulders slump. "Thanks." She takes a few stiff steps over to the chair beside the office desk, sinks into it. Her knees are trembling. Holding her ground against Bell took more effort than she realized. "I think Carter is going to say yes."

"Are you prepared for that?" Kristin asks softly.

Emma meets her gaze. "I'd better be."

CHAPTER SIXTEEN

"Close your eyes for me," Kristin whispers.

Emma closes her eyes. The feel of the soft brush on her eyelids is exotic, foreign. She can smell powder, and a hint of perfume. Moments later, a larger brush swipes against the edge of her cheek.

"What are you painting on me?" she murmurs back.

"Something interesting," Kristin says, and Emma can hear the grin in her voice.

Word came back from Carter early this morning that they'd been given approval to participate in the Paradise operation. A field office agent named Reyes gave them a full briefing on how it would be staged, how she and Bell would be protected, and how things were supposed to happen.

But when Kristin realized that nobody had thought about Emma's wardrobe requirements, she promptly took over those aspects entirely. Now they're here, in the echoey women's bathroom of Pittsburgh police headquarters, doing Emma's makeup.

Emma's not sure what Bell has been up to, because she's only seen two glimpses of him. Once last night, when she and Kristin were escorted by Francks to their accommodation, where Emma sat up watching the hotel parking lot as city lights flared in the Pittsburgh darkness. Once this morning, in the HQ bullpen, when she spotted Bell deep in conversation with three other detectives.

She's tried seeking him out, because she doesn't want them to go into this situation without being able to talk. But he disappeared for hours, and now it's nearly 9:45 PM. Vans begin rolling at ten. Maybe it's too late. The idea makes her chest ache, but she tries to stay focused.

"Don't make me look too different," Emma says, her eyes still closed. "If I'm going in there, I should look like the old me. The same hair, the same everything. That's the person the College Killer is interested in."

"That's true." Kristin's thin brush applies a layer of gloss to Emma's lips. "But won't that make you feel too vulnerable?"

"I'm already vulnerable." Emma swallows, tasting wax. "Just by walking into the club. But the old me... That's not who I am anymore. It's just another disguise."

"You're a different person."

"Yes." Emma opens her eyes, looks up.

Kristin shrugs. "Then one disguise is as good as another." She drops the brush into her makeup bag, selects an eyeliner pencil, leans forward. "When was the last time you were in a club? Close your eyes again."

Emma complies, considers the question. She was sixteen, not yet old enough to club-hop with friends, when her life changed forever. Since '79, clubs are the kinds of places she's stringently avoided.

"Never," she admits.

"Then you'll need to get the lay of the land. Nightclubs are noisy and dark."

Emma is intrigued. "Clubs don't really seem your thing."

"That's true. Open now." Kristin wields the eyeliner expertly, touches the kohl to Emma's lower lids. "But I really like parties. All that energy! I like gatherings."

"I'm basically the complete opposite of that," Emma points out.

"Fortunately for this operation, it won't matter." Kristin finishes, straightens. "All right, it's time for the hair."

She passes over the wig, helps Emma center it and pull it on. Emma doesn't need a wig cap—her buzzcut makes everything easier—but the hair is the part Emma is most nervous about.

It brushes against her ears and shoulders now: disconcerting fake hair. Kristin bought a wig with a blunt fringe, but it's been impossible to style, so they've left the body of it as a long fall of dark brown.

Kristin checks the fit of the wig, finishes her makeup job with a brushed dusting of some kind of gray and silver sparkles along the side of Emma's cheekbones. Now she takes in the angles of Emma's face, assesses her whole appearance. "There. You look like you, but different."

Emma stands and faces the bathroom mirror and sees . . . a ghost. A gaunt, pale girl with huge eyes, dramatic makeup, dark hair with aggressive bangs. She blinks, and the stern-looking girl in the mirror blinks back. This is someone she used to look like, someone she doesn't know at all. The dissonance of it is staggering. Emma desperately wants to take a Valium, but that would be idiotic.

She's wearing a pair of her own acid-wash jeans, cinched tight at the waist—a good six inches of bare waist. Emma thinks the skin of her midriff looks white and exposed and taut with tension. The black top is something Kristin bought when she bought the wig. It's a kind of scrunched stretchy fabric, just a boob tube with spaghetti straps. The main familiar element is the shoes: Emma's wearing her own clean socks and white running shoes.

She catches her breath, touches the spill of the wig self-consciously. "The hair is the weirdest."

"It's perfectly lovely." Kristin smiles. "You look a little like Kate Bush."

"Who?"

"Never mind." Kristin checks the clock high on the tiled bathroom wall. "It's time. Are you ready?"

Emma straightens her clothes in the mirror. Her new hair keeps brushing her shoulder blades, startling her. She pulls a dark men's suit jacket over the whole ensemble. Kristin wasn't sure about the jacket, but it has useful pockets.

Kristin nods approvingly. "You look good. Are we meeting Mr. Bell and the others in the police pen?"

"I guess so—I don't wanna wander around headquarters looking like this for too long." Emma feels herself flush, fights the urge to press her hands to her face and smear off all this makeup. She keeps her chin down as she pulls on tight black leather gloves with the fingers cut off. "I haven't seen Travis. I think he's still mad."

"He'll be all right," Kristin reassures. "He's just anxious."

"I feel guilty that he's coming with me. I didn't mean for him to do that." Emma adjusts the belt at her waist, flinches; her fingertips are cold.

"I'm *glad* he'll be with you," Kristin counters, packing up her makeup bag. "I don't wholly trust the police to look after you, but I know Mr. Bell will. Come on, now—let's go."

Emma walks out of the bathroom first, while Kristin collects clothes hangers and equipment. Down the hall, toward the bullpen area, Bell stands a dozen feet away.

He's dressed to go out—because they're going out, Emma realizes with a jolt. He's in black pants and sharp buffed shoes, with a midnight-blue dress shirt. The shirt has a thin, shiny black stripe, and is unbuttoned to his collarbones. The column of his neck is smooth and brown and strong. Emma's breath escapes her for a second. She feels another flush, this one closer to her stomach.

Bell turns and notices her. His mouth opens, but he doesn't say anything before shutting it again. Emma sees his throat move as he swallows. She comes closer, and his face softens.

"You look good." His voice is gruff. "Your hair is..."

"Weird," Emma says. "I know." Her next words are impulsive. "You don't have to do this."

He sighs. "Well, you're not doing it without me."

Emma presses her lips together. "Are you still angry?"

"I'm worried." Bell shifts on his feet, uncomfortable with what he's about to say. "It's not just the danger of being in the club. Doing this stuff is bad for you. Emotionally bad. You know that, right?"

Emma takes a breath, releases. "I know."

"Just tell me...." He turns his head, eyes closing briefly, before looking back. "*Explain* for me why we're doing this. Is this about feeling guilty? Because of the other girls in Huxton's basement?"

"No." Emma shakes her head, emphatic. "It's not about guilt. I feel a responsibility. If we can stop this guy, if we can save even one victim..."

"Okay." Travis seems more settled in his mind, or at least more accepting.

She lets him really see her, hopes he can read beyond the paint on her face. "Travis, no one should have to live through the things I did."

He nods, and his expression shows more understanding. Then he sighs again. "I still think this is a terrible idea."

"Every FBI operation we've ever been involved in has been a terrible idea." Emma gazes into his eyes. "That's us, Travis. We make the best of terrible ideas."

When he gazes back, she feels as if they have reached a moment of accord.

Kristin arrives with her armful of clothes and the makeup case. She smiles at them. "Oh goodness, you look fabulous. Travis, your shoes are very fancy, I love them."

Bell's cheeks redden. "Okay, we should get moving. Kristin, you're staying here at headquarters—there's enough bodies in the field, and it'll be safer if you stay. Emma, they've got some equipment for us, Reyes is going to explain in the van."

"Then we should get going." Emma turns to Kristin. "Thank you for... all this." She indicates her outfit with an awkward gesture.

"It was no trouble at all." Kristin envelopes Emma in a hug. "Be careful. I know you'll look after each other, but please be careful."

Kristin's hug is peach-smelling and soft. Emma appreciates the hug on a number of levels, not least because it gives her a brief respite: She can hide in Kristin's hug, just for a few seconds.

Then those seconds are gone, and Special Agent Carter has appeared in the hallway entrance to the bullpen. "Mr. Bell, Miss Lewis, are you ready?"

Bell nods in return, before turning back. "Emma?"

He holds out his hand. Emma is shocked to find herself taking it. His hand is warm and large and calloused, but clasping it feels natural, and above all reassuring, as they walk down the hallway to the bullpen.

Emma clears her throat, tries to stay focused. "Okay, so we're both underage. How are we going to get into this club?"

The corner of Bell's mouth lifts. "The same way underage kids all over America get into clubs. Fake IDs."

Reyes has the fake IDs. He's a slight, bandy-legged man with large spectacles who walks with Carter and Horner as they all move downstairs and outside to the staff parking lot of police headquarters. The nighttime air is cool and damp.

A group of black-uniformed SWAT are prepping beside a white van in a nearby bay—Emma sees caps and rifles, hears barked commands. Last time she was involved in a law enforcement strike, she wanted to be close to the action, not just listening to the radio communication at police headquarters. Now, she wishes she were anywhere else but here.

"Mr. Bell, you'll have a wire," Reyes says, moving briskly with them to an unmarked navy Ford Econoline with dark-tinted windows. He yanks the rolling side door open. "Miss Lewis, we've got something else for you. Jump in, we'll get you set up inside."

The interior of the van is red-lit and dim, and modified with a bench stacked with recording devices and headphones, plus surveillance equipment niches. Carter nods at the driver in front before he climbs in with them in the back. He's removed his suit jacket and added a tactical vest. Clyde Horner is in operational black; he pulls the door closed and takes a rear seat.

Once Emma and Bell have found their places—Bell nearer the front, Emma on a side bench—Reyes resumes his explanation, holding up a small appliance with a coiled wire.

"Here's the radio frequency transmitter we're going to use with you, Mr. Bell." Reyes has a small roll of athletic tape in his other hand. "Could you open your shirt, please? Thank you."

Emma sees Bell begin to unbutton, looks away quickly. The van has already started moving, and she can smell gasoline fumes and the fungal scent of old sweat. Tension permeates the van interior and spins in her chest. All the occupants brace as the vehicle exits the parking lot and sharply corners.

"Miss Lewis, we have a Dictaphone that will go in your jacket pocket." Carter hands her the device. "It's only good for regular recording, so it's not useful for real-time surveillance. But if you get a hit, we'll be able to analyze the conversation after the event."

"No wire for me?" Emma checks the cassette, presses the buttons to familiarize herself before slipping it into her jacket pocket. There's a small lurch as the van stops for a traffic light.

"We thought it might be harder to conceal," Reyes says over his shoulder. He's fixing a tiny microphone to Bell's bare chest with the athletic tape. Bell meets her eyes briefly, lifts his arm so Reyes can position the transmitter and the wire.

"You'll need to stay by Mr. Bell," Carter advises. "That's both practical and a safety issue. Listen, I've been on the phone with Alan Kraus all morning—we only have seventy-two hours. After that, the city has reserved the right to inform the public of the risk. That's all Kraus would agree to, and we can't really argue."

"So we have three nights to stake out Paradise," Emma says.

"You might see a suspect tonight, or tomorrow night, or Saturday night—or you might luck out." Carter puts a hand against the wall as they go over a bump. "But if we've got three nights, we're going to use them."

Horner hunkers forward on his seat, showing a clipboard with a miniature schematic of Paradise nightclub. It's hard to make out details clearly in the reddened interior light of the van, but Emma saw the schematic earlier, so this is just a refresher.

Horner points to the locations on the schematic with stubby fingers. "SWAT will be located here, at back of house, here in this alley, and we'll have an officer on the inside mezzanine and two more on the floor. Squad units will be stationed here, here, and here. Agent Carter and myself will be in this van with Agent Reyes, listening to the transmitter feed—so if you get a hit, or you feel your safety has been compromised, call it and we'll send in the cavalry."

"Did we come to a resolution about weapons?" Bell asks, buttoning his shirt back up.

Carter shakes his head. "No weapons. The crowd, the location... There's too many variables."

Reyes rummages in his boxful of gear. "I've got something that might help. Have a look."

He holds up what appears to be the grip of a bicycle handle—a straight brown cylinder with a metal tip. Reyes uses a flicking motion to extend the barrel into a dull metal baton about ten inches long.

"It's a friction-lock design." Reyes presses the baton tip against the floor of the van to collapse it back into the grip. "You can use it for strikes, blocks, and takedowns. It's not going to be a problem in a crowd, like a revolver could be, and if the perp manages to get it off you, it's less damaging than a knife. Good for close encounters. Check it out."

Emma takes the baton he offers: She likes the feel of the grip in her hand. She nods at Reyes and pockets the baton in her jacket. Bell declines with a shake of his head.

"Two minutes," the driver calls from the front.

"Thanks, Mark," Carter says. "All right, this is it. You know what you're doing?"

"We go in, look around," Bell recites. "Get a better understanding of the layout of the club, and where the perp might exit. Watch for patrons who approach. Watch for girls that fall within the victim demographic, see who approaches them. Keep our eyes and ears open."

"You got it," Horner confirms. "The club closes at oh three hundred. If nothing happens tonight, tomorrow night we do it all over again."

"Take care and good hunting." Carter nods at Emma and Bell in turn as the van eases to a stop. "Okay, folks, here we go."

Bell is collecting the IDs and some cash; Reyes pulls the door open. Emma steps out into the night and unfolds. She's still not used to having hair; it catches on her collar and brushes against her ears. They're parked in a quiet alley off Sixth Street, near a parking lot with a blue dumpster. A pizza place on the corner has winking bulbs on the facade. She can smell the Allegheny River, faintly boggy. Behind her, the sound of the van door rolling shut.

Emma has a moment of jittering weakness, like motion sickness. She's miles outside her comfort zone here, dangling on a wire, relying entirely on law enforcement to protect her. It runs completely counter to her natural instincts. She reminds herself of what Kristin said—that Bell will look after her, even if the police don't. Emma centers herself: The soles of her runners scrape on grit, and her nostrils flare. She reaches for the baton in her pocket, takes it out. It's solid in her hand. She flicks her wrist to extend the baton, weighs it through a sharp swish.

Bell walks up beside her, gives her the ID. "You ready?"

"As I'm gonna be." She tucks the ID in her jeans, braces the baton point against her leather-gloved palm, collapses and pockets it. "Let's go."

Up to the corner, turn right. Emma controls her breathing as they walk, trying to take everything in. There are decorative trees planted on the sidewalk. Ahead, the imposing storied structure of the Fulton Building, people crossing the street to reach it. She can feel the pulsing thrum of music in the pavement.

"One second." Bell puts a hand on her arm to halt her progress. "Are you all right?"

Emma locks her jaw and nods, unwilling to disclose her real

response. They're in gloom under the awning of a closed business, a flower shop.

"Emma…" Bell's hand is still on her arm, steadying. He stands close on the sidewalk, and she can feel his warmth. "I'll be right here. I'm gonna be with you the whole time."

She nods again, curt.

"Stay by me, okay? I mean it. I don't wanna lose you in the crowd, that would be… That would freak me out."

She looks up. Bell's cheeks are hollowed by streetlight and shadow, brown circles under his eyes. He still seems shocked that Carter has agreed to her suggestion, that they are really doing this— he is learning a hard truth about the FBI right now. But he is still the boy she knows: the boy who backed her up at St. Elizabeths, the boy who held the watch in the Cool Room while she slept two nights ago.

He's as scared as I am, she realizes, and it makes her feel better, somehow. "Okay. I'll stay by you."

Bell exhales. "Good."

"One thing." She bites her lip. "Your hair."

"What's wrong with my—"

She reaches up, ruffles his combed hair into something less staid.

He gives her an amused look. "Is that better?"

"Yes." She allows herself to dwell on the soft darkness of his hair against her fingers for a moment, then she redirects her mind. Focusing on the task before them is not as calming. She blows out air to settle herself. "Now we're good. Come on."

Paradise is in the Fulton Building lobby. There are stone gargoyles at the entrance, which Emma thinks should be a red flag right there, and a milling crowd. Girls in tight pants and high heels, boys in denim with teased hair. Emma catches the smells of cigarettes, and perfume, and weed being smoked nearby. She sees overcoats, and bomber jackets, and Hawaiian shirts, and pleather, and gold lamé. There's lots of excited chatter, some shrieking, a group of girls calling for friends just arriving.

Cars pull up and disgorge occupants onto the street. "Kids in America" is booming out of the golden doors at the entry, and there's a line with a large-muscled bouncer who looks like Sylvester Stallone.

Emma discovers that their names are on some kind of list, which gets them in straightaway. There's a chorus of groans from the line as the bouncer lifts the red rope for them. She and Bell walk through the golden doors—inside, the whole world is thumping beats and laser purple: tinted purple marble underfoot, swagged purple drapes, blurred purple people, purple lights flashing. The music becomes exponentially louder, then the purple changes to red and yellow. Emma looks around wildly, startles when Bell takes her hand.

"Over here." His voice has somehow raised over the music. He pulls her toward a woman in a top hat and a rah-rah skirt and a red velvet smoking jacket, behind a wooden lectern.

"Got ID?" The woman is a little older, about thirty. She waggles a plastic stamp block in Emma's face.

Bell shows his ID, encourages Emma to do the same. He pays,

CHAPTER SEVENTEEN

The club is a nightmare.

Emma can see straightaway that it's going to be incredibly difficult to surveil: Apart from the darkness, flashing lights, thronging bodies, and loud music, the layout is a mess of columns and private nooks and shadowed corners. Great for a nightclub, terrible for a tactical police operation.

In front of them, the huge dance floor. Everyone is staccato-lit, surging and writhing now as the previous song bleeds into "I Ran" by A Flock of Seagulls. Left of the dance floor, a dramatic rococo staircase to the mezzanine level, where people stand by the marble balustrades with their drinks and wave at people below. To the right, a DJ platform. Behind that, farther right, an arch leads through to a bank of elevators. Crossing the space in front of the DJ takes you to the bar.

"Jesus." Bell has to yell over the guitar riff and the squeal of a girl in a leopard-print miniskirt who's fallen over in her heels and is being helped up by her friends. "Where do we start?"

Emma rolls up her other jacket sleeve. "Let's get a drink." She looks at Bell's shirt, where the transmitter mic is taped, and says loudly, "Something nonalcoholic."

She leads, Bell follows. Pushing through the packed bodies is harder than she expected, and she struggles with the unwanted physical contact. Her fake hair is maddening, obscuring her peripheral vision. The atmosphere is thick with body heat and perspiration, and the funk of spilled beer. Passing under another arch and reaching the bar feels like a significant accomplishment.

She stands by Bell's elbow as he waits for the bartender, scans the landscape. Her eyes are gradually getting used to the combination of darkness and strobes. Tables and chairs are here near the bar, couches in the rear of the drinking area. More seating dotted around against the walls, only visible intermittently through the bodies on the dance floor. The areas on each side of the staircase look especially dicey.

My god, the music is deafening. She examines the curve of the staircase up to the mezzanine. There must be another bar up there, probably a little quieter.

She tugs Bell's shirtsleeve to get him to lean down. "Where do you think this guy targets his victims?"

Bell is paying for two sodas. "How should I know?"

"Think about it, Travis. Look around. If you were trying to chat up a girl, where would you locate?"

Bell gives her a reproachful glance along with her glass of soda. Then he turns against the bar to examine the space. "Okay, um... Here at the bar. At the couches. Corners of the dance floor. Up on the mezzanine level."

"He drugs them, remember." Emma takes a sip of soda, tart on her tongue. Looks at the glass in her hand. "I think he buys them a drink. I'm going to say here at the bar, or on the mezzanine."

"But then he has to get them out once they're drugged." Bell frowns. "They may not be unconscious immediately, but he'd have to guide their steps...."

Emma follows his reasoning. "Easier to get them out on this level, rather than bring them down from upstairs?"

Bell nods. "Sounds about right."

They stand, holding their drinks, watching. Emma can't identify the planted field agents from among the other patrons. She'd like to talk with Bell more—she wants to know what he was doing all day, where he disappeared to while she was worrying about his emotional state. But it's hard to talk with the music so loud, and maybe it doesn't matter. They seemed to have reached a détente back at police HQ, and they're here now in Paradise, a Bosch painting brought to thumping, pulsating life.

"You a nightclub person?" she asks over the music.

"No," Bell says bluntly.

"Me either."

"What did Gutmunsson say about motive?"

She looks at Bell quickly. "You know, I can always tell which sibling you're talking about when you say 'Gutmunsson.'"

Bell rolls his eyes. "So what did the asshole say?"

"He said that the College Killer is looking for a mate, which we knew, and that he doesn't hate women like Huxton did."

"Sure," Bell says, scoffing. "He doesn't hate women, he just murders them. That's some real insight there."

Emma can't disagree; her own reaction had been the same. And the next piece of information makes her uncomfortable. "Simon thinks the College Killer is looking for me because I survived Huxton. Because my survival makes me *worthy*."

"That is such bullshit." Bell's expression is sharp now. "The College Killer is looking for his own warped idea of the perfect woman, which he'll never find. *Worthiness* is just another fucked-up criteria on his list."

Emma stays silent.

Bell scans around at the insanity in the club. "You didn't survive Huxton because of worthiness, Emma." He looks at her. "I don't know how you survived. But what really matters is that you're surviving now, in spite of everything. *That* survival is all down to your strength of character and will. That survival makes you a fucking force of nature."

Emma finds she's at a loss for how to reply. She didn't know she needed to hear this, didn't realize it would give her such a visceral reaction. Something amorphous and sticky has swept out of her, on her shaky exhale, and been replaced by something hard and clean. She feels a powerful urge to cry, blinks it back as Bell bumps her gently with his shoulder.

"You still with me?"

"Yeah." She uses the edge of her glove to swipe at the side of her eye, makeup be damned, before clearing her throat. "Okay. We should probably be getting more proactive here. Let's go scout around."

Bell pushes off the bar. "I'll come along."

Emma touches his elbow with light fingers. "If the College

Killer is here, he's not going to approach me if he sees I have an escort."

Bell instantly tenses. "I don't want him approaching you at all." Then he grimaces. "All right, I'll walk you to the ladies' room, then when you come out, I'll keep some distance."

They do a tour of the floor, pushing between bodies, stepping around dancing couples and spilled drinks, dodging lit cigarettes being waved by careless patrons, observing everything. By Emma's watch, it's just after 11:15 PM. She wonders if "John" sets himself a time limit—does he need to find his prospective bride before the clock strikes midnight? There are lots of marriage themes like that in fairy tales; Emma makes a mental note to talk with Kristin about it.

Bell lets her enter the ladies' room unguarded, gives her a chance to wander into corners on her own afterward. She can feel him just a few paces back, as she scopes out other girls who might be potential targets—white, slender, long dark hair, within the right age range. Then she holds position on one of the couches while Bell does a tour of the exits. They even dance, briefly and unconvincingly, but after a few minutes, Emma decides enough is enough, and she leads Bell away from the floor.

"Do you want to check the mezzanine?" He's behind her, holding her hand, being pressed into her back by the crowd.

Emma turns, smelling the warm, crisp notes of amber and orange and bergamot in his shaving lotion. She pulls her gaze away from his neck, peers up at the mezzanine floor. There's an agent up there somewhere, but they haven't made contact.

She and Bell have seen no signs, nothing to suggest that the College Killer is even here. Carter pointed out they might not get lucky. But something inside her is on high alert, lifting the hairs on her arms—prey animal instinct.

She has a feeling. If the College Killer is here, he'll be on the mezzanine looking down. The certainty of it lives in her gut.

"We don't need to go up," she says. "He'll come to me."

Once they're hunkered over a three-chair table near the dance floor, Bell looks around and shakes his head. "I don't think it's gonna happen."

"If we have to do this tomorrow, and again on Saturday, that's what we'll have to do," Emma says, although the idea exhausts her.

Bell sits back and sighs, his olive skin and dark hair blued by the lights. Occasional sparkles of white spill onto his clothes from the spinning mirror ball. He glances between Emma and the dance floor. "Where'd you get the wig?"

She's surprised by the question. "No idea. Kristin bought it, and I didn't ask."

"You look real different."

Emma thinks he finds the hair almost as unsettling as she does. "I'm not the same as the girl who had long hair back in '79."

"You seem more like you without the hair." Bell grins, shrugs. "But what do I know. You want something else to drink? It's hot in here."

Emma pushes up her jacket sleeves. "Water, if you can get it."

"Stay here, where I can see you, okay?"

She nods, tracks his progress to the bar, which is busier than when they first arrived—lots of thirsty dancers. The bartenders are working double time. From the look of the crowd, Bell's going to be a while.

When she turns back to face the dance floor, someone is blocking her view.

"Hi," the guy says, sliding into Bell's vacated seat. "I haven't seen you around here before. Are you new?"

Emma examines him: on the tall side, rangy, with slightly bouffant blond hair. His chambray shirt is open all the way to his navel, and his pants are some kind of faux white snakeskin. He's giving her a wide, insincere smile.

"Beat it," she says. This is not her guy.

"Don't be like that, honey," the guy says, reaching across the table as if he's going to take her hand. "I just wanted—"

"I know what you wanted," Emma says flatly, withdrawing her hand, "and the answer is no. Fuck off. My boyfriend is at the bar. Touch me and I'll scream for security."

"Bitch." Snakeskin Guy makes an unpleasant sneer, but he leaves.

Emma tracks him as he slides away into the crowd. "Call Me" has started pulsing from the speakers—her sister, Robbie, always a Blondie fan, would approve. The colors on the dance floor change again, a mix of green and blue that makes all the dancers look like they're underwater. Their bodies are sinuous, hands waving like seaweed on the air, teeth and eyes flashing a sharp, unsettling neon in the dark.

Bell is taking a long time. She looks back; he's part of a crowd moving closer to the bar, but still about three people away from actual service. Calling him "my boyfriend" came out quite spontaneously. Of course, it works in well with their operational camouflage. She thinks of the necessity of it with Snakeskin Guy—the irony that she has to claim connection with one man to avoid another. It's the kind of thing that drives her up the wall. She redirects her mind, recalls the expression on Bell's face when he said that her survival makes her a force of nature. *That* is destined to become one of her good memories—like the memory of Robbie's hugs—to help balance out the bad.

Emma dabs her glove against her dry lips, catches Bell's eye as he glances back for her, searching her out. She smiles and lifts her chin. He raises his eyebrows and nods in reply, before a surge in the queue pushes him forward and he turns away.

A voice sounds behind her. "Is someone sitting here?"

Emma's smile winks out like a frozen star, and her breathing slows.

She doesn't know what process in her head makes the alarm go off: She doesn't know how she just *knows*. Her instinct is a product of a complex experiential knowledge set that was born in terror and despair. But she registers all the physical signs, the same ones she experiences standing near Simon Gutmunsson: her skin goose bumping, the way everything seems to decelerate, the sense of freefall as she topples into the abyss.

Purple strobes make large, unhurried revolutions around her. Emma exhales once, to calm herself, and pivots in her chair to face the College Killer.

He's standing right in front of her.

She bears down to quiet the claxon in her head, tries to absorb details. He's white, of medium height and build, brown hair in a conservative cut. Brown pants, white shirt. He's in his late twenties. Holding a bottle of Evian. Wearing glasses.

So ordinary. *But you're not ordinary, are you, John?*

Engage. Keep him talking. Get everything you can. Please, god, let Travis be seeing this. Emma swallows against her dry throat and meets her target's eyes. "Um, sorry?"

He smiles, nods toward Bell's chair. "I was just wondering if someone was sitting here."

Her right hand is on the sticky surface of the table, her left hand is free. She slips it into the pocket of her jacket, finds the Dictaphone, presses the record button.

Smiles back. "Yes, my b"—she backpedals quickly—"my brother is coming back from the bar soon. Eventually." She waves her right hand toward the third chair at the table, trying to make the gesture natural. "But you can have that chair if you want."

The College Killer slides into the spare seat across from her.

Emma controls her breathing. *Observe observe observe.* He's pale-eyed behind the glasses, with dark brows and hair. Not unattractive, but there's a fullness to his lips that she finds unnerving. He has a dimple in his chin, and smooth cheeks from a recent shave.

He leaves a gentlemanly space between them, in a way that would make a regular girl feel reassured. No grabby hands like Snakeskin Guy.

He gives her a casual smile. "Cool place, right?"

Emma glances back quickly, searching out Bell near the bar. No dice. She nods on automatic. "I guess. I don't usually go to night-clubs, but this is cool."

He tilts his head. "You don't like clubs?"

Painful experience has taught her the right ways to respond—the pliant, necessary reactions. She shrugs placidly, wrinkles her nose. "I like to dance. I just don't like…all the noise and people."

She hates that she knows what he wants, that she is so good at producing the required gestures and facial expressions. She tamps that feeling down. *Focus.*

He draws a pack of Virginia Slims from his shirt pocket. "Cigarette?"

Clever targeting—the brand is popular with women. Emma declines gracefully. "No, thanks."

He lights one for himself with a Bic from inside the pack. He has bitten nails, short damaged cuticles. "So, I guess if you don't like clubs, you don't come here so often."

"It's my first time," Emma acknowledges.

The College Killer grins, exhales smoke. "Me too." He holds up his wrist, and the nightclub stamp glows in the darkness. "First time getting my wings. What's your name?"

This is not your first time. Emma smiles, replies to a lie with a lie. "Kelly."

"Peter." Even now, he doesn't reach over to shake, or do anything overtly pushy or aggressive. He cranes to look toward the bar. "Wow, your brother is taking a while."

This guy is good. It's no problem at all for Emma to let some of her nervousness show. "Yeah, he might have seen his ex. He knew she was going to be here tonight." She rolls her eyes. "I told him to hurry up, too—I'm thirsty."

Peter sets his bottle of Evian on the table. "Here, take my water. I only sipped out of it once, I swear."

It's the first time Emma sees a flash of something in his face: a glinting, vulpine look behind his glasses. Now she has to pretend she hasn't seen it. Her heart trip-hammers in her chest.

I think he buys them a drink. That was wrong. He gives them the Evian—innocuous, unthreatening. What could be dangerous about water?

Emma feels his hunger on her skin. This is the choice: take the water, risk the drug she's sure is swirling inside, or block his play, maybe scare him off. *Don't blow it now.*

Then she remembers—she's not alone. Her choice is not about the water. Her choice is whether to trust Travis and drink, or withhold trust and delay.

Emma reaches for the bottle with a convincing smile. If she can find a way to keep the bottle, Peter's fingerprints will be on it. "Thanks."

She unscrews the cap, brings the glass lip to her mouth. Her hand is shaking, but she doesn't think Peter will notice in the gloom of the club. Then it's too late for second thoughts: The water is cool, refreshing, with a bitter aftertaste.

Peter is leaning forward now, his glasses opaque in the purple light. "You remind me of someone."

Emma sets the bottle back on the table, closer to her. She's unable to prevent her voice from becoming deadpan. "Really? Like a famous actress?"

She watches the lines of his face as he examines her dispassionately. "I don't think you'd know her."

"You're right," Emma says, aware that he is comparing her to an image of her own sixteen-year-old self, lost to time. She fights the urge to throw up. "I probably wouldn't know her."

She checks her sensations to see if the drug is taking effect, but there's too much adrenaline in her system. Her pulse is thumping, and everything inside her is skating on a thin, sharp edge.

She needs to keep this conversation going. "Are you from Pittsburgh?"

"Born and bred," he replies with a smile. He finishes with his cigarette, steps on it. "You, too?"

"Ohio." The truth slips out, unbidden. "I just moved here to my brother's place for college."

"It's a great city. I'm sure you'll come to love it."

"I hope so."

"There's lots of cool things to do—Primanti's, Mount Washington, all the art spaces. Kennywood amusement park is really fun...."

He keeps talking about the delights of Pittsburgh like some kind of bizarre tour guide, and she notices how his voice is pitched a little lower, forcing her to lean forward to hear. The details of what he's saying are blurred, but the cadence is hypnotic.

"...could go together to Light Up Night, what do you say?"

"Uh, sounds good." What did she just agree to? Some of what he's saying got lost. She finds herself horrifically transfixed by the shine on his lips as he wets them. Sweat pops at her hairline, under her fake fringe. "Gosh, it's hot in here."

"Take off your gloves," Peter suggests.

Sounds sensible. Emma peels off her fingerless gloves and immediately feels better.

Wait.

"Hey..." Peter raises a finger, like he's just had the thought. "Would you like to go someplace else to dance? Someplace a bit quieter?"

Emma makes a helpless little shrug. "I would, but my brother..." She nods toward the dance floor. "We could dance right now?"

Peter grins. "I'd like that."

He stands, and Emma realizes he is tall.

No—that's the drug. That small moment of altered perception gives her a jolt of terror, yet she's unable to do anything but comply.

Peter extends his hand, and Emma finds herself reaching up and taking it. His hand is soft and powder-dry. His fingertip brushes against her palm gently, like a wriggling worm, and she feels an indescribably powerful revulsion.

Breathe. Travis, where are you?

She stands, knees wobbling. *Whoa.* This isn't... She tries to steady herself on the table, sees one of her gloves, the bottle of Evian. There's something she has to remember—it's not coming to her. As Peter leads her to the edge of the dance floor, Emma slips her right hand into her jacket pocket. She's surprised to find a hard cylinder there, curls her grip around the baton absently.

Walking is far more complicated than she anticipated. Her legs are watery. Around her, people are lurching and lunging in slow motion, bumping into her. Only Peter's hand feels solid.

He turns back and frowns at her, almost theatrical. "Come on, Kelly. What's the matter?"

Emma focuses on his lips. *Whaaat'sss the maaatterrr....* Her head is really foggy now. Very strange indeed. *Travis—where is Travis?* She looks back, can't see him. All the purple lights look like crystals.

Everything is slow, slow, slow, and Emma flicks her right hand behind herself, feels the baton extend with a comical *shloop.*

When the flash-bangs happen, they look like part of the strobe pattern. But they're not coordinated with the music—the timing is off. And they're white, not purple, not red. People are screaming, teeth gleaming, sparks arcing in the dim light. Staccato movement around her.

Peter's breath is sour, his grasp tight on her wrist. He casts around, alarmed. "What the—"

Somewhere in the stratosphere, voices yelling, *"Freeze! Everybody stay where you are!"* and some garbled words she can't make out.

Emma looks at the College Killer mildly. "What's the matter, Peter?"

In one smooth, slow action, she brings her baton down on his hand, and his hold breaks.

The crowds around them surge. She doesn't see whether he's surprised at her, and it doesn't seem to matter now. He melts away into the mass of screaming, panicked people.

Emma's mind is hazy, and her legs no longer support her—she sinks down onto the dance floor. Brief flashes of pain as people step on her. But the pain is transient, and it's cooler on the floor, and she's so heavy. Maybe she's dreaming all this.

"Emma. EMMA."

That's her name. The realization is somehow important. Then strong arms are scooping her up, carrying her, and all she can think of is *Paradise Lost*, in which Milton said that the mind is its own place, and in itself can make a heaven of hell, and a hell of heaven.

CHAPTER EIGHTEEN

Travis clutches Emma in his arms, pushing through people, his brain boiling inside his skull.

—the FUCK, the goddamn ever-loving FUCK—

Then the door to the nightclub office is there, and he boots it open and angles his way inside, Emma's sneakered feet bouncing off the door lintel. The office is bright, with a standard fluorescent strip light, and it's beige-painted and looks normal. More than anything else in the world right now, he needs some normal.

He kicks a chair to face him, it's a wooden chair with a padded seat and a horseshoe-curved back, and he eases Emma into it. She flops in his arms like a doll, her eyes only half-open.

"Emma." He holds her upright with one arm, snaps the fingers of his other hand in front of her face. *"Emma."*

"I can hear you." Jesus, her words are slurring all over the place. "Bell, I *saw him*. Peter. His name is Peter."

Travis wants to break something in half. "Goddammit, I know you saw him. Look at me. Focus."

"Did they catch him?" He gaze swings wild. "He gave me...He gave me a drink of water...."

"He gave you more than that." Travis tastes blood on his lip from where he bit it earlier, feels his anger threatening to spill over. He glances back toward the door. "We need a— *Medic! Someone get us a goddamn medic!*"

Emma—all pinned pupils and strange, beautiful hair—grabs his arm hard. "Take a blood sample. Then we'll know for sure what he's drugging them with. And there's an Evian bottle—"

Travis drags his gaze away to holler at the door again. *"I need a fucking medic!"*

Emma jerks, wincing. "Not so loud, Travis—"

But she's interrupted when a SWAT guy barges into the office. Black riot gear, helmet, Heckler & Koch MP5 in a forward drop. The guy's stance softens when he recognizes them, and Travis is mollified by the immediate response: The guy side-slings his weapon, sinks to one knee in front of Emma to check her over.

"Are you feeling faint?" Travis knows that SWAT officers have first aid training. He watches the guy examine her breathing, take a pulse reading at her wrist. With a penlight fished out of his vest pocket, the guy illuminates Emma's eyes. "Follow the light for me. How are you feeling, ma'am?"

"Dizzy...sleepy...a little nauseous." Emma's still slurring, and her voice is throaty. "Tell me you caught him."

"We're checking ID, but a lot of people scattered."

"That sounds like no." Emma sags, closes her eyes. "Travis, I'm tired."

"We don't know what he gave her," Travis says through gritted teeth.

The SWAT guy nods. "Seems like a benzodiazepine."

Emma shakes her head, stops when it makes her whole body reel. Travis keeps his hand on her shoulder. "It's not Valium—I have a prescription. It's not that. It's different. Take a blood sample."

The SWAT guy frowns. "Okay, I need to get some medical equipment from the truck. Son, can you look after her a second? Don't let her lie down or fall asleep."

"I…" The SWAT guy marches out of the room without waiting for a reply. Travis rubs a hand across his face, looks back at Emma. "Hey, stay awake. Look at me."

"I'm okay," Emma says, when she clearly isn't.

Travis wants to burn down the world. "No, but you will be. We're all right now." He examines her eyes carefully. "Don't go to sleep on me."

Emma seems like she's in shock, her stare vacant. She grimaces, reaches an unsteady hand to her head. The fake hair spills from her shoulders as she drags off the wig, drops it to the floor. "That was crazy."

"I saw you fold under that crowd and I…" Travis runs his other hand down Emma's arms. "Did you get stepped on? Are you okay?"

"My wrist is sore," she admits. She leans into the hand he's using to steady her shoulder. "My mouth is dry. But I'm okay. I'm fine."

"I swear to god, you'd be saying that if you got shot." He looks over the rest of her. "Are you hurt? Look at me, Emma."

"I'm okay."

He clutches at his forehead. "Jesus Christ. Let's stop doing this, all right? Let's find a way of catching the serial murderers without getting ourselves nearly killed in the process."

"Okay."

Emma seems very agreeable, which is unlike her. His hands brace on her shoulders as he lowers his head to find her eyes. "That's the fourth time you've said 'okay.'"

With what looks like a concentrated effort, she grasps his forearms. He changes his grip so she's propping herself on his arms, their hands at the crooks of each other's elbows. Their faces are close and Travis can feel her breath on his lips. Her eyes are still hazed, and he doesn't think she's back inside her body yet.

"Travis..." she whispers.

"What do you need?" he whispers back.

"I'm dizzy." She's trembling, and her eyes are very wide and dry.

"It's okay. Emma, it's all right. Hold on to me."

Her mouth works for a moment before she finally gets it out. "Can you hug me?"

"Jesus, of course I can hug you, come here."

Travis shifts his hands again, draws her close. And it's...perfect. It's what they both need, he realizes. He doesn't know why they weren't doing this sooner. All this time he's wasted, when he could have been hugging Emma.

Her whole body is shaking, the curve of her cheek tucked into his neck. Her tiny earrings are cold on his throat. "It was him."

"I know. I saw you with him, and I just..." He pulls himself back from that edge. "I called it in over the transmitter. That's how the unit arrived."

"How did he get away?"

"I got no idea."

"It was scary." Her breath, humid on his skin.

"I know." He holds her more firmly. "This okay?"

"Yes." She's still shivering. "*God*. Oh *god*, Travis."

"Hold on to me, Emma. It was scary, but it's over. We're safe now. You're safe. Just breathe."

Emotion spilling out of her, making her words choke. "I was down there. He grabbed me, and..."

"It's all right." He cups the back of her head, makes steadying strokes over her shoulder blades with his palm. "You're not down. You're not down."

"I get stuck down there." Tears in her voice now. "I get stuck in that goddamn basement...."

"I know," he says quietly. "But you're not there anymore. You got out. You're here in the real world, with me."

She presses a hand against his chest, squeezes like she's trying to sink her fingers into the earth, trying to find solid ground. Then she runs the same hand up his neck and digs her nails through the hair at his nape, into his scalp. He swallows hard. Through the open door of the office, he can hear a slow ballad by Foreigner—in the aftermath of the raid, they've let the music continue.

Residual panic seeps out of him, into the air. He's on his knees, cradling Emma in this dingy office. She is warm against him, bony and delicate as a bird. Their breathing has synchronized, rising and falling together. He keeps stroking her back gently, and then he remembers that she's not allowed to fall asleep. And he remembers the transmitter, realizes that nothing about this moment is private, feels a shattering pulse of resentment.

"Emma..." He has to clear his throat. Even then his words come out gruff and soft. "You're not going to sleep on me, are you?"

She shakes her head against his neck. *Oh my god, this girl.*

"Okay." He has a heightened awareness of every point of contact. Fights it, because she's drug-impaired and vulnerable, and he has no right to be feeling this stuff. He's also aware that these quiet minutes are about to be interrupted, and he needs to warn her. "They're gonna be back in here soon."

"I know." Her voice is a drowsy whisper. "Stay with me?"

"As long as you need me."

But in the end—after the SWAT guy returns and takes a sample of Emma's blood, after Carter arrives with questions—the EMTs load Emma onto a gurney, and it's Reyes who's tasked with traveling with her to the hospital.

Travis can argue all he wants, but he's not a full-fledged agent yet. He can't protect her, and it eats him up all the way to UPMC Mercy.

―――――――

"It was Rohypnol," Carter says. "He's drugging them with Rohypnol."

"Yeah, I know." Travis scrubs a hand through his hair. "The doctor told me. He said it wasn't a dangerous dose, and they could give her flumazenil or pump her stomach to get it out, but it was probably easiest on her if they just let her sleep it off."

Travis can see Emma in her hospital bed through the plate-glass window. She looks small, half-buried under the white sheets and blankets. They've got her on IV fluids, with an antiemetic to help with the nausea. A Hecla bar heater above the bed casts her room in a dim, orange glow.

Out here, in the hospital corridor, the temperature is cooler. Travis is still in his dark shirt and trousers, his shiny shoes, no jacket. Next to Carter, he feels chilled and grimy.

Carter has divested himself of the tactical vest. "Were you able to get any more information from her about the target?"

Travis can still taste aluminum in the back of his throat, from the flash-bang smoke. Carter's question about more information pisses him off, but this is why Emma went into Paradise in the first place.

"She gave a full description—hair, eyes, build." Travis thinks of Emma's pulse beating fast in her neck, the way she held his hand after they finished hooking her up to the IV. The way she said, *I saw him, Travis. I talked with him. I know him now.*

"That's great news," Carter says.

"She said she'll work with the sketch artist tomorrow to get a composite." Travis catches himself. It's three o'clock in the morning. "I mean, today."

"Do they know what time she'll be out of sedation?"

Again, a flash of resentment, burning like magnesium. "They don't know exactly. Look, she's drugged up, exhausted...." Travis gets a better grip on his temper. "Give her some hours. Were you able to bring that paperwork about the Huxton case?"

Carter pauses. "Miss Gutmunsson found it for me." He passes over Travis's satchel full of notes. "Got something stuck in your craw, Mr. Bell?"

Travis slings his satchel strap over his shoulder, not meeting Carter's eyes. "You didn't have to send her in. We didn't have to do that."

"She volunteered. And it worked."

"That's not—" Travis reins himself firmly so he can make this clear. "Emma's *driven* to do this stuff. She'd tell you to shoot her to the moon, if she thought it'd help catch this guy."

Carter nods slowly. "She and Miss Gutmunsson are both highly motivated, especially in this case."

"Of course they are." Travis rubs a hand over his mouth. "But you can't take advantage of that. You can't treat the girls like agents. They're not agents. And they both have complicated history. They deserve respect."

"You have complicated history, too," Carter points out.

"I signed up for this. They didn't."

Carter thinks, nods. "Understood."

For the first time, Travis wonders if that means Carter really understands or whether it's just a stock phrase, meant to placate. The idea makes him cold.

Carter takes off his suit jacket and settles it over the crook of his arm. "You going to stay here tonight? Francks is on duty, and you look like you could do with some rest."

"I'm gonna…" The satchel on Travis's shoulder suddenly feels like an anvil weight. He rubs his mouth again. "I'll stay a while. I want to be here when she wakes up. And she got some information from Simon Gutmunsson that I want to chase, something about a camera tripod at the Huxton crime scene. I need to go through the old evidence logs and find out what it means."

"All right." Carter ponders. "Listen, we didn't catch our man tonight. But we got closer than we've ever been, and now we have crucial information about him."

Travis just nods.

Carter claps him once, gently, on the back. "You did well. It was a tough situation, and you did everything right."

"Thank you, sir." Travis feels numb.

"I know the parents of the victims would give you their appreciation if they could. We *will* catch this guy. And when we find him—"

"Mr. Bell!" Kristin Gutmunsson is jogging toward them from the direction of the hospital elevators. Her white hair is spun behind her in a long cloud, and her dark jacket whips as she hurries. "Travis! Oh, and Mr. Carter, I'm so sorry—"

"Quiet, please." The nurse at the nearby staff station looks up sharply.

Behind Kristin, Clyde Horner, still in tactical black. His face is lined and tired and grave. "Howard, we got bad news."

Travis finds that Kristin has taken his hands. "What's going—"

"Another girl," Kristin says, holding tight. "Travis, the College Killer has taken another girl."

CHAPTER NINETEEN

Emma feels hungover. She's sitting up in the hospital bed, her head pounding like she was smashed in a hit-and-run. She'd feel embarrassed about the hospital gown, but Bell saw her in the midriff-baring outfit last night. And none of that stuff really matters, now they have this news.

"So she fits the profile?"

"To a tee." Bell looks wrung out and sallow. It's seven in the morning, and he's still in his clothes from the club—Emma saw him dry-swallow two Excedrin a few minutes ago. He holds up the ID photo. "Linda Kittiko. Dark hair, white, slim. She's twenty years old. Her roommate said that she and Linda snuck out of Paradise when the raid happened and went to a coffee shop. She went to use the bathroom, and when she came back into the coffee shop, Linda was gone."

Emma sinks back onto her pillows, squinting against the morning light. "But how do we know it was him?"

Kristin twists the rod to open the window blinds. "He left one of your gloves at the scene."

Bell shows her the photos: the coffee shop booth, the ball of black leather on the bench table, scrunched like a dried leaf.

"Fuck." Emma wants to scream it: *FUCK*. But this is a hospital, and her head is sore enough.

She spreads the photos over the blanket on her knees. There's a terrible taste in the back of her throat; she's already tried making herself throw up, but expelled only bile. She's been drinking glass after glass of water, trying to get rid of it. Now, reaching to drink again, she finds the glass shaking in her grip.

"Emma," Kristin says, frowning. "You cannot imagine that this is your fault. There's nothing you could have done to—"

"I held his goddamn hand!" Emma thumps the glass back on the nightstand. "He was *so close*, Kristin. *So* close!"

"You were drugged out of your mind," Bell says flatly. "It's just a fluke that he didn't take *you*."

"I could have *tackled* him. I could have done *something*." Emma chews the edge of a thumbnail, her other arm wrapped around her waist.

"Will you just listen to yourself for a second?" Bell shoves the photos aside, sits on the bed. "It's not on you. SWAT should have caught him, but he slipped through the net. Someone screwed up, sure, but it wasn't you."

"Travis is right." Kristin has approached on the other side. "If anyone shoulders the blame, it should be the police."

But Emma knows the truth: For Carter and the police, this is a horrifying fuck up. For her, it's a body blow. *Another girl.* How could they have let this happen? *How?* And what more could she have done to prevent it?

Bell angles his head lower to find her eyes. "You want to do something? The sketch artist is all ready to go—Francks can take you to the station to do the composite. We'll release it with an all-points BOLO. It's gonna be a lot harder for the College Killer to walk the street from the moment that sketch goes out. Then do a full debrief with Carter. The team couldn't locate the Evian bottle, but you can go through the Dictaphone tape, every word that was said—"

"There wasn't anything in the conversation," Emma says. "It was all just bullshit and lies."

"You don't know what's important," Bell reminds her gently. "Every detail adds to the picture. Maybe one of the Pittsburgh locations he mentioned is significant."

"And something has changed." Kristin has wandered back to the window, to watch the sun come up on the redbrick buildings of Duquesne University student residences. "He's changed his pattern, Emma. He's taken three girls from nightclubs, but this time, he took a girl from a coffee shop in the aftermath of the police raid. He could have gone to another nightclub, or at least waited until things died down. Why didn't he bide his time? Why did he change?"

"Okay." Emma scrubs a hand over her head. Among other strange, disturbing dreams last night, there was one set piece in which she couldn't get the wig off, and she's relieved to feel her usual short buzz. "Okay, I'll…I'll do whatever needs doing." She tugs at the blanket Bell is sitting on. "Get up. I have to get dressed."

"Has the doc cleared you to leave?"

"Yes, I'm fine. Come on." She ignores her headache as she tugs more urgently.

"I'll come with you to the station." He slides off the bed and stands.

"Yeah, no way." Emma flips back the covers, skewers him with her eyes as she slings her bare legs out. "Go get some sleep."

"This is more important," Bell objects.

"Travis, you look like you're ready to fall down."

Kristin glances over, shrugs. "She's not wrong. You do look rather awful."

"Kristin can come with me," Emma points out. "Go back to the hotel. I'm telling Carter you're out until you get some rest. Don't even think about arguing." She ignores his shitty expression, holds her hand palm up. "Just give me some of those Excedrin before you go."

That's how it plays out: Emma finds her feet, Bell gives her the Excedrin. Kristin passes over a shopping bag full of clothes, Emma's usual ones this time, before walking with Bell to the elevator, to make sure he gets into it.

Emma is left to shower and dress. She waits until no one else is around before she picks up her water glass, clenches her fingers around it, weighs it in her hand. The urge to throw it at the wall is almost overpowering, but in the end, she sets the glass down again.

⸻

The sketch artist is a younger Black guy called Wilson, and he's very patient with her.

"Okay, his eyebrows are as dark as his hair. Full lips like this?" He sifts through the composites, offering her options.

She squints at the images, points. "More like this guy. But you got the chin. The chin is good."

She's never worked with a police artist before, and the amount of time and detail involved is staggering. Face shapes, eye shapes, noses, cheeks, brows. They've been at this over three hours, and all she can think about is Linda Kittiko, strung out and terrified in the College Killer's basement. She takes another slug of her to-go coffee.

"So kind of a smaller mouth, with fuller lips. Okay, try this." Wilson draws fast, his brown hand moving quickly across the page with astonishing accuracy.

He keeps encouraging her to correct and adjust as the sketch emerges. When it's done, Emma sits back. The bustle and noise in the bullpen fade out around her as she stares into the eyes of the man she saw last night. The man who told her to remove her gloves, and then used one of them to decorate the scene of his latest kidnapping. The finished likeness is only pencil and shadow, but it still makes her shudder.

She nods at the completed image. "That's him. That's Peter."

Wilson waves across the room to flag Horner down. Horner takes the sketch and hands it off to another officer to photocopy, then calls for a detective.

"We've got an identification picture to go out with an APB—tell highway and foot patrols to check the fax. Put some language together for a broadcast, but don't let it go without my sign-off." He gesticulates at Kowalski two desks over. "Get me Alan Kraus on the phone, I want to see this sketch in the papers."

Kowalski nods. "You got it, Chief."

Emma retreats as the wheels of law enforcement process begin turning. She dumps her coffee cup and goes back to the spare interview room where Kristin is sitting at a table, reading the report from last night's Paradise operation while eating kung pao chicken from a takeout container. The windowless room reeks of soy sauce and chili peppers.

"Oh, Emma, here, you must have some of this, it's delicious." Kristin passes her another container, with a paper napkin and a set of chopsticks. "I can't say I'm terribly impressed with the way the search was carried out last night—there was nobody covering the elevators at all."

"Is that how they think he cut loose?" Emma takes the lid off her lunch, ditches the chopsticks for a plastic fork. She's not sure her stomach is enthusiastic about anything right now, but she starts picking at the chicken.

"Yes." Kristin slides the club schematic across the table with her elbow, points with her chopsticks. "Although there were a couple of other gaps. The mezzanine had a fire exit stairway used only by staff, but it turned out some of the nightclub patrons had propped it open so they could bring in friends rejected by the bouncer."

"Paradise was full of problems. It would have always been a tough venue to lock down." Emma's tired and headachey. She's sick of being around herself, and she just wants this day to be over.

"Apparently it was well above patron capacity," Kristin says. "It was only licensed for three hundred people, but there were at least a hundred more on-site. Mr. Horner said that it would be hard to argue that point with management, however, as they were so cooperative about allowing the police operation to proceed...."

Kristin keeps talking, but Emma tunes her out. The dark-glazed chunks of white meat in the takeout container have become suddenly unappetizing. She needs to breathe awhile, and she's not sure how to do that in Pittsburgh.

She borrows a copy of the report from Kristin, plus the folder on Linda Kittiko, and goes out to find Francks. He's been replaced by a young, stocky guy called Napier, who agrees—after phoning in to the local field office—to allow Emma to go for a walk to the park. There is no nearby public park, so Napier drives her in a field office Dodge Diplomat to Duquesne's Gumberg Library, where she can sit in the sun on a park bench in Brottier Commons and see green grass and feel warmth on her shoulders.

The breeze on the Commons is stiff, but Emma doesn't care. It's clean air. No stale cigarette smoke in the bullpen, no stuffy interview rooms, no other people nearby—if she ignores Napier sitting in the Diplomat with the door open, drinking a Tab.

There's a scattering of college students walking around on the grass, who at least don't make her feel like the youngest person in the vicinity. She herself is a college student; she should be at Ohio State right now. She turns her face up to the sky and inhales, keeps breathing deeply until she realizes that this attempt to release tension is only going to make her cry. Then she blots her eyes on the sleeve of her Henley, pulls her jacket more firmly around herself, sets the report and the Kittiko file on her knee.

She reads for about an hour. Linda Kittiko is a second-year student at Carnegie Mellon, with excellent grades in music theory. She plays the oboe with a band on campus. She is one of three children; her parents are flying into Pittsburgh from Youngstown, and the Ohio connection is probably significant. She is white, and slim, and dark-haired, and pretty, and it's driving Emma crazy that this girl, this poor fucking girl, is screaming somewhere in the city because of a superficial resemblance and police incompetence and some really shitty luck.

Feeling sick, she puts the file aside, picks up the Paradise report. After a while, the warmth of the sun overpowers the breeze;

Emma lets the light fall on the nape of her neck. When she's done, she sits for a minute to let it all sink in. Her mind spins through the information, and through her garbled memories of what happened at Paradise.

Gosh, it's hot in here....

Take off your gloves.

That is the part of her own encounter with the College Killer that she finds most distressing. That moment when he told her to take off her gloves, with the same tone he'd tell her to take off her dress, and she complied without resistance. It is a moment she finds shameful, and she wishes it hadn't been caught on tape. Yes, the Rohypnol in her system, but it was an instant of extreme vulnerability, of a kind she would normally never allow.

Emma exhales slowly, tries to narrow down what she's feeling. Guilt, that Linda Kittiko was taken instead of her—as a *substitute* for her. Shame, that she was so vulnerable in front of the killer. Emma understands emotional responses, knows that shame is a screwed-up way of exercising control—because feeling guilt and shame, believing you're at fault somehow, is a way of saying that you can stop it from happening again. But she had no idea how the Paradise operation was going to go down when she volunteered to participate. She was there as bait—she trusted SWAT and the FBI to do their jobs. She couldn't have anticipated that Peter would take another girl. She couldn't have stopped what happened at Paradise last night any more than she could have stopped what happened to her three years ago. Audrey has been over this with her so many times. It's still incredibly hard to process those feelings.

Emma does her breathing exercises again. No matter what

happens, she's going to find Linda. She makes it a commitment, writes it on her bones. She reminds herself that vulnerability itself is not a weakness, that it's possible to be vulnerable without regret. That she also asked for help last night. She asked for help, and Travis hugged her, and it was good. It was *really* good. Maybe she shouldn't be thinking this way about her partner, but she wishes she could remember more about it. All she has is the sensation of being held, and the warmth of Travis's chest, and the scent of him. But that is enough of a balm, enough to cling onto for a while, so she spends some time searching her memory for more traces of the hug until a shadow falls nearby, and when she looks up, he's there.

"Hey." Travis is dressed in fresh clothes—dark suit pants, white shirt, tie hanging open—and his hair is damp from a recent shower. He seems less haggard now, but somehow more sad.

"Hey."

Suddenly it's like she can see him, really *see* him: his defined cheekbones, athletic strength from physical training, the specific way he's been honed. She can see him at twenty-five, in sharper suits, his social intelligence channeled into administrative politics, being a better agent than every other man in the bureau because with his dual heritage, he has to be. She can see him at thirty-five, with extra scars, and reading glasses from squinting at all those reports, his expressions confined and FBI-neutral.

Blinking hard, she brings herself back before she sees any further into his future—it's making her too emotional. She indicates the bench beside her and he sits down. His posture is loose, like they are two college friends about to discuss afternoon classes.

"I went back to headquarters, but Kristin said you'd come here."

"Yeah." She looks away blankly to the green lawns. "It's nice. You get a little rest?"

"A couple hours. Not enough, but it'll hold me until tonight."

Emma lets the pause spin out. She hugs the folders to herself and tilts her face into the light. The sun on her skin and the fresh air all put her in mind of home. "Travis, how long has it been since you went back to Texas?"

He tips his head up and closes his eyes. "I was there a week, after St. Elizabeths. Since then . . . It's been about three months."

"D'you miss it?"

He makes a weak laugh. "Every goddamn day."

Thank you for hugging me last night. It's on the tip of her tongue to say it, but she sidesteps. "Why did you come out to find me?"

He looks at her, his expression changing, face falling. "Emma, I'm sorry, but we need to go back to the office. I found something in the old evidence logs, and we need to talk about it."

Emma feels the spit in her mouth dry up, just like that. She can't reply, so she only nods.

He presses his lips together. "I always seem to be the one giving you bad news."

"Don't take this personally," Emma says, "but I'm really sick of hearing it."

The news is very bad. When they get back to headquarters, Carter meets them and they go into one of the side offices to talk. It's a long room off the hallway, with a viewing window and two Formica-topped tables plus a bunch of file boxes, and Emma suspects it's used mainly for legal depositions. Carter is unshaven, and looks like he needs about twenty-four hours' additional sleep.

"All right, Miss Lewis, there's no easy way to say this," Carter starts. Obviously reluctant, he frowns and glances at Bell, who assumes responsibility with a nod.

Emma stands near one of the tables and braces herself.

Bell has knotted his tie, and his expression is bleak. "I went through the evidence logs in the Huxton case. The tripod you mentioned, after the interview with Simon Gutmunsson, was a Velbon Victory 480 video camera tripod. From the crime scene photos and the description of where it was located, it looks like it was set up for secret filming, and agents recovered an RCA BW003 video camera in the kitchen of the mountain house."

"A video camera." Emma suddenly feels everything slow down. "You're saying that Huxton made videotapes."

"Yes," Carter says. "It appears that way."

There's a pause, during which she forces her mind to work. "This was never looked into before?"

"Not to my understanding," Carter says. "We knew he took some Polaroids, but this is the first time we've examined the idea of videotape. It was extremely rare in '79, which is why it wasn't originally considered. But Mr. Bell found the details in the evidence logs, then realized that Huxton's job as a TV and projector repairman had significance."

"Okay." She holds steady by pressing one hand hard onto the top of the table. "So Huxton was filming videotape. Then, where are those tapes?"

Bell says, "We don't know yet."

"What do you—" Emma feels pressure building inside her head, white noise. "What does that mean? Did the bureau *lose* them?"

Bell is taking in her whole face with his eyes. "We don't have a record of them being recovered from the scene."

"Are you saying Huxton destroyed them?"

"Mr. Bell is saying that we suspect they were sent elsewhere. To someone else." Carter's expression is very grave. "During the inquiry, it was established that Huxton was part of a circle of collectors...."

Emma reaches for a chair, sinks down into it. "Collectors."

Carter squeezes the nape of his neck. "Yes. We're going back over the evidence logs again, and reviewing file notes to see if we can dig up any of Huxton's contacts or correspondence, or find any record of packages he might have sent. I'm sorry, Miss Lewis, but it appears those tapes may have been in underground circulation for some time."

Bell comes closer, crouches down on his haunches beside her. "Emma, we think that's how the College Killer knows the Huxton murders well enough to replicate the details. That's how he knows about the dresses, the rings. And it's maybe one of the reasons why he's focused on you."

Emma finds that her voice seems to be coming from a long distance away. "Because he saw a videotape of me. Me inside Huxton's basement."

Bell nods. The white noise in her head reaches a deafening pitch, and for a moment it crowds out all other sensory input. Her vision becomes opaque. She can't feel, or see, or hear, or think.

But when the totality of it recedes, the room blinks back. She checks Bell and Carter. She can only go by their expressions. Carter looks solemn, tense. Probably worried how she's going to take it. When she turns toward Bell, his eyes hold her.

"I'm not gonna ask you if you're okay," he says softly. "Can I help?"

Emma looks away to the tabletop. "I need an external phone line, and some privacy in this room."

Bell stands and shifts, places the phone from the neighboring desk in front of her.

"I'll ensure you're not disturbed for a while," Carter says quietly as he moves to the exit.

Bell speaks before closing the door. "I'm gonna be right across the hall."

Emma nods, and he's gone.

She dials Dr. Audrey Klein's number, which she knows by heart. Usually, the phone is answered within about five rings. This time, the phone keeps ringing. She redials, and the phone rings on and on. Emma's breathing goes high on her ribs, and her vision goes white once more, and she has to ride through it. Then she dials another number from memory.

"Yes?"

"Robbie?"

"Oh my fucking god—*Emma*? Is that you?" The sound of her sister's voice almost tips her over the edge. "Are you okay? Where are you?"

Emma's shocked to find her own voice shaking. "Robbie, I'm in Pittsburgh."

"*Pittsburgh?* Holy Jesus, Emma, I've been trying to get in touch with you for *days*. Every time I call the number they gave us, I end up talking to some guy called Kirby—"

"Jack Kirby." Emma has to work hard to keep her words level. "From Behavioral Science."

"He wouldn't even tell us where you are!" The rustle of Robbie changing the phone over to her other ear. "Listen, I'm glad to hear your voice, and I'm fucking pissed at the FBI, but we're okay. Dad and Mom are okay. Are you okay?"

"I'm..." Emma can't answer that. "Robbie, I need to talk to Audrey. But when I call, nobody answers—"

"Oh Jesus." Robbie expels a harsh sigh. "Emma, that's why I've been trying to contact you. Audrey was admitted to hospital on Wednesday. She had a—"

"What?" Emma presses her hand against the tabletop, can't feel it.

"—some kind of episode while she was out grocery shopping. The doctors found cardiac arrythmia, so they admitted her. Listen, Emma, it's gonna be okay. Where you are in Pittsburgh, do you have support?"

Support. Emma is confused by the question. This table is supporting her hand, and the phone. The chair is supporting her weight. The rest of her is coming in and out of focus, like an image in a camera lens....

Videotapes. Collectors.

Her lips are numb. "Robbie, I have to go."

"Emma, wait—"

"If you need me, call Kirby and tell him to get a message to Travis Bell." She repeats, the sounds feeling strange in her mouth. "Travis Bell."

"Emma—"

Emma hangs up. She can't feel her fingers, so the receiver clatters back into the handset cradle. The white noise is returning. She knows that when she starts experiencing dissociative symptoms, she needs to move to release them. It's important that she move. So she stands up from her chair, which falls over behind her.

The crash of the chair hitting the floor ripples out, and the echoes in her head domino together, and the whole world shatters into pieces with a sound like the smashing of a thousand water glasses.

CHAPTER TWENTY

It's ironic, Kristin thinks, that law enforcement is the service everyone is supposed to call in an emergency, because law enforcement
personnel are truly dreadful at dealing with a crisis.

She was the one who dealt with Emma's collapse in the side
office: finding a blanket, turning off the lights, speaking in soft,
quiet tones—basic things that Kristin wishes someone had done for
her when she was upset, on the day of Simon's arrest. She ushered
people out of the room, and told Travis Bell to find some ice for
Emma to hold. That was helpful, but when Emma began hyper-
ventilating, Kristin moved to stage two. She made Travis bundle
Emma up and carry her outside, where the FBI agent, Napier, met
them in the parking area. Napier drove them all back to where
they've been staying at the Hampton Inn, and being at the hotel has
made things easier.

Kristin gave Travis strict instructions that he was the one in
charge of Emma's prescription bottle for the moment, and he was
not to allow her any more Valium than what she'd already taken.
Then Kristin borrowed some money from him and caught a cab to
the nearest mall for necessary supplies. The best remedy would be

a puppy, but of course that option was not available; Kristin made do with ice cream and a few other items. Back at the hotel, Emma couldn't be persuaded to eat any of the ice cream, so Kristin made her walk on the carpet in bare feet and drink some soda.

Now the immediate crisis is over, and Kristin is sitting on one of the ghastly plastic chairs outside her and Emma's ground-floor hotel room, leafing through a copy of *Vogue* she found at a newsstand near Kroger. She's already examined and disapproved of the Valentino looks in the magazine. Her eye lingers on a lovely ensemble from Ralph Lauren as Travis Bell emerges from the room. He settles on the second plastic chair on the other side of the glass-topped table, rubbing his face.

"She's resting." He drops his hands. His tie is loosened in front, and he looks hideously tired. "She seems better, but she doesn't want to talk."

"I don't imagine so," Kristin says, perusing the lipsticks in a Lancôme advertisement, turning the page.

"I said I'd stay with her." His voice is ragged. "But I don't know what to say to her."

"Say nothing," Kristin suggests. The Giorgio Armani spreads are not her style at all; Oscar de la Renta, however, is divine. "I don't think much of what you say is getting through right now. Just be present. Tuck the blankets around her. Hold her hand, if she's comfortable with that."

Travis talks as if he hasn't heard, looking away across the concrete parking lot behind the hotel. "Today is the worst possible day. It's September tenth—the anniversary of when she was taken. She's here in Pittsburgh, miles from her family, everything compounded by what we're doing...." He rubs a palm across his jaw again. "Seeing her disconnect like that, back at headquarters, it scared the shit out of me. I'm so used to Emma being together."

"She's not a robot," Kristin points out. The Chanel colors are like jewels this season.

"I know that," he says.

"Does she need to be strong for you to feel comfortable?"

"Of course not," he says sharply. Then his shoulders lose their stiffness. "I just...I want to be there for her, but I don't know what she needs."

Kristin, who has had more experience with dissociation than most law enforcement personnel, finally loses patience.

"Don't you?" Kristin can't fathom his thought processes. "It's very simple, Travis—she needs to know that you're on her side."

Travis's expression is wounded. "I *am* on her side. She knows I'm on her side."

"But you're not." Kristin doesn't know how to break it to him gently. This is the best she can do on short notice. "Your loyalty is to the bureau, not to Emma."

"I can still do my job and be her friend." His forehead is screwed up.

"No," Kristin says, turning another page absently. "You can't."

"That's *bullshit*. I'm in a better position to help her—"

"She doesn't want to be *helped*. She's not a project."

"I never said—"

"Anyway, I don't think that's true." Kristin lifts her chin. "The bureau employs you. If you had to make a choice, you'd choose your job, wouldn't you?"

Travis scrubs through his hair. "That's a hell of a hypothetical."

"Being in law enforcement is what you've always dreamed of."

"I don't know." He seems genuinely torn.

"Well, Emma can see your uncertainty."

"What kind of choice is that anyway? The bureau or my friend?" Travis's cheeks are flushed, but at least he's showing some higher brain function.

In return, Kristin tries to be as honest as she can. "I had to choose like that once. I stabbed Simon in the neck so he could be arrested. I chose the law over my brother. I don't know anymore, if I would make that choice again."

She knows saying this will cut him because when she chose the law back in 1980, his father was a casualty of her decision. At least it's something that will get his attention.

Predictably, he glowers. "What are you saying, Kristin?"

"Just that you're in a difficult position. You're divided." She sees him take this in, but there's no way of knowing if her words will have any impact. "Look, I'm going to sit here for a little while longer. Then I'm going to check that Emma's all right, and offer her more Valium, and then I'm going to ask Mr. Napier if he can arrange some room service. It's getting on five o'clock, so I think—"

The phone is ringing. Travis moves first, going back into the hotel room to answer. Kristin assumes the call is probably his, so she continues leafing through *Vogue*. She's very surprised when he steps out of the room again and says, "Phone for you."

She's even more surprised to hear Mr. Carter's baritone on the other end of the line.

"Miss Gutmunsson, we're at the end of our rope here." Carter clears his throat. "How would you feel about going back to talk to your brother?"

The flight to Philadelphia is sparsely occupied, and Kristin has a row to herself. She is not even slightly bothered by the FBI agent who is accompanying her: She has lived her life under supervision at Chesterfield for most of the last two years, and was overseen by teachers or tutors or parents quite often before that. And of course, before his arrest, Simon was her constant companion.

So this is certainly the most free she has been for some time, and it gives her an exuberant feeling. She has nothing with her but her little handbag, with a notebook and a pencil which Mr. Carter insisted on, and the copy of *Vogue*. During the flight, she spurns the articles and editorial opinion pages in the magazine to spend more time with the photographic spreads. She looks at the colors and the textures, examining everything in detail, including the backgrounds of the exterior shots, the flowers in the fields. Some of the pictures were taken in Sudbury, she's quite certain. Once they're back on the ground, she folds up the half dozen pages she's torn out and tucks them away in her handbag, leaves the rest of the magazine on a table in the passenger boarding area as she walks on toward the waiting car.

Byberry is not a welcoming place, and Kristin can't help but feel a chill every time she enters the gates. Now, as the sun goes down on the day, it's like the whole facility is edged with sharp-cut shadows. It makes her tear up to think that after their conversation, she's going to have to leave Simon alone here in this bitter place once again.

Her steps fly as she descends toward Men's Secure General. As she gets closer, her heart wants to beat itself out of the prison of her ribs. But she has learned to conceal her emotions from people who might cause Simon harm, so she is sedate with Mr. Grenier in the tiny bunker office.

He has just finished eating the dinner he brought from home. While eyeing her, he rolls up the remains in a brown paper sack and picks at his teeth with the edge of a fingernail. "Weren't you just here?"

"Two days ago," Kristin confirms. She smiles, with a hundredth of the enthusiasm she'd normally use for smiling at her sibling. "Now I'm back."

"Must be some kinda scintillating conversation you folks are having with *Mr. Artiste....*" Grenier wipes his fingers on his shirt before logging her visit. When she doesn't rise to the bait, he prods further. "But I guess there aren't so many conversations left now, are there?"

Kristin imagines Mr. Grenier—with his slicked-back hair and his tattoos and his unpleasant food smells—being consumed by fire as he hurtles into the sun.

"I'd like to see my brother now," she says, still smiling.

"You and your brother look too much alike." Grenier's cheeks cave as he sucks his back molars. "It's damn unsettling."

"Yes." Kristin is not of a mind to talk with him further.

Grenier shrugs, lifts his chin at Randy. "Let her through."

Kristin stands in place as Randy works the heavy metal door open. She tries to fix her concentration on where she is, and which side of the yellow line is the correct side. She can never recall.

"Stay to the right," Randy says.

Kristin grins. "Of course. Silly me."

Then she is slipping down the passage, as though the dull concrete is carpeted with lawn. Kristin tunes out the cold white and metal bars and wire, thinking instead of the long arbor walk to the garden of the Massachusetts house in the spring. All the purple vetch shifting in the breeze, mosquito bites on her ankles, the scent of cut grass.

Simon is sitting at his metal shelf desk, working on something with his pastel crayons, but he turns when she arrives, a soft smile playing on his face. "I can always tell when you're the one coming to see me. Your footsteps are so light."

"Simon." Now *she* is the one consumed by fire, her heart glowing out of her chest.

"Hello, dearest."

They do their ritual, which has gained more poignance over the last two years: Simon stands and holds up his hands, palms open, and Kristin does the same on her side of the bars. Hands aligned, saying nothing and everything, communing with their eyes alone, energy sparking between them like they're sharing lightning.

Simon puts a hand to his own cheek, and it's like Kristin can feel it. A hand to his chest, and it's like he can sense her heart thumping there. He is dressed in his blue jumpsuit, a color that has always looked so well on him. Kristin only wishes he would eat a little more; he doesn't appear to have regained any of the weight he lost in St. Elizabeths, and his white hair seems stiff and dry.

She wills energy and care through her palms in his direction. Kristin is very aware that the bars are no barrier, that air is permeable; it flows between them freely, carrying Simon's love for her and hers for him. If they were just allowed to stretch out their arms, they would be touching right now, in this moment.

With this knowledge, it takes Kristin a few breaths to regain her composure. "I have the most amazing thing—a picture of Sudbury. Would you like to see it? And you must show me what you're making."

"Certainly." Simon sits back at his desk chair, waves a hand at the papers. "It's a transcription of a poem, with some decorations along the side."

Kristin can't stop smiling. "That sounds lovely."

"I'm thinking I might send it to Emma once it's complete. I only have her college address, of course, but perhaps she will be back there soon. Do you think it would cheer her?"

"It might," Kristin acknowledges. "She could certainly do with some cheer, she's been having a terrible time lately. Poor Emma."

"Poor Emma." Simon's blue eyes are shining. "Is she with you?"

"Not today," Kristin says proudly. "I came all on my own. Well, except for the FBI escort fellow, but he's waiting outside in the car. Do you want to see my Sudbury picture?"

"In a moment, dearest. Does the bureau want more information?"

"Oh, you know them." Kristin rolls her eyes. "They always want *something*. Actually, this time it would be useful if we could give them more. Things are moving very fast in Pittsburgh. Emma met the killer! His name is Peter."

"Of course it is." Simon smiles, wolfish.

"But before they could talk more, the SWAT team arrived. He ran off and took another girl. Now everyone is up in arms."

"I imagine so." Simon inclines his head gracefully, touches a finger to his bottom lip. Her brother is graceful in all his movements. "What should we give them this time, do you think?"

"Well, there are any number of options...." Kristin considers. "I think we're looking for a very lonely young man, don't you?"

Simon smiles. "I don't imagine you would kidnap young ladies and squeeze all the life out of them if you weren't lonely. It would be a lot of trouble to go to if you were simply doing it out of spite."

Kristin laughs. Simon always understands things so well. "Can you imagine? But I really think this fellow has his heart set on Emma, which is why his pattern changed after he saw her in person. It would have made him angry, too, don't you think? There she was, and she didn't fall into his arms—it's so awkward when you're fixated on someone and they don't even seem to know you're alive!"

"You've had that sad experience," Simon says, kissing his fingertips and casting the kiss her way. "And if this new rebound girl—"

"Linda."

"The rebound girl, yes—if she was taken hurriedly, in the aftermath of meeting Emma, then she's bound to be unsatisfactory, isn't she? He will finish things with her quickly, I think."

"That would make sense," Kristin agrees. "But do you believe there's a chance we can find her, before he loses his temper completely?"

Simon tucks his arm against himself and holds his chin with his other hand. "Well, it would be very tricky....Has the FBI considered looking into vital records in Pittsburgh? Perhaps this fellow has had a loss recently that's made it harder for him to endure being alone?"

"That's what *I* said!" Kristin exclaims. She's almost vibrating with excitement. "But I don't think they've checked at all. There would be lots of people in Pittsburgh who've had a loss, though. I suppose we could narrow it by the age range of those left to deal with the estate? Would there be anything else to search for, do you think?"

"Well, if Emma saw him, then surely the FBI have a composite by now." Simon shoos the rest away with a gesture. "But let's not waste any more time talking about extraneous things—show me your picture, dearest, you know I'd love to see it."

"Oh yes, please." Kristin claps her hands in front of her face and smiles.

She fishes the folded magazine pages out of her little handbag. Then she sits down on the concrete, skirts tucked over her knees, and peels the paper apart carefully.

"Here it is—look." She smooths the creases against her thigh, holds one page up. In the foreground, a woman reclines against a post-and-rail fence, showing off her Laura Ashley dress to perfection, but Kristin is not interested in that aspect at all. "Do you see? There's the edge of the building, and I'm just sure it's the grist mill."

Simon, too, is now sitting on the floor cross-legged. "You know, I think you're right."

"And if you look around the fence post edges, there are star-flowers and wild columbines...." Kristin examines the picture again, feels her eyes getting hot. All she can do is look to her brother. "I was so happy in Massachusetts. Do you think we'll ever go back there again?"

"No, Kristin." He is gazing at her lovingly, sadly. "No, I don't believe so."

"But... have you heard any word from Mr. Jasper about the execution appeal?"

"Mr. Jasper commends me for assisting the FBI with their inquiries, but advises me not to get too excited."

"That's not right." Kristin feels her cheeks pale, then heat. "You've been *helping*. Simon, that's not fair!"

"Life isn't always fair, dearest." He sighs gently.

"This feels so inhumane—both of us staring at each other across this distance." She can't help her eyes filling, her bottom lip quivering, no matter how strongly she tries to rein it in. "And in two months, they'll expect me to stand by your grave with an armful of flowers...."

"Hush, darling," he says gently. "You know I won't let that happen."

But Kristin will not be consoled. "And all the stories they'll tell about you will be the bad stories, the awful things, and I will have to listen to them over and over.... People will just *swoop* in, you know, trying to explain you, to pin you down like a bug in an insect collection, and me with you, and I don't think I will be able to stand it. I won't be able to stand it, Simon."

"I wish I could hold you right now," Simon whispers. "Flesh of my flesh, bone of my bone."

"My brother." Kristin's voice is hiccupping softly in her grief. "My twin, my love. My other half, the part of me I cannot live without. They *can't* kill you. Please tell them not to keep us apart, or I will die, too."

"You cannot die." Simon's eyes are flaming. "You can't die, Kristin."

"Simon...Simon." Kristin cups her own face, her palms filling up with tears. "What are we going to do?"

A pause in the cell. Then sinuous movement, as her brother stands from his cross-legged position on the concrete floor, unwinding fluidly to his full height.

"Darling." Simon flicks dust from his blue scrubs. Behind the bars, his face is calm. "I think the time has come for me to share what I really know. Go and fetch Monsieur Grenier."

CHAPTER TWENTY-ONE

E mma? Kristin?" Travis knocks again, opens the door of the hotel room a little wider. The wedge of sunlight on the beige carpet in front of his feet seems intensely bright in the dark entryway. "Hey, it's me."

He steps in, closes the door with his free hand as he balances the cardboard tray with three to-go cups. Now it's possible to see that the only illumination in the room is from the glow of the television. Cartoons are running, but the sound is so low it's a barely audible hum.

The room's twin double beds, separated by a nightstand, are both messy. Emma is sitting in a nest of blankets and pillows on the farthest one; her head is resting back on the wall, her face a moon of blue shadow. She looks wiped. She's wearing the gray sweatshirt he's seen her in before, over a white tank and a pair of black athletic pants. He's wearing athletic pants, too, with a USMS T-shirt: Maybe she's running out of clean clothes the same way he is.

One blanket is wrapped around her like she's cold. Last night, she couldn't stop shivering. Now she looks over, her skin waxypale. "Hey."

"I got coffee," he says.

"Yay, coffee." Her voice sounds threadbare.

"Where's Kristin?"

"Beats me." Emma shrugs, and the collar of the sweatshirt slips down her shoulder. "When I woke up, she wasn't here. But I only woke up about a half hour ago."

It's ten in the morning; Travis thinks she absolutely deserved to sleep late. He's surprised she didn't sleep until noon, after the stress she's experienced and the amount of medication she took yesterday.

Last night was an endurance test for them all: Kristin didn't return from Byberry until after eleven, and by that stage Travis had slept only two hours in the previous thirty. As soon as Kristin took over with Emma, Travis phoned and left a message at headquarters explaining that Saturday morning would be a slow start, before returning to his own room and crawling into bed in his clothes.

"Maybe Kristin's gone for a walk or something." Now he comes closer to the bed, easing a to-go cup out of the embrace of the cardboard tray. "Coffee. Sweet, with cream—you need the sugar."

"Okay." Even Emma's hand seems limp with tiredness as she reaches up, sets the warm cup on her knee.

"And here." Travis digs in the pocket of his pants, comes out with an orange pill bottle with a white lid. He thinks it's safe to give it back to her now. "Your prescription."

"Thank you." Emma takes the bottle, tucks it under her leg. She inclines her head to the space on the bed beside her. "Take a load off."

He slides his own coffee out, puts the tray with Kristin's cup on the nightstand. Then he settles on the bed, careful not to dimple the mattress too much. He sat beside Emma like this for most of last night, and the intimacy of it no longer feels strange. They're just sitting here, watching soundless *Schoolhouse Rock!* together.

Emma sips her coffee. "You get some sleep?"

"Yeah. I feel more human now."

"Good."

"How are *you* feeling?"

"Exhausted." She rests the cup on her knee again, lays her head back. Light shifts on her face from the television. "Nauseated. Embarrassed."

"I guess we're not going out for breakfast in the hotel restaurant, then," Travis joshes her gently, before sipping from his cup. "Hey, don't be embarrassed."

"Easy to say." She examines the lid of her coffee.

"Seriously. If people don't understand, fuck 'em. They're stupid. *They* should be the ones who're embarrassed."

Emma turns her head, deflecting. "I need a shower."

"Drink your coffee first."

Scooter Computer and Mr. Chips are talking about baseball on the screen; Travis isn't trying to make any sense of it. He listens to the little noises—tiny rustles and sighs—that Emma makes as she slowly comes back to full function. He thinks he's getting better at just being present with her. It's quite comfortable here on the bed.

Emma's voice emerges quietly. "Travis, why haven't you been home to see your family?"

A graph appears on the TV, and Travis watches it turn into a rocket ship. He can't say "I don't know" in answer to her question, because he does know. It's just hard to express. Hard to be vulnerable.

But Emma has already had to reveal way more about herself to him than she is comfortable with. The least he can do is be honest in return.

"Mom talks about my dad like he's still around," he says finally. He keeps his eyes on the television. "'Your father always says' or 'Your father is so proud of what you're doing'—that's the way she talks about him. I know it's a small thing, and it's important for her. It's nothing I can change. Nothing I should *want* to change. It's what she needs. But it hurts every time I go home. Every day, it's like a dozen paper cuts." He swallows more coffee. "So I thought maybe a little space and time would help."

Emma nods slowly. She takes another sip from her cup. "You want to go back eventually though, right?"

"Yeah." He leans his own head against the wall. "Maybe I'll go see my uncle first."

"Your uncle?"

"He has land in Guanajuato. Good land. He keeps horses." On-screen, Scooter Computer and Mr. Chips zoom around on their skateboards together. Travis watches them absently. "When this case is all over, I think I'd like to go spend some time with the horses."

Emma nods. "Sounds nice."

"Yeah." Travis lets the pause spin out a little, before he leans his shoulder against hers. "You don't want to pull the plug here and go home?"

"No." Emma sighs out a long breath. "I can't. Linda Kittiko is still out there."

"We'll find her," Travis says softly. "We'll find this guy. It'll all stop. It'll be over soon."

Emma tilts her head sideways, until it's resting on his shoulder. "I really hope so."

Travis finds his own head turning, until his cheek rubs against her crown. "It'll be okay." He brushes his lips against her stubbled scalp and it feels very natural. "Go have a shower, Emma."

While she's in the shower, the phone rings. He sets down his coffee and switches on the bedside lamp, debates for a moment whether to answer the phone again in Emma's hotel room—people might get the wrong idea. Then he realizes it doesn't matter and he's being stupid, so he stands and walks over to pick up the receiver.

It's Carter, who talks for some while. After the conversation is over, Travis is glad that Emma didn't have to deal with it. Problem is, now he has to tell her.

Bad news—bad news, every goddamn time...

As he's thinking that, the bathroom door opens and she emerges, barefoot, in jeans and the white tank. Steam puffs around her in the lamplight, bringing with it the tang of her soap. She looks fresher, and she's scrubbing at her head with a towel in a way Travis has seen her do before, and for a dizzying moment, he's very aware that he is in her room, and they are alone. Then sanity returns and the conversation with Carter floods back, and he realizes that he has to tell her.

But Emma has already seen it in his face. She tosses the towel onto a chair. "What is it?"

"Carter called. Kristin's been negotiating in his office all morning." Travis can't believe he's saying this. "Her brother has new information about the College Killer case."

Emma takes an unthinking step forward. "What information?"

"Something about the Huxton videotapes. Gutmunsson says

234

there's a link. He says he'll only provide details about it if we bring him to Pittsburgh."

Emma presses her lips, releases them. "Simon can't seriously believe—"

"Carter's doing it. He's arranged prisoner transport from Byberry for this afternoon."

She goes very still. "Simon's getting out of Byberry."

"They're gonna keep him at Allegheny County Jail."

"That's the worst idea I've ever heard."

Travis just looks at her. "Do you want to tell Kristin that?"

CHAPTER TWENTY-TWO

The jail population intake area resembles a garage, because that is what it is. Emma stands beside Howard Carter in the cold metal guardhouse overlooking a set of stairs descending to the garage's concrete floor, where a white GMC Transit van is parked, its rear bumper facing the platform.

Beyond the Transit van, the massive oak doors of the intake area are open, showing a rectangle of sky, a glimpse of normalcy on Forbes Avenue. Outside the jail, the clouds are low and purple: There's the growling electric pulse of a coming storm.

Emma watches through the guardhouse viewing window as two Pennsylvania state troopers in gray shirts move to close the oak doors. She tries again with Carter, although she knows it's impossible.

"There's still time." Her tone is restrained. "You could turn this van around and send it back to Byberry."

Carter stands impassive in his most official suit. "Miss Lewis, I know you've had some bad experiences dealing with Simon Gutmunsson, but I guarantee you we'll handle this in a methodical, orderly way. Before you know it, he'll be back at Byberry awaiting his execution."

Emma watches as the gap between the oak doors shrinks, shutting out sky and normalcy and freedom. The gap gets smaller, smaller, turns into a sliver...

Slams shut.

Emma lets out a shaky breath.

"How are you feeling today?" Carter asks.

Like I've been kicked in the head by a mule. "Peachy." Emma closes her eyes against a wash of claustrophobia and the throb of a headache before turning again to Carter. "You still haven't told me what it is about Simon's information that makes this transfer so important."

Carter straightens the chain of his glasses. "As I've explained, once we've had the opportunity to question Mr. Gutmunsson further, I'll call in both you and Mr. Bell to discuss it."

Emma firms her knees, steels herself. "Is this because it's about the videotapes? Are you worried I'm going to flip out again, like yesterday?"

Carter gives her a loaded glance. "Miss Lewis, I can't give you more just yet. But I can guarantee that Simon Gutmunsson's information is pertinent to the College Killer investigation and it will be helpful for the case."

"Fantastic." Emma wants to rake her fingernails down her cheeks in frustration.

She's distracted from the urge when four correctional officers with batons make a semicircle around the rear of the Transit van. At the top of the stairs, a SWAT officer with a rifle aims squarely at the van doors.

Emma clenches her teeth to stop them from chattering and

wishes she'd thought to bring a thicker jacket. "You haven't met Simon Gutmunsson before, have you?"

Carter shakes his head. "I haven't, no."

"Well, if you're committed to doing this, let me make some suggestions." Through the open doorway of the guardhouse, rounded like a submarine's hatch, Emma can hear the muted crackle of handheld radios. "Put Simon far away from other inmates. Make sure the duty guards are briefed about him, and about his escape attempts. Make sure he's not given any concessions."

"I've read the file," Carter says. "And I've been given advice from the warden at Byberry."

"The warden at Byberry doesn't know shit." Emma sighs. "Talk with Dr. Scott at St. Elizabeths, she's seen what Simon's capable of."

"Dr. Scott is no longer working at that institution," Carter says, "but I'll make an effort to reach out to her."

"Simon made four escape attempts under Scott's care." Emma experiences a slippery flutter in her skull just thinking about it. *Anthony Hoyt's screams. The blood on Simon's teeth as he smiled. And she was the one who let him loose....* She blinks it all back. "The last attempt nearly worked."

"Who's going to break him out here at Allegheny? His sister?" Carter makes a faint snort.

"Simon can manipulate anyone. He looks harmless, but I've seen him..." *The gleam in Simon's eyes as he ripped Hoyt's face apart.* Emma shakes her head. "I've seen him do terrible things."

"And I'm taking that very seriously, Miss Lewis." Carter gestures at the combined forces on the floor of the intake garage. "My men, these guards—they're all highly trained professionals."

A state trooper begins unlocking the door behind which Simon is confined. Sweat breaks out on the nape of Emma's neck, despite the jail's chill.

She turns to face Carter directly. "Are you going to speak with Simon yourself?"

Carter shifts on his feet, which is the only tell that reveals his irritation. "His sister is acting as liaison, but I'll speak with him once he's gone through intake."

Emma moves so Carter can't just keep her in his peripheral vision. "Look, I know I'm just a college student, and you're FBI, and you think I'm emotionally compromised. I'm sorry if this seems like I'm trying to tell you how to do your job. But if you haven't dealt with Simon before, please be careful."

"Miss Lewis, let me say this again—I've worked with a lot of maximum-security prisoners, a lot of serial offenders. I treat them all the same, with the utmost caution." Carter switches a clipboard from his right hand to his left, retrieves a pen from his inside jacket pocket. "Excuse me, please. I need to deal with the documentation for the transfer."

He exits the guardhouse through the hatch and is met at the top of the stairs by a skinny figure with slicked-back hair. Emma's startled to recognize Grenier. She can hear their conversation through the open doorway.

"Ayuh, paperwork is moment-of-transfer, so we both gotta sign it." Grenier has a clipboard of his own, although his papers look more wrinkled and the pen he fishes out of his white asylum-staff shirt is a plain ballpoint, not a fancy Sheaffer Targa.

"Absolutely," Carter says, slipping on his glasses, making his mark. He offers his corresponding papers. "Sign here and your duty's done."

"Wonderful." Grenier signs off Carter's documentation, tucks his pen away. "Okay, he's all yours. Hope you have a fun time, listening to him recite some poetry bullshit all night long. Enjoy."

"Thank you, Mr. Grenier."

Grenier clears his throat and spits off the side of the stairs. His expression is sour. "Y'all won't care, but I gotta say it. This is dumb. This guy is one of the sharpest characters I ever had the pleasure of keeping locked up. At Byberry, we could handle it. At Allegheny, who the hell knows. You want him, you got him, but don't screw the pooch here, or someone's gonna end up getting hurt."

For once, Emma finds herself in agreement with the man.

"Thank you, Mr. Grenier," Carter repeats stiffly. "We'll give your advice due consideration."

Grenier shrugs, raises his hand. Six feet below, the bolt on the Transit van's rear doors cracks back like a double-tap hammer.

Fighting against instinct, Emma steps out of the metal cocoon of the guardhouse to stand beside Carter and watch the proceedings. Her extremities still feel limp from last night's Valium, but her stomach is hard as a rock as the van doors swing wide.

One of the state troopers unlocks the mesh grille separating Simon from the outside world. The trooper takes a long implement with a curved attachment like a bail hook from the side of the van. He reaches into the van with it, drags it back. The motion of the hook pulls forward a steel-plate floor section that slides along a set of rails.

Atop the raised section, like some kind of satanic god worshipped by deranged heretics, Simon Gutmunsson sits strapped to a wheelchair.

The chair is locked down to keep it from rolling, and Simon is secured to the chair with canvas webbing. In addition to his blue asylum scrubs, he is wearing a white straitjacket and leg restraints. He has also been fitted with a grotesque mask, like a veterinarian's dog muzzle. Behind the wire of the muzzle, his lower face—mouth, chin, cheekbone to cheekbone—is entirely covered by a thick band of black leather. Above all this, the blaze of his freakishly white hair and arctic blue eyes.

Across the room, Emma feels a crawling sense of dread when Simon's gaze searches, finds her, locks on. He gives her a slow nod. She nods in return, unblinking, careful to keep her face completely expressionless.

Beside her, Carter shifts, uneasy. "All this for one boy."

"Don't think of him as a boy." Emma's voice comes out faint. "Think of him as a rattlesnake in a boy suit."

But there are no disasters, and no mistakes. Simon is smoothly lowered on the steel platform. When his chair is wheels-down, he's rolled up a ramp on the other side of the intake garage to the platform, and through an archway to a corridor leading away from general population, toward an assigned cell. The dark corridor is lit by large round lamps the size of crystal balls: Emma watches the shadows shift in the corridor as Simon and his entourage pass each lamp in turn.

"Okay, that's done," Carter says with quiet satisfaction. He turns his back on the process Grenier and his crew are going through to close up the van and return to Byberry. "Now it's time to meet Miss Gutmunsson."

He walks Emma out the way they came in, but turns them both before the jail exit to take a set of stone steps down to an external door that opens onto a courtyard with high stone walls, flat concrete pavers, lanky elms that smell like sap. Some kind of family waiting area, or maybe someplace for inmates to stare at out their windows with tortured longing. Kristin is standing by one of the trees, swinging her hands and peering up into the yellow leaves as if she's at the park.

When she notices them, she smiles and approaches. "Oh hello! I hope you don't mind that I didn't attend the transfer, Mr. Carter. I simply can't stand to see Simon in restraints." She shudders. "It bothers me so much."

"We didn't need you there," Carter reassures. "It all went fine."

"I'm so glad," Kristin says, then looks at Emma. "Did Simon seem all right?"

"He seemed...just the same." Emma's words stay level.

"But where is Mr. Bell?" Kristin asks, casting around as if Travis might magically jump out from behind Emma's back. "He didn't come with you?"

Emma blinks at her for a moment. *Did you really think Travis would come to see his father's murderer?* But she can't say that. In her personal joy, Kristin appears insensible to the sensitivities at play.

"Travis is still at headquarters," Emma says finally.

Carter draws Kristin's attention back. "Now, Miss Gutmunsson, I've kept my part of the deal, so I believe you have something for me."

"Goodness, yes, I do!" Kristin rummages in her purse for a moment and comes out with a somewhat crumpled letter. "Here you are—all the names."

"What names?" Emma asks.

Carter ignores her question, takes the letter. "This is extremely helpful." He opens it and peruses the contents. "Yes. Good. All right, Miss Gutmunsson, much appreciated."

Kristin is beaming. "You're very welcome. I don't know what the names mean, but Simon said that you would." She turns her smile on Emma. "This is such a wonderful day! I can't believe Simon is so close—oh, Emma, it's so exciting!"

Kristin steps in for a hug, and Emma awkwardly obliges her. In the chill breeze of the concreted courtyard, surrounded by the dense stone walls of the jail, Emma realizes that she can't be angry at Kristin. Simon is her brother, her twin. More crucially, in two months' time, Simon will be dead. Kristin deserves to spend as many final moments with him as she can.

Kristin steps back, her face radiant. "I'm going to visit Simon now. They should have settled him in. Mr. Carter, thank you again for making this happen. Emma, I'll see you back at the hotel later on."

She swirls away, shoes tapping on the ash-colored pavers. Emma watches as Kristin's slim figure and white hair are swallowed up by the dark interior cloisters of the jail.

"I know you consider this transfer unwise." Carter's deep voice resonates behind her. "But so far as I can see, this is a net good. Miss Gutmunsson acts as an intermediary and gets to see her brother. We get the benefit of his insight in the case. The College Killer is brought to justice and Miss Kittiko gets rescued faster. Everybody wins."

Everybody wins. Emma feels numb. She turns and looks back at him blankly. "Right."

Carter holds up the crumpled letter. "I'll have this information analyzed and contact you later about results." He nods toward the courtyard gate. "Mr. Francks is waiting just outside. I'll be in touch again soon, Miss Lewis."

He follows the route Kristin took, back into the jail. Emma stands in place, surrounded by autumn elms and a glowering sky. Far off, the rumble of thunder. Her senses feel heightened by yesterday's panic attack—her exterior shield walls abraded, all her skin raw and rippling with unease.

Carter's nonchalance and Kristin's smiles don't provide reassurance. It's like Grenier said: This is dumb. This is not a net good. This is a horrific mistake.

Simon Gutmunsson is in Pittsburgh, and anything could happen.

She goes back to the hotel and takes a Valium and tries to nap, surprising herself by falling into a dead man's slumber until Kristin's return at six.

They start a takeout dinner at the glass-topped table outside the room, retreat inside when the storm breaks. The background drumming of the rain provides a counterpoint to Kristin's excited chatter about her visit with her twin. Emma finds it hard to sustain a pose of neutral interest, wants to press Kristin about the names in the letter, knows nothing will come of it. Finally, she excuses herself to call headquarters. No one is available to talk, so she yanks on a rain jacket to go for a walk.

Accompanied by Francks and the smell of wet asphalt, Emma sees the way Pittsburgh lights up in the evening rain like a box of costume jewelry. The city looks good if you ignore the heavy industry areas. She skirts flooded drains as workers in white hard hats find their way home on streetcars and buses.

The walk is not as good as a run, and only proves useful as a way to get very damp. On her way back, she detours past Bell's room, but he isn't there. She gives up at last, returns to her shared room with the faux wood-grain dado and brown blankets and apricot-colored comforter she's come to loathe. She tidies a little, watches an episode of *The Greatest American Hero* with Kristin—who stares at the television, mouth agape—then turns off her lamp and goes to sleep.

At midnight, the phone rings.

Kristin is snoring. Emma fumbles for the noise in the dark, feeling like she's in a coma.

"Lewis, you ready for some news?" Bell only calls her Lewis now when there's police business. "We found the videotapes. Gutmunsson's names hit pay dirt, and we confirmed via tax records of the delivery services Huxton used to distribute the tapes—he claimed the videotape deliveries as a fucking tax deduction."

"Where are you?" Emma wipes the corners of her eyes, still groggy. "What does this mean?"

"It means we're conducting raids—tonight, right now. We've got three targets." Bell's voice is charged, despite the line's faraway crackle. "Emma, I'm in Columbus."

"You're in Ohio?"

"Yeah. Look, try to go back to sleep—I'll call you again in the morning, once it's over. I just thought you'd want to know straightaway."

"Wait," she says, before he can hang up. "What about Linda Kittiko?"

"Martino says these new leads should help us find her. I'll call you first thing tomorrow, okay?"

"Okay. Good hunting," she manages to say before he disconnects.

Emma feels her way back to bed. She lies there in the dark and does not think about videotapes. Then she does not think about Linda Kittiko, and pink nails, and the round opaque lenses of Peter's glasses in the Paradise nightclub. They flash the burgundy of fresh blood, hiding his eyes from view....

Close to 3:00 AM, and frustrated by lack of sleep, Emma tries another strategy. She pretends that Bell is sitting on the sofa nearby, quietly reading reports, turning pages, holding the watch, like he did that night back at Quantico. Finally, her mind relaxes and her subconscious takes over, pulls her back under.

At 8:00 AM, Bell calls with an update.

CHAPTER TWENTY-THREE

That morning in Pittsburgh shows all the yellow fall colors echoed in the paintwork on Liberty Bridge. The streets are full of pedestrians in flat caps and beige coats, and the smell of rotten eggs wafts around as the city steams.

Carter's makeshift office at headquarters in the Public Safety building has a wooden desk, two nondescript chairs, a metal filing cabinet, a ceiling fan. The window behind him is covered with a closed pearl-gray venetian blind with a crack in one of the slats, and a shard of squintingly bright light stabs Emma right in the eye as she eases through the door.

The man himself is on the phone, standing with the receiver wedged between neck and shoulder as he simultaneously talks and hunts through paperwork on the desk.

"...then make sure they hold him." Carter sees her, waves her closer. He finds what he's been searching for on the desk, puts it aside. "Don't let them go to Justice without—"

"Bell said I should come see you." Emma speaks in an undertone.

Carter covers the phone with a hand. "That's right, thank you."

He removes his hand to complete the call. "Jack, I've gotta go. Call me again in an hour when we've got the deposition." He sets the receiver back in its cradle, gestures to a chair, smooths down his tie as he takes his own seat. He's in the same suit as yesterday, without the jacket. "So Mr. Bell told you what happened last night?"

Emma finds her posture straightening. "Bell called and said you got suspects."

"We found tapes, and we arrested three men." Carter's face is tired but pleased. "Now I should stress that we've compared the arrested men to your composite picture, and none of them are a match. None of these men are the College Killer. But we think these arrests will generate a lot of new leads related to the videotapes— who owned them, who distributed them, who they were distributed to. And that should lead us to Peter."

"Okay."

"Of the men we arrested, one is in Ohio—Bell is still on the ground there with Mike Martino. Another man we arrested in Massachusetts—Jack Kirby is currently coordinating a full search of that man's residence. Do the names Todd Benneau or Vincent Chavez have any meaning for you?"

"No," Emma says.

"Okay. I have some mug shots I'd like you to look at, Miss Lewis, if you think you're up for that."

"Sure." Emma arrows in. "This is all the result of the information you got from Simon Gutmunsson?"

"That's correct," Carter confirms. "Gutmunsson has been very helpful."

"That'll be a first. Usually he just jerks law enforcement around. And you said you'd consult me on it. Am I allowed to know the details of that now?"

"I'm afraid we had to move quickly, which is why you weren't consulted." Carter leans his forearms on the desk, shirtsleeves rolled. "There were names of videotape collector contacts, and some suggestions about delivery services, which we'd already begun work on anyway. But the names were very useful. We're hoping to talk to Gutmunsson again this afternoon—"

"You said three men," Emma interrupts.

"The third man, Derrick Brosky, was arrested here in Pittsburgh."

"Here?" Emma startles. "Is he—"

"He isn't Peter." Carter takes on a calming tone. "You can look at his mug shot, too, but as I said, physically Brosky bears no resemblance to the composite you helped create. We've spoken to him briefly—"

"He's in this building?" Again, Emma experiences a light shock, as if she's missed a step going down.

"Yes. I hope that doesn't make you feel uncomfortable."

"Derrick Brosky's here in the building, and you've spoken to him." Emma controls her breathing. "Okay, so he's not the College Killer. But he might be the link between Peter and the videotapes. He might have *given* Peter the videotapes."

Carter opens out his palms. "Well, that's what we're trying to establish, but he's exercised his right to an attorney."

"He's not talking?"

"It's going to take some time," Carter admits.

"But we don't *have* time." Emma thinks this should already be mind-blowingly obvious. "Linda Kittiko doesn't have time."

"We're very close now—"

"How long are you able to hold him?"

Carter remains patient. "His arraignment is scheduled for tomorrow, but he's unlikely to walk."

"Unlikely?" She presses harder. "So he could still skip out."

Carter shakes his head. "It's a federal obscenity case, and possibly an additional charge of intent to distribute."

"But he's not a physical threat, and there's no concerns about violence."

"We think, considering the seriousness of this case and the graphic content of the videotapes, the judge will be understanding."

New suspects, further steps, more delay. Emma feels her stomach flutter with tension and fatigue. "So you're going to sweat Brosky for information about his contacts in Pittsburgh. How long will that take?"

Carter shrugs. "It depends on his level of endurance. It could be a couple hours or a couple days."

"A couple *days.*" Emma closes her eyes, breathes out, opens them again. "No. Send me in there."

There's a pause. The chattering sounds of the fax machine and male voices echo from the bullpen down the hall.

"Miss Lewis, I can't do that," Carter says quietly.

"Can't or won't?" Emma counters. "Look, I've talked to serial killers, the insane, and the incarcerated. I can talk to this guy. I can get answers out of him faster."

Carter's brown eyes regard her solemnly. "I don't think that's a good idea."

"That's what you said about Paradise," she reminds him.

"And I was right. Paradise was a mess."

"We got good intelligence from it."

"We lost the target. And this is not the same." The fan spins above them. Carter wets his lips, preparing to rebuff. "I can't send a civilian consultant into an interview room with a suspect. It would imperil the legal case. I could lose my job. It's illegal, unethical, and most probably for you, unhealthy."

"Don't you think an *abducted girl* is in a *more* unhealthy position? In *more* peril?" Emma can't understand how he doesn't feel her sense of urgency.

"If Brosky doesn't talk about who he sent the tapes to, we've got his phone records, delivery records, known associates...." Carter's whole manner has firmed. "Let us do our job, Miss Lewis. We'll find Linda Kittiko faster that way."

"How?" Emma finds her anger is taking on a hard, glassy shape, like a lump of obsidian. "You're going to spend forty-eight hours digging through records, waiting on court orders, hoping Brosky cracks and gives you Peter's address.... Peter's not going to hold her too long. She could be *dead* already."

"Miss Lewis..." Carter pinches the bridge of his nose before looking at her again. "Emma. I understand your motivations here. I know you don't want another young woman to suffer. I know this case is a terrible reminder of what you went through—"

"God, shut *up*." Emma stands abruptly, shifting away. The

corners of her eyes are wet, and she can't let Carter see. "This case is not 'a terrible reminder.' I don't *need* a reminder—I *lived* through it. And I live with the aftermath *every goddamn day*."

She is the reminder, Emma realizes—a living, breathing reminder to the FBI of what can happen when they fail.

She turns to face Carter head-on. "The College Killer has already had Linda Kittiko for almost as long as Huxton had me. Send me in to talk to Brosky."

"No." Carter sits back in his chair, regarding her. He considers a moment, then seems to come to some kind of decision. "Miss Lewis, I'm going to arrange for you to have some time off."

Emma jerks like she's just been slapped. "What?"

Carter leans forward and pulls a paper closer, puts on his glasses. He doesn't look at her. "This case is an enormous strain and you haven't been able to see family or receive personal support—"

"You're not serious." She steps nearer the desk. "You're taking me *off the case*?"

"I'm sending you home for a few days," he says quietly, beginning to write.

"I don't believe this. You brought in *Simon Gutmunsson*, and you're sending *me* home?"

He glances up. "Emma, I know you're upset—"

"Of course I'm upset! A girl is going to *die*!"

Carter stops writing, holds her gaze. "But pushing yourself into another panic attack, or some kind of nervous breakdown, isn't going to help us find her."

"Please don't do this."

Carter goes back to writing. "The agent on your security detail can take you back to the hotel. You can pack up and catch the next flight back to Ohio."

"Don't do this," Emma pleads again. It's disorienting to realize she never wanted to be here and now she's fighting to stay.

"See your folks," Carter says. He signs off the paper, glances up. "Get some rest. Come back in a few days if the investigation is still continuing."

"After Linda Kittiko's body turns up at another bus stop?" Emma wants to scream.

Carter merely holds up the paper for her. His dark, somber stare has weight. "I'll see you in a few days, Miss Lewis."

―――――

Francks escorts her down the escalator and outside to the car, which takes her back to the hotel. Emma watches the traffic signs pass as they drive the watercolor streets of Pittsburgh, gets the same sensation she had when all this started, like she's in some kind of waking nightmare.

Kristin is not in the hotel room—she's at breakfast, or maybe visiting with her brother. Emma shoves her clothes and other belongings into her black overnight bag, shoulders her backpack, and returns to the car. Her hand dashes at her eyes. She wishes desperately that Bell was here.

Francks, at the car, has a page: He asks her permission to use the hotel room phone. Emma, still dazed, just waves her hand. When he returns, Francks explains that Carter has arranged Emma's flight and that they're headed straight for Pittsburgh Airport.

On the drive, she looks out at the leafless branches of silver birch trees beside the Penn-Lincoln Parkway, the high, rippled cirrocumulus clouds. Her uppermost feeling is anger, then tearing grief for Linda Kittiko. She thinks about Simon telling her she has to learn to wield her power.

At the airport, she goes to check-in, collects her boarding pass. Behind her, Francks collects his own. They have to wait forty-five minutes before the boarding call.

Emma sits quietly for a moment, looking at the people moving around near the Southwest counter on the airport concourse. Then she stands and tells Francks she's going to the bathroom.

"You want me to stand by the door?" Francks asks. He's a good man, and conscientious.

"It's okay," Emma replies evenly. "I can go to the bathroom by myself."

She leaves her overnight bag on the chair beside him.

The women's bathroom is all fawn floor tile and shiny silver stalls. She goes into one of them, opens her backpack on the lid of the toilet. Changes her shirt, pulling on a black T-shirt she borrowed from Bell when she was sick. She dons Kristin's dark blue cardigan, and the Paradise wig, and a pair of sunglasses. Leaving the stall, she turns side to side in front of the bathroom mirror, checking that the alteration seems different enough.

Then she takes a breath, shoulders the backpack again, and leaves the bathroom. She keeps her head down, walking quickly away from Francks and toward the airport exit.

Outside, the sun is glaring. She walks fifteen yards to the nearest taxi rank and jumps into the first available cab. The driver is an elderly man with a cauliflower ear.

"G'morning, Miss, have a nice flight?"

"Absolutely." Emma pulls off the wig and stuffs it in her backpack, along with the cardigan.

"Heh, nice hair." The driver grins as he pulls the car away from the curb. "Where're you headed?"

She passes him a twenty. "Take me to Allegheny County Jail."

CHAPTER TWENTY-FOUR

Seeing it from the outside now, Emma thinks Allegheny County Jail is like someone took a medieval barbarian's castle and thumped it down in the middle of a modern Pittsburgh city block. The jail is entirely constructed out of brown granite, which its founders probably thought looked dignified but which Emma thinks looks forbiddingly bleak. She asks the cab driver to go up Forbes Avenue and onto Ross Street, passing beneath the Bridge of Sighs, the ancient stone walkway that links the jail to the red-roofed turrets of the courthouse. She alights just outside the external jail gate.

The gate is decorated with elaborate Romanesque ironwork, and is followed by a wooden door, a steel door, other doors. She submits to the standard search and consents to them holding on to her backpack. She shows her FBI identification, explains that she's visiting in connection with Agent Howard Carter's ongoing investigation—it's very fortunate that Carter failed to repossess her ID when he sent her packing. A correctional officer on the admin desk recognizes her from yesterday's prisoner transfer, which is also helpful.

Once she gets past the elegant ironwork and stout doors and

appropriate checks, she arrives at a kind of lobby area, where the walls are thick stone and soundless plaster painted an unpleasant yellow, reminiscent of tobacco-stained teeth. Emma is the only person waiting on the solitary church-like pew for an audience with her chosen inmate. On the wall in the lobby, an old-fashioned sign outlines the GENERAL BLOCK RULES TO ALL INMATES: *In here, individuals cannot choose at will those rules they will abide by and those they will disregard.* It's impossible to imagine Simon Gutmunsson observing such an injunction.

Emma wonders how long it will take Francks to realize she has eluded him, how long before Carter finds out, how soon until they deduce her location. She presses her tongue against the roof of her mouth and waits.

Shortly thereafter, a correctional officer escorts her through a barred door and down a branching corridor. Finally, they arrive at a matte-gray door made of solid metal, which is stenciled in red: KNOCK ONCE ONLY. The conducting officer knocks once with his baton. Emma hears locks clicking on the other side.

The door slides open on tracks. Emma is ushered inside, the door is rolled back and locked behind her, and another officer—a man in his fifties, dependable-looking—issues instructions.

"Okay, your guy is the only inmate on the range here." The officer stands by the hatch of his metal station box, similar to the guardhouse in the population intake area. "The rules are real simple. Don't pass him anything, and stay in the center aisle. See the white lines on the floor? That's the center aisle. You can step back a little, but don't step forward or you're within arm's reach."

"I understand," Emma says.

He waves her onward. "Okay, mind the aisle, like I said. Go on down now—you got twenty minutes."

Emma looks at the sixty-foot stretch of dark stone corridor with its guiding aisle. A single lamp shines above a cell at the end. She can feel cold air; the hairs on her arms prickle. A flash of clarity tells her that she doesn't want to be here.

Go. Don't go. Linda will die if you don't go.

Emma makes a fist of her heart and begins walking toward Simon's cell.

She smooths her black T-shirt and tries to order her thoughts. It's important to have a clear understanding of what she wants and why she's here: She wants any final information Simon has about the case so they can find Linda Kittiko quickly. She is here only to get this information. Nothing more.

Her anger about Simon's connection to the videotapes is so close to the surface, though. Like cactus spikes under her skin. She reminds herself that the issue of her videotape is a subsidiary matter: She is not here to be angry or accusative. Simon knows what he is; there is nothing she might say that will be a revelation to him. Showing fury or frustration will not move him in any way.

But...can she use her anger somehow? Withholding fury and frustration means denying Simon his chance to gloat, and it might be advantageous to prod his ego in such a way. Won't he *expect* her to be angry? Yes, of course he will.

With each step, Emma thinks quickly. She is accustomed to using anger for fuel. Perhaps this is an opportunity to turn it to another use. She has been shoving down her rage toward Simon for hours now—maybe it would be good to just let things out, and watch how he reacts and what he is goaded into revealing.

Emma allows a whippy tendril of her anger to emerge. It feels satisfying. It powers her final steps, blood heating in her cheeks as she arrives in front of Simon Gutmunsson's cell.

This cell is a ten-foot-square box with three solid walls, and a barred front wall—like Byberry, but stone instead of concrete. It is very spare: a bunk, a chair, a toilet bowl. Simon is sitting on the chair in the perfect center of the cell, wearing the same blue scrubs and long-sleeved white T-shirt he wore in the asylum. Deep shadows in the creases of his blue scrubs make them seem like Baroque drapery. Simon's posture is upright, his ankles crossed. He holds a small hardcover book open in one hand as he turns pages with the other. He looks studious and neat, like a cleric.

Emma hears crows cawing at the sight of him. For a moment her head is full of the sound, like a flock has nested inside her skull.

Simon looks up from his reading material with a gracious smile. "Good morning, Emma. How lovely to see you."

She recovers her fire. "Don't you 'good morning' me, you lying, discourteous *asshole*."

"Oh, Emma, so cruel." His eyebrows lift. "Although it certainly makes your visits lively."

She decides to go in hard and fast. "Why didn't you tell me you knew about the videotapes?"

"You never asked." Simon closes his book, shoulders straight. "And I resent being called discourteous."

"I could call you worse things." Emma stalks to the edge of the white line. "And I could expend a lot more energy being angry at you, but I don't have the time for that." She shakes her head, watching his face. "It's the *pointlessness* of it that I find hard to take. A twenty-year-old girl, Linda Kittiko, is going to die—and for what? Because you enjoy watching the FBI scurry around and jump when you say so?"

"That does have significant appeal." Simon sets the book on the floor. His eyes are shards of turquoise, never leaving her.

"You've trashed any kind of connection we had." Emma introduces a note of disgust. "*Why?* For no reason at all? It's just a waste."

Simon holds himself very still. "It's the nature of life to be pointless, Emma. Mayflies fluttering for a single glorious day . . . Existence has no real meaning—I thought you knew that. We shine briefly, and are extinguished."

"Well, you've only got two more months to shine," she says harshly. "I hope the fun was worth it."

She turns and walks back toward the station box. Gets three paces away. Four—

"Emma." Simon's voice behind her.

She stops, as if arrested mid-flight. She wants him to think she's angry; she *is* angry. *God, let this work.* She's abruptly aware that her energy reserves are low.

"Please don't go, Emma. You've only just arrived." Simon's words are soft and echoey in the jail corridor. "I'm sorry I was discourteous. I can give you the information you need to find the College Killer's newest abductee."

Yes. Emma closes her eyes, waits a beat, opens them. Turns back. "Why should I believe you?"

Simon is standing from his chair now. He has stepped up to the bars, gripped them with his hands. The cell's spotlight casts the planes of his face in sharp relief. Everything white about him—his skin, his hair, his long fingers—glows with overexposure.

"Because you must." His eyes are gentle beneath his shadowed brows. "It's branded into you, to return and try to save. You returned to Huxton's basement for Vicki and Tammy. You return now for Linda...."

Simon tilts his head, with a slice of a smile.

"And maybe, just a little, you return for me. You wonder, don't you, if there's a sliver of light remaining inside of me. But I'm not all bad, Emma. I'll help you save this new girl."

Emma forces herself to look open to persuasion, forces her taut muscles to relax. She is walking a fine line here. "I don't know if I can trust anything you say." That's certainly not a lie.

Simon spreads his hands. "And yet, here we stand—distrustful and dishonorable, both. It's a kind of cosmic joke, isn't it?"

"I don't like being used as a punchline," she replies flatly. But this is not a moment she can waste. She takes two considered steps back toward Simon's cell. "You gave the FBI names. Those names led directly to arrests. The men arrested had copies of the Huxton videotapes."

"Naturally."

"So you had access to this world of 'videotape collectors.'"

"Why yes," he acknowledges.

"Did you make your own videotapes?"

"Of course." He examines his nails. "I love new toys."

Emma files that information before steeling herself. She can see the trajectory here. She has to do this, has to have this confrontation, but she's afraid of it. *Don't stop now—keep going.*

"And you watched the Huxton tapes."

"Yes," he says.

It's important that she doesn't reveal how much this affects her, but it's very difficult. She exhales, slow and even. "I should have known when you gave me that hokey prompt about the moving pictures."

Simon bites his bottom lip, coquettish. "I've been waiting for you to realize. Then time began to grow short."

"And you figured you'd better turn things to your advantage before Linda Kittiko showed up dead."

"Well, Kristin informed me that Pittsburgh is a city of grand delights, so I simply couldn't resist a visit...." His grin falters. "It's as you said, Emma—I have only two more months left to shine."

"Then tell me what you know, before the clock runs out." It's running fast: She needs to be gone before Carter realizes she's absconded, before Simon intuits she's here without authority. She reins her impatience hard.

"But if I tell you everything, what incentive do you have to come back?" His expression becomes coy. "You might break up with me entirely."

He imitates real emotion with disarming sincerity. *Oh, Simon, you goddamn drama queen.* She keeps her voice defiantly anodyne. "I guess you'll just have to go on trust."

Simon's chin lifts. "You're wrong, you know, about our connection. It's not tarnished at all. We know each other too well. I've seen your strength in the face of adversity, I've heard you cry in pain—"

"I don't want to talk about that." *Too abrupt. Compensate.* Stiffening her knees, Emma steps closer. "Tell me what you know, Simon."

He looks up at the ceiling of the cell, clasps his hands behind his back. Sighs, like this is all terribly wearing.

"All right, then. Special Agent Carter should check vital records for a list of Pittsburgh residents who died in the eight weeks prior to the first murder. Check their beneficiaries for young men in the target demographic—poor Peter simply can't *stand* to be alone. There will be a link to Brosky, although you may have to dig a little. Use the composite you've created to match identification. It should all be fairly simple."

There it is. Emma feels a crushing weight lift, but flooding in to take its place is a pall of exhaustion. Does it show on her face, how tired she feels? She needs to get out of here.

"Is that everything?"

Simon shows his large, empty palms. "That's everything I have. You've wrung me dry of truth. All that stands between us now are these bars."

Emma says a silent prayer of gratitude for the bars. "Okay. Thank you, Simon."

She nods, preparing to turn. But Simon has already moved nearer, the folds of his blue scrubs pressing against the cold steel of the cell bars.

"Will you come to my execution, Emma?"

She blinks, caught off guard by the question. "I... I don't know if I can do that."

"I would like to see you one last time. And someone should be there for Kristin."

Go with honesty. "I don't like watching people die."

"You would deny my final request?" Simon straightens, and his eyebrows lift. His expression shifts in subtle ways. "Am I not the only one to have seen your agony and looked you in the eye afterward?"

Emma feels her hackles rise. "Are you expecting applause?"

"To view is to witness—it's not a passive act." Simon's eyes peer out from below the fall of his white hair. "I ask only that you stand witness to my throes, as I stood witness to yours."

"I didn't ask you to *witness* anything." A pulse of pain at her temple, a lightning bolt. "If you watched the videotape, you only witnessed a version of me that Huxton constructed. Not the real me. Not the me I am inside, not the me I am now."

"Indeed?" Simon's full lips are sly at the corners. "But so much of the current you was prologued in that construction, dear Emma."

Her spine goes rigid immediately. "That's not true."

"You were then as you are now. You held nothing back."

"Simon, don't." She feels his attention on her like a thick tongue lapping at her brain stem.

His voice slithers in the space between them. "The other girls were catatonic from long use, but you were fresh and raw and *real*. You fought so hard—"

"Shut up." She is losing control of this conversation.

"Do you remember the ritual of it? The sliver of light would enlarge as the door opened. He would come down the stairs. . . ."

Emma closes her eyes. "Don't do this."

"He removed his rings, one by one."

I was down there. He grabbed me, and I went down.... She grips the back of her neck. All her muscles are wires. The brown granite of the jail presses on her, and Emma scrapes for energy to combat it, comes up dry.

"Stop now," she whispers.

Simon presses against the bars, greedy for her reactions. "The girls would start to cry. There must have been a smell—"

"Sweat." Her throat is like a desert. "He smelled of sweat."

"Vicki and Tammy could only make the sounds of crying, with no tears. Were they too dehydrated?"

Emma shakes her head, furious, then nods, helpless.

"But you made tears with no sounds." Simon seems curious about it.

"I wasn't going to give him that." Her voice rasps with anger.

"He hurt you for it."

"You think he needed an excuse?" Her eyes are open now, but her vision won't focus.

"You scratched and bit—how strong you were! You had disadvantages, though. The threat of hurting the other girls made you compliant."

With a last, violent effort, Emma struggles awake. "I never *complied*. I never *consented*."

"No," Simon allows, "you were forced to submit. But you maintained control. Do you remember our discussion about control? Hold and release—in the face of Huxton's brutality, you still had the power." He moves his head so the light falls on his expression just so. "Do you feel shame, Emma? There's no need. I admired you, for the way you battled and endured."

"You fucking shit." Heartsick, she stares Simon full in the face. "You watched a *videotape*. Don't assume that means you know me."

"Oh, Emma." Simon's shadow looms in the cell, and when he smiles, his teeth are ivory-sharp. "I believe I know the real you better than anybody. And you know the real me. We're *drawn* together, Emma—murderer and victim, predator and prey. We understand each other in ways others can't."

Her cheeks feel cold. The sound of cawing magnifies inside her head, a buffeting maelstrom.

Simon pauses, considering. "Huxton formed that connection, so I must give him some credit, I suppose. Although his video skills were of the crudest sort. No artistry at all."

Emma stiffens. Carefully managing her anger when she first arrived, now she hears the leash snap off her rage with a clear, crystalline ring as she steps forward. "You son of a bitch."

"He did, after all, have a wealth of material to play with." Simon grins, his eyes alight as she comes closer. "All those interchangeable girls."

"Don't you say that," she whispers. She's shaking, control disintegrated.

"But your appearance is the highlight, Emma. No wonder Peter is so obsessed...."

"DON'T YOU SAY THAT!" She takes another unguarded step, her face contorting. *"Don't you say—"*

"EMMA." A strong grip on her shoulder, a familiar scent: crisp

266

notes of amber and orange and bergamot. Travis Bell wrenches her backward, holds her firmly, his arm wrapping around her collarbones.

She did not hear him come. His body presses against the length of her back; the warm contact immediately makes her want to cry. Vision swimming, she sees the white aisle marker on the floor, and Simon's grasping hands, finally realizes how far she'd strayed over the line. Simon looks at her and grins.

She can't breathe. There's fabric against her cheek. Over her shoulder, Travis's other arm extends as he aims a Smith & Wesson Model 13 revolver at Simon's forehead.

"Back off." The sound of the gun cocking in the stone corridor is loud, and Travis makes the action look very smooth. "Right now."

"Mr. Bell." Simon transfers his attention, sneering. "What a nice surprise."

"Don't you start." Travis's face is more stone than the granite around them. "Don't you even fucking start with me."

Simon's grin is thinner now. "I see you're no longer wearing Daddy's suits."

"They should've just shot you on arrest." Travis's lip twists with revulsion before he exerts control, eases Emma closer to his side. "Okay, come on, Emma. Come on now, let's go."

She's shaking hard, terror and fury still thumping through her blood. Her limbs feel like they've seized up. She hears the quick steps of the station box officer coming their way.

Travis squeezes her, while his eyes stay glued to Simon. "Emma, focus. Breathe now. It's time to go."

She breathes once, twice, unsteady. Manages to squeeze back

at last. The station box officer is calling out. Travis lowers his right arm away, holds the hammer of the revolver with his thumb and returns it to a safety position. Once the gun is clear, he slides it into the pancake holster under his jacket.

"Okay, we're done here." He turns them both abruptly and starts walking with Emma back up the long corridor.

After a few steps, her legs are more cooperative. She flinches when Simon's voice sounds behind them.

"Goodbye, Emma. See you in November. . . ."

"Just keep walking," Travis says softly. "Don't give him anything."

When they meet the station box officer, Travis does the explanatory talking. They return to the station box, where the officer rolls the metal door to allow them exit. Now they're in the branching corridor. Emma finds it easier to move forward with Travis's arm around her.

In the lobby area, she makes him stop so she can rest against the wall and lean over. She puts her hands on her knees and waits for her vision to clear. Concentrates on the victory of getting the information. Tries not to think about the things Simon said, the way she responded.

Tries not to think about how there are only five doors between Simon Gutmunsson and the outside world.

CHAPTER TWENTY-FIVE

here is no Francks, just Travis in the bureau Fairmont, and he has remembered to get her backpack from the jail admission desk, throwing it in the back as she clambers into the passenger seat. He's shaking almost as much as she is, gets the car started but guns it too hard pulling away from the curb.

Emma is numb. She works to settle her shaking by clenching and unclenching her fists. "I thought you were in Ohio."

"I just got back." Travis scans traffic, looking like he wants to ram something. "I called Carter, he said you gave Francks the slip at the airport. I figured this was the place you might be."

"Carter kicked me off the case."

"I heard. I told him it was dumb. Don't know if that was the response he wanted, but I guess that's too bad." He takes the intersection at Forbes Avenue too fast, exhales, eases off the accelerator. He's a good driver.

"Simon gave me the rest of the information we need to catch the College Killer."

"I'm glad you got something. Carter's pretty pissed."

"I'm sorry." Emma feels her eyes getting wet. "I'm sorry you had to deal with Carter, and I'm sorry you had to go in there and pull me out...."

"Hey, any day I get to hold a gun to Simon Gutmunsson's head is a good day." Travis snorts. They're coming up to Fourth, and a red light. He slows the car to a stop, glances at her. "He got you pretty good, huh?"

"Yeah." Emma feels her breath trembling in and out. "Yeah, he did. He watched the videotape."

"I know." Travis pauses. "I figured that, too."

"He's known about it all this time." She swallows, looks out the window. How to ask this? "You were at the bust in Columbus. You never saw... You never watched—"

"No. No." When she looks back, Travis is shaking his head, eyes doggedly forward to the red light. "I heard your deposition, Emma—I heard it in your own words. I reviewed the evidence photos. I never want to... see it." His jaw clenches, his expression sickened. "No."

"Simon just..." Her skin feels very thin, almost transparent. "He kept... talking about the things that happened in the basement, and I—"

"You got overwhelmed," Travis says quietly.

"Yes."

"It's okay," he says. "Emma..." He looks as if he's about to say more, but then he shakes his head. "Come 'ere."

He reaches out with his non-driving arm, drags her into a sideways hug. Emma leans into his warmth as much as she can in the confines of the car. She tries not to cry, and mostly succeeds.

The light changes to green. The car behind them honks.

"Okay," Travis says, easing them apart, putting the car in gear. "Let's get to headquarters and put that info of yours to urgent use."

They drive forward.

It takes more than four hours, once they reach the Pittsburgh Public Safety building and Emma gives her report, for the combined investigative team—detectives from the Pittsburgh PD, and agents from Quantico and the local field office—to pull the information they need out of vital records, and begin putting it all together.

During that time, Emma reconciles Carter to the idea of her continued involvement in the case. Both Kristin and Travis weigh in. There's a lot of fast talking, and a lot of huffing from Carter, but Emma hopes that one dumb thing cancels out another dumb thing, and that she and Carter will be able to maintain eye contact again soon.

It helps that the intelligence she got from Simon is crucial; Carter quickly becomes too busy to huff. As more news emerges, the tone in the bullpen changes, snowballs. Every officer on the floor is aware that they now have enough information to give them a window—they're close. They have a chance for a collar. The general atmosphere is buzzing with the feeling of *we can catch this guy*. Emma senses the baying energy of a disparate group of people who've learned to hunt as a pack.

Kristin orders Chinese food, and she and Emma sit on chairs in the glassed-in deposition room, watching men rush around, listening to the phones ring. As the likelihood of finding Linda increases, Emma's anxiety ramps and she finds it hard to concentrate. But she changes her shirt, makes herself eat, and drinks water from the cooler while Kristin expresses her indignation about Emma's almost-removal from the case. Emma refrains from talking about the fun and games with Simon. But that conversation is going to have to happen soon. She's gotten to know Kristin better while they've been sharing a room: Kristin is eccentric, but she's a good person. She's also valuable as a conduit to her brother. But it's as if Kristin's still connected to Simon in a tangible way, as if the membrane between them is porous. It makes Emma nervous.

Around 5:00 PM, Bell trots over to the deposition room and leans in the doorway. "Hey, you might want to hear this. They searched vital records for recently deceased residents and got the name of a Vivian Kirke, who died in May. She left her son, Peter Thomas Kirke, as sole beneficiary. House, car, the works."

"What?" Emma stands, sets her mug of water down. "So Peter used his real name in Paradise?"

"Looks like it." Bell nods. "We still need to confirm. He's the right age, and we're waiting on a copy of his driver's license from Pennsylvania Department of Motor Vehicles. If his photo is a match with your composite, things are gonna start happening. Come on out—there's gonna be a briefing."

The noise level in the bullpen is getting loud. As she and Kristin emerge into the scramble, Emma notices a couple of guys in black fatigues and realizes that Carter has called SWAT into the briefing. Carter's standing in shirtsleeves at a table near the front, calling instructions and accepting information as men mill around.

"Here, sir." A young gray-shirted officer hands him a folder.

"Thank you. Is this—" Carter checks the papers in the folder. "Okay, this is good. Ask the chief if he's done on the phone, please."

"Yes, sir."

The briefing area has a corkboard—the same one from the City-County Building, it looks like—which has been plastered with all the latest new data. Emma and Kristin watch the action from the end of a row of filing cabinets, behind and to the left of Carter. Bell stands beside them, his eyes restlessly scanning.

Once again, Emma realizes, she and Kristin are the only women in the room: Faye and the other women from the switchboard are all downstairs. While there might be female officers in some department here somewhere, Emma has never seen them and they're not in attendance now.

"Do you think Carter will—" Emma starts.

"Hold up." Bell lifts his chin at someone walking in the main entrance. "Kirby's here."

Jack Kirby leads a group of three agents into the room, one of whom is Mike Martino. All of them are wearing dark suits with somber ties.

"I haven't met Mr. Kirby yet," Emma says. Kirby is a man with very pale eyes in a wide face, and blond Germanic hair. He conferences with Carter as people start to gather.

"I'll introduce you," Bell says.

Kristin cranes her neck. "Is it starting soon?"

"I think they're just waiting on the info from the DMV."

Horner arrives; there's a lot of handshaking going on. Like Kristin, Emma wants them all to cut to the chase and get moving.

The phones around them are ringing off the hook, and Bell gets pulled away to answer a call.

Kristin chafes her fingers together, looking around. "Such a lot of delay."

"Lots to coordinate," Emma reassures her. But there's a hard fizz of nervous tension under her ribs, gaining strength.

The fax machine chatters. Another detective—Simmons— brings the papers over.

"Is that what I'm hoping it is?" Carter asks. He slips his glasses on to look, nods at the paper solemnly and passes it to Horner. "We got it."

Horner peruses the fax. "Who made the ID?"

"Merrill Grantham, Vivian Kirke's attorney and executor. He knows the family. Confirmed identification from the composite, in comparison with the DMV shots."

"That's it, then."

"Yes, it is." Carter looks both pleased and relieved. "We're good to go."

"Outstanding," Horner says. He turns and faces the room, claps for quiet. "Okay, people, let's form up. Listen here."

There are thirty men in the bullpen, and most of them are gathering in this corner; detectives, task force officers, SWAT, and FBI. Bell arrives back to stand by the girls.

Everyone settles as the chief begins to speak.

"All right, gentlemen, we have a positive identification of the target. His name is Peter Thomas Kirke, white male, twenty-seven years old, brown and brown. Address is 198 Union Avenue, Crafton.

Now, we don't want to spook him. He's still holding a twenty-year-old girl hostage. We want everything to go nice and fast and clean."

Carter takes a step forward and continues. "Pittsburgh SWAT and the Hostage Rescue Team will be heading for Crafton. Ground transport is being provided by the DEA, we've got a couple delivery and utility vans prepped. Ten-man teams, stun grenades for forced entry, hard-shell armor. The gentleman standing over there"—he gestures with his hand—"is Special Agent Jack Kirby, he'll be our hostage negotiator if things go south."

Emma hears a nearby plainclothes detective murmur to his desk mate, "Or you could just shoot the fucker, put him out of his misery."

"Pittsburgh PD backup teams will be stationed at street intersections—check your maps." Carter's eyes move over the group, intent. "Gentlemen, this is not going to be like Paradise. Peter Kirke is not going to slip through again. Like the chief said, we want this smooth and by the numbers. Hostage gets rescued, perp goes down, nobody gets hurt. Does that sound preferable?" Agreement from his audience. "Good. It sounds preferable to me, too."

Horner takes over. "All right, people, this is what we've worked for. You know your jobs. Backup teams, I want five minutes in the deposition room real quick. SWAT is with Special Agent Carter. This operation kicks off in ten—get to your stations."

Officers and agents disperse with a sense of purpose. It's nearly 5:30 PM. Behind the blinds over the big bullpen windows, the sunlight is starting to gray. Emma's not sure how far away Crafton is, but she guesses the teams will arrive right at dusk. She doesn't know if that's a strategic advantage. She imagines they'd prefer not to be chasing Peter Kirke through the Pittsburgh suburbs in the dark, if things don't go to plan.

"But what do *we* do?" Kristin asks, watching the movement of men and uniforms and weapons.

Bell looks distracted. "I don't know yet."

"We're probably gonna be sitting this one out," Emma says to Kristin. The awareness gnaws at her, but she works to control it. She follows Bell's line of sight, sees Kirby in serious conversation with Martino as they walk toward the exit.

"I guess we'll have to save the introductions for later," Bell says quietly, before turning to Emma. "You're *definitely* gonna be sitting this one out. Question now is, whether I will be." He glances up toward Carter. "Sir?"

Carter breaks off giving instructions to one of the SWAT officers to walk over. "Mr. Bell, you were wondering about your assignment? It's to stay and supervise Miss Lewis and Miss Gutmunsson."

Bell wets his lips. "Sir—"

"I don't know that we really *need* supervision," Kristin says in an undertone.

Carter catches the comment, looks pointedly at Emma.

"Hey," Emma says, palms open, "I am on good behavior here, I swear."

"Please try not to sneak out on your security detail this time." Carter turns back to Bell. "Mr. Bell, we need you here. Everyone else is on assigned duties."

Bell seems resigned to the idea. "Francks and Napier are assigned?"

Carter nods. "But I feel pretty confident about Miss Lewis's safety in the middle of Pittsburgh police headquarters, especially now we're grabbing the guy who's made her a target." He checks in with Emma. "Are you comfortable with that?"

"Yes." Emma feels she has to fly the flag for the team. "But Bell misses out on the action."

"This isn't a punishment." Carter looks between them. "This is about doing our job. You won't be blind—you can listen in on the radio chatter, there's a VHF scanner on Kowalski's desk."

"Emma, it's fine," Bell says. "Don't worry about it."

"You've trained for this." She's not convinced that Carter's claim that "this isn't a punishment" holds water.

"I can stay," Bell insists. He turns to Carter. "I'm okay to stay."

Kristin straightens, cheeks pink with excitement. "So we can listen in to the radio and hear what's happening?"

"That's correct," Carter says. "You can't contribute to the conversation, but you can hear us talk on the scanner."

Emma looks him in the eye. "The last time I listened in on an FBI operation, Ed Cooper ended up as a casualty."

Carter's manner becomes reassuring. "Every precaution will be taken, Miss Lewis, I guarantee." He turns again to Kristin. "The information from your brother has been critical to this case, Miss Gutmunsson, and I appreciate the work you've done as liaison."

"And when this is over?" Kristin brightens hopefully.

Carter hesitates, trying to be gentle. "When Peter Kirke is apprehended and all the links to the videotapes have been followed up, then we'll begin the process of returning Simon to Byberry. After that, it will be a matter for the court."

"Oh." Kristin's cheeks are pink for a different reason now. "I . . . I understand. I mean, of course."

Carter pulls on his FBI tactical jacket. "Miss Lewis, Mr. Bell— it's time." He looks at both of them seriously. "We'll see you on the other side."

CHAPTER TWENTY-SIX

The bullpen is largely deserted; the sky out the window is a silvery canvas, and the colored sequins of the city lights are beginning to sparkle. Travis already pulled the blind to get a glimpse of the teams leaving, but it wasn't dramatic, just a collection of vans and patrol vehicles. No lights, no sirens; they don't want to scare the quarry away.

He sighs and looks over his shoulder at Emma. "You want coffee?"

She's sitting at Kowalski's desk in front of the scanner, with a notepad and pencil. Having stripped off her green vest in the warm office, now she's just down to her gray Henley, plus jeans and runners he's seen her in a hundred times. Her left leg jigs compulsively; it stands out because she's usually so controlled. Travis can almost see the tornado of barely suppressed nervous tension whirling inside the envelope of her skin.

She glances up from fiddling with the frequency knobs on the scanner. "Did you say coffee? Coffee would be good."

Travis considers the wisdom of giving her caffeine when she's like this. Across the big room, a phone rings. Another Pittsburgh officer, the lone man on the floor, answers the phone, then goes out the door with paperwork.

Travis turns to the right. "Kristin?"

At another detective's desk nearby, Kristin's white silk blouse and dark blue pants are drooping. She looks washed out, but everyone looks washed out under the fluorescent lights. She curls a long strand of her white hair over and over in her fingers as she stares straight ahead at nothing.

Travis tries again. "Kristin?"

She blinks like she's waking from a dream. "I'm very sorry, what did you say?"

"I asked if you want coffee."

There's a pause as she looks at his face, like she doesn't recognize him. Maybe he needs to ask a third time. The fax machine chatters on its desk near the hallway entrance.

Kristin's eyes suddenly seem to find focus. "I have to go see my brother."

Travis frowns. "Your brother?"

"Kristin—" Emma starts.

"You heard what Mr. Carter said." Kristin sits up straight, her expression shifting into a new intensity. "They're going to send him back to Byberry. Throw him on the mercy of the judge."

"Yes." Emma tries again. "But hey—"

"And once this investigation is over, I return to Chesterfield." To Travis, it's as if Kristin has found a clarity she's been missing. "This might be the last chance I have to see him." She stands abruptly, turns for the hall. "I'm going to get my things."

Travis steps forward. "Kristin, I don't think—"

"Travis." Another phone rings somewhere. Emma just looks at him. "Let her go."

They both watch as Kristin swirls up the hallway toward the deposition room, her pumps clicking on the linoleum. Travis doesn't know what to think. His primary responsibility is with Emma, so technically, Kristin can do what she likes. But still. He puts his hands on his hips, blows out air.

Emma meets his gaze. "Come on, Travis. Simon's a bastard, but he's her twin."

"She should stay close."

"Don't worry about it." She raises her eyebrows. "Coffee?"

Travis sighs again, sucks his teeth, goes to get the coffee. While he's finding mugs near the Brewmaster, he rolls his neck. They're about to get their wish—they're catching the College Killer. He should be excited. Why isn't he? Is it because he's here, not in the field? Or is anxiety about the outcome of the operation deadening his response? That's not it. He's not sure what it is.

He glances over at Emma. Now she's chewing the end of the pencil. "Are you still rattled from this morning with Gutmunsson?"

"Not anymore." She leans closer to the scanner, which gives out a hiss and crackle, and presses a button. The machine makes a brief earsplitting squawk. Emma throws the pencil onto the desk. "God*dammit*. What's the point of having a scanner if it's not *working*?"

Travis looks at her, bemused.

Emma sees him looking, flushes. "Fine—maybe I am still rattled.

But I won't feel better until I know the strike team has got Linda out safe. And I can't do it with this piece of *crap*." She gives the top of the scanner a frustrated slap.

"All right, calm down. Lemme see."

He comes back with the two hot mugs, sets them on the desk so he can pull up a chair. It's Simmons's chair, with the wheels. Travis feels like he's been living in this dress shirt, these suit pants, for months. He loosens his tie.

Emma grimaces. "I've got no idea how to get reception on this thing."

"One second—let me look. There should be headphones." He squints around at the items on the desk near the scanner.

"There's no headphones." Emma throws up her hands, stands to search behind the unit.

There's a clatter and an almighty crash near the hallway entrance, and they both jump.

"Oh my goodness—I'm sorry!" Kristin has reemerged with her small, odd handbag and her long jacket: It's the jacket that obscured her vision so she knocked over the metal trash can near the fax desk. Now she falls to her knees to fix the mess. "That was my fault, I'm so sorry."

"Forget about it." Emma makes a face as Kristin attempts to gather screwed-up paper and cigarette butts. "Kristin, leave it. I'll find the broom."

Kristin clambers to her feet. "Oh, Emma, I'm sorry—"

"Stop apologizing. You want to get to your brother."

"I do." Kristin bites her lip, wipes her palms on her pants. "I'm going now. Will you be all right?"

"We'll be fine," Emma says gently. "How long will you stay?"

"As long as they'll let me. I have a special permission letter from Mr. Carter, giving me admission to the jail at any time." She dithers a little, before getting herself aimed for the exit.

"Kristin?" Emma waits until the girl makes eye contact. "I'll see you back at the hotel when this is all over."

Kristin nods, conjures up a weak smile, then hurries off. Travis watches her pass through the exit. The sway of Kristin's white hair gives him all kinds of conflicting feelings.

"Those two are like…" He can feel his lip twisting. "It's like they never cut the umbilical cord."

Emma finds her seat again, looks at him with what seems like recognition as she reaches for her mug. "I know. I need to talk with her about it." She glances down at the scanner again, her expression thinning out. "But I guess they don't have much time left."

"Guess not."

And it's only then that Travis realizes: Simon and Kristin Gutmunsson aren't the only ones running out of time. This investigation is about to reach a conclusion. Travis knows how invested he is in catching Peter Kirke, in saving Linda Kittiko from torture and death. He's also suddenly, achingly aware that once everything is resolved, he'll return to Wisconsin and Emma will go back to Ohio.

"You must be exhausted."

"What?" Travis turns blindly to look at her.

Emma's head tilts as she examines him. "Well, you were up all night in Columbus. Got back just in time to race over to the jail and pull me out. Now you're here."

Travis makes a production out of sipping his coffee. "Yeah, but this is the good part—when we get to catch the bad guy."

"What was it like? Columbus?" Tension in her muscles, as if she's braced to hear.

Travis blows out air again. "It was...weird. Being on the strike team was, like, a massive adrenaline rush. But I couldn't..." He takes another sip. "I wasn't prepared for dealing with the guy. Benneau."

"He resisted?"

"No, it wasn't..." Travis doesn't know how to phrase this. "It wasn't like that."

"What was it?" Emma's expression changes, and he realizes she already knows. "He was normal."

"We arrested him at home. His wife and kids were there...." Travis stares at a place across the room. "I just can't reconcile it. How a guy with those kinds of...*predilections*..." He rolls the term in his mouth; such a courteous-sounding word for the urge to enjoy the rape and torture of women. "I didn't know a guy like that could have such a smooth facade."

"I've been used to that idea a long time." Emma cups her mug on the desk, as if she needs the warmth. "Monsters don't always look like something from a horror movie. Mostly, they just look like... normal guys."

Travis can only lean back in his chair and nod. The last time he and Emma worked together, he had to come to terms with the idea that the monsters were real. This is just a variation on the theme: Monsters are people, and they're living among us.

"Not all of them can fake it," she continues. "A lot of them aren't smart enough. But the smart ones...Huxton managed to do it, for a limited time. Simon Gutmunsson probably seemed completely normal to his friends and acquaintances."

"Somehow I kinda doubt that." Travis lets his shoulders settle in the chair, rests his mug on his knee. "And I don't know how we combat it. We can find and catch them, but..."

"There's always more," Emma agrees. Her expression turns cold. "In a civilized society, we'd just put them to death and be done with it."

He wonders if she's joking. Her expression says she's not. "What, and hang their heads on the wall as a deterrent?"

"I could live with that." She sips her coffee.

"Jesus, Emma." Travis hadn't realized she was so bloodthirsty. Then he thinks of Simon Gutmunsson, and wonders if his own position on the matter is really any different. But working with law enforcement, doesn't he need to have more balance? It's hard to disagree with her, though. "Is this spillover from seeing Gutmunsson at the jail?"

Emma puts her mug aside, returns to the knobs on the scanner. "I don't think I've been so angry in the past three years as I was with Simon this morning. He got in my head."

"You knew when this started that would happen," Travis points out gently.

"I know—you warned me." Emma glances at him, rueful. "But it all got a little too close."

"You wanna talk about it?"

She presses her lips together, looks down, her cheeks a muted pink.

"Hey, if you don't want to talk to me, there's someone else you can call."

"No, there isn't." Emma examines her hands. "I talked to Robbie on the phone, and—"

"I know. Me too." In the flurry of everything, he forgot. Now Travis sits forward and sets his mug on the table, digs for his wallet.

"You spoke to my sister?" Emma's eyes are bright and wary.

"Just before the briefing. She's okay. And she said to give you this." He finally finds what he's searching for, flips open his billfold to fish out a scrap of paper, which he pushes across the desk. "Dr. Klein is out of the hospital, she's in a recovery unit at OSU Medical. She contacted your family to say you can call her anytime."

CHAPTER TWENTY-SEVEN

Kristin thinks it's very convenient that the jail is situated so close to police headquarters. It makes sense, of course. But it's wonderful to be five minutes away from Simon, and her permission letter allows her to breeze in despite the hour. It's nearly 6:00 PM, and the shadows of Allegheny County Jail are cool and dark.

Once inside the jail, she is asked to explain the purpose of her visit and show her letter and her ID—she has her FBI identification on its lanyard. The officer at the desk scans her and the ID photo carefully, while Kristin peruses the giant mural that says REMEMBER YOU WILL BE SEARCHED! Then there is another door, where she duly surrenders her jacket and handbag. She is given a tag for her belongings and a prominent VISITOR badge.

She waits in the lobby with the unpleasant yellow paint, until a correctional officer enters through a steel-barred door and examines a clipboard.

"Kristin Gutmunsson?"

She raises her hand like she's still in school. "Yes! Yes, that's me."

"Follow behind, please."

She follows behind as he goes back through the barred door,

then down the corridors. Finally, they arrive at the metal door that says KNOCK ONCE ONLY.

By the time the metal door has rolled aside, and the officer in the odd little barometric chamber has given her his talk again, and she has walked down to her brother's cell, Kristin feels ready. Her shoulders push back, and there is not a breath of nervousness about her anywhere.

She walks past Simon's cell, collects the hard wooden chair left nearby for her convenience, arranges it as close to the white aisle line as possible. She seats herself, composed and elegant, with her hands clasped in her lap.

The spotlight glares inside the front of the cell, and the rest of the space is dingy. But she can see Simon, fully reclined on the bunk shelf at the right. His long limbs are relaxed, his eyelids violet with shadow and closed as if in sleep. His book lies open facedown on his chest. Kristin watches the book rise and fall with his slow breaths, hears the foxed pages rustle faintly against the blue fabric of Simon's scrubs.

"You came." Simon's voice is like a sigh in the oppressive quiet of the jail corridor. His eyes are still closed.

"Of course," Kristin replies, equally soft. Her heart fills up with an overwhelming tenderness.

She has done everything right. She has visited on four occasions since her brother arrived. Whenever she has attended, she has been a model of decorum. She speaks politely. Submits willingly to each demeaning search and process step. Allows her belongings to be confiscated. Smiles at all the correctional officers.

She has prepared well for this moment.

"So." Simon's eyes open, languid. "It's time for us to begin."

CHAPTER TWENTY-EIGHT

Emma raises a fist to cover her mouth, takes it away again, staring at Travis's scrap of paper on the desk. She picks it up carefully, like it might burst into flames. "This is my therapist's number?"

"Yeah." Travis lifts his chin at the scrap. "Apparently, she's doing fine. When you get a chance, you should talk with her. Tonight, even."

Emma's expression transforms: shock, relief, gratitude, all skimming across her features so fast it makes his breath catch. Finally, she seems to settle on happiness, and her whole face glows. She smiles, presses her lips for restraint. Her mouth opens and closes a few times before she can get words out.

"I appreciate this." The control in her is fierce, but her eyes are glistening. "Thank you, Travis. I mean it."

Why, Travis thinks, *why why why would anyone find any pleasure in seeing women hurt, when it's a billion times more pleasurable to see them happy?* He doesn't have the answer to that question.

"No problem." He clears his throat, drags his gaze away. Takes a gulp of coffee. "Maybe *I* should talk to her. Maybe she can make the psychology of perps like the one in this case make sense to me."

Emma scrubs her eyes quickly with the back of her hand, squints at him. "I mean, you can talk to her, if you want."

"Nah, I'm just kidding," he demurs.

"No, really." Paper scrap clutched tight, Emma reaches to squeeze his forearm with her other hand. "But look—the reason you don't understand Peter Kirke isn't just because what he does is outside your experience. It's because you're you." Her cheeks color, but she's staunch. "It's because you're a good person, Travis."

He's not sure what's more compelling: the words she's saying, the depth in her eyes, or the gentle pressure of their contact through his shirtsleeve. He swallows hard, shakes his head.

"Doesn't make me a very good law enforcement officer, though. I need to understand to investigate." He rubs a hand across his lips. "And I've had a lot of trouble compartmentalizing stuff during this case. I can't seem to keep things...neat."

"Maybe it's just not neat."

"No, I mean..." He tries to phrase it correctly. "I can't seem to keep the stuff I see separate from my emotions. From my daily life. It makes it really hard to do the job."

"You're worried about it," Emma prompts.

He feels bleak. "Law enforcement's the only path I've ever had."

"Well, you shouldn't quit it yet—this case is different." When he makes a noncommittal noise, her hand slides down to find his own. "Hey, hear me out. Maybe it's hard to compartmentalize because it's *my* case. Because you know me."

"Maybe," he admits. Her hand is very soft and warm in his.

Animation and color have given Emma's stern face a kind of radiance. "Travis, you're as close to me as anyone. That might make it tough to detach. Maybe you're not doing anything wrong. Maybe this case is tough because... it's personal for you."

You're as close to me as anyone. She doesn't just mean proximity— they're emotionally close, and it's been this way since they first met in June. The one bright spark for him in this whole mess has always been Emma.

"Yeah," he whispers. "Maybe it's personal."

Emma's breathing seems high in her collarbones. She wets her lips. "Travis—"

The phone rings on Kowalski's desk.

CHAPTER TWENTY-NINE

Kristin sits up straight in the wooden chair and gives her small report to her brother.

"The police and the FBI have gone to capture the man they believe is the College Killer. His name is Peter Kirke—they found out through vital records, just as we knew they would. Mr. Carter took a hostage negotiator with them to Crafton. Travis and Emma are still at headquarters."

Simon slowly moves a hand. Touches a single finger to his bottom lip. "Crafton, you say."

"Mm-hmm." Kristin feels a little shiver go through her. "I don't think that's the right place, though."

She hears her brother's breath stall. In one smooth, graceful motion, he pushes the book away and rolls to sit up. His white hair is tousled, but his eyes are alert.

Simon braces one hand against the thin cotton mattress on the bunk. "Why do you think that, dearest?"

"A message came through before I left," Kristin says. "A message on the fax machine. I saw it."

Simon smiles. Nothing of the languorous sleepiness of a moment before is visible in his movements and expressions now.

"And what did that message say?"

CHAPTER THIRTY

The phone's bray makes them both startle, but Travis is the one who recovers first. Hot blood still in his cheeks, he disentangles his and Emma's hands, grabs for the receiver.

"Uh, hi. This is Travis Bell.... Hey, Faye, no, he's not.... Uh, sure, put him through." He covers the phone and lowers his voice. "Gerry Westfall's trying to reach Carter." He clears his throat, returns to the call. "Dr. Westfall, it's Travis Bell here—I'm gonna put you on speaker, okay? One sec." He glances at Emma, sees her look down to straighten her shirt—she's blushing. He finds focus somehow, presses the button on the cream Rolm unit and replaces the phone, speaking a little louder. "Okay, me and Lewis can hear you now."

"Great." Westfall's voice crackles down the poor-quality line. "I'm checking in to see if you got the data I just sent. Carter said if—"

"Hello, Dr. Westfall, excuse me," Emma interrupts. "What data?"

"The data I just..." Westfall makes an annoyed noise. "The fax. I sent a fax about twenty minutes ago. With the latest information about the trace analysis. Is Carter there?"

"You sent a—" Travis feels his forehead crease. "Um, I'm gonna check the fax machine, okay?"

As he gets up to walk to the fax desk, he sees Emma lean forward to the phone. "Dr. Westfall, Special Agent Carter isn't here. He's leading a strike team to a place we think is the latest address of our suspect."

"I just love how people keep me in the loop on these things," Westfall mutters, before increasing his volume. "So it's only you two?"

"Pretty much," Emma admits.

"Okay, well, if Carter thinks he's found the guy, then maybe the new data isn't relevant."

"What's the new data?"

"The nail polish." Travis speaks over his shoulder; he's found the fax now. He rips it off the roll and walks back to the desk with it. The flag of paper curls around his hand as he scans the page for the information they need to keep up with Westfall. "You tracked it to a few places here in Pittsburgh?"

"I mean, there's a whole subculture of ladies who like vintage nail polish, who knew?" Westfall's tone, warming to his subject, turns serious. "But look, there was a bulk order placed with a Revlon sales supplier in Pittsburgh about eight years ago, before the color was discontinued, which wouldn't have been noteworthy except the supplier remembered it was all the one color, and all for a single customer—a woman's name, Vivian Elyse Kirke."

Emma sits up, spine stiff. Travis hears the ping inside his head. He props himself on the desk with one hand, uses the other to keep the fax paper flat.

"Doctor, that's a direct link to our current suspect." He reads further. "I've got the fax here. You got the name of the supplier—"

"Yeah," Westfall says, "but check my note right at the top. The shipment order was for a dozen cartons—that's six hundred and fifty bottles of Frosted Pink Cloud nail polish. It went to a receiving warehouse in Beechview for her to pick up."

"You think it's all still there?" Emma frowns.

"Whether it's still there or not, I don't know," Westfall continues. "But it might be where your perp is getting his supply."

"How far away is Beechview?" Emma whispers to Travis as their eyes meet over the phone unit.

"It's not far from Crafton." Travis's voice is low. He returns his focus to the phone call. "Dr. Westfall, I think this might be important. Thanks for sending it through."

"No problem," Westfall wheezes. "But you really need to start calling me Gerry, before this 'Dr. Westfall' stuff starts going to my head."

Emma makes a faint smile. "Sure, Gerry. Thanks again."

"You're very welcome, Miss Lewis. Ask Carter to check in with me when he gets back, will you?"

"Will do," Travis says, and then the call ends, and it's just him and Emma staring at each other.

CHAPTER THIRTY-ONE

Interesting, very interesting…" Simon is still seated on the bunk. He leans back now against the wall of the cell, fingers pinching at his bottom lip. "And you think Emma and Travis Bell may explore this alternative address?"

Kristin considers, nods. "Emma would want to. And I think, where Travis is concerned, she can be very persuasive."

Simon snorts. "I'm sure." He sighs. "But that information doesn't help with our more immediate problem, I'm afraid."

"I know." Kristin's voice is small. She watches her twin's gaze focus and settle on her. It feels like the wings of a great moth fluttering inside her head. "You were right. *Nothing* you have done on this case assisted with the execution appeal—and the FBI remain profoundly ungrateful."

Simon smiles faintly and drops his hand, opens his palms wide. "You know my feelings about the bureau, Kristin. With one hand, they giveth, and with the other, they taketh away."

Kristin feels her face contort with grief—but there's no time for that. She blots her eyes with her sleeve and composes herself for what's to come.

Simon's expression now is so gentle it makes her heart ache. "Do you still have doubts about all this, dearest?"

Kristin senses emotion moving inside her, a deep-swirling current. It's as if she is a mote on a vast, dark sea. Her eye turns inward and she grasps her own forearms, tucking them against her midriff to keep herself balanced.

"There was a storm last night," she says quietly, "while Emma and I were having supper. Perhaps you felt the thunder, here in the stones. Emma went walking, so I had the moment entirely to myself. I sat outside the hotel room, smelling the storm, watching the lightning...."

She closes her eyes and remembers the brilliant sizzle and crack of ice-white, the metal scent of ozone on the air. Her twin, her brother, trapped in lightless correctional caves, has not seen a storm in over two years.

She opens her eyes. "I have doubts, Simon, but they are not about you."

CHAPTER THIRTY-TWO

N ail polish." Travis looks at Emma, then back at Westfall's fax. "Same brand and color as Kirke used on the victims."

"Westfall said it went to a warehouse space." Emma takes the fax off him to see. "It's listed as a receiving warehouse on the shipment order."

"That's gotta be where Kirke is getting it from."

"From an order his mom placed eight years ago?" She examines the paper, rubs the short hair at the back of her neck. "Who orders six hundred and fifty bottles of one color of nail polish?"

"Maybe she clipped coupons?" Travis shrugs. "I don't know. It's weird."

"His mother." Emma chews at a fingernail.

"What's that?"

"I just remembered what Simon said about the College Killer— *he's had some unfortunate experiences with women, most likely with the first woman he ever knew.*" Emma's leg has started jigging again. Travis doesn't think she's realized. "Peter Kirke started killing after the death of his mother. It wasn't only that he got access to means—a car, a house. It's because that connection was severed."

Travis frowns, following her thread. "You think she kept him in check?"

Emma nods. "I think Kirke probably has a really complicated family history. And if we dig further into his life, I'm guessing we'll find evidence of earlier minor transgressions—trespass, public exposure, peeping Tom behavior—that his mom managed for him."

"That would track."

"So this nail polish, and the connection to his mother, would have importance for him." Emma's eyes move as she considers. Then she pushes away from the table to stand. "Travis, I think we should go to Beechview and look at this warehouse."

"What?" He blinks at her. "No. Why would we do that?"

She grabs her vest from the back of her chair, starts pulling it on. "To find additional evidence that Kirke used in the murders. To close the loop. There could be a link there. Kirke could work at the warehouse, or someone there might have seen him."

Travis knows he should rein this in. "Yeah, but that's something the Pittsburgh PD can follow up once Kirke is in custody."

"Then let's save them the trouble." Emma is already zipping up her vest.

"Emma, we can't."

"Look, if it's just a warehouse with a dozen boxes of nail polish, what does it hurt?"

She's radiating nervous energy, and he tries to go gently. "We're supposed to be staying here, listening to the scanner and—"

"This scanner?" Emma pokes the softly hissing machine, raises her eyebrows. "The scanner that doesn't *work*?"

"Emma—"

"Travis, I can't just sit here." She swallows at the admission. "I'm sorry, but I can't. When I sit here, all I can think about is Linda, and what Kirke might be doing to her." Her expression flickers, and he sees the bubbling desperation she's trying to control, how it's wearing on her. "I've got to do something. Please."

He presses his lips. The way she said *please*, the tension spilling out of her, it all gives him pause. He sighs. "Carter wouldn't like it."

"Carter isn't here."

"What happened to good behavior?" He tries to turn it into a joke.

Emma just looks at him.

"I'm not a fully-fledged agent," he says softly. It's a reminder to her and to himself. "If something goes wrong, I'm not qualified to protect you."

"You're qualified enough for me." She holds his gaze for a long moment, before breaking eye contact to gesture at the phone. "Okay—call Faye, ask for a patch through to the strike team. Get Carter's permission."

"Really?"

"I don't want you to do something you're not comfortable with." She nods at the phone. "Really. Go ahead and ask him."

Travis reaches for the handset, makes the call to Faye. Emma listens, pacing. Faye tries the patch—it's unsuccessful. Travis hangs up, considering his options.

"It's just a warehouse." He tries to see if saying it out loud makes it more palatable.

Emma nods, hopeful. "And we've known from the beginning that Kirke keeps his victims in a house, with a bathroom and a kitchen and the privacy he needs." She shifts foot to foot. "Look, call Faye back. She can keep trying Carter so he knows where we are."

There's a long pause in the quiet room. Travis can hear the hum of the fluorescent lights above them. He has to make a decision now, and he wants it to be the right one.

He stands, grabbing the phone again. "Okay, let me make this call to Faye and we'll go."

Emma lets out a massive breath. "Thank you."

"No problem." He glances at her as he dials. "But between here and Beechview, you need to figure out an answer to the biggest question."

"What's that?"

"What are we gonna do with six hundred and fifty bottles of nail polish?"

CHAPTER THIRTY-THREE

S imon, you must listen now." Kristin lifts a hand to prevent interruption. Her voice is soft. "I need to say something, and I don't know if I'll be able to articulate it so clearly again."

She sits forward on the wooden chair, fingers clutched together, ankles crossed, everything symmetrical and neat. What she wants to explain is not neat. She takes a breath and dives deep within herself for the words she requires.

"We have always been together. We were in Mother's body together, we were babies together, and then children, sleeping curled up in one bed. We have lived and loved in unison our entire lives, which is one reason this separation has felt so cruel...." Kristin glances away and swallows down tears. Tears are of no use now. "We are two people, but we are one. I know you feel the same."

"I do." Simon's whisper carries through the bars. He holds his spine straight, with a controlled tension.

"Yes." Kristin nods. She hunts for her words, her thread. "So I know you will understand when I say that every individual is a spectrum. From light to dark, we all hold goodness and evil inside. Even the most holy man has flaws—petty grievances, weaknesses, vices, faults. It is what makes us all human." She looks into Simon's eyes, finding her direction. "Even the gods are not pure. Do you remember our old history tutor, Ram? How he told us the story of the Mahabharata, when the prince Arjuna has the god Krishna as his charioteer? Arjuna has a crisis of conscience about going into battle to kill his cousins, and to appease him, Krishna reveals his godly form—"

"Yes—the Vishvarupa." Simon leans forward, knuckles white on the metal edge of his bunk, and recites. *"Behold now, Arjuna, the entire universe...assembled together in my universal form."*

Kristin nods excitedly. "And Arjuna was both dazzled and terrified, for the form of god extended immeasurably in all directions."

Simon smiles. "And the Supreme Lord said: *I am mighty Time, the source of destruction that comes forth to annihilate worlds."*

"Even the Christian god is not all golden harmony."

"The Christian god of sacrifice." Simon's eyes light. *"Think not that I am come to bring peace on earth: I came not to bring peace, but a sword."*

Kristin knows that she is understood. "The form of god contains everything—it is a spectrum of light and darkness. And each human being is a reflection of that form, that spectrum." She feels her own yearning show in her face. "Simon, we are one being. One person. And we contain a spectrum. I look at you, and I see the lightning I witnessed in the sky last night—wild and brutal and unrestrained. You are my twin. My other half. Without each other, we live only pitiful half-lives. Without each other, the excesses of our natures exist out of balance. We must exist together, or fall apart. I love you, Simon. I *am* you—and you are me."

Simon's eyes are glistening with tears. *"Our state cannot be severed, we are one, one flesh; to lose thee were to lose myself."*

"You ask me if I have doubts." Kristin finds her own eyes blinking wet. Without moving her gaze from her brother, she raises a hand to her hair and begins unwinding the razor blade she has hidden in her ice-white tresses. "Simon, I have no doubts. I only want to get you out of here."

CHAPTER THIRTY-FOUR

In the dark interior of the Lincoln, Travis is driving because he knows the roads best. Emma grips the door handle of the car, feeling tough vinyl, and sweat on her palm. They're driving through the Liberty Tunnel; she watches the white tile and tunnel markings and identical lights go backward, as though she and Travis in the car are standing still, and their surrounds are in motion.

The air in the Lincoln smells stale and she still feels antsy, but it's infinitely better than pacing the bullpen. Just moving toward a destination is providing a measure of relief. She knows that Travis has done everything he can to ensure this all follows procedure: He's got Faye calling Carter until she gets through, and he's sent a message to the local field office. He even argued to get the use of a Motorola phone pack, now stashed on the back seat in case of emergencies.

Everything is squared away. Anxiety is still gnawing at her, though.

Emma tries to calm her mind. Carter has a solid lead in Crafton, and this Beechview address is just a warehouse that has some dusty cartons of nail polish. It's a distraction—Emma recognizes that, but she also recognizes that in this moment, it's a distraction she needs. Better to be moving, acting, than dwelling on what's happening with Linda and the strike team. She can't save Linda, but she can still do something.

It's branded into you, to return and try to save.

"*Shut up.*" Emma doesn't need Simon's voice in her head right now. And she doesn't realize she's spoken aloud until Travis glances at her sharply.

"Sorry?"

"Nothing." Emma shakes her head. They're coming out of the tunnel. Travis's hands are firm on the steering wheel.

"Are you okay with this?" Emma asks suddenly.

"Nope." He's leaning to see better through the windshield, eyes forward. "I'm not really okay with any of this. But I'd rather be here than sitting in the squad room, listening to you cuss out the scanner."

"Huh." Emma sees his mouth twitch up, feels strangely comforted. That Travis passed on Audrey's number, that he's going along with this—it means a lot. She lets her shoulders settle. "All right."

There's a pause.

"And I just..." Travis chews on his bottom lip. "Kristin said something to me. She said that I'm divided. That my loyalty is torn between working with the FBI and my connection with you. It's been bugging me."

"Why would she say that?" Emma frowns. "And why has it been bugging you?"

He is determinedly looking away. "Because it sets up those things as contradictory. Like I can't be FBI and also support you. As if doing my job and following orders puts me in opposition with you. I don't know what to make of that. But it feels uncomfortable, so maybe there's something in it."

Emma watches the buildings as they navigate off West Liberty Avenue onto Brookside, then toward the traffic lights at Sebring Avenue. She thinks about how to reply. "I can't make a judgment on what Kristin meant, or what it means about your job. I can say that I've never felt supported by the FBI. I've always felt that they're...kind of ashamed of me. The fact I escaped Huxton without their help, and then reminded them of it, rankles them. We raised some hackles during the Hoyt investigation, too. And I feel like they think I'm a means to an end—a useful tool in their arsenal."

Travis glances over. "I'm sorry the bureau hasn't treated you right. I saw it during the first Pittsburgh briefing, and after Paradise, and it pissed me off. It sucks, and I understand why you felt used."

She has to say it. She watches the traffic lights turn from red to green. "I worry that if you keep working with them, you'll change. Become more official, less...you. Institutions have a way of changing people."

Travis makes the turn. "I don't want to change the kind of person I am. I got into this job because of my dad, and what he stood for. For me, it's always been about both catching bad guys *and* helping people."

Emma glances down at her lap. "My grievances against the bureau are mine. I think they can do good work. But they're part of a system. They use people up, and they don't listen."

Travis looks at her long enough that she worries he's not paying attention to the road. "I want to be someone who listens."

Emma experiences a sudden clarity, and it resembles their trip through the tunnel: like everything around her is in motion and she is momentarily suspended. Something inside her, some awareness about the way she regards Travis, is shifting—she can feel it. Maybe it shifted a while ago, and she's only just realized he's more than simply her partner. She wants to prolong this conversation to its natural end, but Travis is back in action, navigating over Broadway and turning at the T-junction. Now they're on Rutherford Avenue.

In the sealskin twilight, the houses around them are large, double-storied, mostly brick. They're spaced well apart, with big sloping yards. Lots of trees and large gardens. Emma frowns, uneasy. This doesn't look like a warehouse area.

"What number?" Travis asks, as they crawl down the street.

She blinks, turns on the internal light, and checks the note she's holding, with the information from the fax. "Three sixty-eight."

"There." Travis lifts his chin.

He pulls the Lincoln in to idle at the curb. On the right, 366 is a vacant lot covered in grass and dotted with beech trees and hornbeam saplings. The structure they're looking at on 368 is set back from the road, made of pale brick, double-storied with mullioned windows, on a generous-sized lot. There's a semi-wild garden plot out front, with a winding concrete path. Forty feet behind and to the right, a large outbuilding.

Emma knows her expression is worried. "Travis, what do you think about this?"

He turns off the car and peers out the window. "I think this isn't a warehouse."

CHAPTER THIRTY-FIVE

Hey. Hey there!" Fifty-four-year-old Allegheny station box officer Gil Pasternak, husband of Ann, father of five, calls out
as he walks the stone corridor toward Kristin Gutmunsson, who is
hugging her brother through the bars of his cell. "Miss? Miss, you
need to step away now. We don't allow that here."

Kristin has her face tucked against her twin's blue scrub shirt,
but she turns her head to see Pasternak's approach. "I want to hug
my brother."

Pasternak looks uncomfortable. "I'm sure you do, miss, I'm sure
you do. But there can't be any physical contact with prisoners in this
part of the jail, I'm real sorry. Please step away."

"Can we not allow the bonds of affection in the halls of punishment?" Simon asks quietly.

Pasternak draws his baton. He steps onto the very edge of the
white aisle line. "Miss, you need to step back now. Right now."

Kristin does not step back, but instead turns her face against her
brother's chest once more. Pasternak leans and taps the end of the
baton against the bars near her arm.

"Come on now, miss—"

It happens in a flash: Like a striking snake, Simon grabs the baton, pulls hard. Taken off balance, Pasternak tilts toward the bars. Simon seizes him by the collar and says, "Step back, dearest." Pasternak gasps, eyes wide. Kristin steps back quickly and turns around.

There's a thrashing, a gurgling sound. A clatter as the baton hits the floor. Kristin keeps her face covered with her hands. She knows what her brother is, but she does not wish to see it.

"It's done, now." Simon is barely breathing hard. "Turn around, Kristin, and collect the keys."

Kristin turns around. Gil Pasternak lies slumped on the floor of the aisle, most of his blood volume drenching his white shirt, dripping into the puddle at his feet. His eyes are glazed, but his mouth opens and closes like a fish. Where his throat meets his collar, there is a dark red gap that reveals flashes of glistening pink and white.

Simon is half bent over, holding Pasternak's shirt, easing him gently back against the bars. The razor blade, and Simon's left hand, are both covered in horrifying crimson. Simon's left pinky finger is raised, as if he is holding a teacup made of fine porcelain.

"*Kristin.*" Simon's voice forces her to look at him, not at the man dying on the floor. "The keys."

Kristin nods mutely, bobs down, and follows Simon's directions to find the keys clipped to Pasternak's belt.

CHAPTER THIRTY-SIX

Emma sits with Travis, staring at the house at 368 Rutherford Avenue like she's hypnotized. Her throat has gone suddenly, horribly dry.

"Westfall said it was a warehouse. That's what it said on the shipment order."

Travis lifts his chin toward the building out the window. "That is not a warehouse. It's a house."

"Have we got the wrong address?"

"Nope. I checked."

"This looks bad, doesn't it."

"Yes, this looks bad."

Travis runs his hand over his face; Emma hears the rasp. She's busy looking across the street at the house that is not a warehouse, and a terrible feeling is coalescing inside. She doesn't want it to be true, but her certainty is growing roots.

"Travis, do you remember what I told you when we first met, about why it took so long for the FBI to find Daniel Huxton?" She can hear how her voice is trembling and soft.

"Lack of strong evidence," Travis says quietly. When she looks over, he's staring straight at her. "And they didn't know about the mountain house."

"That's right."

A long moment of quiet in the warm car. Then they both speak at once.

"Linda Kittiko could be—"

"We don't know if that's—"

"*Travis.*" Emma tries to settle the shake in her voice. There's a light tremor in all her limbs. "If she's in there, we have to go get her. Right now. We can't afford to wait."

"I agree with you," Travis says immediately.

Emma gapes. "What?"

"I agree. If Carter's got the wrong lead, and Linda Kittiko is being held in this house, the strike on the Crafton address could tip Kirke off."

"He'll kill her, Travis." Emma feels a dizzying surge of vertigo.

"I know."

"Okay, then." Emma forces herself to steady. She takes a bracing breath. Reaches for the Lincoln's door handle, tugs on it—

"Hold on," Travis says, and he leans across her and pulls the door closed before the interior light has barely had a moment to shine. "Hold on just a second."

Emma wants to push his restraining hand away. *"What?"*

"We can't go in there yet. There's stuff we need to do. We probably shouldn't go in there at all."

"But Linda—"

"She may not be in there. But if she is, she isn't going to thank

314

us if we charge in and get killed before we can do any good." Travis frowns. "If Peter Kirke is in that house, we need to go prepared."

Emma manages to control herself. "Okay, what do we need to do?"

"Give me the phone pack."

Travis makes two calls, one to Faye at police headquarters and one to the Pittsburgh FBI field office. He keeps his hand on Emma's arm the whole time. She looks out the window, quivering with the need to move, to do something. Finally, Travis puts the phone pack away and turns to her.

"Faye's sending an urgent message through to Carter and Horner in Crafton. Someone on the team will get it to them. The field office is sending out an agent to our location, and he'll be here in thirty minutes." He keeps going when Emma opens her mouth. "He's coming from another assignment across town, he can't get here any faster. Look, I agree we should go in, but at least now we know that in thirty minutes, we'll have backup."

Emma turns to face out the window again. Linda Kittiko, abused and terrified and possibly trapped in that pale brick house, may not have thirty minutes. "Now what do we do?"

"We need to go in armed." Travis's tone is grim. "When was the last time you shot a revolver?"

"Three months ago, when I shot at Anthony Hoyt. I missed both times." Emma's hands are shaking as she stares out at the location in the dim light of early evening. And she notices something else. "Travis, look at the garden. What do you see?"

He looks. "Flowers. The lawn's too long. I don't know, it's getting dark, what is it?"

"Chrysanthemums, dahlias, bud roses." Emma points, then curls her pointing hand into a fist in her lap so her shakes don't betray her. "I can see some Christmas fern in there, too. They're some of the flowers from the girls' bouquets. I'm betting if it were full light, we'd see them all."

Beside her, Travis exhales slow. "Okay, that's it, then. That's the house."

Emma wets her dry lips. "Give me a gun."

"I have an FBI field kit. You can have that, I'll take my own gun."

"Okay."

He shrugs off his suit jacket awkwardly in the driver's seat, unclips and sheds his pancake holster, passes her the Model 13, plus the speedloader off his belt. "Check the load. Anytime someone hands you a gun, check the cylinder."

She nods as if she knows what she's doing, as if she remembers what a cylinder is. The revolver is small and heavy, like all handguns are heavy, and it has a wooden grip. She lays Travis's jacket over her knees and holds the gun carefully, with the speedloader resting on the jacket. She is not comfortable with guns, and she's nervous about holding this one.

Travis looks at her for two seconds, then reaches over and takes the gun off her. He opens the cylinder, tips the ammunition load into his hand, clicks the weapon shut, gives it back. "Hold it firmly. There's the safety. Remember our firing range sessions—Weaver stance, point and aim, watch your breathing."

Emma feels more comfortable holding the unloaded weapon.

She leans back to give herself enough room to point it into the passenger footwell between her feet. Getting accustomed to the feel of a weapon in her hand again. She takes a deep breath. "Okay, give me the ammunition."

He gives her the handful of bullets. Then he reaches across her once more, cracks open the glove compartment, and retrieves a box of ammunition and a large stainless-steel Colt Python with an accompanying gun belt. He has worn this gun around her before.

"You got your dad's gun back after St. Elizabeths."

"Yep." He glances between her and the pale brick house. "You sure you want to carry? I don't want you to shoot me by accident."

"I'm not going in there unarmed. I promise not to shoot you." Emma swallows hard, hoping she can keep that promise. She opens the cylinder of the Smith & Wesson. She needs to focus her mind. "When this is over... When this is over, are you going to Guanajuato to see your uncle?"

Travis nods as he cracks the box of ammunition and starts loading the big silver gun. "I think so. I think I'd like to see the horses, and just spend some time being quiet."

"Quiet is good." Emma has never practiced with a speedloader. She gives it back, puts her handful of bullets into the Smith & Wesson one at a time.

Travis clicks the six-shot cylinder back into the frame of the Colt. "You can come, if you want. My uncle has a big house. Lots of room. Lots of horses. They lean over the fence and whicker at you. It's warm. You can go swimming in the river."

Her breathing is ragged and she needs to calm it. "I'd like that."

There's a short pause.

"I came here with you to show you," Travis blurts suddenly. "I want you to see that you can trust me. That I'm on your side. That I choose you. Emma, I would choose you over an FBI order every time."

She glances at him, her bottom lip clenched hard between her teeth as she continues to fumble ordinance. Her fingers are shaking so much the metal taps together. She exhales to speak. "I know. I've always known. But don't talk to me about that now. I'm having a hard enough time getting these bullets in."

She can feel Travis radiating energy beside her. Finally, she manages to get the Smith & Wesson locked and loaded.

"You're doing great," Travis whispers. He looks up at the house. "Okay, time to get out."

They exit from their respective doors, into the cool dusk of the silent street. Emma gives Travis his jacket back, and he slips it on. She is sweating in her clothes, but the perspiration chills on her skin immediately. Her knees are wobbling bad. She keeps the gun low, pointed at the road. When Travis joins her, they both look at the house.

"How do we always end up in these situations?" Emma feels the panic riding high in her chest.

"We don't have to go," he reminds her.

"No, we really do."

"Come 'ere." Travis transfers the Colt to his left hand, gives her a side-on hug. "Breathe. It's all right."

"It's all right," she repeats, muffled against his shirt. She breathes deeply a couple times, inhaling his scent.

"You okay?"

"Travis—" Before he moves away, Emma does something she's been thinking about for a long time. She leans into him. Kisses his neck, where his skin smells hot and good. When she steps back, everything feels better. "Now I'm okay."

Travis is looking at her with his mouth open. Hectic color in his cheeks.

"You ready?" Her lips are warm. Her hand, holding the gun away, feels more solid.

He blinks at her. Doesn't seem capable of speaking. Transfers the Colt back to his right hand, closes his mouth and nods.

"Okay," she says. "Let's go."

CHAPTER THIRTY-SEVEN

Lobbies are supposed to be places where people sit, quietly bored, while waiting to enter another space and encounter the thing that happens next. No one expects anything to happen in lobbies.

Which is why the correctional officer in the lobby of the jail is not prepared for Simon and Kristin's arrival. He is perhaps anticipating that action might happen in the more obviously punitive areas of the jail, or maybe he is thinking about what he will have for dinner after his shift is over.

Kristin can't know, will never know, what the officer is thinking, now that Simon is slashing the man's face. When the officer turns his head, hands going up self-protectively, Simon slashes his throat.

"Don't look, don't look," Simon whispers as it happens.

But Kristin had to look at the second guard, back in the corridor, and she has to look at this third guard, too. The lobby man gurgles. Wet spatters slap across Kristin's chin and shirt. Simon's ferocity and accuracy are astonishing, terrifying. *And Arjuna was both dazzled and terrified, for the form of god extended immeasurably in all directions.* Kristin struggles with stars in her vision.

Her god is a more efficient killing machine than she could ever have imagined.

CHAPTER THIRTY-EIGHT

They walk around the left side of the house, rather than knock on the front door.

There's a tinkle of glass as Travis cracks one of the small rectangular panes on the back door to reach through and unlock the catch. A portico covers them with shadow. The windows here at the rear have their blinds closed, like sleeping eyes.

Travis withdraws his arm carefully, and no glass catches on his suit jacket sleeve. "Okay, come on."

"What are the rules on breaking and entering if you're trying to rescue an abductee?" Emma whispers.

Travis grips the doorknob and recites in a low voice. "Officers of the law may enter a home without a warrant in exigent circumstances, in which a reasonable person may believe that entry is necessary to prevent physical harm to someone, or prevent the destruction of evidence, the escape of the suspect, or some other consequence improperly obstructing legitimate law enforcement efforts."

Emma swallows. "Except you're not graduated yet."

"Except that, yeah."

He turns the doorknob.

CHAPTER THIRTY-NINE

Simon rests the dead officer against the floor, straightens and gestures to Kristin with blood-smeared hands. "The next area is admin reception?"

"Yes. Yes." Her whole body is trembling with little aftershocks.

Simon transfers the razor blade from hand to hand as he wipes his slippery fingers on his pants. "Kristin. Sister, look at me."

She looks up. "Simon?"

He walks closer, cups her against him, croons into her hair. "Just a little further, love. We're almost at the end now. It will all be over soon."

Kristin cannot speak. She grabs at her brother's shoulder, smears the blood on her face onto his shirt. This is the first time in two years they have hugged without bars between them, and Kristin finds the closeness, the feel of her brother's arms around her, utterly intoxicating. They are here together. She is whole again.

"Kristin," Simon whispers. "Can you be strong for me?"

"I can." She has come this far. She presses into her knees, down through her feet into the floor. Pushes back from her brother to stand independently. "I can be strong. I can be strong for you."

"You're amazing." Simon smiles gently, gazes into her eyes. "Will you be my willing hostage once more, dearest?"

What can she do but give her assent?

CHAPTER FORTY

The kitchen of the Rutherford Avenue house is all scuffed, dun-colored tile and fake wood-grain Formica, mixed with slabs of darkness. No lights. The air is still, the space feels spooky. There's a wooden table and two chairs. A white coffee cup and a bowl sit in the sink, already rinsed.

It's a straight shot through the kitchen to the front door; Emma can see the dark wooden banister of a set of stairs to the upper floor. Another door to a basement is here on the left, past the refrigerator.

"Up or down?" Travis whispers.

"Up." Her eyes move between the basement door and the stairs. If they descend to the basement first, she'll lose all her nerve. "But block the basement door, just in case."

Moving quietly, Travis wedges the basement door handle with one of the chairs. Emma waits for him by the newel post. Her weapon is clasped across her chest.

"Point that thing at the floor," Travis reminds her quietly. "Put your left hand in support, pressure front to back to keep steady, trigger finger on the frame. Let me go first."

Emma nods, lets him pass.

The stairs are carpeted but creaky in the centers. The house has white walls, thick with plaster: Emma suspects the plaster over the solid brick makes the building highly soundproof. A small amount of slate-colored light is reaching them via smoky glass bricks around the front door behind them. It disappears when they reach the upper floor.

Now, the dark hallway. There's the same carpet, dado paneling that matches the banister, pictures along the walls. Emma wants to look at the pictures, but she doesn't want to get distracted. Her body is electric with nerves. There are four doors up here, only one of them open. Travis moves away abruptly to get a better angle on the interior of the open room. His arms extend with the Colt as he scans, then drop as he returns.

"That's a bathroom. I'm gonna check—"

"Wait." Emma has her gun pointed to the carpet with her right hand; she lifts her left, palm open. "Can you hear that?"

Somewhere nearby, a muffled thump.

CHAPTER FORTY-ONE

Kristin does not protest when Simon spins her around to press himself against her back. Her eyes are wide and frightened, because she is frightened. But not of him, never of him; only that this ruse may not work.

Simon tugs her hair aside, rests the razor on the artery throbbing under the white skin of her neck.

"Don't speak," he whispers in her ear. The deep sibilance of his voice, his lips at her earlobe, make her shiver. "Just dance with me, and let me lead."

And so the stage is set, the dance begun.

There is much yelling in the reception area, and people moving fast. Shouting, the crackle of radios, weapons drawn, the acrid musk of anger and fear, the cool thread of her brother's voice.

Kristin is insensible to all of it. She lets Simon lead. There are times when she closes her eyes and lolls, as if she has swooned. Her paleness and the blood on her clothes make her performance seem entirely convincing.

Then the brisk air of evening is on her face, and she knows they are outside the jail.

Simon's arms around her are like iron bars. Kristin stumbles when he drags her off the sidewalk and into the middle of Ross Street, putting them both in the path of an oncoming vehicle. She feels detached from fear, squints at the glare of the headlights as the car screeches to a stop in front of her knees.

"Get out!" Simon screams. *"Or I'll slit her throat!"*

The car's driver complies without question, hands raised. Kristin doesn't even see his face. Simon pushes her into the rear seat and slides himself behind the wheel.

She slumps down in the back, enervated from the furor of the last ten minutes. The car bucks and surges forward, and she sways on her side on the vinyl seat, watching the streetlights flash in passing. She can hear sirens. Simon takes a number of fast corners, and she has to brace. Cold air rushes in from the open window. Kristin feels her hair stir around her face like lemurs' tails.

Within a few moments, everything is quiet but for the sound of evening traffic and the burr of the engine. Kristin lies on the back seat of the dark car, listening to her brother's heaving breaths.

"I didn't know you could drive a stick shift," she says softly. "Simon, you're so clever."

In the front seat, leaning over the wheel, her twin begins to laugh.

CHAPTER FORTY-TWO

Emma's breath catches.

"There." She lifts her chin at the door near them on the right.

"I hear it." Travis moves to the door, stands side-on. Tests the knob, shakes his head. He transfers the Colt to his other hand and shifts away a step. "Get back."

Emma gives him room. He throws his right shoulder against the door, keeping the gun pointed down and away. The first time, the door only creaks. He tries again, with his full weight. The door is solid, but the locks are old: The door bursts open with a crack.

A muffled cry. Emma can see past Travis, into the room. On the right, a window with a drawn blind, a radiator. On the left, a nightstand with a bucket underneath, an old wooden bed frame, a mattress. On the mattress, a girl in a dirty white dress with a strip of duct tape over her mouth. She's tied to the bed frame. She's screaming behind the tape.

Emma comes into the room and straight over, puts her gun on the nightstand, starts working on the bonds. The girl keens and thumps against the bed. Her eyes are straining. A ragged cloud of dark hair, the scent of sweat and urine, a girl who went to a night-club and is now in hell. A girl who plays the oboe, a girl who looks like Emma.

Emma sits on the bed, wanting to weep, fingers trembling as she tries to unpick the knots. "It's all right," she says. "It's all right. We're here for you. Are you Linda?"

One of the girl's hands comes free. She rips off the tape, her voice hoarse. "He's outside. He's outside. Oh please, get me outta here, oh please—"

"We're getting you out," Emma confirms, finally loosing the other knot. She goes to work on Linda's ankles, feeling an aggressive urgency. "Stay quiet. I'm not leaving here without you." To Travis, she says, "The other doors?"

Travis seems numb with shock, staring at Linda Kittiko, at the conditions in the innocuous beige room. He snaps out of it. "Two more across the hall."

"I'm the only one here," Linda rasps, scrabbling and scratching at her wrists where the remainder of the rope makes pink, bleeding circles.

"Let him check," Emma says as Travis goes back to the hall.

"Stay with me!" Linda shrieks out, she's crying. "Oh god, please—"

Emma shifts quickly, puts a finger against the girl's open mouth. "We're not leaving you. Quiet now. He has to check." She renews her efforts with the ropes. "Linda, think for me. Where is the man who did this?"

"Outside, outside." Linda rocks on the bed, seems delirious, desperate to get out.

"How long ago?"

"I don't know. Hours. I don't know where. I only saw this room and the bathroom. He goes out and down the stairs, and then I hear a door down there near the back of the house."

"Okay, that's good." The last knot is done. Emma helps Linda swing her legs over the edge of the bed. "Lean into me. We're getting out of here."

CHAPTER FORTY-THREE

Kristin braces herself as the car corners sharply again. The smell of exhaust and the bog of the Monongahela River tears through the car with the breeze. She listens to Simon's laughter crest and sigh away, feeling happier than she has in years.

This is what it is to be complete. This is what it means to be free.

"Where do we go now?" she wonders, speaking half to herself.

"Anywhere." Simon's voice is light with release. "We can go anywhere at all."

"First, we should leave Pennsylvania." Kristin lifts a weak hand and swipes her hair away from her mouth. "Maybe go toward Lake Erie into Canada. We could be in Toronto in five hours."

"And then where to?" Simon sounds amused, all indulgence.

"Europe first, I think." Kristin considers. "Lisbon. And then Morocco—it has no extradition treaty with the United States. I've already made arrangements to get the money that belongs to us."

She clambers to sit up. Simon is driving fast along Boulevard of the Allies, smeared blood drying on his face, his gaze moving to take in the traffic lights, the cars around them, the glow of the city. He seems enraptured.

"Or we could do something completely unexpected." In the rearview mirror, the ultramarine of Simon's eyes turns thoughtful. Mischievous. "Don't you want to see what Emma Lewis and Travis Bell will do next?"

Kristin's mouth opens in surprise.

"Dearest, where do you think is the *last* place the authorities will look for us right now?"

Kristin lets out a snort of laughter. Controls it with a palm against her lips, gives up and allows a smile to emerge. "You think we should go to Beechview?"

Simon grins. "I think we should go to Beechview."

CHAPTER FORTY-FOUR

Emma adjusts as Linda braces against her, then remembers her gun on the nightstand. She scoops it up and it's fine, she can hold the gun in her right hand because Linda is on her left. But the girl is in rough shape, and when she tries to rise, her knees won't stiffen.

Just as Emma manages to get them both up, Travis comes back in. Linda jumps.

"The other bedrooms are empty," Travis explains.

"Carry her," Emma says, and helps with maneuvering as Travis holsters the Colt on his gun belt and scoops the girl into his arms. They leave the room, go back out to the hall.

"Careful on the stairs," Emma warns.

Travis handles the shadowed carpet on the stairs while carrying Linda. She has her mouth mashed against his shoulder, the fabric of his jacket absorbing the sound of her sobs, her arm a taut band of tendon around his neck. Emma takes the lead, gun forward, as they go through the kitchen and out the back door. Her sense of urgency doesn't fade until they're outside in the cool evening air, hurrying along the concrete path.

The night is dark now, only moonlight guiding them to the Lincoln. Emma works the rear door handle, puts her gun on the roof of the car, muzzle facing away. Travis sets Linda carefully on the back seat, moves aside so Emma can take his place.

"You're out, you're out." Emma chafes Linda's hands. The girl is crying, leaning her head into Emma's shoulder.

Travis has raced around the hood of the Lincoln to get to the Motorola pack on the other side of the seat. "I'm calling the field office. It's been twenty minutes. The agent should be here soon."

Emma nods, still consoling the girl in her arms. "It's okay. It's all right."

She doesn't hear the call Travis makes, although she senses him talking on the other side of the car. She's focused on Linda, helping her drink from a bottle of water in the back passenger footwell, hugging her to calm her. Linda tries to talk, but she's shaking too much; she can only make garbled scraps of words.

"It's okay," Emma says, rubbing her back. "I understand. Just rest for a second. Talk later."

Travis comes back around to stand near her. "I've gotta check that outbuilding."

"How long before the cavalry arrives?" Emma thinks Linda might have stabilized for now. She wishes she had a blanket.

"Maybe twenty more minutes. There was some kind of emergency action in downtown, everyone's scrambling. They might have to send a local patrol car on hot response."

"Can you wait?"

"The whole property is a crime scene now," Travis reminds her. "I'm supposed to secure it."

"Okay." Emma presses her lips together, detaches from Linda, and stands to face him. "You shouldn't go in there on your own."

Travis glances at Linda. "We can't bring her with us."

"No." Emma, torn by the conflicting desires of her heart. "I'm giving you ten minutes. If you're not back in ten, I'm coming after you."

Travis nods, shucks off his jacket, unholsters his gun. "Both of you stay in the car. If Kirke is still around, if he runs back this way—"

"Hey, I've got a weapon," Emma says, grin weak. "And really shitty aim."

"Don't shoot me, shoot the bad guy." Travis gives her his jacket, his eyes very clear under the moon. "And we're talking about that kiss when I get back."

"Be careful," Emma whispers, clutching at the fabric.

"You know it." He breaks eye contact, backing away. "Stay in the car. Lock the doors. I'll call out when I'm close."

The shadows under the trees in the garden swallow him up.

CHAPTER FORTY-FIVE

Emma takes her gun off the roof and locks the doors of the Lincoln from the inside.

On the rear seat, Linda is crying and scratching at her hands. "I can't...."

Emma puts her gun on the driver's seat and sits back with her, notices the problem: the glinting gold band on Linda's left ring finger. Emma grabs the girl's hand. The ring is tight, constricting. It makes Emma shudder.

"Get it *off*, get it *off*." Linda scrapes at her fingers, eyes red and wild.

"Okay, we're getting it off," Emma reassures. She pulls the girl's knuckle back, pulls the ring forward. Linda is moaning. Their harsh breathing reverberates in the car. The damn thing won't budge.

"Spit on it," Emma commands.

Linda spits. With saliva and the sweat on Linda's skin, they make progress. The ring slides, scrapes over the knuckle. Pops suddenly off, flies and clinks against the dashboard. Rolls somewhere into the front passenger footwell.

Linda wails abruptly, loud in the car.

"Okay, it's gone, it's gone." Emma hugs Linda as she cries. The disposal of the ring feels like a relief for both of them.

Linda's voice is hiccupping. "I want to get this dress off, too."

"I know," Emma says, "but we don't have a blanket. The dress is keeping you warm. Wait, this might help."

She removes her green padded vest, helps the girl ease into it.

"He hurt me." Linda says suddenly. Her voice is hoarse and she clutches Emma tight. "*He hurt me,* oh god..."

"I know." Emma's eyes are wet, too. She hugs and hugs. "I know. I'm so sorry. It's awful. But it wasn't your fault. And you're here now. You're safe."

Linda's distress hitches, slows, becomes more coherent. They calm a little together. Emma has to keep blinking tears away. Nobody gave her those words when she needed them. But she can give them now to another girl, and feel them unfurl inside, feel them take root.

"Are you..." Linda wipes her nose on her sleeve, takes a shuddering breath. "You're a cop? The guy, is he a cop?"

"I'm Emma." She smooths her hands down Linda's biceps. It's a miracle they got her out alive. "I'm not a cop. I'm just a girl like you. He's Travis, and yes, he's a cop."

"Okay," Linda says, cheeks chafed red. "Is he coming back?"

CHAPTER FORTY-SIX

J ogging to the outbuilding, Travis considers the risk that Kirke might still be here. He goes through everything he knows about solo-officer response tactics: silent approaches, threshold evaluation, blind corners. Approach, assessment, and firing accuracy are important. But solo entry is dangerous, and officers are frequently shot.

He is not fully trained; he has never done this before. His gun hand is trembling a little, and he tries to control it.

Not wanting to walk in completely exposed, he circles the big shed quickly, looking for windows—there are none—and entry points: There are two doors, front and rear, as well as a roller door. Moonlight washes everything of color, deep shadows are like vaults. His shoes are soundless on the grass. Finally, there's nothing to do but go inside.

Travis listens, inhales deep, opens the door, and ducks through the entry.

All quiet. He closes the door. It's dark as hell in here. He keeps his gun forward, feels with his free hand. Metal corners; a shelf. Concrete gritty underfoot. The smell of rust. After a few seconds, his eyes adjust. The front area here is full of industrial junk and building materials. A pile of bricks, a mound of boxes, a big shape that looks like a car covered with a drop cloth. In the corner, a drill press. There's a cleared path through the mess, and Travis takes it, picks his way forward.

The space is big. Up ahead, the junk thins out under a high skylight. Toward the back of the building, just past a piano, a wide set of metal steps is offset on the right. It leads up to a loft area, where a light is glowing.

Travis listens. Quiet. The occasional scurry, probably mice. He inches forward—

A thin scream.

Travis startles, moves swiftly, gun down, two-handed grip. Scans for movement. Nothing. His mind is racing. *Another girl? Where's Peter Kirke?* He almost trips over a bunch of cement bags, corrects.

He skirts left, then crosses past an old armoire and a rolled carpet and a huge pile of folded canvas tarps, reaches the foot of the stairs. Behind him, the piano and a pile of rebar. Another sound, like crying. *Where the hell is the noise coming from?*

He's halfway up the stairs when he realizes: There's a television set up in the loft. He can see the top edge of it, alongside an old standing lamp with a heavy shade. That's where the glow is coming from, and also the noise. He should—

Flash of movement.

Downstairs on the left, the rear door opens, admits a shaft of moonlight, closes.

Travis backtracks swiftly and follows. Under the loft, around a coil of wire and a pile of boxes, careful toward the door. He's covering the door with his weapon, doing the wide swings left to right, like he was taught. No tall furniture or shelves nearby, which is good—no hiding spaces, no deep shadows.

But he has to go out that door.

No point in delay; he takes a low side position, turns the door handle, and pushes—the door swings out. Take a peek, retreat. No suspect. Now, a fast lateral movement straight out, making a moving target. He's outside again, spinning.

Nothing. No movement. Fuck.

The air is cold on his sweaty face. *Where the hell is Kirke?*

Should he go back to the Lincoln? Protect the girls? But Kirke is the primary target. He must be here somewhere. Maybe he went to the house. Maybe he spooked and skedaddled.

Or maybe he circled back to enter the shed again from the front....

Travis whirls, returns to the door, enters.

Gets clobbered from behind, and it's all over.

CHAPTER FORTY-SEVEN

Emma holds on to Linda, checks the clock on the dashboard. It's 6:39 PM. Travis's time is up in three minutes.

She exhales hard. "Linda, listen to me. Travis might need my help."

Linda blanches. "No, no—"

"Linda, it's okay. Listen, Linda. Listen to me."

The girl calms. Emma tries to prevent her own frantic energy from leaking out. She exhales again, more slowly. Levels their eyes.

"Linda, you're strong. Incredibly strong. You survived. The man who did this—" Emma firms her arms around the girl when she gets heightened. "It's okay. You're safe. He's not here. But we need to get him, or he'll do this again. Linda, please help me. If Travis doesn't come back, I need to go find him."

"You're leaving me alone?" Linda's lip trembles.

Emma squeezes her. "More police are coming, but I need to find Travis. He might be in trouble. I'm going to give you the keys to this car—"

"Will you give me the gun?"

Emma breathes. "I can't give you the gun. Linda, I've got to—"

"Will you shoot him?" Linda's voice is rasping, but her eyes are charged now. "Will you shoot him dead?"

Emma feels emotion spear through her heart, hot as a laser. "If I find the guy who did this, yes, I want to stop him. But I've gotta find Travis first."

"Give me the keys," Linda says.

Emma digs in her jeans for the keys. She shows Linda the door locks, tells her the ETA of law enforcement. Shows her the Motorola pack. The pack is too complicated—but Linda can drive. That's good. The car is solid.

"Listen," Emma says, "if you get scared, drive away. Drive to a hospital, or a police station, or even a 7-Eleven. Somewhere crowded. Get in the driver's seat now."

Emma always feels safer behind the wheel of a car than sitting in the back. Linda moves, scrambles through the console space to get in front. Her white skirts swish on the vinyl. Emma retrieves her gun from the driver's seat just in time.

"Look, don't wait if you don't want to," she says. "But the police will be here in ten minutes, maybe sooner. The FBI are coming."

"Are you gonna be okay?" Linda looks back, hair bedraggled, eyes huge. Injured and desperate, pink rings around her wrists leaking new blood. "I want you to stay. I'm scared. But I want him gone."

"Me too. So much." Emma reaches over and puts the keys in Linda's hand, curls her fingers over them. Squeezes gently. Emma blinks against the blur in her eyes. "Okay, are you ready?"

Linda's teeth are chattering, but she seems determined. "Yeah. Yeah, I think so."

"Okay. Lock the door soon as I get out."

Emma opens the door, exits the car, feels the cold night air, shuts the door. Inside, Linda scrabbles over the console to press the button. The lock clicks. She scrambles back.

Emma nods at her through the window glass, receives a nod in return.

She walks away.

CHAPTER FORTY-EIGHT

A worn path in the grass from the back of the pale brick house to the outbuilding. Emma sees it by moonlight, feels it under the rubber soles of her shoes.

The outbuilding is a large steel shed, like a garage or a barn. Almost as tall as the house. It'll have a mezzanine level inside, Emma's sure—she's seen a lot of sheds in Apple Creek, and she recognizes the style. There's a front door, beside a roller door large enough to admit a big Chevy or a truck. A short concrete ramp lips up to the roller door, but it doesn't look well used, and there are no tire ruts outside.

The front door is the most terrifying part. Walking up to it, Emma feels electric. She keeps moving her head, scanning for scurrying figures. Has to keep reminding herself to hold her gun properly, trigger finger on the frame, left hand in support. Her palms are sweaty. She loosens her left hand to grab the doorknob. In the moonlight, her skin glows almost blue. She listens, hears nothing. Turns the knob and opens the door, inches inside.

She closes the door. It's very dark. But there's a glow somewhere farther back, up high. The space inside feels big. Echoey.

Some faint noise coming from somewhere, maybe the same place as the glow.

Travis. Stupid to call for him, but that's her first instinct. She has to suppress it.

She picks her way through the debris. An old car, a pile of bricks, an abandoned sink. She can smell bagged concrete and dust. Furniture and mothballs. Up ahead, a pile of canvas, and to the right, an old upright piano, a pile of rebar. A set of stairs to the mezzanine.

Noises on the mezzanine level. Her heartbeat drowned them out when she came in, but now that she's closer, she can hear them. They sound tinny, like a TV show soundtrack. Something about them is familiar, and her skin prickles.

She takes the stairs slowly, keeping her back against the rail near the right-hand wall, scanning up, down, every direction. Her eyes move all over, and she tries to settle. Stay in control. She doesn't want to jump at nothing, shoot and give herself away by accident, shoot Travis by accident.

From the second-top stair, she sights with her gun over the mezzanine level. Like she thought, there's a TV: It's set up on a rug, in front of an armchair and a standing lamp. The unsettling noises are loud now. She's been trying to block them out. Dread rises in her, like damp fog. There's no one here. She steps onto the mezzanine, edges closer.

It's as if someone has arranged a diorama of a living room, here on the mezzanine. The rug is circular and plush, some kind of ginger shag pile. An armchair is facing her—brown leather, solid, with wide arms. Beside the armchair, an adjustable dress form on an old-fashioned wooden stand—the tall lamp nearby casts it in a dull orange glow. Emma feels her heart stutter: The dress form has a veil draped over it, a headband with a fall of white tulle.

She catches her breath. Looks at the furniture. Everything is at least a decade old. Emma immediately thinks of Vivian Kirke, and where you'd put household items from a deceased estate. The final piece in the diorama is a big console TV set. Emma can see illumination radiating from the TV, which has its back to her.

She hears a tinny cry from the television. There's a silver JVC videotape player on top of the TV.

Now she understands.

Sweat on her skin. Her mind quails, but she has to know for sure. She takes a shaky breath, walks onto the rug, and skirts the console TV until she's facing it.

On the big screen, in the grimy gray light of a cinder-block basement, a man in overalls shakes a girl by her long, dark hair. The girl clamps her lips together to stop herself from crying out. The man bangs the girl's head against a wall—once, twice. The third time, the girl finally makes a cry.

Emma puts a hand to her mouth, makes a small, desperate noise in shock and sympathy. Spots in her vision, resolving wet. Gun down, forgotten at her side, she watches through tears.

It's *her*. The girl is her.

This is the videotape.

Emma drops her hand, lets out a sob. Can't help it. This is a horror show. This is her life. For a moment, she is wholly back in that basement. Back in those moments she has tried so hard to forget.

Her ribs squeeze together, her chest is compressed. She knows what comes next on the screen. She watches as the girl is dragged by her hair. As the man slaps her. As the girl's arms rise and flail so the zip ties on her wrists are clearly shown. As the man tears the front of her white dress—

Emma bites down on her lip, tastes blood. Consciousness returns. Her heart is pounding. She raises her gun, aims it, shaking, at the TV.

Shoot it, shoot it dead.

She is going to blow this memory apart, and the feelings that come with it. Destroy these bones of her past. She's going to put it all to the sword.

Her arm trembles. Finger on the trigger. Hard to aim, her vision blurry.

On-screen, the girl on the videotape turns her head. Stares in the direction of the camera she doesn't know is there. Her lips are sealed, her eyes full of mute appeal.

Emma gasps again. Loses breath. Her arm wobbles, dips. She watches the girl. This girl who endured so much. Emma has tried to run from her, in the last three years. Has tried to bury her. To be rid of her.

But doesn't this girl deserve more?

She did nothing wrong. She fought, and escaped, and tried to save. It was not her fault. It was awful, but she survived. She doesn't deserve to be forsaken. She deserves compassion, and respect, and gentleness, and care.

She deserves rescue. She deserves love.

And she deserves recognition.

Emma lets out a broken wail, ready to pass out. Can't get enough air. This is her experience. This is all she has.

Something inside her snaps.

Emma drops her gun arm again, muscles limp. Cries now, loudly sobbing without restraint. Shoulders shaking, hand raised to her face. Part of her knows she should be quiet, but she can't. She can't hold back anymore. Tears blinding, racking. Ugly but necessary. A moment of total vulnerability. A final sense of release.

Once the storm dies out, Emma's rasping breaths hiccup and slow. She feels exhausted. Weakened and gutted, but washed clean. Peculiarly light. She wipes her nose and face on her sleeve. She's a mess. Her body is trembling. Her eyes are sore, and her knees won't stay strong.

But there's something she needs to do. Emma swallows, straightens. Steps forward to the television. Quivering, she reaches up to the videotape player and presses the button marked STOP/EJECT.

The screen goes black. The top-loading cassette bed lifts high. Emma slides the videotape out.

Behind her head, the ratcheting click of a gun being cocked.

CHAPTER FORTY-NINE

The night air feels raw on Kristin's skin, and all her surfaces are quivering as she stands, twirling gently, under the glow of a streetlight in the middle of Rutherford Avenue, Beechview.

Part of her yearns to be with Simon, who has gone off to explore the house and shed nearby—even this momentary separation from her twin feels hard and wrong. But another, larger part of her is drawn like iron filings to the black FBI Lincoln just ahead. She stops twirling, regards the car. Its metal panels look cold. No light shows inside—only the shadow of a girl. A girl with dark, messy hair. A unique girl: whole and complete and alive.

How astonishing.

Kristin cannot resist. Her shoes crunch on the blacktop as she steps closer, bends like a willow to tap on the front passenger-side window. "Hello?"

The girl inside jerks and lets out a small, strangled scream before focusing on Kristin's face.

"Oh goodness." Kristin smiles. "I didn't mean to startle you. I'm Emma's friend. Are you Linda?"

"What?" The girl is shivering, hard to understand. "You're Emma's friend? Are the police coming soon?"

"I'm Kristin." This half-heard conversation, muffled by the car window, simply will not do. "Let me in," Kristin coaxes gently.

Linda looks at her, glances front and back to check the street. Leans over and unlocks the passenger door. It takes a few tries; her fingers are swollen and unsteady. Kristin is finally allowed to open the door and slide inside.

"Shut the door," Linda says. Her voice is quite hoarse up close. "Lock it."

"Oh, certainly." Kristin complies, turns back. At last she can see Linda directly, and it makes her smile in wonder. "Goodness. You do look so much like her."

Linda shudders, clings with both hands to the steering wheel. "Are you here with the cops? Did they catch him?"

"I'm here with my brother." Kristin isn't really following the thread of Linda's questions; she is much more fascinated by the way the girl's eyes catch the light in shards of translucent white.

"Your brother?"

"He's gone to help." Kristin waves toward the house and shed, then her hand falters.

Will Simon really be helpful? That is not his nature, but she knows he holds Emma in a certain regard. Surely he will be considerate of her, in some small way, now that he is free....

Simon's arm descending, slashing with the razor. Blood on the walls, cries of terror. The pink, exposed meat of a man's throat... Kristin has a sudden urge to scream, high and loud. She closes her eyes against the barrage of mental images. Pushes in her mind, and it is like pushing against the sea, but finally she folds all the images and thoughts together into a thick black mass.

She ties a red ribbon around the writhing black mass to keep it controlled. Then she thrusts the mass deep into her subconscious— it is like shoving her arm down her own throat, all the way to the elbow.

But now everything is gone.

Kristin swallows, recovers herself. Blinks and looks over. Linda is staring, her eyes wary, the shards in them flashing.

Linda wets parched lips. "Are you okay?"

"Why yes." Kristin takes a calming breath. What were they discussing? Oh, of course—Simon's small, considerate thing. Relieved to have remembered, she fishes in her pocket. "Linda, I have something here for Emma. If you would be so good as to deliver it to her, I'd be ever so grateful."

Linda accepts the square of paper cautiously. "You...want me to deliver a letter?"

"Thank you so much," Kristin says. "You're a darling."

Her smile is big, and bright, and not of this world at all.

CHAPTER FIFTY

t's so nice to meet you again," Peter Kirke says in Emma's ear. "But I think I'll take your weapon now, if you don't mind."

Emma feels a coldness in her core. Her muscles are lax, unready, and her eyes are still swollen from crying. She gets a wash of dizziness. Over the top of the videotape player, she sees the distance from here to the stairs—too far.

Her right hand goes stiff as Kirke's fingers slip over hers from behind, wrenching the Model 13 away. Kirke smells like vinyl and cigarettes and cologne. In her left hand, Emma's still holding the videotape.

"Turn around slowly," Kirke says.

Emma turns. Backlit by the dim glow of the tall lamp, Kirke is a creature of shadow. She can make out some details: the round glint of his glasses, his pale eyes and dark eyebrows, his dark hair. The powdered-looking softness of his cheeks. He's wearing a pastel polo shirt and jeans, with white running shoes. Holding a large shiny pistol. The gun mouth is pointing directly at her chest.

"Ah, there you are." When he sees her, he smiles. "Hello, Kelly. Although we both know that's not your real name."

Emma jerks in place. "Of course it's not my real name," she says. "You already know my real name."

"Emma." Peter Kirke pronounces it with relish.

"That's right." She keeps her face entirely blank. It's difficult.

"I can't believe we're really meeting properly, in person." Kirke seems almost gushing. His eyes flicker over her. He can't stop smiling. "Not in that horrible club, with your costume on. But right here, in this place. My place."

Emma says nothing. She shudders inside.

"I'm honored, I suppose you could say." Kirke wets his lips, still grinning. "The incredible *Emma Lewis*... The girl I've been searching for, for so long. The moment I saw you on-screen, I knew you were the one."

"The one what?" Emma's voice is flat.

"The *one*." Kirke's glasses flash. "The only one. My one and only."

He seems to feel awkward, holding two guns. He tosses the Model 13 over the mezzanine railing. Emma doesn't take her eyes off him, but she hears the weapon hit the pile of canvas downstairs with a puffing thump, then a muted clank as it slides off the edge of something onto the concrete floor.

Unarmed—that's game over. She closes her eyes. Her soul drops into her feet. But her mind is still going. At light speed, in fact. Kirke has a gun, but he never kidnapped his victims at gunpoint. He drugged them instead. And he never shot any of the girls: He strangled them. She notes that he wields the gun like a prop.

Emma opens her eyes. "Your one and only," she repeats.

"I'm sure you've wondered," he says. "Everybody wonders if

there is someone in the world who is perfect just for them. A soul mate. A person designed to be an exact match."

"Right." She wonders if he knows how to shoot properly. She wonders if the gun is loaded. Does she have the guts to find out? She takes a step toward him.

Kirke steps back, just a half step. "Mother always said there was a girl like that, waiting for me."

Emma can't help herself. "Your *mother* told you to kidnap girls so you could rape and murder them?"

Kirke makes an expression of distaste. "Don't be vulgar. Good girls aren't vulgar."

Aren't they? Emma's fingers itch for a trigger.

Kirke glares. "It's important to have exacting standards. To be selective."

Emma's mouth twists. "You need that 'special someone.'"

Kirke blinks, looks suddenly younger than his age. "That's right. Someone who will take away all your pain, who'll be beside you always. Someone just for you." Kirke's lips quiver, but he resurrects his smile. "And you are that person for me. Although your hair is very short now. That's not right. We'll let it grow for a while. You'll be back to yourself in no time."

Emma looks at him, at this man they've chased all over Pittsburgh. This man who is the root of all this death and horror. She feels overcome with a new weariness. There's a seemingly bottomless reserve of these grasping, hungry men. These pathetic, selfish men, who feel entitled to take what they want with no regard for anyone else, and without consequences.

She knows them so well, and she doesn't want to anymore.

355

Doesn't want to listen to their bullshit. Doesn't care about their psychology and their monologues, their histories or excuses. Like Linda, she just wants them gone.

And she remembers: Like Linda, she has survived. Sometimes she thinks her survival has been the result of strength, and courage, and tenacity—all the good, virtuous foundations for survival. But now she thinks maybe she has survived out of pure spite. Because *fuck Huxton*. Fuck him. He doesn't get to dictate to her from the fucking *grave*. She can be happy if she wants to be. She can live. She can be free.

Travis was right—she is a fucking force of nature. She is the maelstrom. And she is mighty.

"Actually, Peter," Emma says, "I think I'm back to myself already."

And she steps forward and swings left fast and hard, with her entire body weight, smashing the videotape in her hand into Kirke's gun.

His arm goes wide, knocked away as the tape's plastic guts splinter. Kirke cries out as his hand loosens on the gun, looks horrified as the tape flies, smacks into the mezzanine railing, falls to the floor in a tangle of magnetic spool.

Emma reacts on instinct sharpened by adrenaline. She grabs his shoulders, knees him hard in the balls. Kirke makes a strangled cry, drops his gun, and doubles over. Emma spins and does something she's had a lot of practice at—she *runs*.

Downstairs—find the revolver—shoot this bastard. Her feet clatter on the wide wooden stairs. The sound of Kirke cursing. She jumps a step. His voice gets louder. A booming shot over her head, and she ducks, screams a little. *Okay—so his gun is loaded.* She keeps going, almost tripping, moving fast.

She leaps down the last steps to the concrete, careens around the banister. There, ahead—the canvas pile, beside a rolled-up carpet. She stumbles onto the pile, stamps on the canvas, scanning for the Model 13 in the gloom. *Where is it? Where is it?* Not here.

She hears a roar from above, Kirke staggering to the stairs. He might not aim to kill, if he wants her that bad. Does she want to take that bet, though? There's not much time.

She drops to her knees, digs between the canvas and the carpet roll, fingers scraping on concrete. *Down here? Oh my fucking god, WHERE IS IT?* Nothing, nothing. She gets up and spins in place, hands wide and desperate.

Out of the darkness, a new voice. "Are you looking for this?"

Emma's head jerks up.

Simon Gutmunsson is leaning on a mezzanine support pole, tall in his blue scrubs and white long-sleeved shirt, holding her gun.

CHAPTER FIFTY-ONE

Her mind skids to a stop.

She stumbles back, her mouth open on a gasping inhale. She is dreaming with her eyes open. She is having a psychotic break. Simon Gutmunsson is in Allegheny County Jail, not standing real in front of her, dangling her gun by the trigger guard.

"Hello, Emma." He grins.

The sights and sounds and smells of the building around her fade out to nothing. All Emma can see is Simon Gutmunsson's terrifying blue eyes, the spill of his white hair, his crisp jawline lit by the moon through the skylight high above, the rest of him in shadow.

Emma feels her eyes go round. And she does what any startled prey animal would do.

She pivots on the spot and *bolts*.

Heedless of what she's running back into, every atom caught up in a blind shriek of panicked horror, she doesn't even see Peter Kirke in front of her. He doesn't have a chance to raise his gun and aim before she barrels into him, she's on top of him, crying out, pushing him to the floor.

Kirke falls backward with a yell, and Emma doesn't hear that either. She climbs over him, the soft give of his flesh only vaguely registering in her senses as she scrambles over him, and off, and she's gone.

Cawing in her head and a great clanging of bells—*Simon Gutmunsson, Simon Gutmunsson*. She needs to *get away*, get away *now*, she'll plunge through brick walls if she has to, the obstacles in the shed are nothing, nothing. She's bouncing off them, tripping over them, her breaths panting loud, her skin alight.

Two cracking booms inside the shed and Emma doesn't care, it doesn't matter, she's sprinting for the front exit. Then her left leg collapses under her and she sprawls, slides on concrete, colliding with a box near a stack of bricks and spinning in the dust.

Even then, the pain doesn't sink in. Her arms still scrabble on grit, she still tries to heave herself up, she's gasping, her heart pounding out of her chest. But her leg doesn't work at all, and she's reduced to crawling to the bricks. The fire that started in her skin is spreading, whirling, concentrating in her thigh. She feels it now like the aftermath of a punch.

Kirke shot me. That stupid asshole shot me. The awareness arrives like an echo of the shot itself, peaking and reverberating. Emma grabs her leg and it's sticky under her hands, warm liquid flowing over her fingers. The wound is a long, open gouge on her outside thigh—she presses her hand against it. That's not going to work. She rips off her belt and cinches it around her thigh. The pain makes her hands shake. Slumped against the bricks, she can see the two figures by the mezzanine pole only twenty feet away.

Kirke is standing. He has dropped his arm, now he knows his

shot hit true. He's smiling. But he turns quickly and raises the silver pistol again in Simon's direction, alive to this new threat.

"Peter, I assume. How nice it is to meet you." Simon puts the Model 13 into his waistband. His voice is quiet, and lightly jovial; it seems to carry in the profound silence after the sound of the shot.

"What?" Kirke says, and his arm wavers. Emma almost feels sorry for him.

"Why, I've heard *such* a lot about you," Simon exclaims, eyes flashing. "And I see you've made the acquaintance of the delightful Miss Lewis."

Her temples make a convulsive throb of pain and Emma gasps, pushes down through her hands, everything in her urging retreat. There's a lightness in her center, like she's been disemboweled.

"She's..." Kirke seems confused. "She's the one. The special one."

"Isn't she, though?" Simon makes a tripping laugh, wets his lips, takes a step closer to his quarry. "They don't make them more special than her. And you've been searching for dear Emma all this time."

"I...I have." Kirke's glasses glint in the low light. "I knew she was out there. I knew."

"Had to sort through a lot of dross to find her, though, hmm?" Simon looks like he's glowing, his skin and hair are so bright. His long, sculpted figure is like something out of a vision. He waves a careless hand. "Girls are everywhere, and none of them the *right* girl. It takes so long to select them, and then they're worthless. It's *exhausting.*"

"That's it!" Kirke seems suddenly energized. "You know what it's like?"

"Of course I know." Simon's eyes are welcoming, beckoning. "I know what it's like to be without the one you love. Without the one who cares for you, makes you complete."

"It's awful," Kirke whispers, gulping.

"It is." Simon nods sympathetically. "How long have you been alone, my friend?"

Kirke exhales, trembling, his voice sighing out. "So long. *So long.* I don't think I can take it anymore."

"Well, now, there's no need to yearn," Simon says softly, and his head lifts, gaze spearing through the gloom to find Emma. She shudders. "Oh, Emma, dear! So wonderful to see you again. Why don't you come and join the conversation."

There's instruction in his voice, and command, and a sense of menace that Emma finds impossible to withstand. She wants to fight it, but her last energy is dribbling out with her blood onto the dirty floor of this shed.

And Kirke wants to press his advantage. He lifts the gun and aims it straight at her.

"Yes, Emma." He looks triumphant. "Come here and join us. *Now.*"

Her stomach does a slow, sick revolution. She's going to throw up. She's going to cry. She has to move. With a monumental effort, keeping her eyes on the two men, Emma slowly clambers up the bricks and then up the edge of an old armoire until she's standing. Her left leg is pulsing, it's agonizing. She makes a choked noise.

But she will not let these two see her weep. She will not lose control again. She has to think. Has to use her wits. Maybe it's hopeless, but she has to try. And if she's going to die, at least she can die on her feet.

With the gun trained on her, it seems to take an age to plod closer to Simon and Kirke. She can put weight on her leg, but very little. And vitality is leaching out of her: She's sweating, but it's a cold sweat. Her hand is pressed over the belt, over the wound, but her jeans leg is wet with blood. Each step burns like hellfire. She leans on obstacles as she goes, finally reaches the pair. She ends up positioned between them, like a carcass about to be fought over by two wild dogs.

When she arrives at her spot, Simon steps in. He leans forward, and Emma recoils as he gets close enough to bite.

"You smell of blood," he whispers.

But his eyes are glinting with amusement, and instead of an attack, he lowers his head toward hers. With a crawling shock of horror, she feels his lips touch her skin as he kisses her gently on the cheek.

Emma swallows hard. "Where's Kristin? What did you do with your sister?"

"Oh, Kristin is visiting with the young lady in the car outside." He straightens with a broad smile. "Now, turn around, Emma."

She trembles. He puts his hands on her shoulders and maneuvers her to face Kirke.

"Let me introduce you to my new friend, Peter."

CHAPTER FIFTY-TWO

When Travis first wakes up, he's pretty sure his head has been disconnected from his body. It's so damn heavy. His brain seems to have ballooned to a couple sizes bigger than his skull.

He manages to lift a hand, finds his head still attached. The hair behind his crown is wet. A vein pulses at his temple. It's dark.

His throat is so dry he can't make a sound; when he tries to turn over, his mouth opens with dizziness and nausea, but no noises come out. After a moment, the feelings pass. Now he just feels like shit.

On his side, vision fuzzy, the dark peels back a little. Shapes and colors coalesce farther away. Strips of blackness at left and right are objects—a tall stack of flattened cardboard tied with string, a table with boxes on it. Between the objects, Travis can see moving figures. People.

Sounds switch on, too, although they're kinda like audio being beamed to him from Sputnik. He blinks, and the voices seep into coherence—male voice, female voice. A voice he recognizes.

Emma.

She's there, limned in moonlight, the curve of her head defined and kinda pinkish—although maybe everything looks pinkish after waking up from being knocked out, when your bones are throbbing and your eyes are bloodshot. Travis blinks a few times more, to clear his vision.

Emma's nodding, her body stiff: She's turned to the left, like she's talking to the stack of cardboard. Then Travis's depth perception improves, and it's clear she's speaking to someone beyond the cardboard, facing her.

She doesn't look happy. That's the first thing that comes into focus, how unhappy she looks. And Travis thinks that's just shameful, because if anyone deserves to be happy, it's Emma. When he's able to scrape himself up off this hard cement floor, he's going to make it his mission in life to ensure she's happy.

Which is when audio tunes in properly, and he can hear her words.

"...more do you want me to say?" Emma closes her mouth into a tight line to swallow. "That talking to you doesn't make me sick? That you're just a nice, normal guy?"

"I *am* a nice, normal guy." The male voice. On the left, behind the cardboard. "I just want what everyone wants—the one person for me."

The owner of the voice steps toward her, and now Travis can see him. A slim, dark-haired white guy with glasses. Polo shirt. Jeans.

And a gun.

Nice, normal guy? Travis is dimly aware that pointing a gun at someone isn't normal. None of this is normal.

"You tortured and killed three women." Emma's voice is bleak.

The male voice replies, but Travis has heard enough. Because it's all coming back. The College Killer. The house. Linda Kittiko in her white dress, screaming behind duct tape.

He has to do something. He has to help Emma.

Getting up is the hardest thing he's ever done. His head is pounding, splitting apart. When he makes it to hands and knees, he has to stop for a minute so he doesn't dry retch. His body gets real thin. He's see-through. Oh Jesus.

Travis focuses on breathing, focuses on the dirt on the floor sanding his palms. Small details. Soon, he comes back. Recalibrates enough to get to his feet.

He sways, puts a hand out. Steadies on the cardboard. His Colt. Where's his Colt? No Colt. Okay, that's not great. Just have to work with it.

The College Killer—Peter Kirke: the name drifts back. Kirke has a gun and he doesn't. What's the solution?

Travis looks at the cardboard he's leaning on. It's a tall stack of other piles. Each pile is tied quarter-wise with thin nylon packing straps. Each pile is bigger than a trash-can lid. About eight inches thick. Big enough for heft.

Big enough for a shield.

Okay, that might work.

Cardboard against a gun. Travis recognizes something alarming about that concept, tugging at him. But it's weak enough he can bat it away. Helping Emma is more important. And Kirke doesn't know he's here, awake.

Travis moves carefully now. Ignores the way his head is screaming at him, ignores the way even his eyeballs are throbbing. He straightens his shoulders, rolls his joints, alleviating some stiffness.

Eases his hand under the tight packing straps on the topmost cardboard pile, palm-up.

He moves slowly so Kirke won't notice. Grips the straps, a good grip. Lifts the pile—it's thick, not too heavy.

Kirke is maybe ten feet away. He'll really have to go in quick.

Travis Javier Bell—son of a dead father, law enforcement by birth, brave by nature—takes a deep breath, lifts his cardboard shield, and focuses on his target. Rounds his shoulders. Holds his energy, lets it build . . .

Releases.

He charges past obstacles, hard and fast, comes in low. His whole body grinds like bone in a dry socket when he collides with Kirke, and normally he'd brace for impact but he's in no shape to really do that. Smashing into Kirke's midriff, he just goes with the momentum, throwing Kirke back and sprawling on top of him.

Kirke makes a startled bark, a guttural *uhhh* when his head bounces off the concrete floor. His hand releases the big silver pistol and it goes flying, spins toward the wall and skitters away under the upright piano.

Travis knows that the only way to do this is to be thorough. He kneels up over Kirke, straddling his body, pushing the cardboard aside. He rolls the guy to face him and starts punching. He punches once, twice, three times, Kirke's glasses falling away, blood on his mouth. Travis keeps hitting, even though his head feels ready to burst apart—

"Travis!" Emma's voice, anguished.

Travis makes himself stop. The guy's face is a mess. Travis wants to be sick. Breaths heaving, he pushes back and off Kirke, lying prone on the floor. *Don't throw up.* Travis hears the words in his father's voice. *Don't throw up and don't black out.*

Travis staggers, turns around to find Emma.

She's standing still under the moonlight in the dark building. Her expression is tormented: pale, pinched lips, dark circles around her eyes. Her hands are shaking.

Behind Emma, with one hand on her shoulder and the other hand holding Travis's Smith & Wesson Model 13, is Simon Gutmunsson.

He's smiling fit to burst.

CHAPTER FIFTY-THREE

O h, bravo!" Simon Gutmunsson's voice rings out in the echoing dark of the shed. "Well done, Mr. Bell! And welcome to our little party."

Emma wants to curl into a ball. Wants to close her eyes, but she can't. She owes it to Travis to stay present. He looks terrible. His hair is a dirty tangle. Smears on his white shirt, tie drooping. Sweat dewing his face, blood on his brow. Standing in place, swaying under the skylight, his gaze is transfixed as he absorbs what's happening. What they're up against. What the stakes are.

"*Emma*," Travis rasps. His hands are still curled into fists.

"I'm sorry," she whispers. "I'm so sorry."

"Nothing to be sorry for." His eyes hold hers.

She wants to cry. He looks green, like he's just woken up, like he's about to pass out. Something has happened to him, and she wants to kill Kirke for that. But she can't do anything now. Can only stand here, feeling the weight of Simon's heavy hand.

"What a touching demonstration of loyalty and affection." Simon is so much taller, she can hear his icy words emanating from over her head. "Although was the pummeling really necessary?

Beating your opponent bloody after he's down—it's like something *I* would do."

Travis's gaze snaps to Simon's. "No, you'd just bite off their face."

Simon is surprised into a laugh. "Well, goodness, Mr. Bell— I suppose you're not wrong. So whose face will I bite off today, hmm?"

He lowers his head; Emma feels his chin touch her shoulder. The way Travis is staring, Emma can only assume that Simon's expression is diabolical.

"Should I ravage dear Emma?" His jaw brushes hers as he speaks, soft, soft. "Tear off her lips, her nose...Strip the skin from her cheeks? If she's no longer pretty, will the foolish boys like Peter Kirke stop hounding her? It's a curse to be lovely, isn't it? Everyone wants a piece...."

Emma holds herself frozen as Simon's breath warms the skin of her neck. He runs his lips gently up to her earring, across to her cheekbone, and she can smell him: dried blood, the harsh bleach of jail laundry, the cold sizzle of ozone. She keeps her eyes on Travis, shaking with the effort of not flinching.

Six feet away, Travis swallows. "How are you here? How did you know where to come?"

Simon straightens, moves his face away, and Emma exhales, trembling. A temporary release of tension.

"Oh, it's a long, tedious story...." Simon waves the gun in his hand. "But in a nutshell, Kristin told me. She saw the fax with the address here, while she was at police headquarters. I'm sure that very boring man, Special Agent Carter, will be absolutely *furious* to discover that Crafton is a dead end, yet another in a long string of spectacular FBI failures...."

Travis's jaw tenses. His fists are so tight, Emma can almost hear the tendons crack.

Simon's tone sharpens, becomes supple. "But surely you can appreciate the poetry of this moment, Mr. Bell. You're standing here, confronting me as I hold a hostage—just like your father did before you. Will you make the same mistake as he? Will you offer to take dear Emma's place and—"

"Yes," Travis cuts in immediately, and Emma's heart breaks into a million pieces.

She can only imagine Simon's raised eyebrows. "Yes? You're prepared to exchange yourself? Even at the risk of—"

"That's what I said," Travis interrupts, stepping a pace closer, face stony and stalwart.

"*No*," Emma whispers, can't stop tears coursing silently, her wet cheeks the only warm spot on her body. "*Please*, Travis, don't do this, he's just playing with us, he only wants—"

"If he wants me, he can have me." Travis drags his gaze away from Simon long enough to burn his eyes into hers. "So long as you're safe, it doesn't matter."

It matters to me! Emma feels like she's being ripped apart. The pain in her leg is nothing compared to this. Simon takes his hand from her shoulder long enough to stroke her left cheek.

"Oh, Mr. Bell," Simon scolds. "See what you've done—you've made poor Emma cry. That's very bad form. Apologize at once."

"*Emma...*" Travis whispers. His bottom lip is trembling. He meets her eyes with an intensity that consumes like lava.

Emma feels her expression crumble.

"Simon, don't do this," she gasps. She knows it's useless, but she has to try. "Simon—"

"Now, Emma, don't be cruel." Simon Gutmunsson raises his right arm and points the gun at Travis's head. "Accept Mr. Bell's apology so he feels better about all this before he leaves us...."

Emma sees dust motes floating in moonlight as everything in the moment slows down.

Pale spots in her vision. In front of her, Travis, the only person in the world still in focus as he steps closer, close enough to reach out and touch. As he gives her a look of almost unbearable tenderness. Simon's hand squeezing her shoulder. The slow leak of blood from her leg. The cock of the gun. Far off, the sound of sirens.

Then rustling movement, a flash of pale shirt in the background. A voice that starts as a wheeze and accelerates, turns into a bellow that accompanies running footsteps.

Travis, in front of her, head in the process of turning as he hears the bellow. His body suddenly pinioned, jerked to a standstill, eyes widening, chest lifting as he arches, everything slow, slow, slow.

Peter Kirke, howling, face bruised and hideously twisted in its rage, channeling all his weight and the force of his sprinting momentum into a sharp length of rebar he grips in both hands. It goes through Travis like a sword, and emerges, bloody, high on his torso, punching through the white cotton of his shirt with a tearing rip that Emma will be unable to scrub from her memory, no matter how hard she tries, for so long as she will live.

Emma screaming, she can't hear it, hands reaching. Travis's

arms open, hands shaking, empty, suspended in air. He looks down at the gore-covered tip of the rebar, trails his gaze back to Emma's.

Simon Gutmunsson, the Artist, gasping with delight at this tableau of devastation, an extraordinary moment he would like to paint in oils—then flicking his right hand to send the gun flying in Travis's direction to add the poignant coup de grâce.

Travis catching the gun, training kicking in on automatic, blood spilling from his lips in a thin, bright stream. He lifts the weapon, lowers it, unable to act, vague with pain and shock, the fluted steel protruding from just below his breastbone. With the last of his energy, he drops the gun into Emma's hand as, twisting to his side like an oak, he topples down.

She grasps the gun, wavers barely a moment—the killer behind her, the murderer in front. Lifts the weapon and shoots Peter Kirke in the face. Steps forward and shoots him again. And again.

Then she breaks the spell of her horror and turns, shoots again into nothing, into darkness and shadow, which is Simon Gutmunsson's substance, the shape of absence and sorrow, a void in her heart as she sinks to her knees.

CHAPTER FIFTY-FOUR

It takes thirty minutes to stabilize Travis at the scene. There's such a long delay that Emma is ready to punch somebody by the time they load him into an ambulance to UPMC Mercy.

Both the SWAT paramedic and the EMT try to stop her from going with him despite how much she tells them that her leg is fine, it's a graze, it's nothing she can't deal with. Before she can press her case further, some goddamn bastard shoots her full of fentanyl against her wishes, and she passes out awkwardly mid-sentence to Carter, who manages to grab her before she hits the floor.

She wakes up in a hospital bed, it's two in the morning, and the only sounds are the faint hiss of the air conditioning and the scuff of nurses' shoes as they walk the linoleum on the late shift. Emma can smell Lysol and a hint of vomit. Then she's vomiting herself as she feels the effects of the fentanyl and the chill sweat of nausea, the memory of the last twenty-four hours—the last three fucking years—coming back to her in a rush.

Once the puking stops, and the mess has been cleaned up by staff, Emma eases back onto the pillows and swipes a dirty hand over her forehead, asks the night nurse her questions.

"Your friend is in ICU. He was in surgery for four hours, only got out of it a little while ago." The woman's hair is done in intricate braids, tied off her face for work, and her gaze is both matter-of-fact and kind. She pats Emma's other arm gently. "He's gonna be in recovery a long time—he's lucky to be alive. As for the rest, honey, I really don't know what to tell you. There's an FBI man out in the corridor, though, maybe he can give you better answers."

Which is how Carter gets permission to come in. He's in shirt-sleeves with no vest and no tie, which is the most casual Emma has ever seen him, although he's carrying his FBI jacket, which he lays over a chair. He pulls up another chair closer to her, his glasses swinging on their chain. She can see that his foundations have been rocked tonight. This isn't how everything was supposed to work out.

"First, I need to apologize," he says, mouth drawn and tired behind an extra day's growth of beard. "We should have learned about the Beechview house earlier. And the communication with Faye at police headquarters should have been straightforward, but there was a problem with the UHF radios in the DEA vans, which didn't synchronize with the FBI VHF radios....Anyway, I'll say there's no excuse for it. We should've done better. Then everything got screwed up when Simon Gutmunsson escaped Allegheny County Jail. That set a lot of things in motion that dominoed into a lack of coordination between you and Travis Bell, us in Crafton, and the men at the local bureau. It was a mess, plain and simple, and you suffered for it. I'm very sorry."

Emma can see that it's not an act, he means it. She doesn't care.

She has to take a drink of water before she can reply, and Carter has to help her with the cup and straw, which rankles her. "Linda?"

"She's fine. We found her in the Lincoln. She was scared and hurt and tired, but she's alive. She's gonna be okay. She's one floor down, and her parents are keeping her pretty protected. But you can go see her if you like."

Emma nods. She's going to do that. "Kristin and Simon?"

Carter sighs heavily and rubs his face. "Another mess. We don't know where they are. They could be halfway to South America by now, for all we know. They just disappeared like smoke."

Like Simon when I tried to shoot him. Emma doesn't want to think about that now, has to keep her head straight.

"That was my fault," Carter admits. "I don't know how we're going to deal with it. The bureau's on high alert, and we've contacted Interpol as well, in case they try to run overseas."

"Europe," Emma says—my god, her voice is raspy. She swallows more water to give her throat extra purchase. "They'll run to Europe."

"Probably via Canada, or do a few hops elsewhere, yes," Carter agrees. "We don't know how they'll get money, but with the world they lived in, it shouldn't be too hard."

"Subpoena their lawyers," Emma suggests.

"I've made a lot of mistakes here." Carter leans forward, elbows on his knees. His expression is solemn. "I should've listened to you, to Bell...." He shakes his head.

"You should've listened," Emma agrees. She knows wisdom is easy in hindsight. "How's Travis?"

"He's okay." Carter drags himself upright, and out of self-reproach. "It was a near thing, a very near thing. They had to take the rebar out of him in surgery, and there's still a high possibility of infection. But he's close to stable post-surgery, and they should be able to extubate him tomorrow. I mean, today," he corrects. The clock on the hospital room wall ticks softly as the second hand revolves.

Carter takes a slow inhale, to continue with the story.

"Miss Lewis," he says, but Emma puts up a hand. She's tired. She's heartsick. She isn't sure if she wants to speak to Special Agent Carter again in this lifetime.

"I don't want to hear anymore." Maybe her feelings will change. But right now, she's over all this Monday-morning quarterbacking. She has something else on her mind. "My clothes are in this room, right?"

"Uh...yes." Carter casts around, spots them somewhere near the end of the bed. "Is there anything you want?"

"My jeans," Emma says, and when he puts the bloodstained denim in her hand, she digs in the pocket a moment before finding what she needs.

Carter stands now, ill at ease. "I can call the nurse, if you'd prefer—"

"I can do that with the button," Emma says, and she waves him away. "Goodbye, Mr. Carter."

Once he's skulked, sheepish, back out into the hallway, Emma eases herself up on the bed. She feels dizzy, but it's okay, she's not going to throw up again. She reaches out and pulls the nightstand telephone closer, hits the button for a line, dials the number on the scrap of paper in her hand. The phone picks up after five rings.

"Audrey?" Emma says, voice halting. "It's me. I'm sorry to wake you, it's so early. And I feel bad because you've been sick—"

"You know I was just thinking about you," Audrey Klein says softly on the other end of the line. "I heard there was some trouble. Why don't you tell me all about it. . . ."

Emma blinks against the tears in her eyes, and feels—for the first time in a while—that everything is going to be just fine.

CHAPTER FIFTY-FIVE

The first time Travis Bell wakes up, the world is light and fire, flames sucking into his chest, flames rampant.

He rolls, and there seem to be arms suffocating him. He thrashes, tries to yell, but all that comes out of his mouth is a bright gush of fire and blood, and before he can do any more damage to himself, he's subdued back to silence and stillness and black—

When he wakes up the next time, the quiet is so loud it's ringing in his ears. He's lying on his back. His eyelids are too heavy to open, but he's determined; he prizes them up a crack. And as his vision stops swimming, he sees an armchair with a girl in it. She's sleeping there, and while he's seen her sleep before, he has never seen her in absolute repose, and it's a revelation; this girl, with the bright-dark eyes that are closed now, her shorn head thrown back, awkward and lovely. She snuffles in her sleep, and he has a moment to think *Emma* before the shutters come down again.

The third time he wakes is the first time he feels awake. Same place, same prone position, but now all his body is part of him again. The pain isn't fun, but it's manageable.

He turns his head, and there is the armchair with Emma Lewis on it, still asleep. *Huh.* But then he realizes she's wearing different clothes—some kind of baggy black shirt and her curled-up legs in black sweatpants with a white stripe—and he knows that time is still messing with him.

The ceiling of the room is unchanged, but the light is different. He moves his hand, his right one, rubs his chin and finds bristles. When he looks at the armchair again, Emma opens her eyes, and he tries his words.

"Hey."

"Holy shit." She uncurls fast. It looks like it hurts. "You're awake."

"Yeah." Words are painful somehow, and his mouth and throat are dry.

"You're awake." Emma, beside him, her eyes getting wet. "God. Oh god."

"You snore," he says on a breath.

"God." She laughs, covers her mouth with her hand, drops her hand, lifts it again. "Oh shit, I should get the nurse—"

"Wait." He lets his fingers open and she clasps them. It's coming back to him now. "Y'okay?"

"I'm okay." She nods and answers at the same time. "I'm okay. Travis—"

"How long's I out?"

"Five days."

"Oof." It takes effort to express even this much surprise. "What happen?" He's not sure how long he has before the dark returns, and he needs to know.

Emma blinks hard. "Simon Gutmunsson escaped. Kristin's gone—he took her. Linda is okay. Kirke is dead."

Travis closes his eyes, breathes. Forces his eyes back open.

Emma bites her bottom lip. "He got you with a piece of rebar. We weren't sure if you... They said you might not..."

Something else he has never seen before: Emma, open. Tears leaking down her cheeks as she clasps his hand and bends closer, presses her forehead gently to his. And my god, what he feels for this girl. His torn heart leaps inside his broken chest, and it should be painful, but somehow it isn't. He releases her fingers so he can cup her cheek, swipe her tears with his thumb—her skin is soft as she leans into his hand.

"*Travis,*" she whispers, and this is another revelation.

Then she makes a wet laugh, and pushes back his hair with cool fingers. Her face is close and real, which is a great time for the nurse to arrive. There's a lot of exclamation, and more nurses, and movement—in the midst of the action, Emma is pushed out of sight. When he lifts his head to seek her out, a shocking pain crunches into his torso, so the next thing he feels is a cold finger in his vein, and then darkness. But he carries the memory of Emma's whisper, the clasp of her hand and the softness of her cheek, down with him into the black well.

The next time he wakes, the light looks like morning, and Emma is there in fresh clothes, with a cup and straw for him to drink, careful, careful.

"How're you feeling?"

"Crummy. But that's probably good, right?" He can't sit up at all, and he realizes he woke because he needs something for the pain.

"Hold on, you've got a PCA pump...." Emma puts the cup aside, presses a button on his IV, which is somehow connected to the monitors nearby. Within seconds, he starts to feel better.

"How ya doin'?" he asks her, nice and warm everywhere now, pleasantly floaty.

"I'm okay," she says, too quiet, and he knows that's not true. But something changes in her face, and she blows out air, resigned to it. "All right, I'm not okay. But I'm trying to get better at this. I just didn't want to overload you so soon after—"

"Tell me," he says, his fingers reaching, finding hers.

She looks at him, presses her lips between her teeth. Finally, she gives up, puts her free hand in her jeans pocket, pulls out a few slips of paper. One of the paper slips is white, with colors on it. The other slip is purple, and looks expensive.

Emma unfolds the purple slip. Cheeks pinking up, she reads aloud. *"Now you're a murderer. Just like me."* She takes a breath, expels it, trembling. Travis can feel the tremble in her fingers. "That one came two days ago. American postmark, so he sent it before they left the country, most likely."

She unfolds the white paper, and a sifting of pastel chalk sprinkles down, onto the bedsheets.

"Here's the other one. Kristin gave it to Linda—she spoke to her in the Lincoln. It's a poem." She reads aloud again. *"Farewell! A word that must be, and hath been—a sound which makes us linger; yet, farewell! Ye who have traced the Pilgrim to the scene which is his last, if in your memories dwell a thought which once was his, if on ye swell a single recollection, not in vain he wore his sandal-shoon and scallop shell; Farewell! With him alone may rest the pain, if such there were—with you, the moral of his strain."*

"Whoa," Travis says. He lost the thread of it about the time she said "Pilgrim."

"It's Byron," Emma explains. "The final stanza of *Childe Harold's Pilgrimage.*"

"Right." Travis feels the awareness in his breastbone. Wonders what comes next.

Emma folds the papers together again, sets them away on the nightstand. She takes Travis's hand in hers.

"Travis," she says, somehow both serene and vengeful. "We really need to do something about Simon Gutmunsson."

AUTHOR'S NOTE

Books are made when an author (that would be me) takes the ideas generated by their own brain and weaves them together in very strange ways with online research, real events, overheard snippets of information, visual images, musical notes, sensory input, and artistic influences.

I'd like to acknowledge the influences of John Douglas, Thomas Harris, Lord Byron, John Milton, Ursula K. Le Guin, Stephen King, and David Fincher in my own work, and encourage others to go look them up.

I deeply appreciate and acknowledge Naomi Shihab Nye for permitting the use of the quote from her poem "Making a Fist," from *Everything Comes Next: Collected and New Poems* (Greenwillow Books, 2020).

I would also like to acknowledge Robert Shatzkin and W. W. Norton & Company for permitting the use of the quote from Adrienne Rich's poem "Power," from *The Dream of a Common Language* (W. W. Norton, 1978).

Thank you once again to David Colón-Cabrera for clarifying and correcting my use of the Spanish language.

I'd like to convey my appreciation to both Richard Diehl (aka LabGuy) and David Gritten for information about the use of videotape recording in 1979.

It was really important to me to portray Emma's experience respectfully. I'm hugely grateful to Philippa McInerney for her generosity in reading parts of the manuscript and for her specialist advice around writing scenes involving therapy, trauma, and recovery from sexual violence.

This book deals with some pretty heavy stuff. If you or someone you know has been sexually assaulted, you can call the 24/7 National Sexual Assault Hotline at 800-656-HOPE (4673) in the United States or 1800RESPECT (1800 737 732) in Australia. For people exposed to sexual violence and those supporting them, more resources are available online from the National Sexual Violence Resource Center in the United States or 1800RESPECT in Australia.

To find a sexual-assault service provider near you, visit the Rape, Abuse & Incest National Network (RAINN) online in the United States or the National Association of Services Against Sexual Violence (NASASV) online in Australia.

ACKNOWLEDGMENTS

First of all, I have to say it—I can't believe this book got published.

There has been a huge outpouring of support for the story and characters of *None Shall Sleep*, and it's been both thrilling and humbling to experience that. People have contacted me online and via email, joined the newsletter, shared and shouted and helped spread the word…and now here we are, with the further adventures of my serial-killer crew.

So this goes out to all the readers and cheerleaders and bloggers and tweeters and tokkers and grammers and podcasters and friends who've screamed for more, especially my Nailbiters and Black Hand gang: You folks made *Some Shall Break* happen. You are the bloodthirstiest and the best—I salute you and offer my profound thanks for giving me the chance to continue playing in this terrifying world.

I'd like to thank my agents, Josh and Tracey Adams, for their unswerving support with this book, even when it didn't seem like it would get off the ground. Much appreciation to Caroline Walsh and Christabel McKinley in the United Kingdom for their hard work, and to Stephen Moore of the Kohner Agency. I am grateful every day that I have such an excellent team on my side.

Massive thanks to my incredibly brave and patient editor, Liz

Kossnar, whom I put through absolute *hell* with this book—I'm really sorry, Liz! But I've appreciated you at every stage of this book's production, and I couldn't have done it without you. Thanks also to the entire team at Little, Brown Books for Young Readers, especially the folks in sales and marketing and publicity, who constantly deserve more credit.

Much appreciation to the lovely Sophie Splatt and Jodie Webster, plus the rest of the team at Allen & Unwin, who have shared my books with my home audience in Australia and Oceania for as long as I've been publishing them. Special gratitude to the A&U sales and marketing and publicity crew, who prove their mettle every time.

Thanks also to the incredibly talented Janelle Barone for taking on the cover art for this series once again, and for once again knocking it out of the park.

Writing is hard and the road is long; you need a good group of friends who give you support, so I have many people to thank. C. S. Pacat encouraged and brainstormed and wrote with me along the way—all love to you, Cat. Lili Wilkinson read the manuscript with a clear eye and gave incredible feedback—thank you, Lili. P. M. Freestone connected me with Philippa McInerney and David Gritten—much appreciation, Peta. Amie Kaufman continues to be extraordinary— massive hugs, Amie. Will Kostakis cheered me on—thank you, Will. And at various times, when I needed to be talked down from ledges, my other House of Progress teammates were there for me—fist bumps and thanks to Kate, Nicole, Liz, Eliza, Skye, and Ebony.

Finally, biggest love and thanks to my partner, Geoff, without whom none of this would be possible, and to my sons, Ben, Alex, Will, and Ned, who are the ones that make it all worthwhile.

xxEllie

ELLIE MARNEY

is a *New York Times* bestselling author of crime thrillers, including *The Killing Code, None Shall Sleep, White Night, No Limits,* the Every series, and the Circus Hearts series. Her books have been published in ten countries and optioned for television. She's spent a lifetime researching in mortuaries, interviewing law enforcement officers, talking to autopsy specialists, and asking former spies about how to make explosives from household items, and now she lives quite sedately in southeastern Australia with her family. Ellie invites you to find out more about her and her books at elliemarney.com.